BIRTHRIGHT

VOLUME FOUR
FAMILY HISTORY

IMAGE COMICS, INC.

www.imagecomics.com

Robert Kirkman *Chief Operating Officer*
Erik Larsen *Chief Financial Officer*
Todd McFarlane *President*
Marc Silvestri *Chief Executive Officer*
Jim Valentino *Vice-President*

Eric Stephenson *Publisher*
Corey Murphy *Director of Sales*
Jeff Boison *Director of Publishing Planning & Book Trade Sales*
Jeremy Sullivan *Director of Digital Sales*
Kat Salazar *Director of PR & Marketing*
Branwyn Bigglestone *Controller*
Drew Gill *Art Director*

Jonathan Chan *Production Manager*
Meredith Wallace *Print Manager*
Briah Skelly *Publicist*
Sasha Head *Sales & Marketing Production Designer*
Randy Okamura *Digital Production Designer*
David Brothers *Branding Manager*
Olivia Ngai *Content Manager*
Addison Duke *Production Artist*
Vincent Kukua *Production Artist*
Tricia Ramos *Production Artist*
Jeff Stang *Direct Market Sales Representative*
Emilio Bautista *Digital Sales Associate*
Leanna Caunter *Accounting Assistant*
Chloe Ramos-Peterson *Library Market Sales Representative*

Robert Kirkman *Chairman*
David Alpert *CEO*
Sean Mackiewicz *Editorial Director*
Shawn Kirkham *Director of Business Development*
Brian Huntington *Online Editorial Director*
June Alian *Publicity Director*
Jon Moisan *Editor*
Arielle Basich *Assistant Editor*
Andres Juarez *Graphic Designer*
Paul Shin *Business Development Assistant*
Johnny O'Dell *Online Editorial Assistant*
Dan Petersen *Operations Manager*
Nick Palmer *Operations Coordinator*

International inquiries: foreign@skybound.com
Licensing inquiries: contact@skybound.com

www.skybound.com

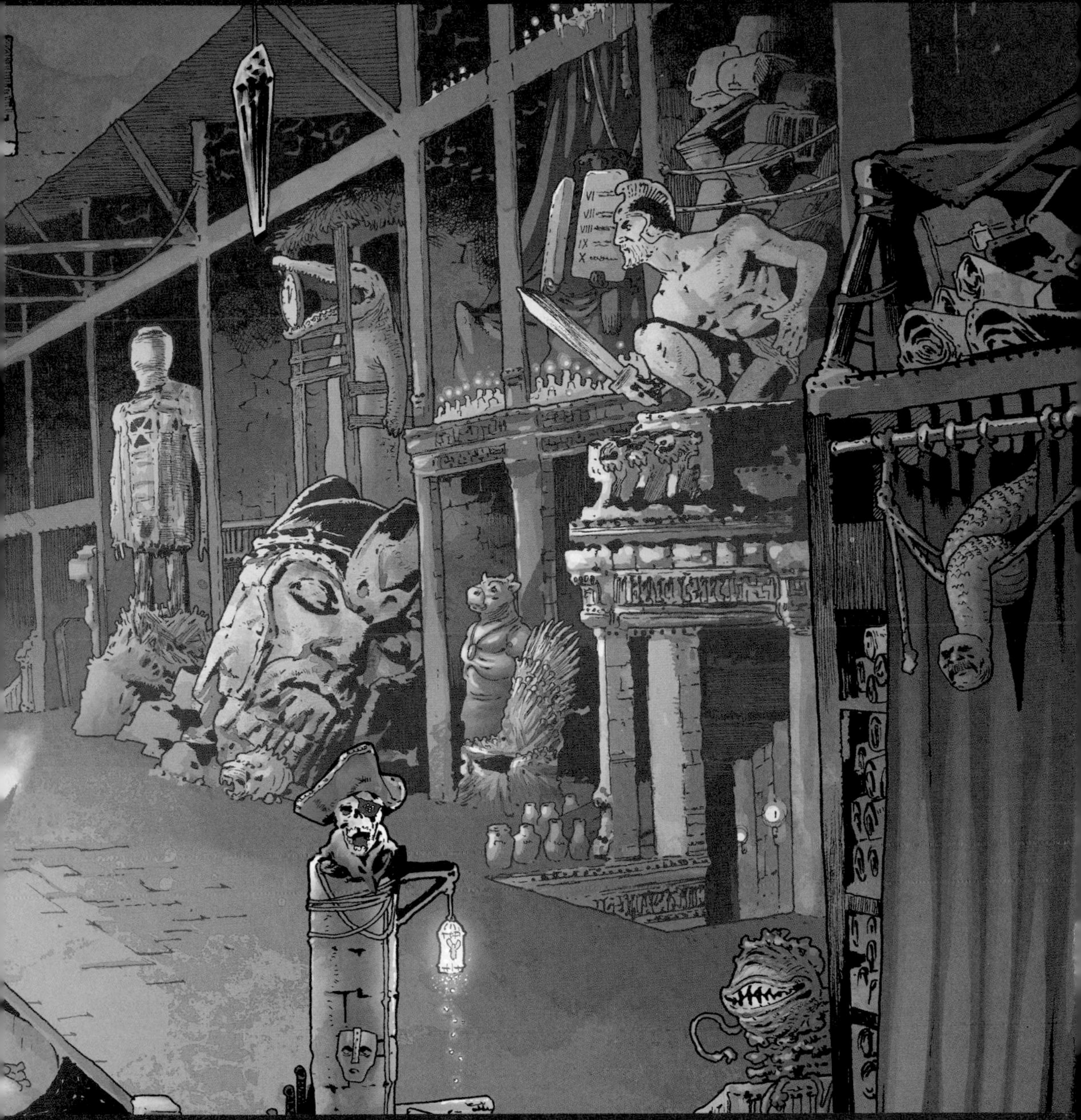

Joshua Williamson
creator, writer

Andrei Bressan
creator, artist

Adriano Lucas
colorist

Pat Brosseau
letterer

Arielle Basich
assistant editor

Sean Mackiewicz
editor

logo design by **Rian Hughes**

cover by **Andrei Bressan** *and* **Adriano Lucas**

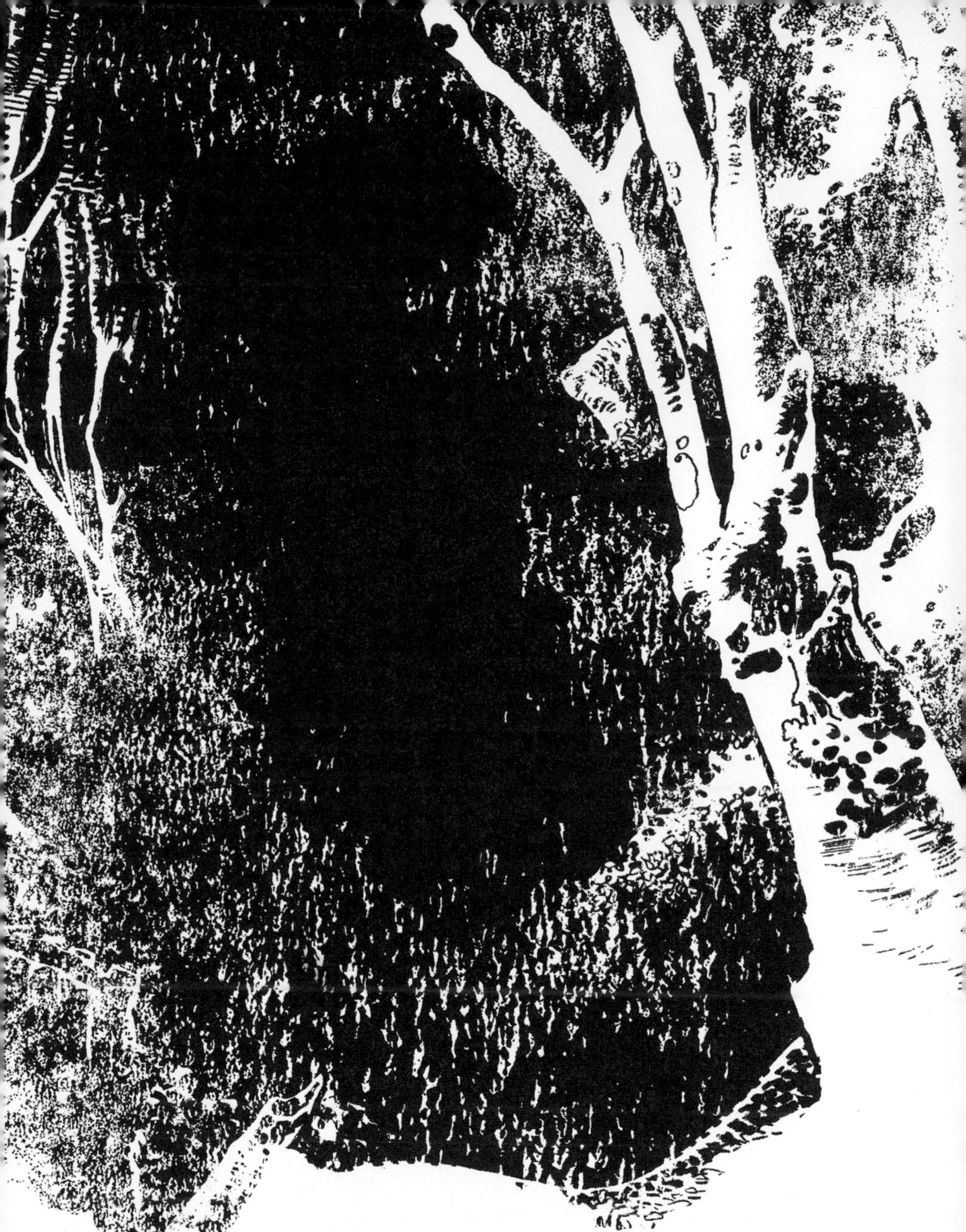

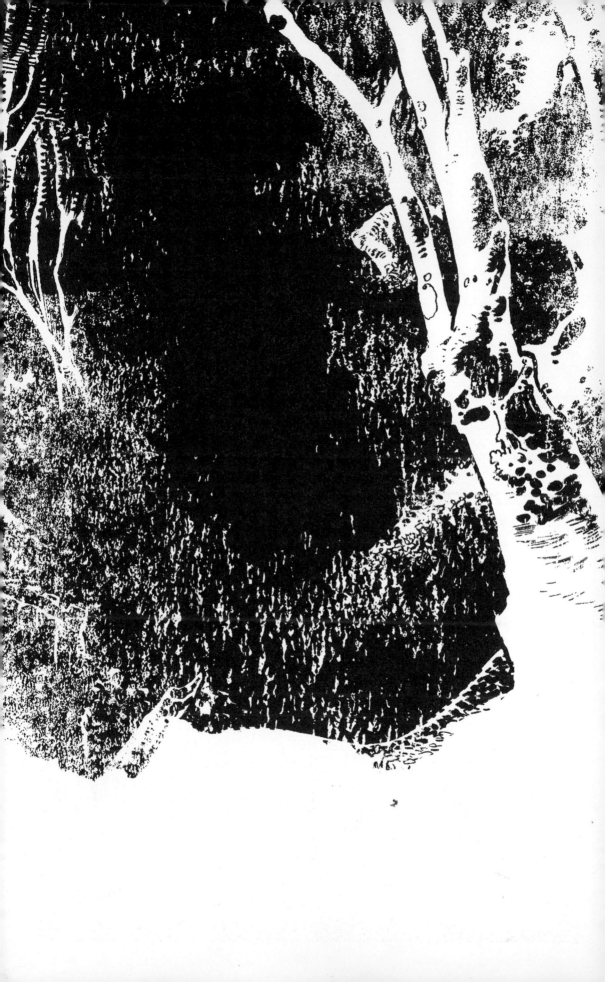

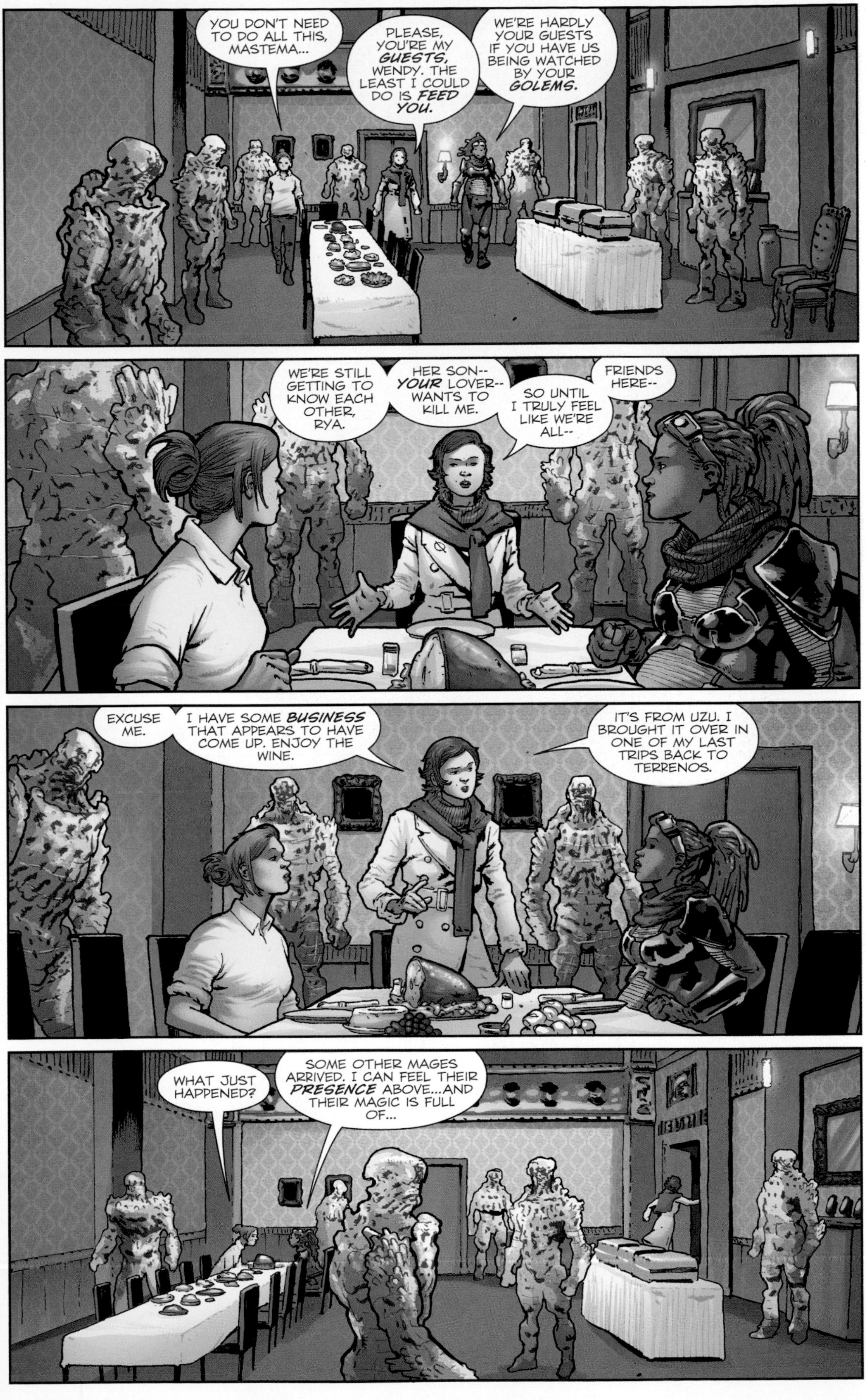
YOU DON'T NEED TO DO ALL THIS, MASTEMA...
PLEASE, YOU'RE MY GUESTS, WENDY. THE LEAST I COULD DO IS FEED YOU.
WE'RE HARDLY YOUR GUESTS IF YOU HAVE US BEING WATCHED BY YOUR GOLEMS.
WE'RE STILL GETTING TO KNOW EACH OTHER, RYA.
HER SON-- YOUR LOVER-- WANTS TO KILL ME.
SO UNTIL I TRULY FEEL LIKE WE'RE ALL--
FRIENDS HERE--
EXCUSE ME.
I HAVE SOME BUSINESS THAT APPEARS TO HAVE COME UP. ENJOY THE WINE.
IT'S FROM UZU. I BROUGHT IT OVER IN ONE OF MY LAST TRIPS BACK TO TERRENOS.
WHAT JUST HAPPENED?
SOME OTHER MAGES ARRIVED. I CAN FEEL THEIR PRESENCE ABOVE...AND THEIR MAGIC IS FULL OF...

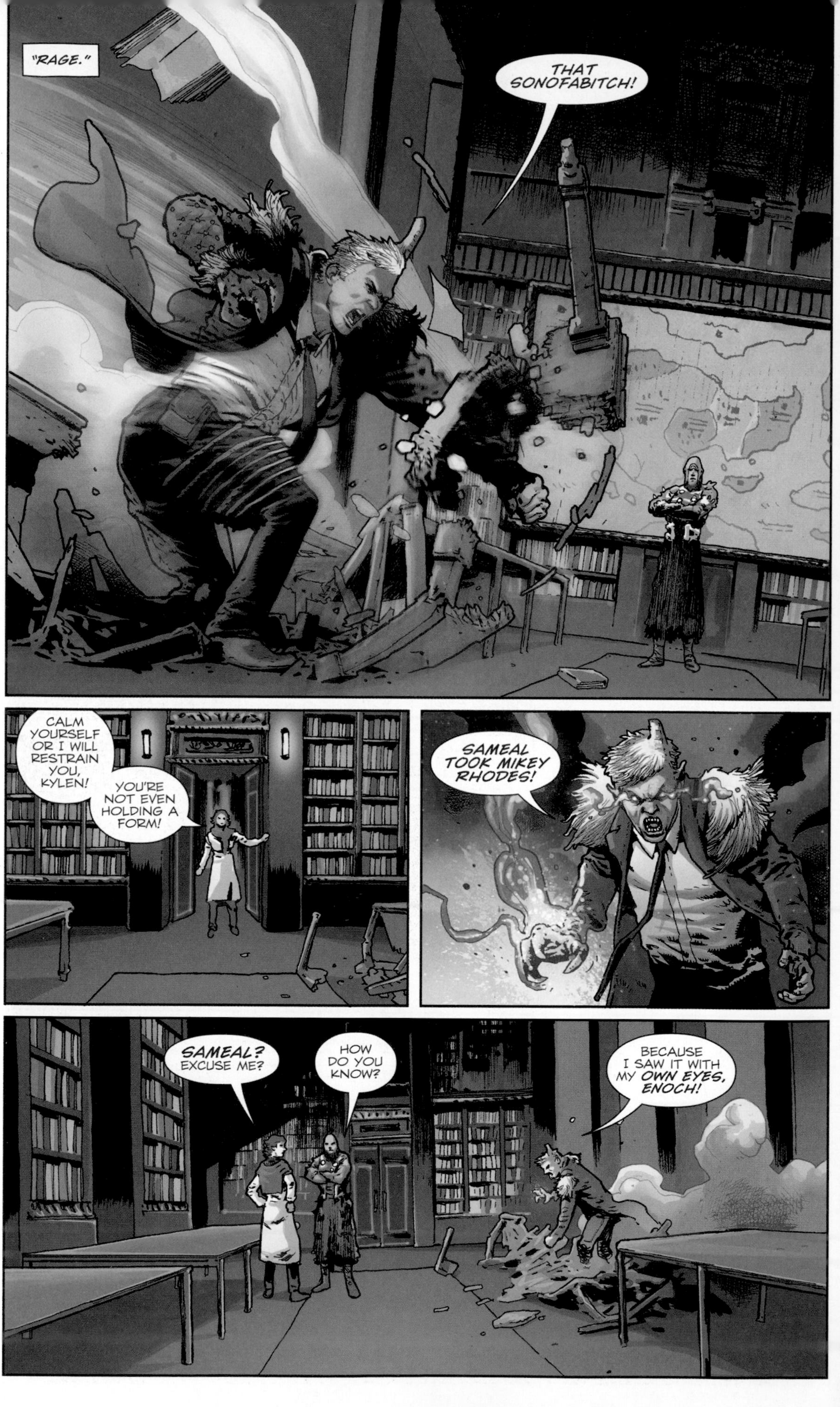
"RAGE."
THAT SONOFABITCH!
CALM YOURSELF OR I WILL RESTRAIN YOU, KYLEN!
YOU'RE NOT EVEN HOLDING A FORM!
SAMEAL TOOK MIKEY RHODES!
SAMEAL? EXCUSE ME?
HOW DO YOU KNOW?
BECAUSE I SAW IT WITH MY OWN EYES, ENOCH!

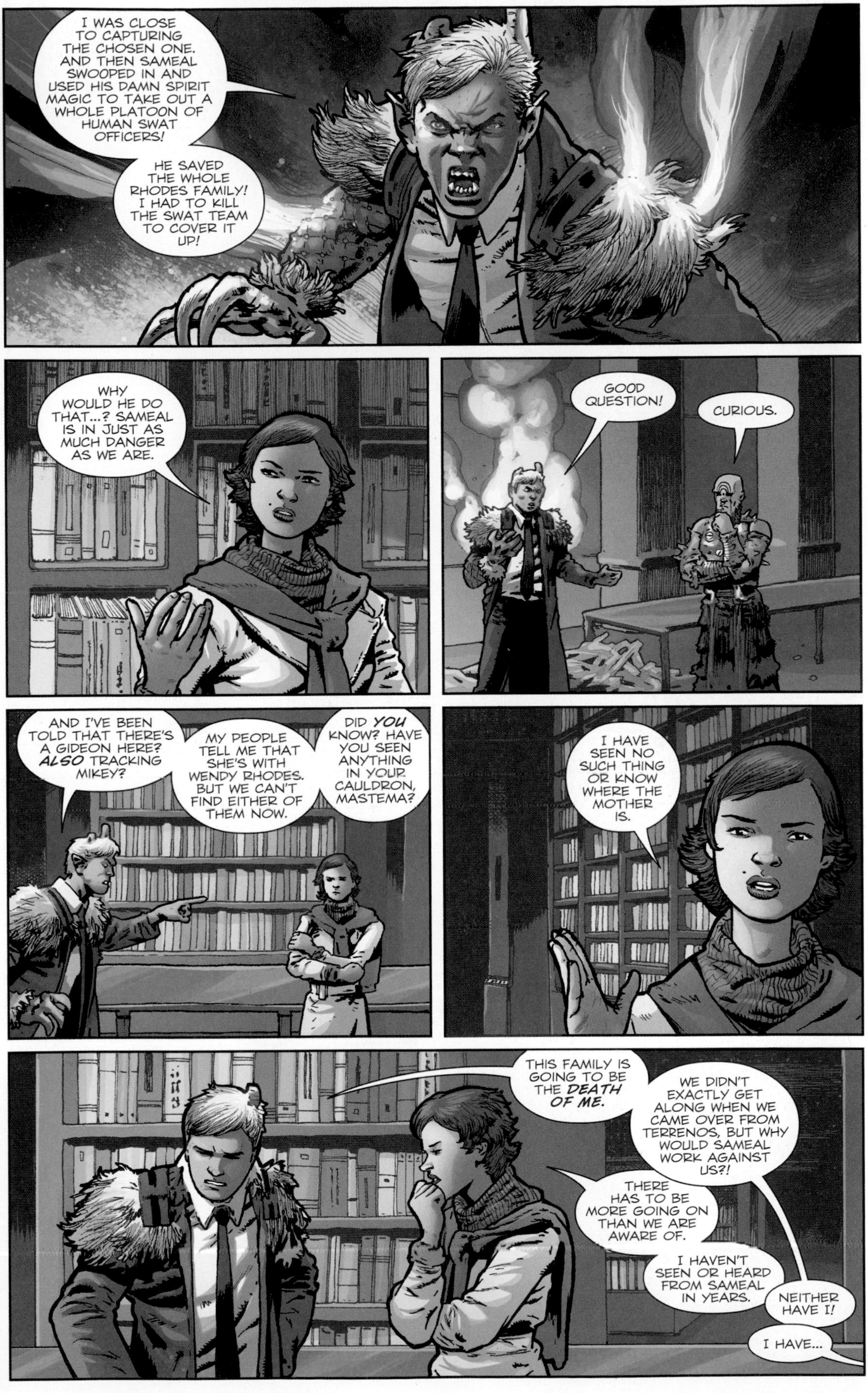
I WAS CLOSE TO CAPTURING THE CHOSEN ONE. AND THEN SAMEAL SWOOPED IN AND USED HIS DAMN SPIRIT MAGIC TO TAKE OUT A WHOLE PLATOON OF HUMAN SWAT OFFICERS!
HE SAVED THE WHOLE RHODES FAMILY! I HAD TO KILL THE SWAT TEAM TO COVER IT UP!
WHY WOULD HE DO THAT...? SAMEAL IS IN JUST AS MUCH DANGER AS WE ARE.
GOOD QUESTION!
CURIOUS.
AND I'VE BEEN TOLD THAT THERE'S A GIDEON HERE? ALSO TRACKING MIKEY?
MY PEOPLE TELL ME THAT SHE'S WITH WENDY RHODES. BUT WE CAN'T FIND EITHER OF THEM NOW.
DID YOU KNOW? HAVE YOU SEEN ANYTHING IN YOUR CAULDRON, MASTEMA?
I HAVE SEEN NO SUCH THING OR KNOW WHERE THE MOTHER IS.
THIS FAMILY IS GOING TO BE THE DEATH OF ME.
WE DIDN'T EXACTLY GET ALONG WHEN WE CAME OVER FROM TERRENOS, BUT WHY WOULD SAMEAL WORK AGAINST US?!
THERE HAS TO BE MORE GOING ON THAN WE ARE AWARE OF.
I HAVEN'T SEEN OR HEARD FROM SAMEAL IN YEARS.
NEITHER HAVE I!
I HAVE...

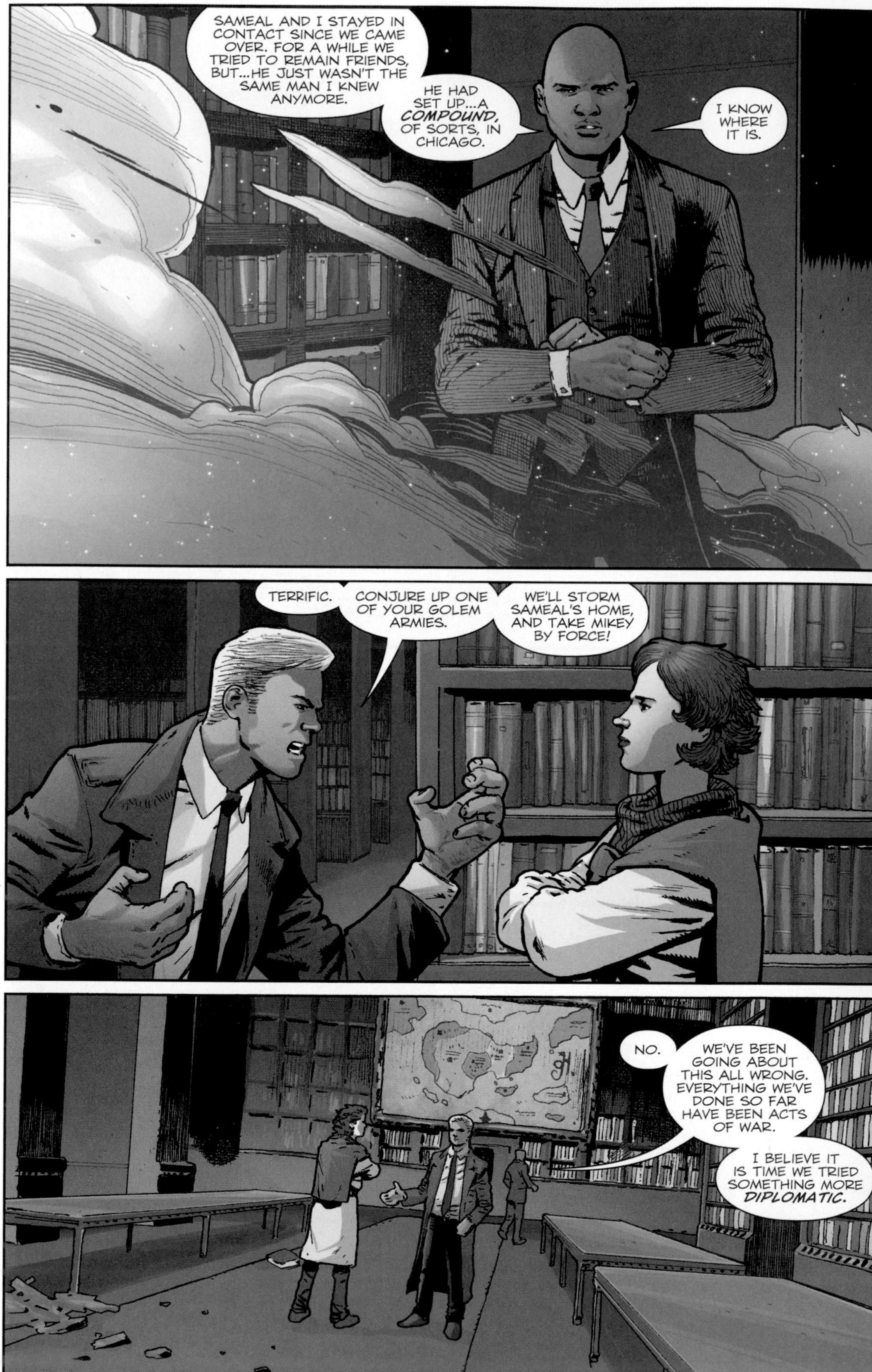
SAMEAL AND I STAYED IN CONTACT SINCE WE CAME OVER. FOR A WHILE WE TRIED TO REMAIN FRIENDS, BUT...HE JUST WASN'T THE SAME MAN I KNEW ANYMORE.
HE HAD SET UP...A **COMPOUND,** OF SORTS, IN CHICAGO.
I KNOW WHERE IT IS.
TERRIFIC.
CONJURE UP ONE OF YOUR GOLEM ARMIES.
WE'LL STORM SAMEAL'S HOME, AND TAKE MIKEY BY FORCE!
NO.
WE'VE BEEN GOING ABOUT THIS ALL WRONG. EVERYTHING WE'VE DONE SO FAR HAVE BEEN ACTS OF WAR.
I BELIEVE IT IS TIME WE TRIED SOMETHING MORE **DIPLOMATIC.**

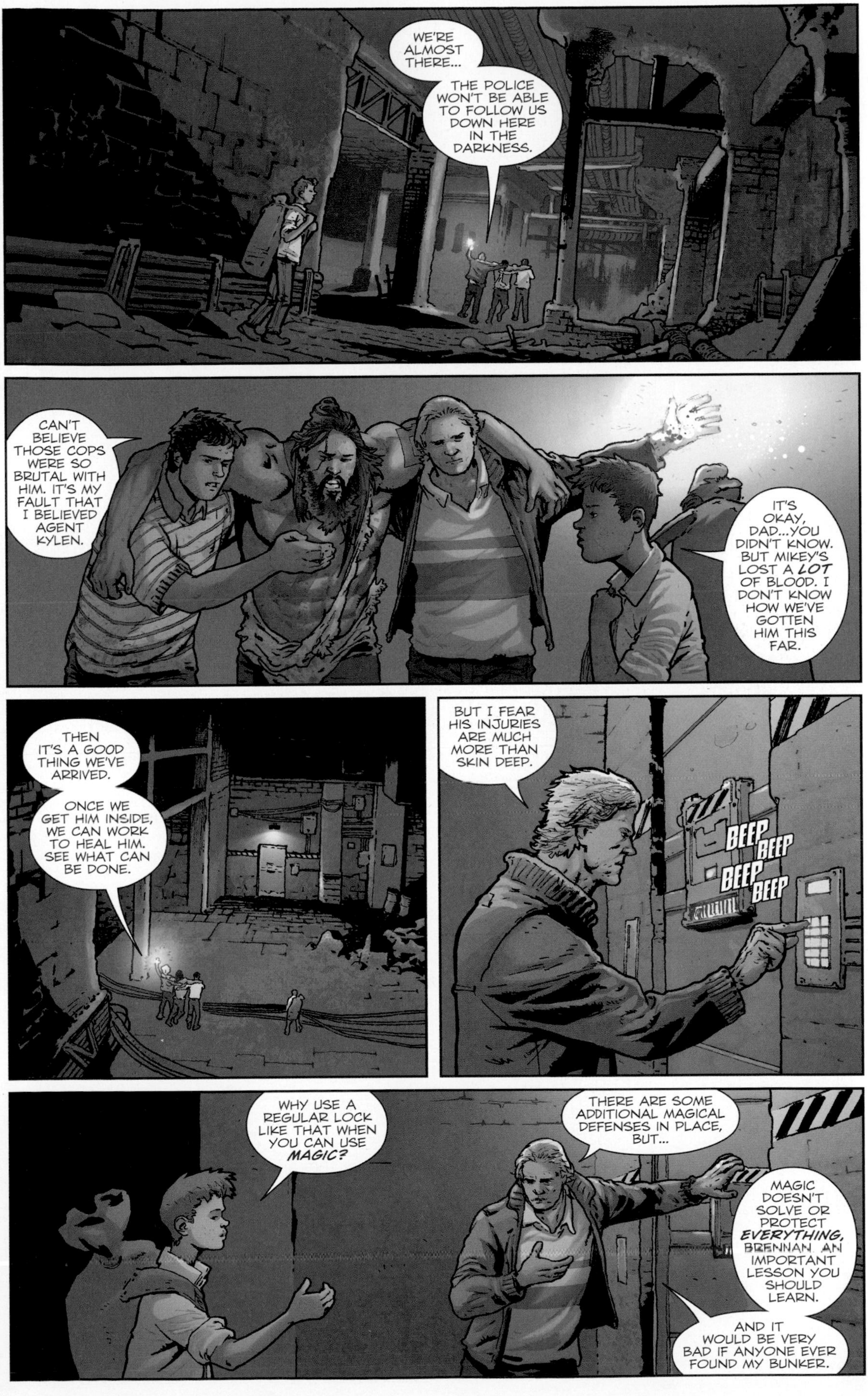
WE'RE ALMOST THERE...
THE POLICE WON'T BE ABLE TO FOLLOW US DOWN HERE IN THE DARKNESS.
CAN'T BELIEVE THOSE COPS WERE SO BRUTAL WITH HIM. IT'S MY FAULT THAT I BELIEVED AGENT KYLEN.
IT'S OKAY, DAD...YOU DIDN'T KNOW. BUT MIKEY'S LOST A LOT OF BLOOD. I DON'T KNOW HOW WE'VE GOTTEN HIM THIS FAR.
THEN IT'S A GOOD THING WE'VE ARRIVED.
ONCE WE GET HIM INSIDE, WE CAN WORK TO HEAL HIM. SEE WHAT CAN BE DONE.
BUT I FEAR HIS INJURIES ARE MUCH MORE THAN SKIN DEEP.
BEEP BEEP BEEP BEEP
WHY USE A REGULAR LOCK LIKE THAT WHEN YOU CAN USE MAGIC?
THERE ARE SOME ADDITIONAL MAGICAL DEFENSES IN PLACE, BUT...
MAGIC DOESN'T SOLVE OR PROTECT EVERYTHING, BRENNAN. AN IMPORTANT LESSON YOU SHOULD LEARN.
AND IT WOULD BE VERY BAD IF ANYONE EVER FOUND MY BUNKER.

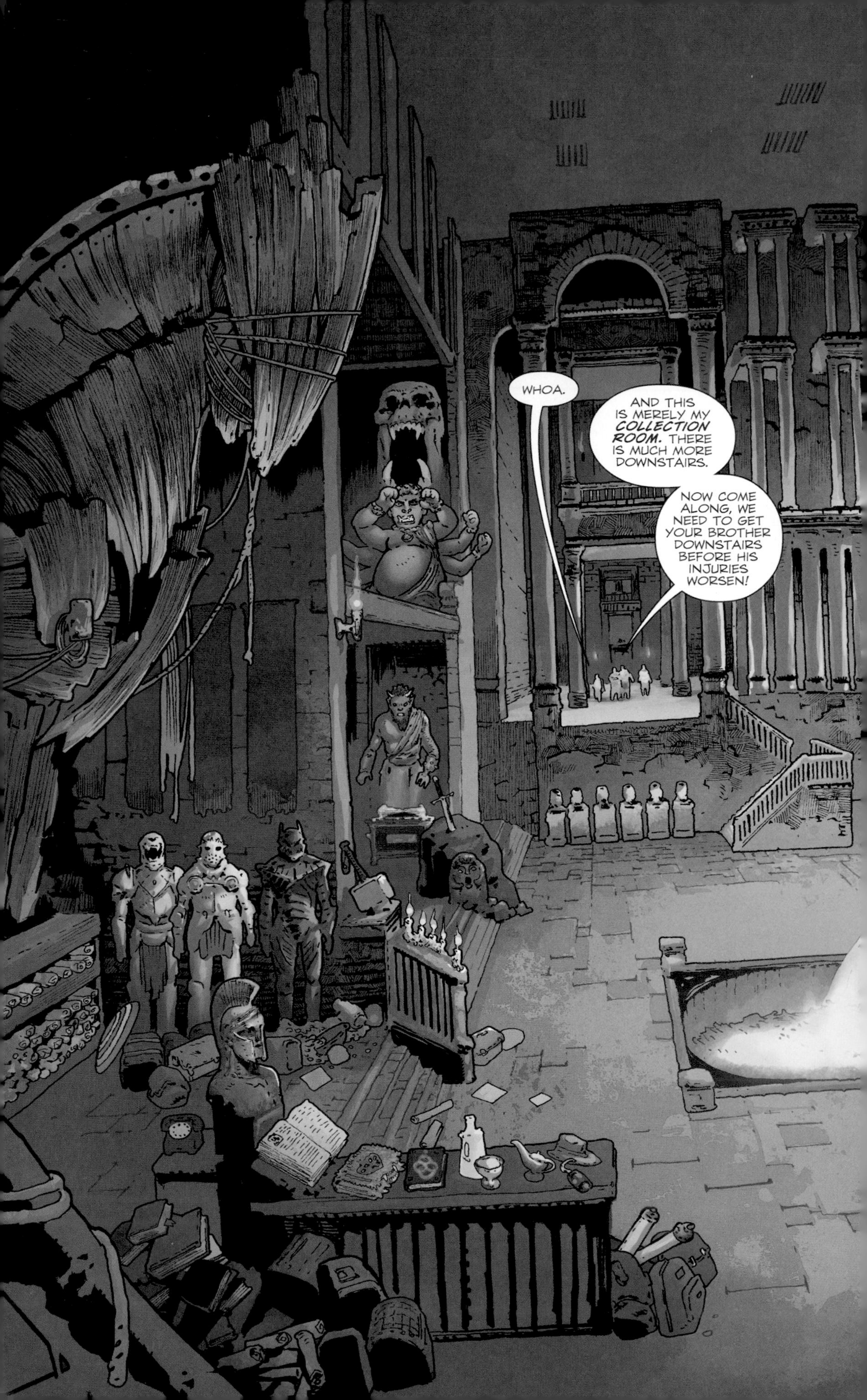
WHOA.
AND THIS IS MERELY MY **COLLECTION ROOM.** THERE IS MUCH MORE DOWNSTAIRS.
NOW COME ALONG, WE NEED TO GET YOUR BROTHER DOWNSTAIRS BEFORE HIS INJURIES WORSEN!

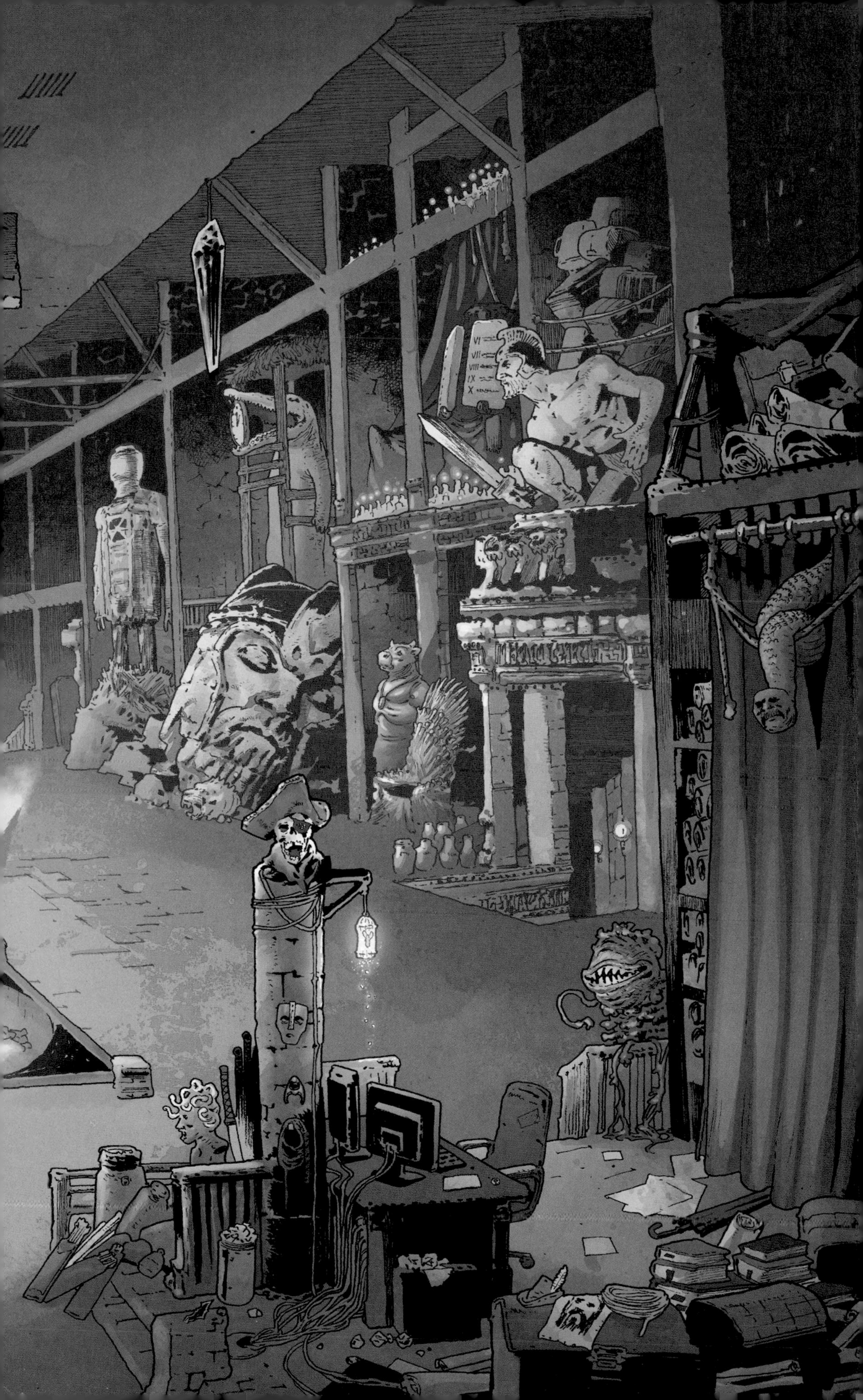

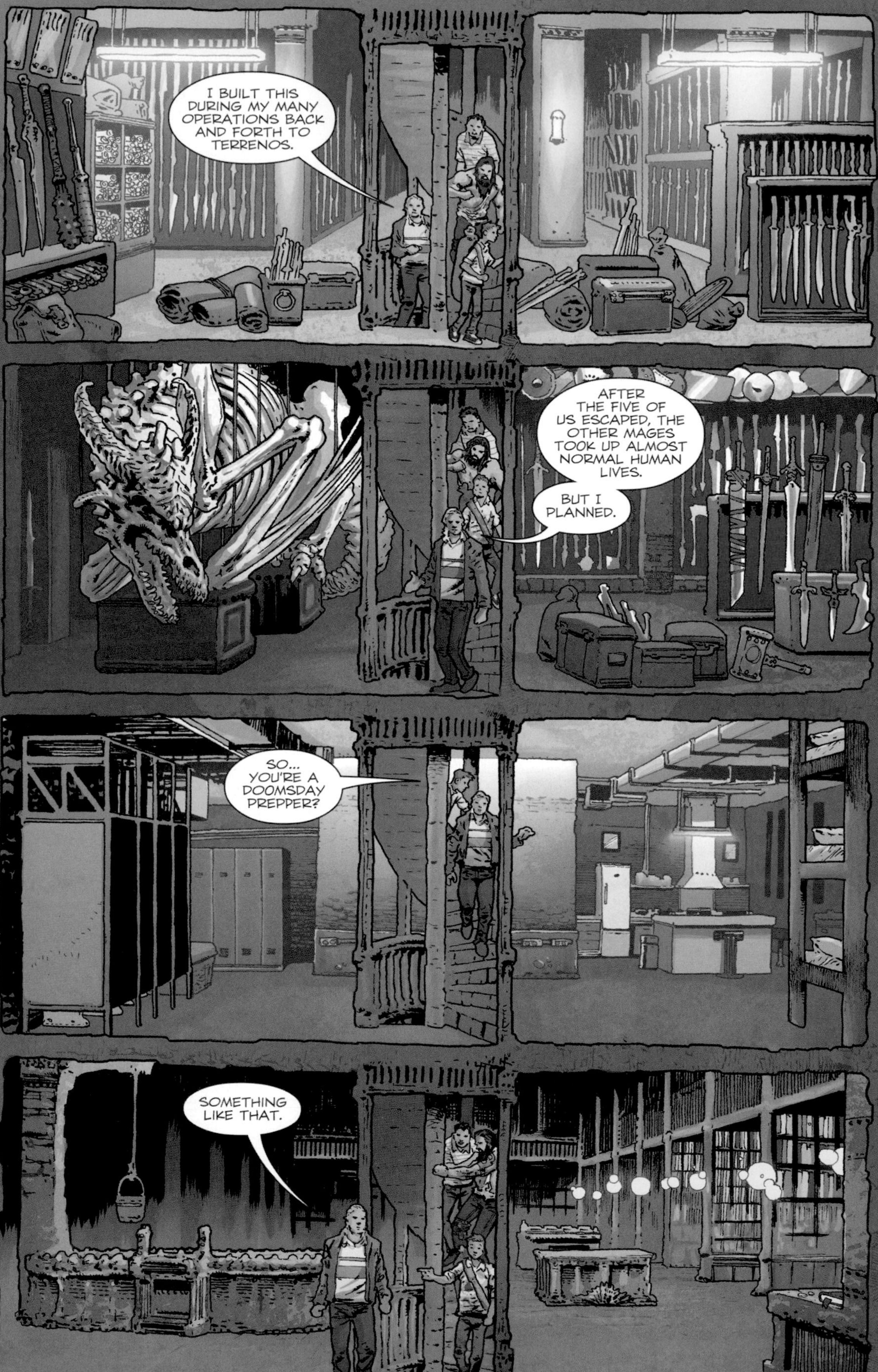
I BUILT THIS DURING MY MANY OPERATIONS BACK AND FORTH TO TERRENOS.
AFTER THE FIVE OF US ESCAPED, THE OTHER MAGES TOOK UP ALMOST NORMAL HUMAN LIVES.
BUT I PLANNED.
SO... YOU'RE A DOOMSDAY PREPPER?
SOMETHING LIKE THAT.

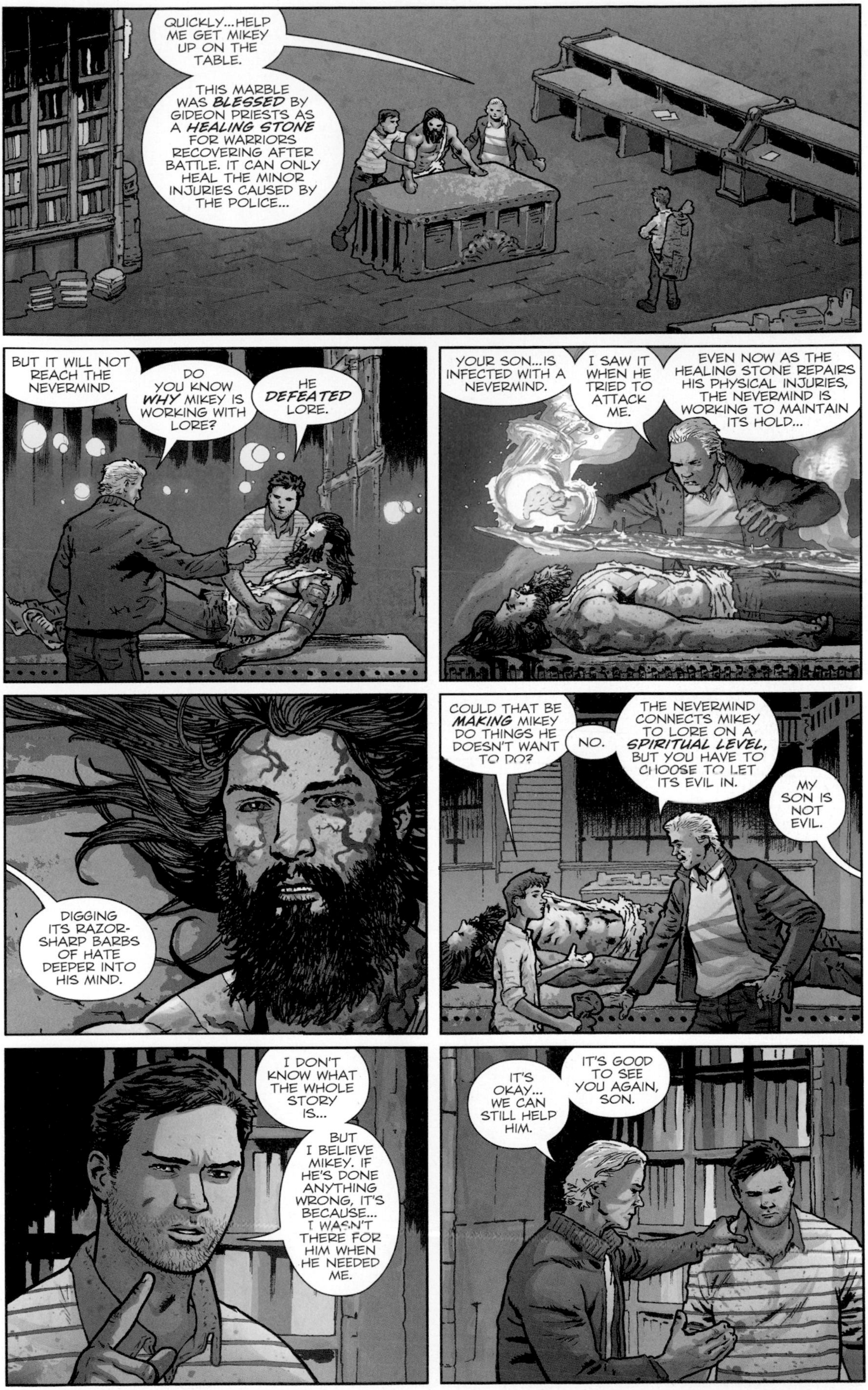
QUICKLY...HELP ME GET MIKEY UP ON THE TABLE.
THIS MARBLE WAS BLESSED BY GIDEON PRIESTS AS A HEALING STONE FOR WARRIORS RECOVERING AFTER BATTLE. IT CAN ONLY HEAL THE MINOR INJURIES CAUSED BY THE POLICE...
BUT IT WILL NOT REACH THE NEVERMIND.
DO YOU KNOW WHY MIKEY IS WORKING WITH LORE?
HE DEFEATED LORE.
YOUR SON...IS INFECTED WITH A NEVERMIND.
I SAW IT WHEN HE TRIED TO ATTACK ME.
EVEN NOW AS THE HEALING STONE REPAIRS HIS PHYSICAL INJURIES, THE NEVERMIND IS WORKING TO MAINTAIN ITS HOLD...
DIGGING ITS RAZOR-SHARP BARBS OF HATE DEEPER INTO HIS MIND.
COULD THAT BE MAKING MIKEY DO THINGS HE DOESN'T WANT TO DO?
NO.
THE NEVERMIND CONNECTS MIKEY TO LORE ON A SPIRITUAL LEVEL, BUT YOU HAVE TO CHOOSE TO LET ITS EVIL IN.
MY SON IS NOT EVIL.
I DON'T KNOW WHAT THE WHOLE STORY IS...
BUT I BELIEVE MIKEY. IF HE'S DONE ANYTHING WRONG, IT'S BECAUSE... I WASN'T THERE FOR HIM WHEN HE NEEDED ME.
IT'S OKAY... WE CAN STILL HELP HIM.
IT'S GOOD TO SEE YOU AGAIN, SON.

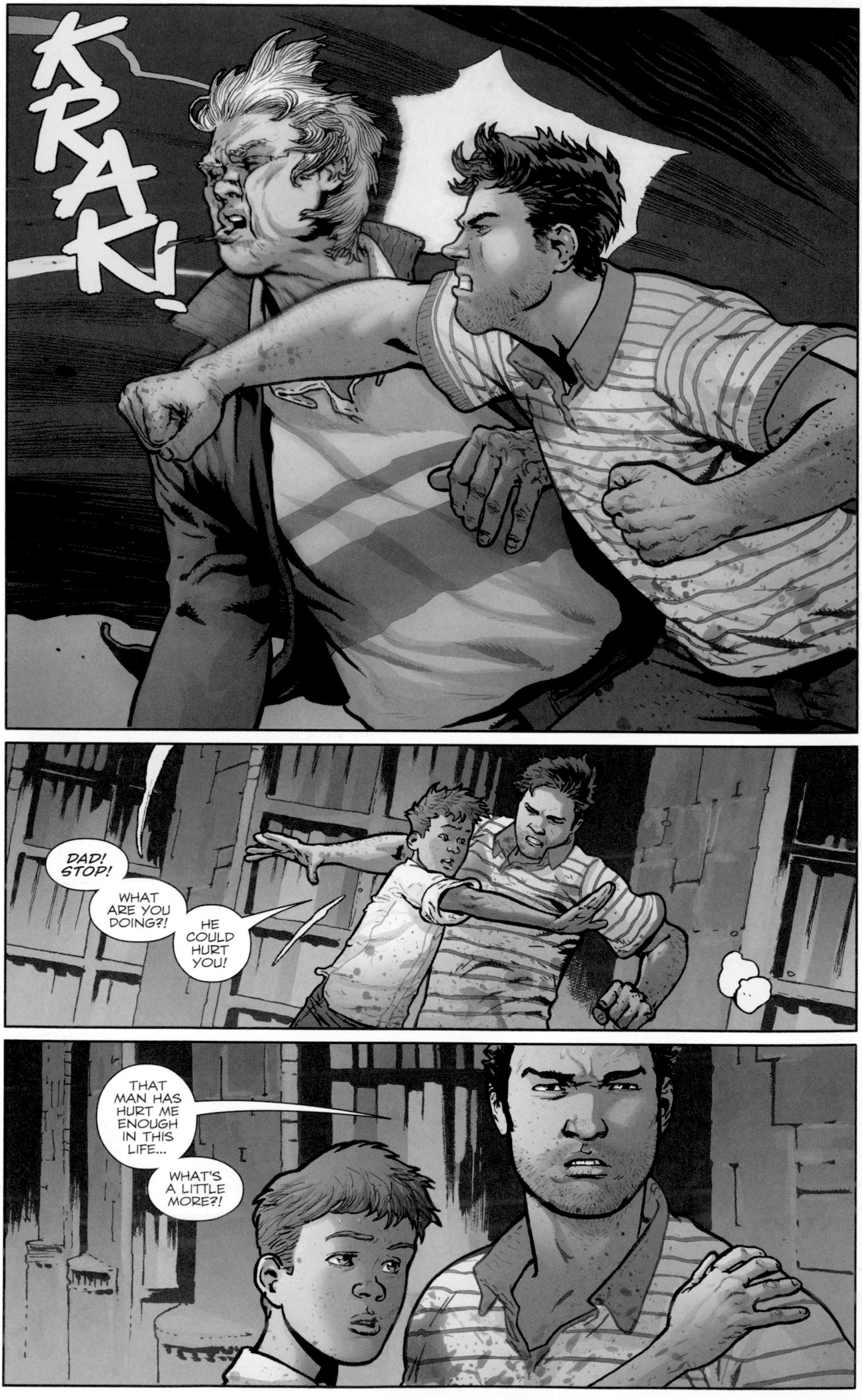
KRAK!
DAD! STOP!
WHAT ARE YOU DOING?!
HE COULD HURT YOU!
THAT MAN HAS HURT ME ENOUGH IN THIS LIFE...
WHAT'S A LITTLE MORE?!

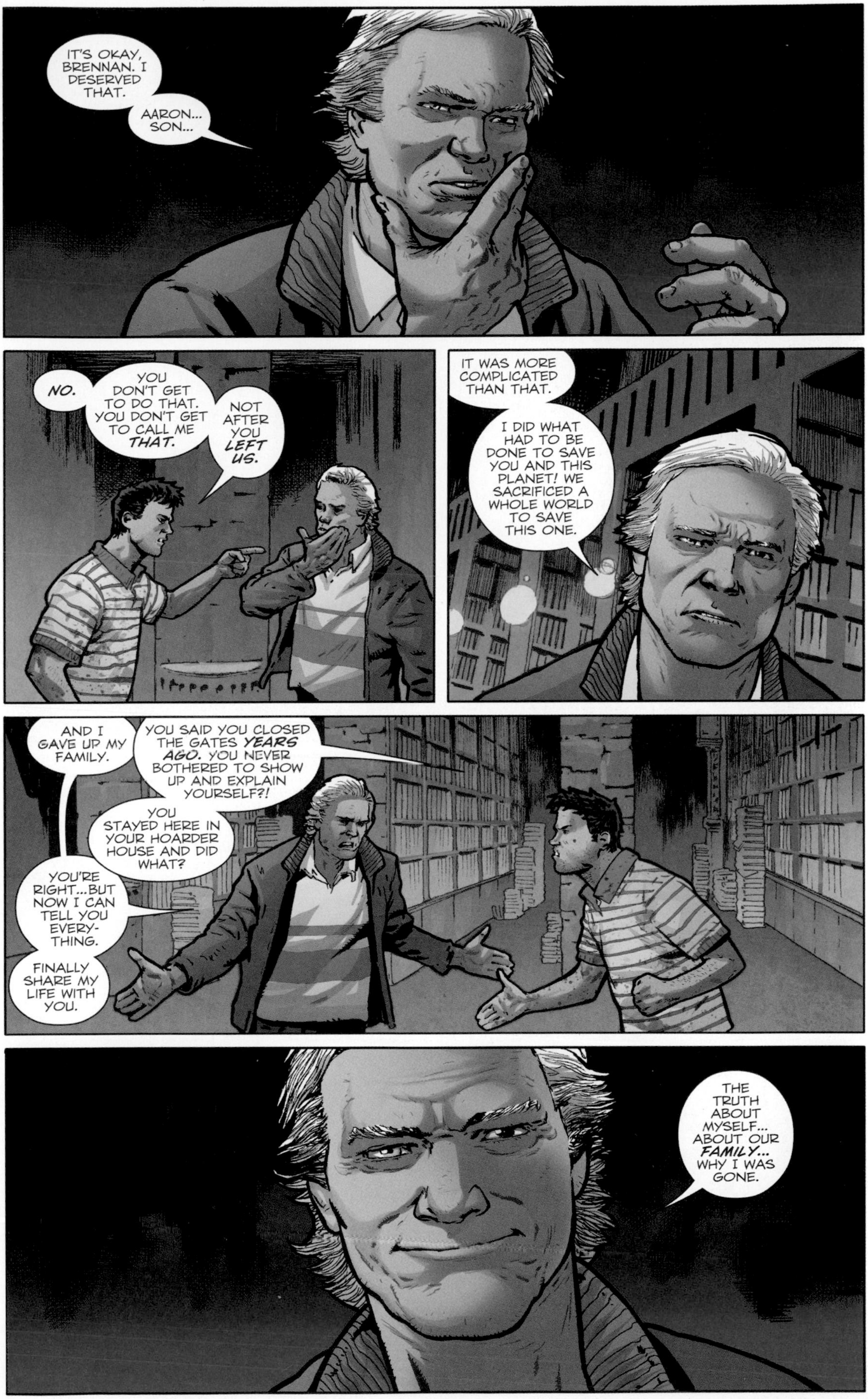
IT'S OKAY, BRENNAN. I DESERVED THAT.
AARON... SON...
NO.
YOU DON'T GET TO DO THAT. YOU DON'T GET TO CALL ME THAT.
NOT AFTER YOU LEFT US.
IT WAS MORE COMPLICATED THAN THAT.
I DID WHAT HAD TO BE DONE TO SAVE YOU AND THIS PLANET! WE SACRIFICED A WHOLE WORLD TO SAVE THIS ONE.
AND I GAVE UP MY FAMILY.
YOU SAID YOU CLOSED THE GATES YEARS AGO. YOU NEVER BOTHERED TO SHOW UP AND EXPLAIN YOURSELF?!
YOU STAYED HERE IN YOUR HOARDER HOUSE AND DID WHAT?
YOU'RE RIGHT...BUT NOW I CAN TELL YOU EVERY-THING.
FINALLY SHARE MY LIFE WITH YOU.
THE TRUTH ABOUT MYSELF... ABOUT OUR FAMILY... WHY I WAS GONE.

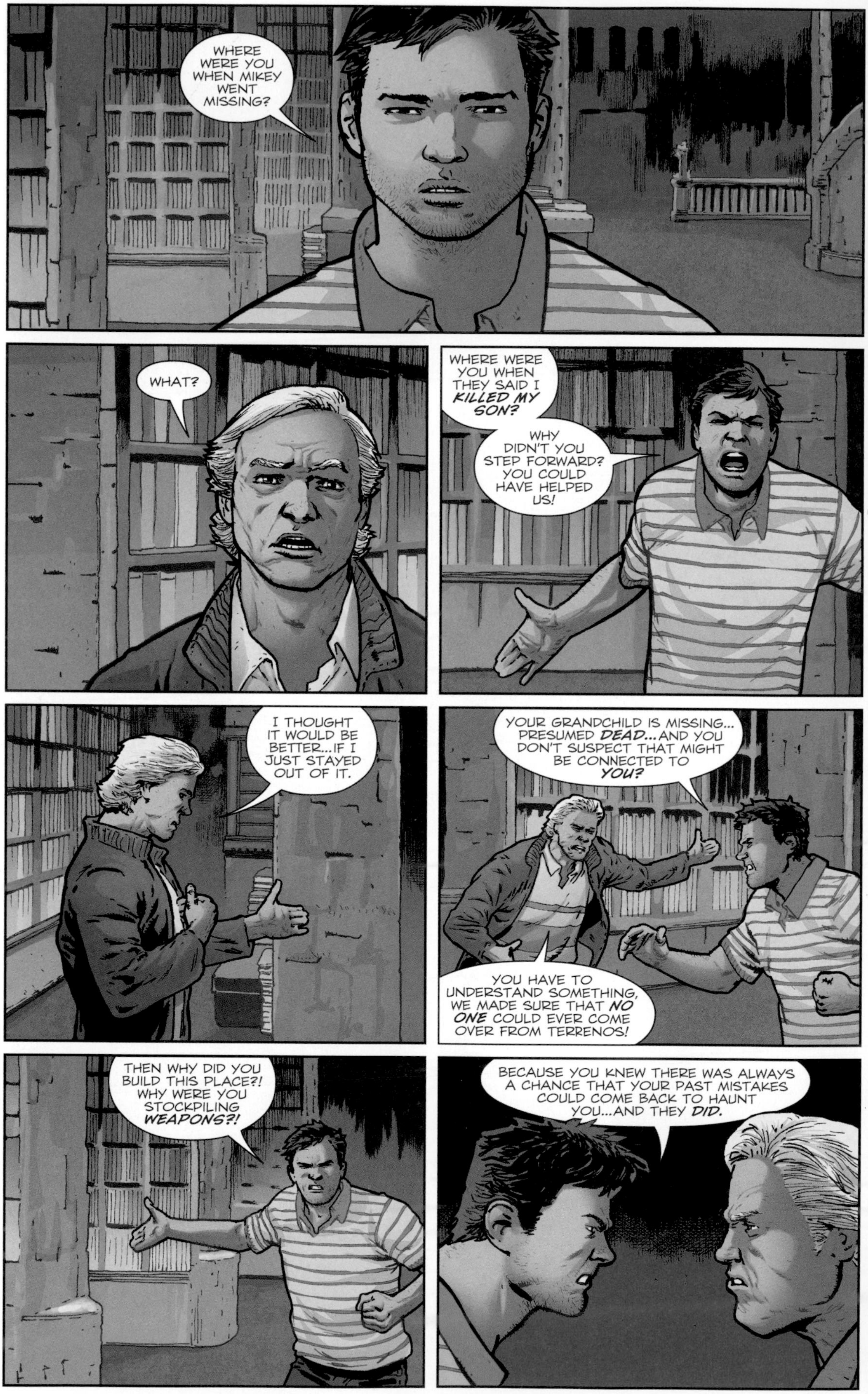
WHERE WERE YOU WHEN MIKEY WENT MISSING?
WHAT?
WHERE WERE YOU WHEN THEY SAID I *KILLED MY SON?*
WHY DIDN'T YOU STEP FORWARD? YOU COULD HAVE HELPED US!
I THOUGHT IT WOULD BE BETTER...IF I JUST STAYED OUT OF IT.
YOUR GRANDCHILD IS MISSING... PRESUMED *DEAD*...AND YOU DON'T SUSPECT THAT MIGHT BE CONNECTED TO *YOU?*
YOU HAVE TO UNDERSTAND SOMETHING, WE MADE SURE THAT *NO ONE* COULD EVER COME OVER FROM TERRENOS!
THEN WHY DID YOU BUILD THIS PLACE?! WHY WERE YOU STOCKPILING *WEAPONS?!*
BECAUSE YOU KNEW THERE WAS ALWAYS A CHANCE THAT YOUR PAST MISTAKES COULD COME BACK TO HAUNT YOU...AND THEY *DID.*

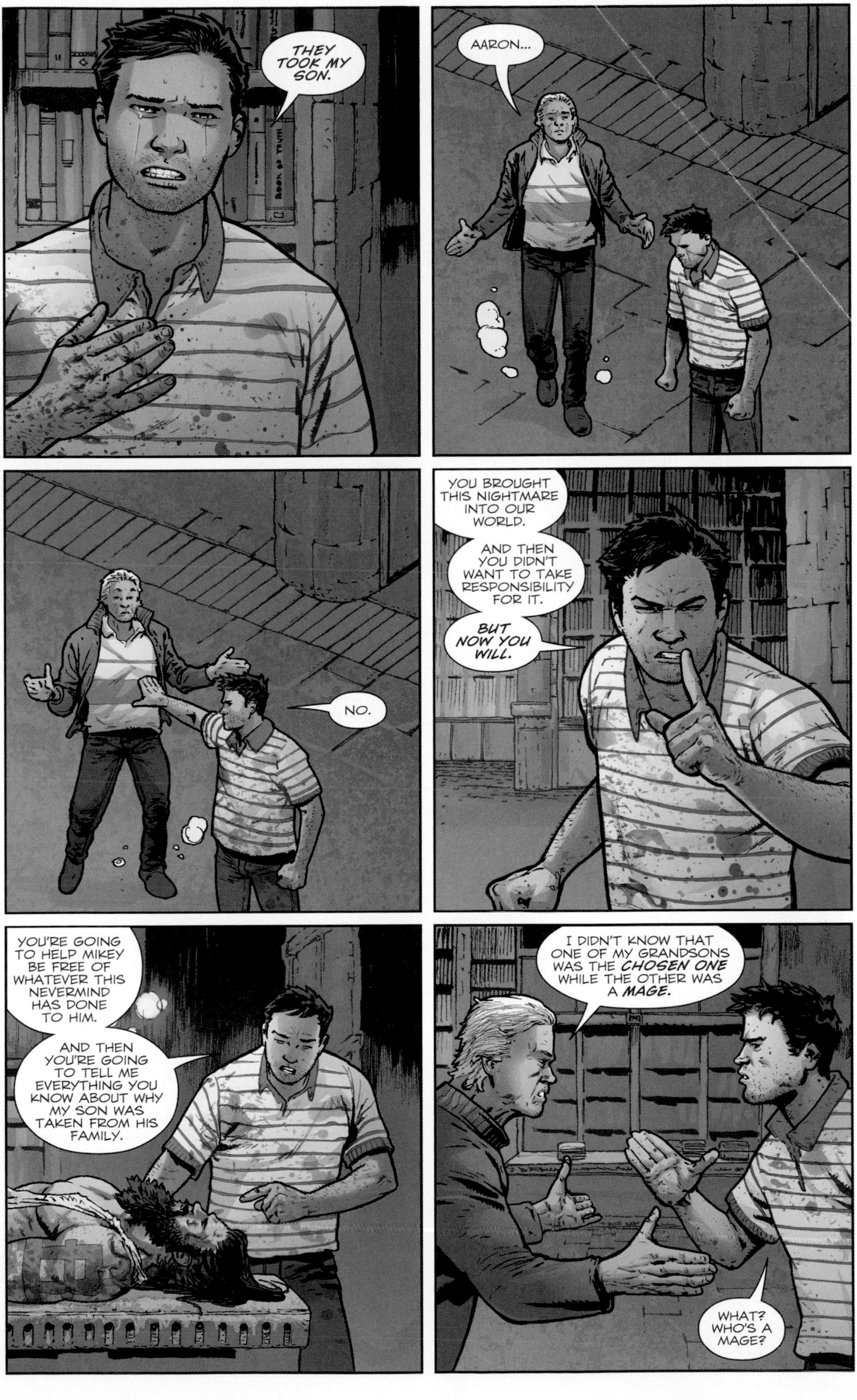
THEY TOOK MY SON.
AARON...
NO.
YOU BROUGHT THIS NIGHTMARE INTO OUR WORLD.
AND THEN YOU DIDN'T WANT TO TAKE RESPONSIBILITY FOR IT.
BUT NOW YOU WILL.
YOU'RE GOING TO HELP MIKEY BE FREE OF WHATEVER THIS NEVERMIND HAS DONE TO HIM.
AND THEN YOU'RE GOING TO TELL ME EVERYTHING YOU KNOW ABOUT WHY MY SON WAS TAKEN FROM HIS FAMILY.
I DIDN'T KNOW THAT ONE OF MY GRANDSONS WAS THE CHOSEN ONE WHILE THE OTHER WAS A MAGE.
WHAT? WHO'S A MAGE?

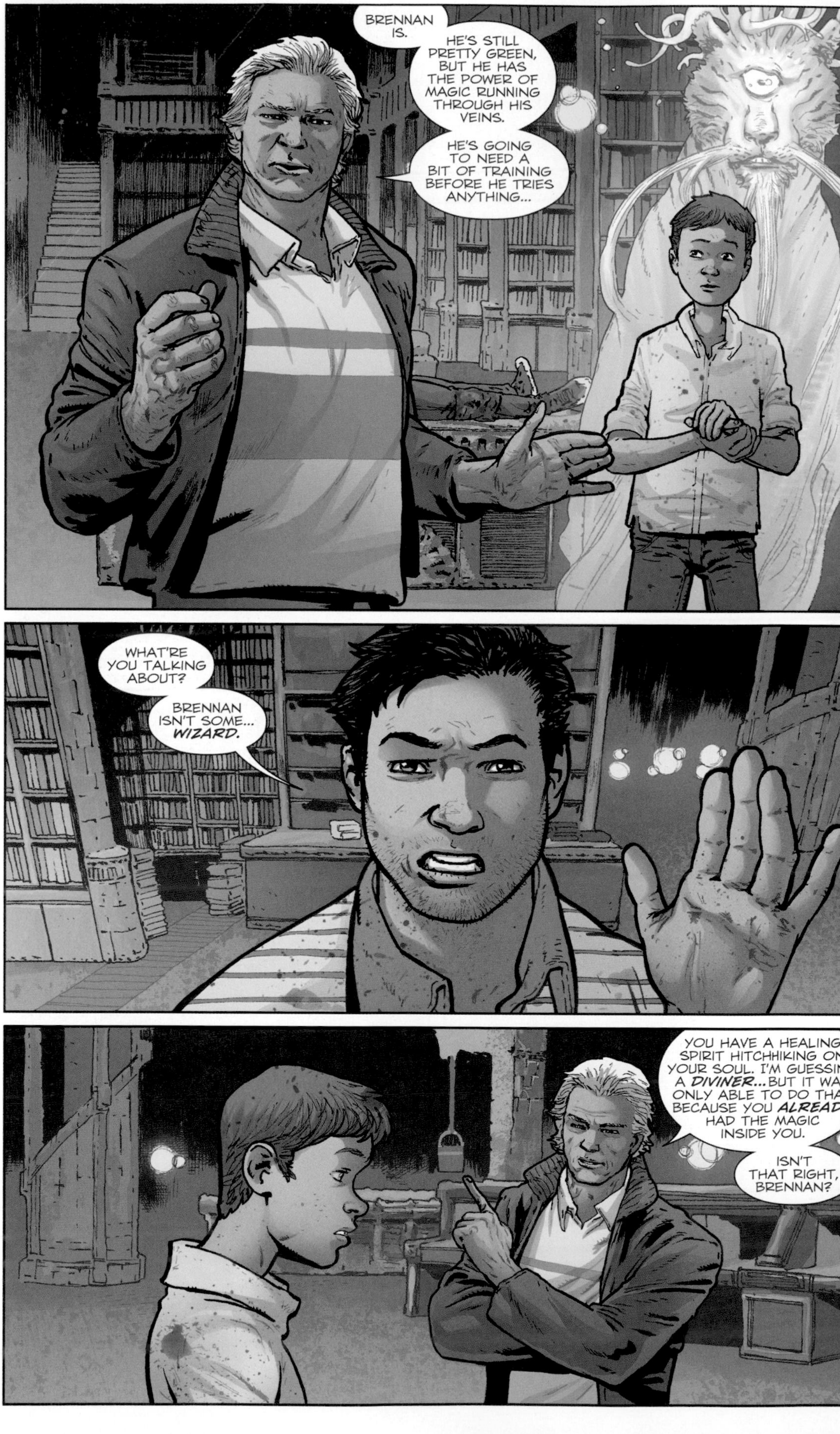
BRENNAN IS.
HE'S STILL PRETTY GREEN, BUT HE HAS THE POWER OF MAGIC RUNNING THROUGH HIS VEINS.
HE'S GOING TO NEED A BIT OF TRAINING BEFORE HE TRIES ANYTHING...
WHAT'RE YOU TALKING ABOUT?
BRENNAN ISN'T SOME... WIZARD.
YOU HAVE A HEALING SPIRIT HITCHHIKING ON YOUR SOUL. I'M GUESSING A DIVINER... BUT IT WAS ONLY ABLE TO DO THAT BECAUSE YOU ALREADY HAD THE MAGIC INSIDE YOU.
ISN'T THAT RIGHT, BRENNAN?

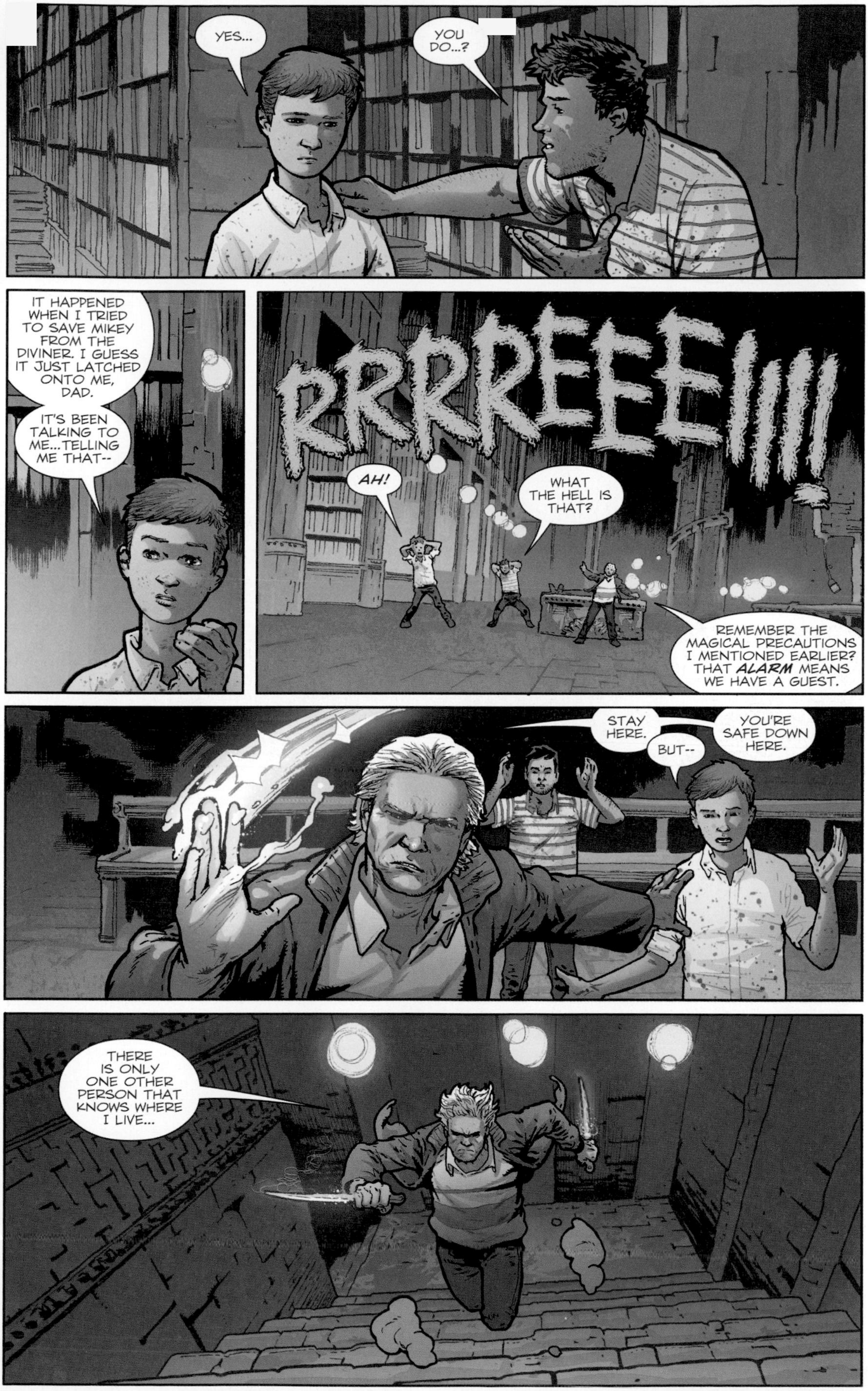
YES...
YOU DO...?
IT HAPPENED WHEN I TRIED TO SAVE MIKEY FROM THE DIVINER. I GUESS IT JUST LATCHED ONTO ME, DAD.
IT'S BEEN TALKING TO ME...TELLING ME THAT--
RRRREEEE!!!!!
AH!
WHAT THE HELL IS THAT?
REMEMBER THE MAGICAL PRECAUTIONS I MENTIONED EARLIER? THAT ALARM MEANS WE HAVE A GUEST.
STAY HERE.
YOU'RE SAFE DOWN HERE.
BUT--
THERE IS ONLY ONE OTHER PERSON THAT KNOWS WHERE I LIVE...

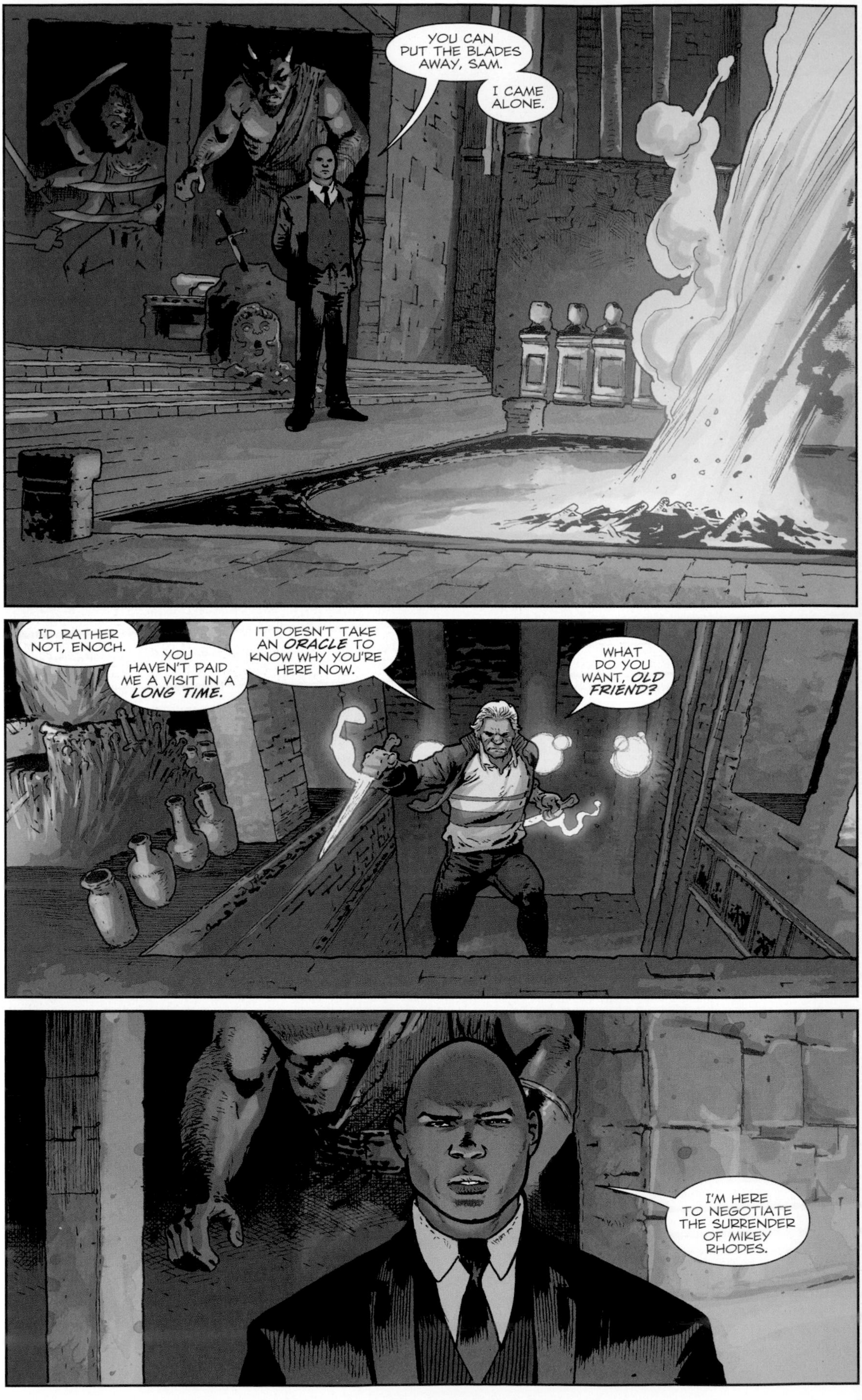
YOU CAN PUT THE BLADES AWAY, SAM.
I CAME ALONE.
I'D RATHER NOT, ENOCH.
YOU HAVEN'T PAID ME A VISIT IN A LONG TIME.
IT DOESN'T TAKE AN ORACLE TO KNOW WHY YOU'RE HERE NOW.
WHAT DO YOU WANT, OLD FRIEND?
I'M HERE TO NEGOTIATE THE SURRENDER OF MIKEY RHODES.

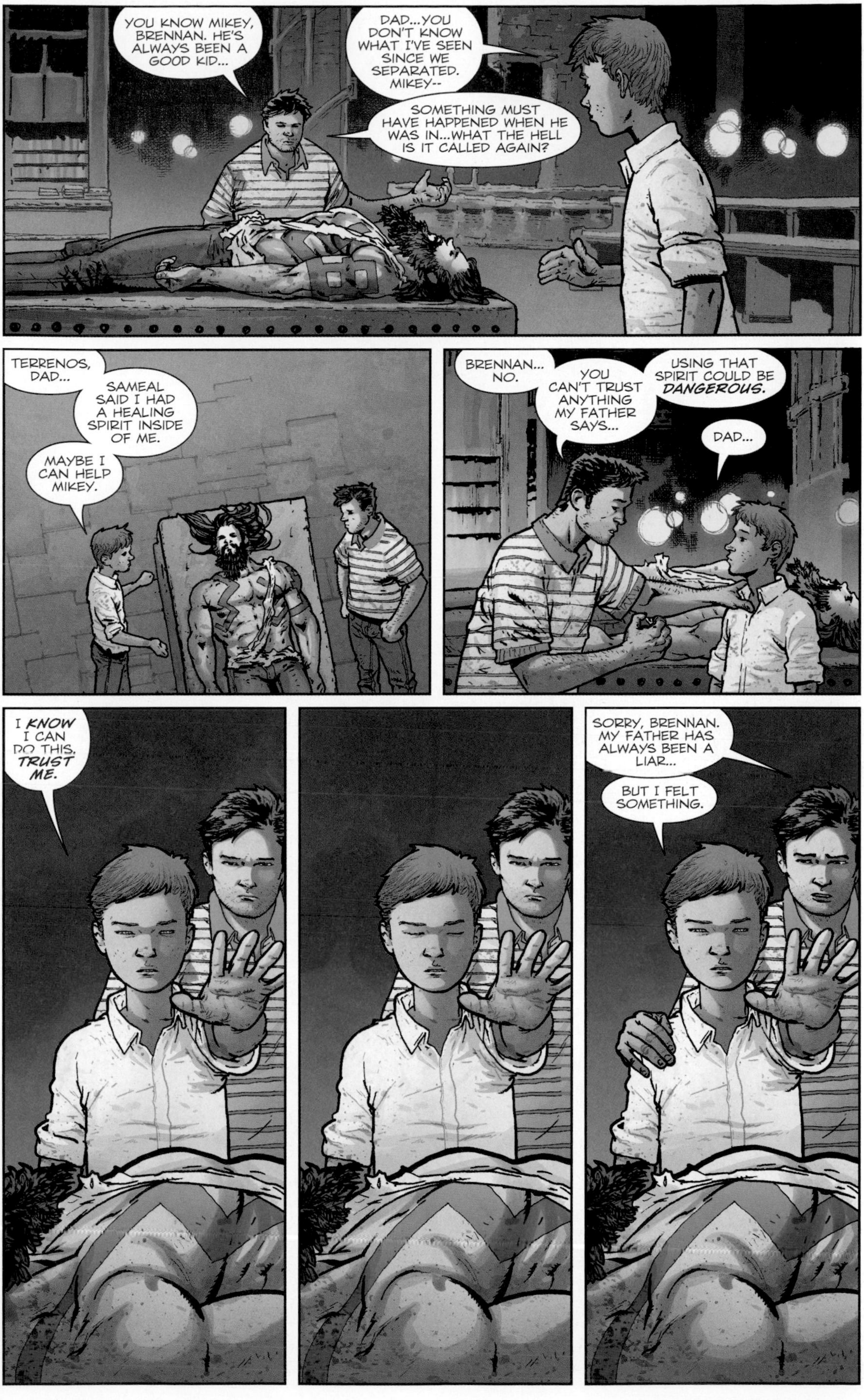
YOU KNOW MIKEY, BRENNAN. HE'S ALWAYS BEEN A GOOD KID...
DAD...YOU DON'T KNOW WHAT I'VE SEEN SINCE WE SEPARATED. MIKEY--
SOMETHING MUST HAVE HAPPENED WHEN HE WAS IN...WHAT THE HELL IS IT CALLED AGAIN?
TERRENOS, DAD...
SAMEAL SAID I HAD A HEALING SPIRIT INSIDE OF ME.
MAYBE I CAN HELP MIKEY.
BRENNAN... NO.
YOU CAN'T TRUST ANYTHING MY FATHER SAYS...
USING THAT SPIRIT COULD BE *DANGEROUS.*
DAD...
I *KNOW* I CAN DO THIS. *TRUST ME.*
SORRY, BRENNAN. MY FATHER HAS ALWAYS BEEN A LIAR...
BUT I FELT SOMETHING.

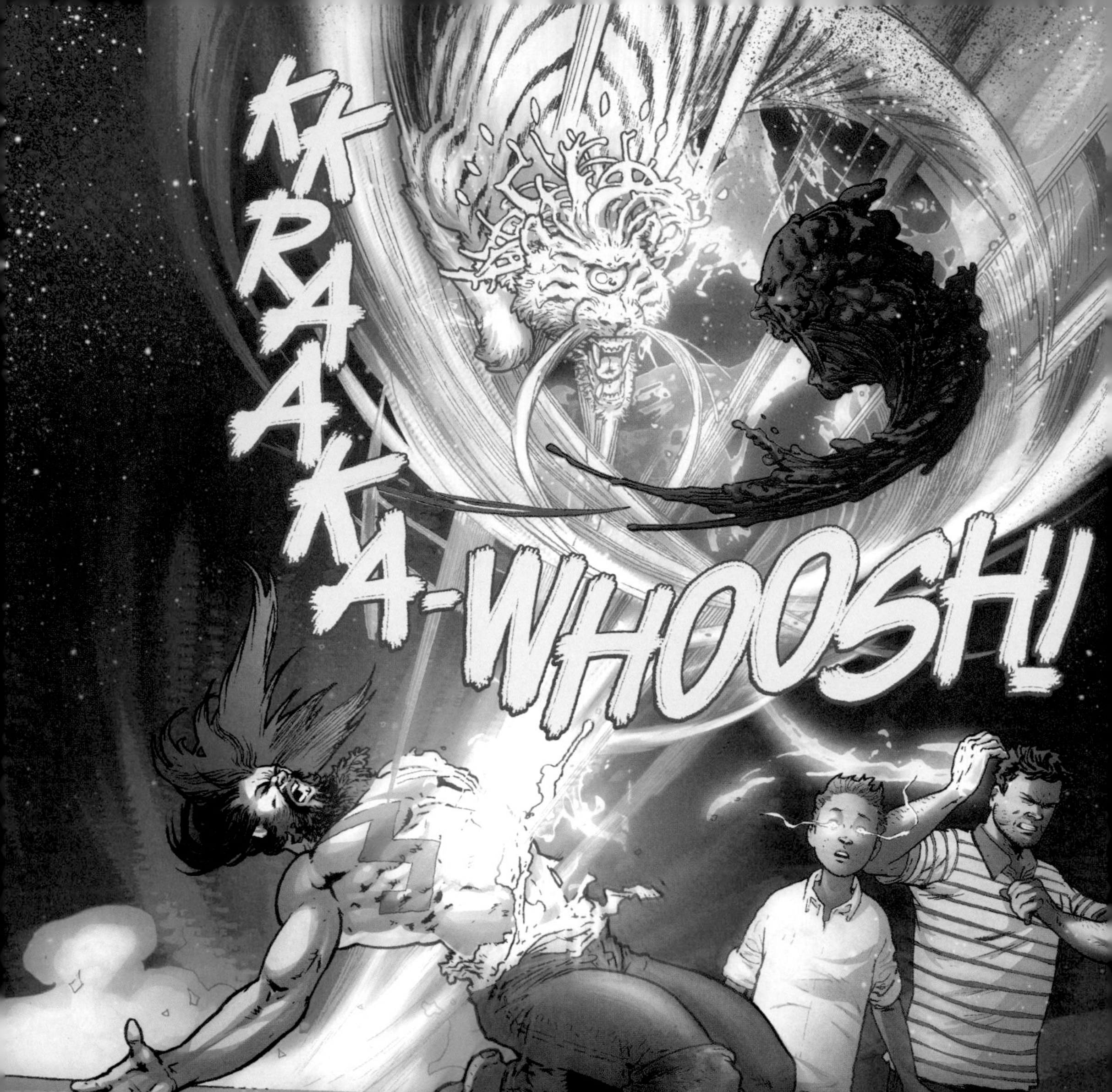
KKRAKKA-WHOOSH!

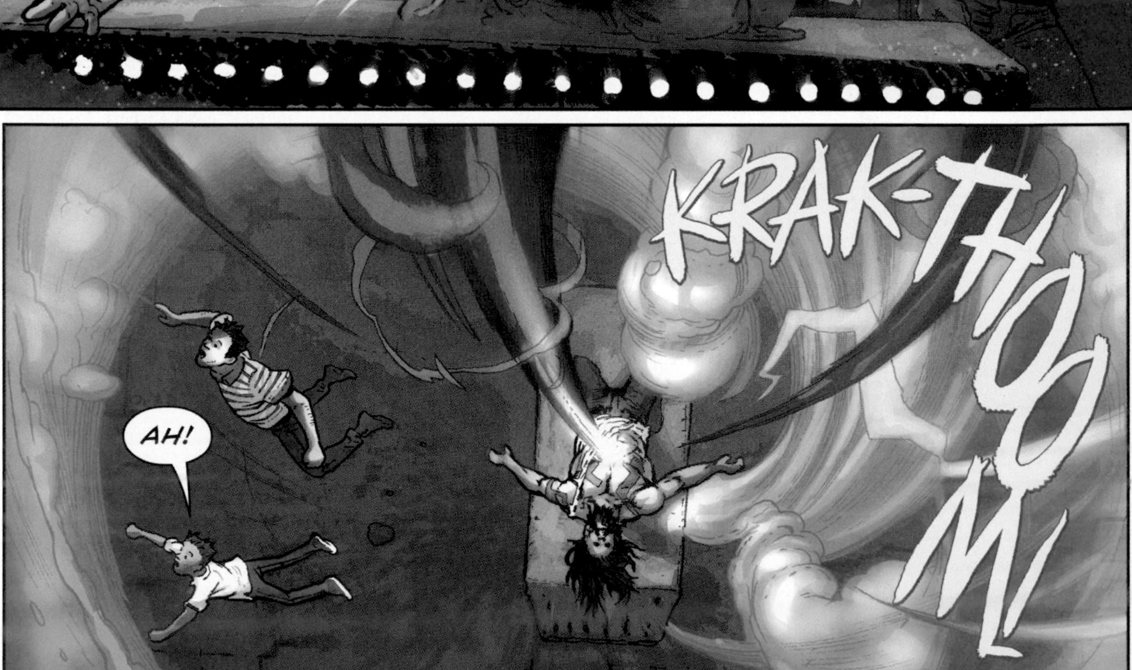
KRAK-THOOM!
AH!

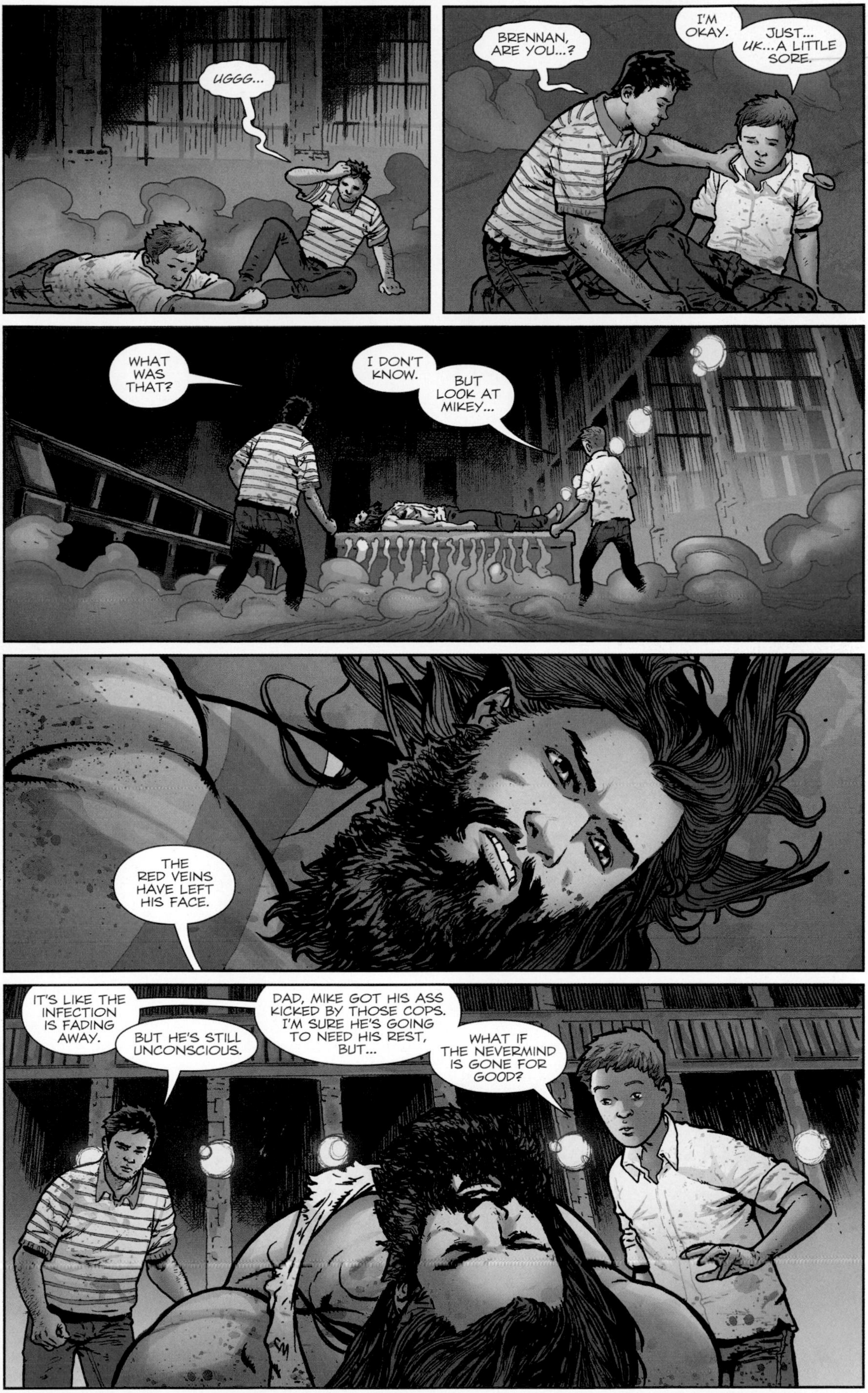
UGGG...
BRENNAN, ARE YOU...?
I'M OKAY.
JUST... UK...A LITTLE SORE.
WHAT WAS THAT?
I DON'T KNOW.
BUT LOOK AT MIKEY...
THE RED VEINS HAVE LEFT HIS FACE.
IT'S LIKE THE INFECTION IS FADING AWAY.
BUT HE'S STILL UNCONSCIOUS.
DAD, MIKE GOT HIS ASS KICKED BY THOSE COPS. I'M SURE HE'S GOING TO NEED HIS REST, BUT...
WHAT IF THE NEVERMIND IS GONE FOR GOOD?

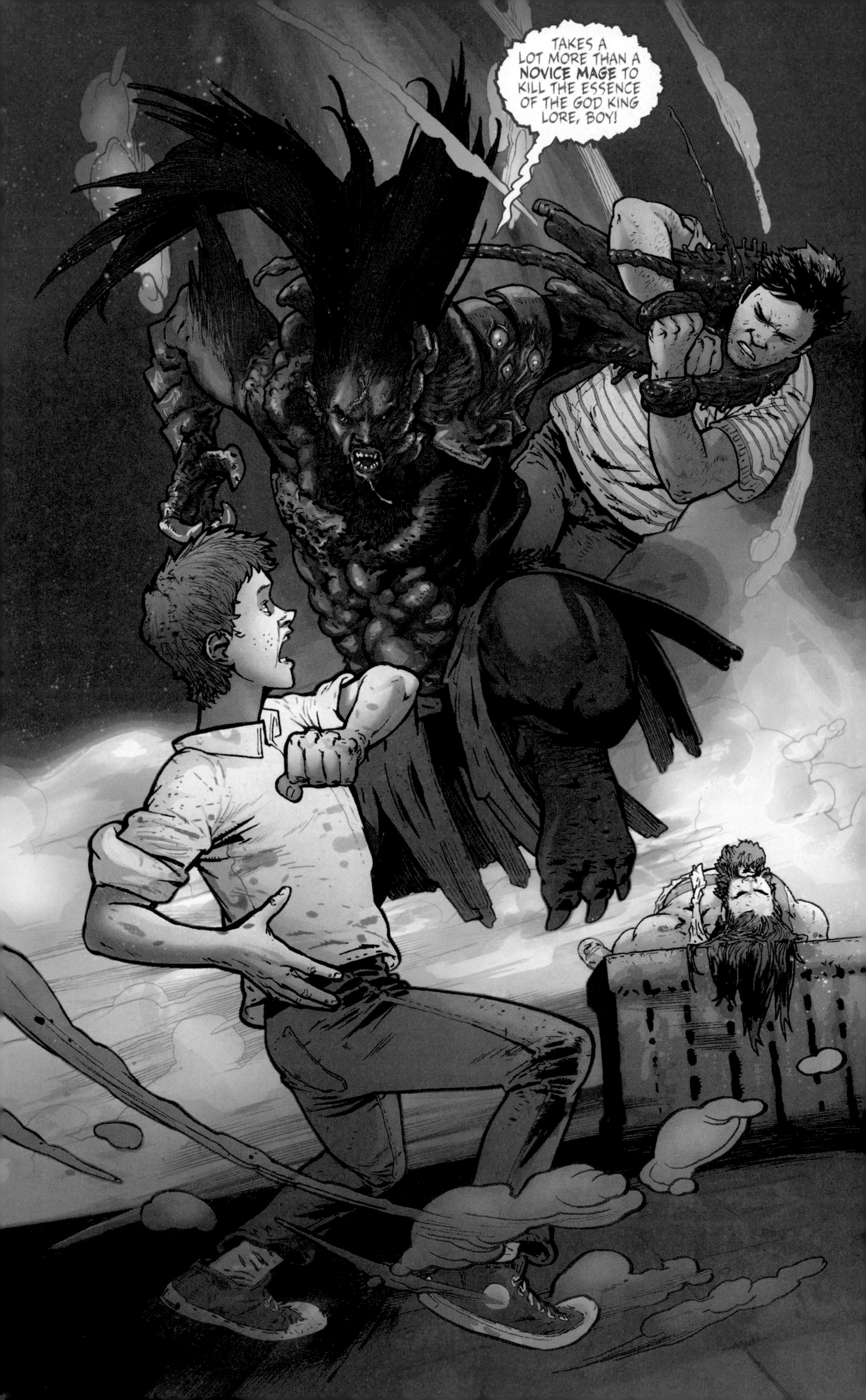
TAKES A LOT MORE THAN A **NOVICE MAGE** TO KILL THE ESSENCE OF THE GOD KING LORE, BOY!

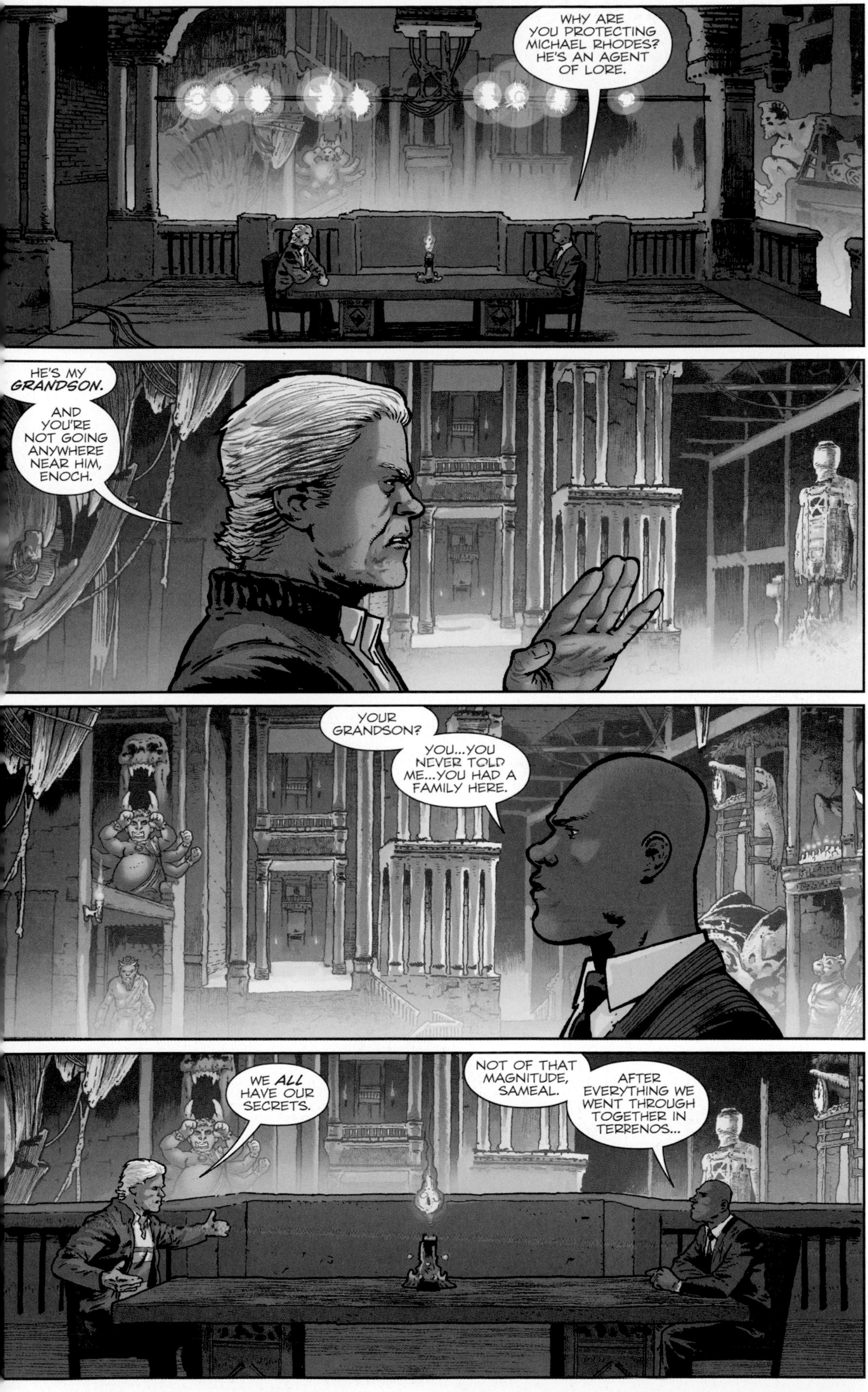
WHY ARE YOU PROTECTING MICHAEL RHODES? HE'S AN AGENT OF LORE.
HE'S MY **GRANDSON.**
AND YOU'RE NOT GOING ANYWHERE NEAR HIM, ENOCH.
YOUR GRANDSON?
YOU...YOU NEVER TOLD ME...YOU HAD A FAMILY HERE.
WE ***ALL*** HAVE OUR SECRETS.
NOT OF THAT MAGNITUDE, SAMEAL.
AFTER EVERYTHING WE WENT THROUGH TOGETHER IN TERRENOS...

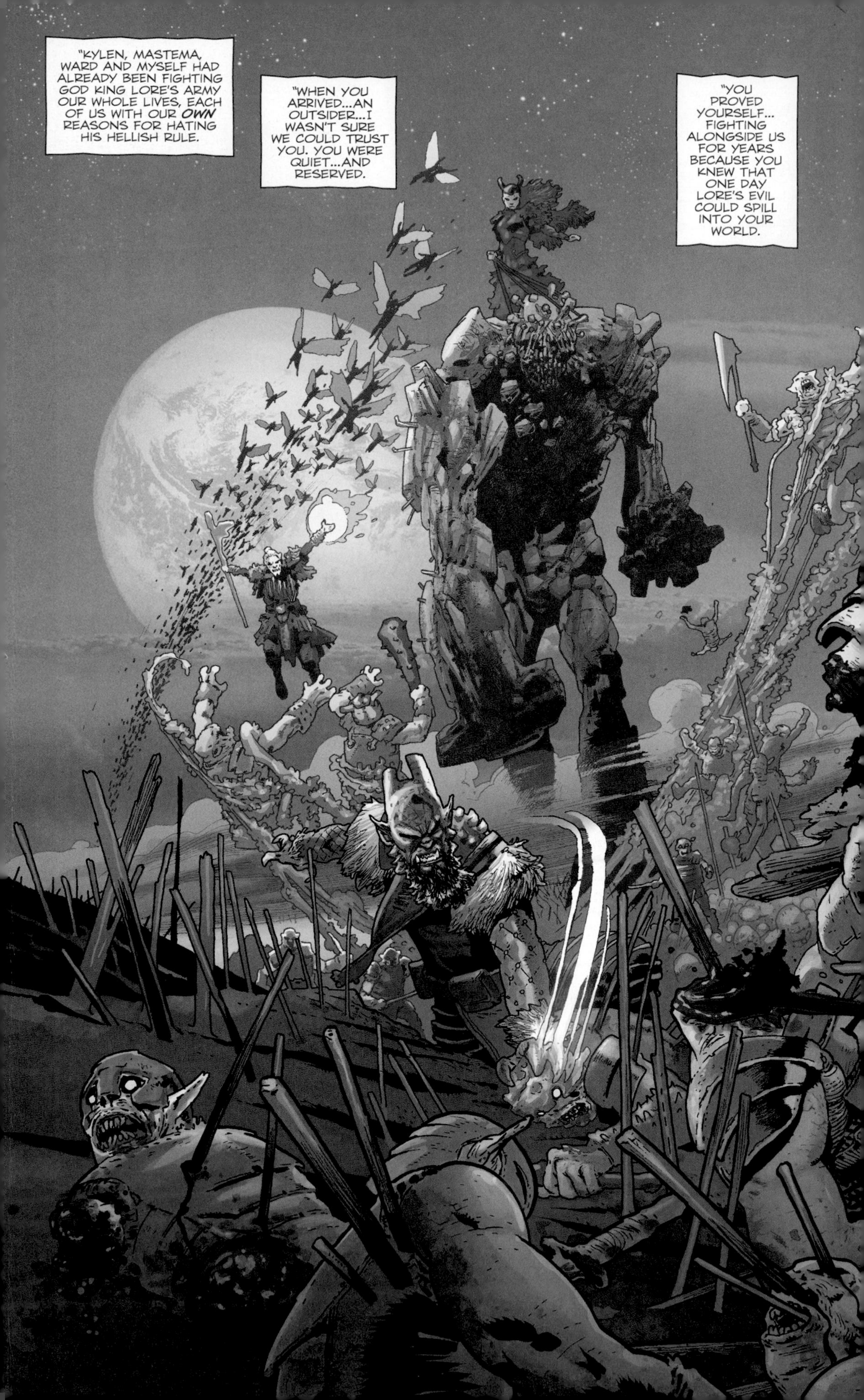
"KYLEN, MASTEMA, WARD AND MYSELF HAD ALREADY BEEN FIGHTING GOD KING LORE'S ARMY OUR WHOLE LIVES, EACH OF US WITH OUR *OWN* REASONS FOR HATING HIS HELLISH RULE.
"WHEN YOU ARRIVED...AN OUTSIDER...I WASN'T SURE WE COULD TRUST YOU. YOU WERE QUIET...AND RESERVED.
"YOU PROVED YOURSELF... FIGHTING ALONGSIDE US FOR YEARS BECAUSE YOU KNEW THAT ONE DAY LORE'S EVIL COULD SPILL INTO YOUR WORLD.

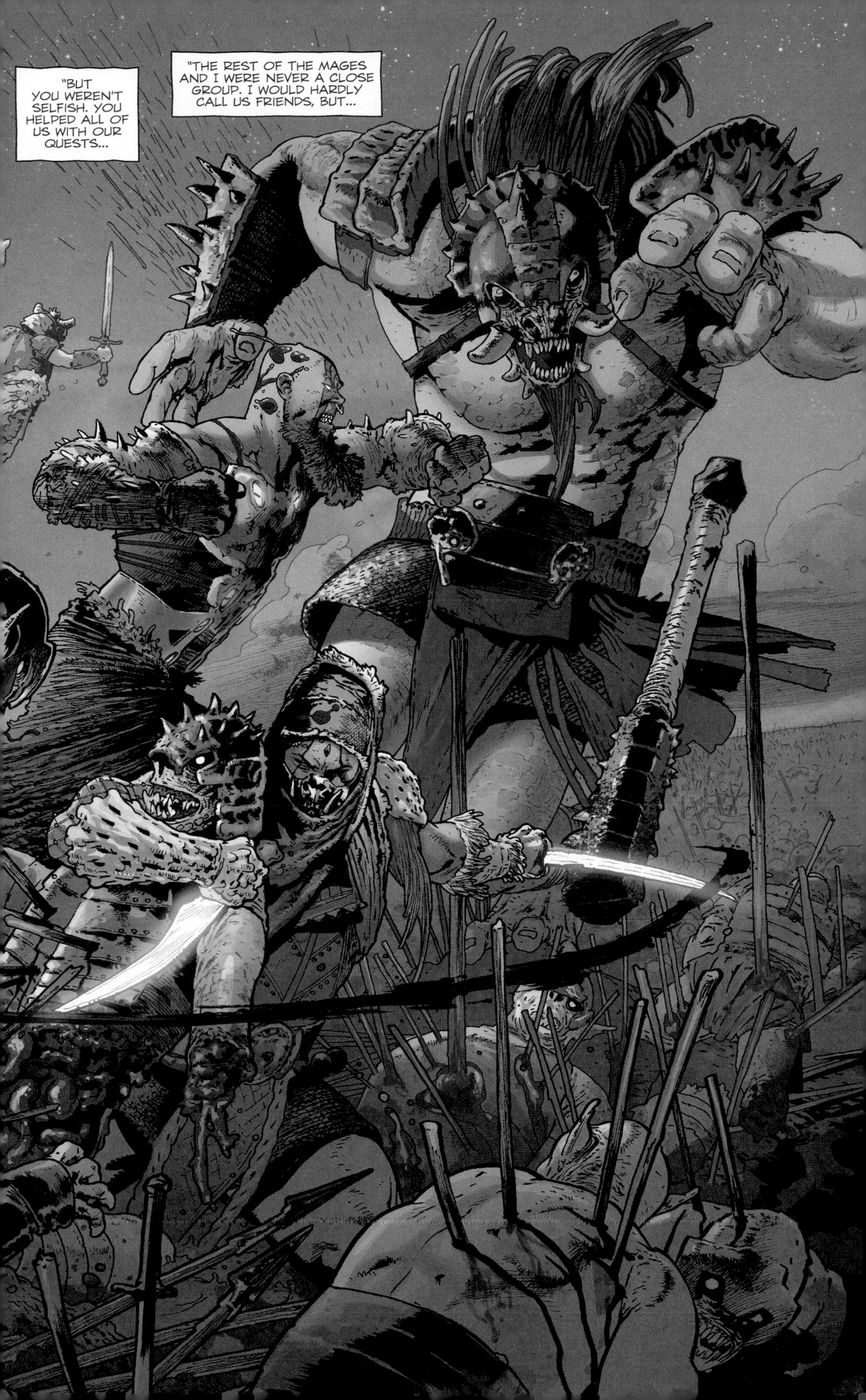
"BUT YOU WEREN'T SELFISH. YOU HELPED ALL OF US WITH OUR QUESTS...
"THE REST OF THE MAGES AND I WERE NEVER A CLOSE GROUP. I WOULD HARDLY CALL US FRIENDS, BUT...

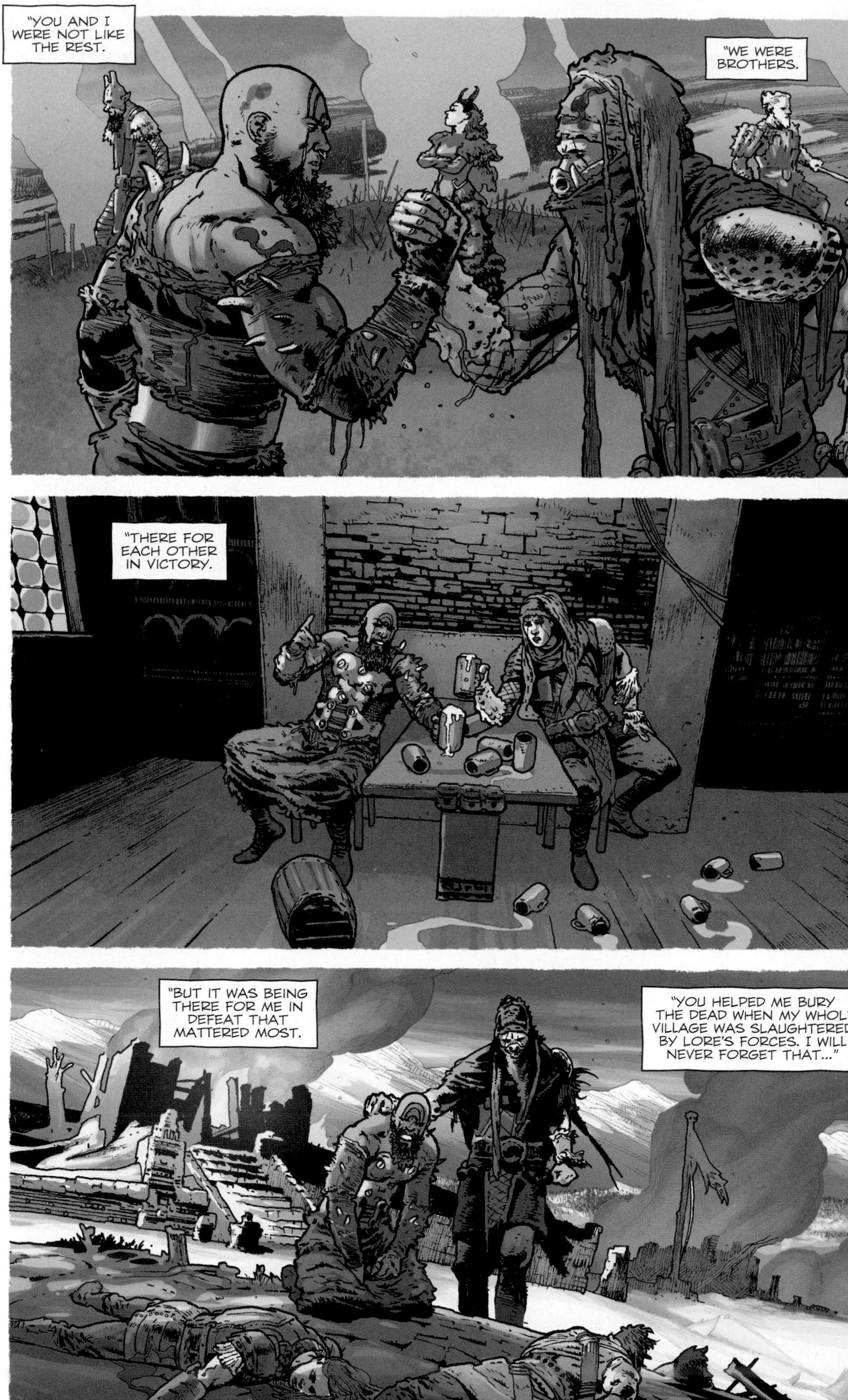
"YOU AND I WERE NOT LIKE THE REST.
"WE WERE BROTHERS.
"THERE FOR EACH OTHER IN VICTORY.
"BUT IT WAS BEING THERE FOR ME IN DEFEAT THAT MATTERED MOST.
"YOU HELPED ME BURY THE DEAD WHEN MY WHOLE VILLAGE WAS SLAUGHTERED BY LORE'S FORCES. I WILL NEVER FORGET THAT..."

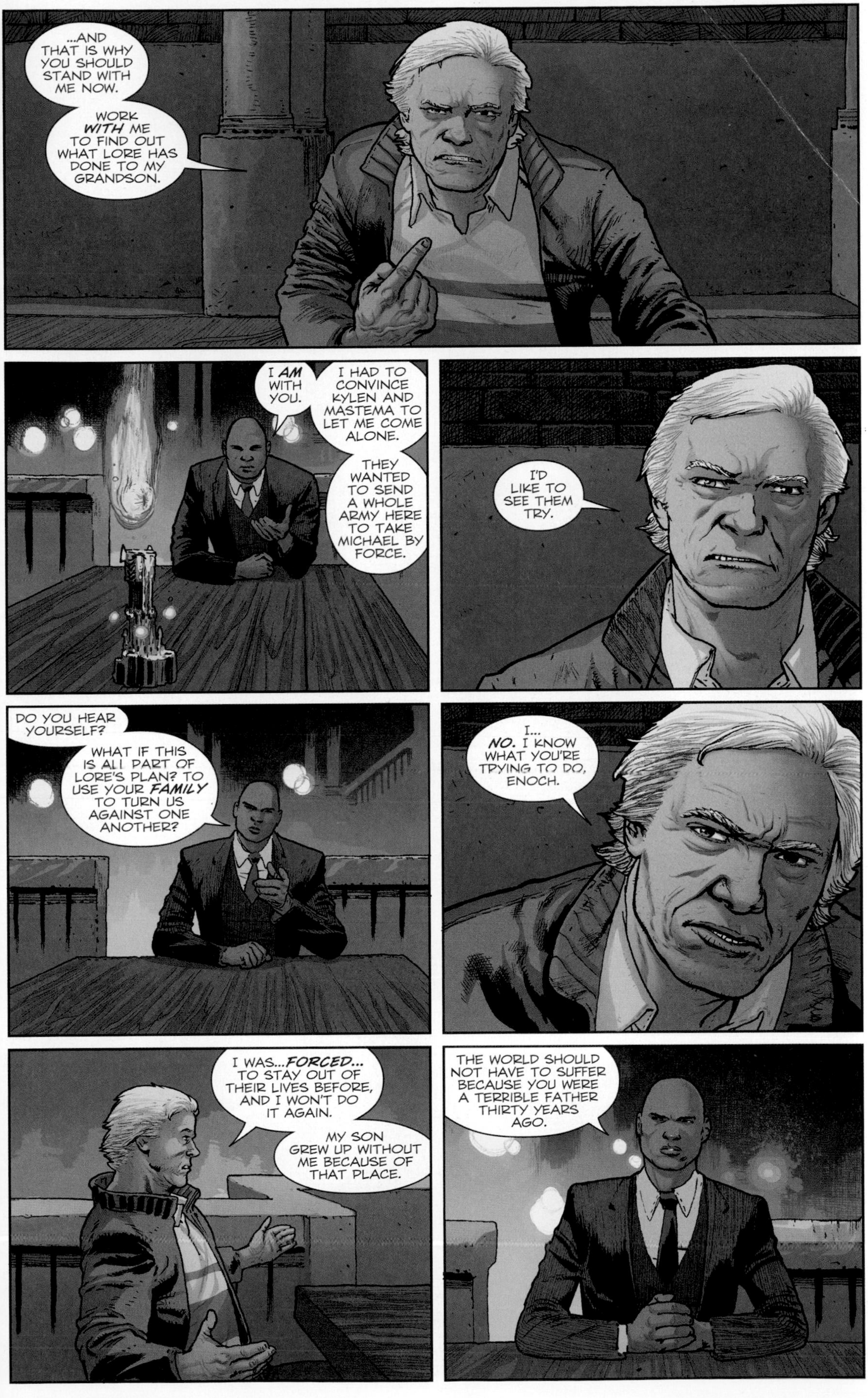
...AND THAT IS WHY YOU SHOULD STAND WITH ME NOW.
WORK *WITH* ME TO FIND OUT WHAT LORE HAS DONE TO MY GRANDSON.
I *AM* WITH YOU.
I HAD TO CONVINCE KYLEN AND MASTEMA TO LET ME COME ALONE.
THEY WANTED TO SEND A WHOLE ARMY HERE TO TAKE MICHAEL BY FORCE.
I'D LIKE TO SEE THEM TRY.
DO YOU HEAR YOURSELF?
WHAT IF THIS IS ALL PART OF LORE'S PLAN? TO USE YOUR *FAMILY* TO TURN US AGAINST ONE ANOTHER?
I... *NO.* I KNOW WHAT YOU'RE TRYING TO DO, ENOCH.
I WAS...*FORCED...* TO STAY OUT OF THEIR LIVES BEFORE, AND I WON'T DO IT AGAIN.
MY SON GREW UP WITHOUT ME BECAUSE OF THAT PLACE.
THE WORLD SHOULD NOT HAVE TO SUFFER BECAUSE YOU WERE A TERRIBLE FATHER THIRTY YEARS AGO.

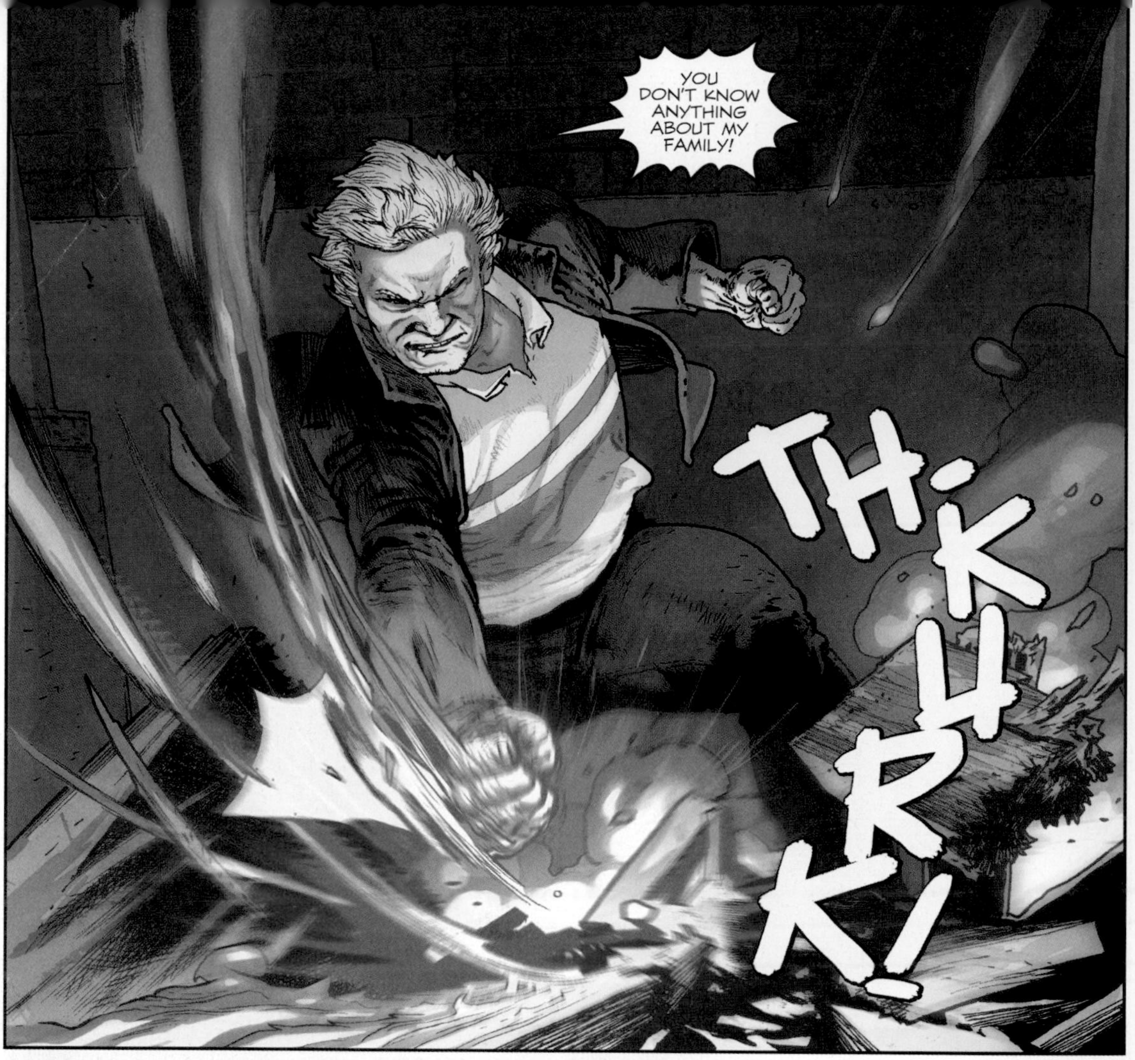
YOU DON'T KNOW ANYTHING ABOUT MY FAMILY!
TH-KURK!

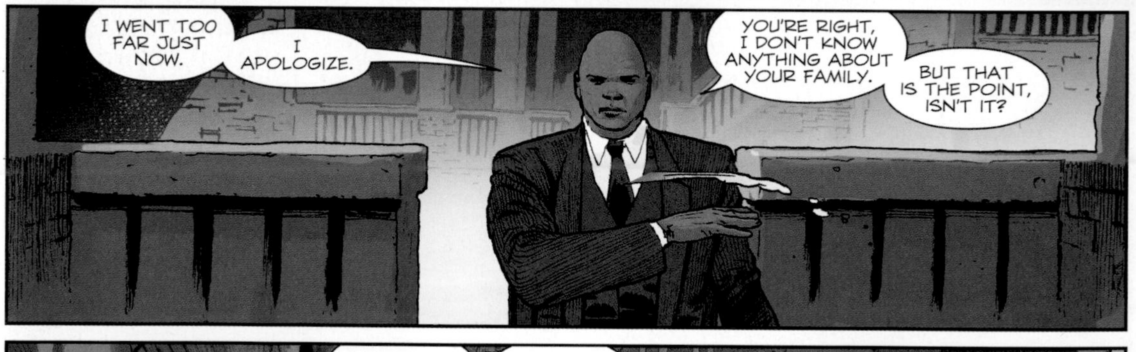
I WENT TOO FAR JUST NOW.
I APOLOGIZE.
YOU'RE RIGHT, I DON'T KNOW ANYTHING ABOUT YOUR FAMILY.
BUT THAT IS THE POINT, ISN'T IT?

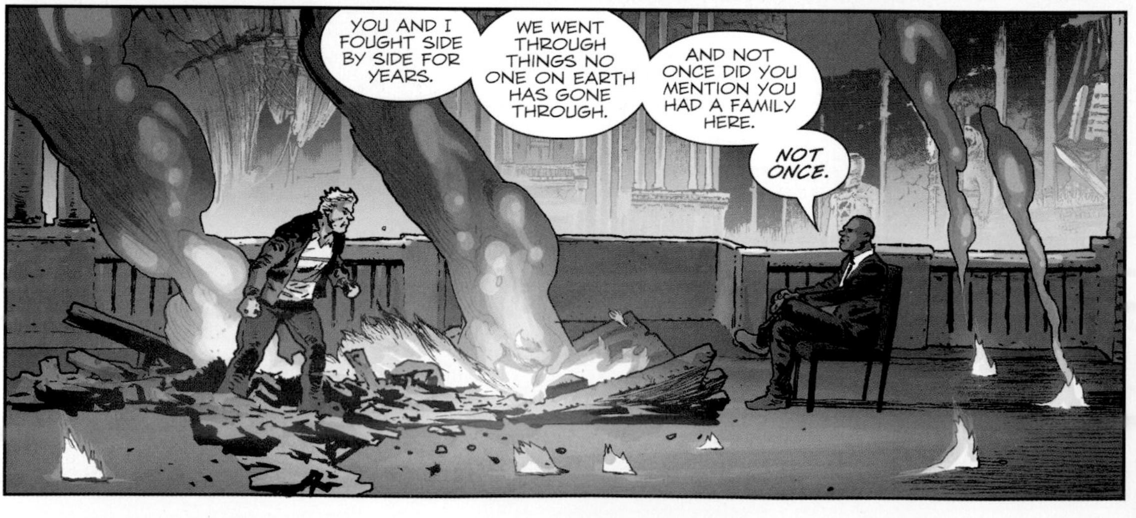
YOU AND I FOUGHT SIDE BY SIDE FOR YEARS.
WE WENT THROUGH THINGS NO ONE ON EARTH HAS GONE THROUGH.
AND NOT ONCE DID YOU MENTION YOU HAD A FAMILY HERE.
NOT ONCE.

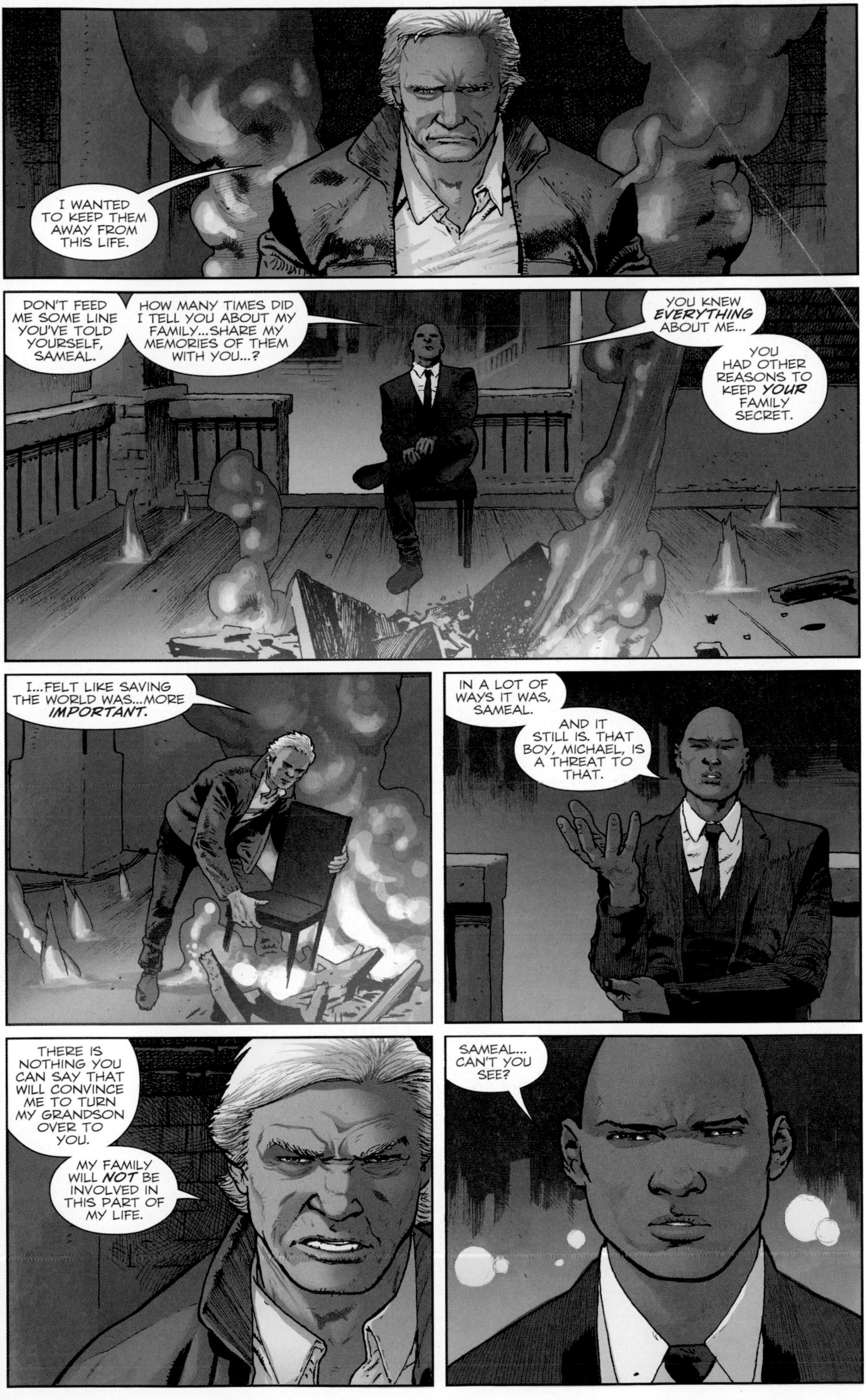
I WANTED TO KEEP THEM AWAY FROM THIS LIFE.
DON'T FEED ME SOME LINE YOU'VE TOLD YOURSELF, SAMEAL.
HOW MANY TIMES DID I TELL YOU ABOUT MY FAMILY...SHARE MY MEMORIES OF THEM WITH YOU...?
YOU KNEW EVERYTHING ABOUT ME...
YOU HAD OTHER REASONS TO KEEP YOUR FAMILY SECRET.
I...FELT LIKE SAVING THE WORLD WAS...MORE IMPORTANT.
IN A LOT OF WAYS IT WAS, SAMEAL.
AND IT STILL IS. THAT BOY, MICHAEL, IS A THREAT TO THAT.
THERE IS NOTHING YOU CAN SAY THAT WILL CONVINCE ME TO TURN MY GRANDSON OVER TO YOU.
MY FAMILY WILL NOT BE INVOLVED IN THIS PART OF MY LIFE.
SAMEAL... CAN'T YOU SEE?

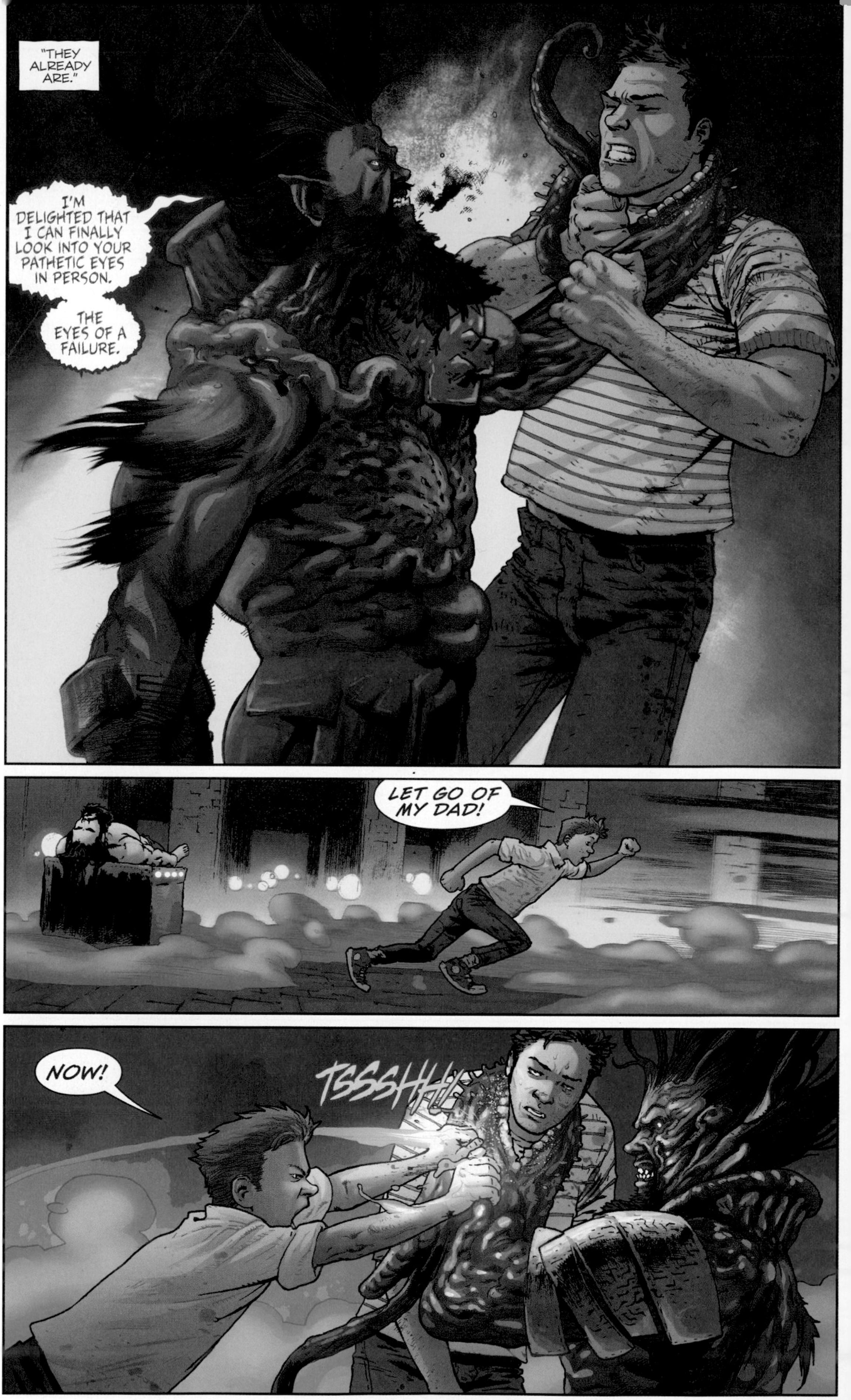
"THEY ALREADY ARE."
I'M DELIGHTED THAT I CAN FINALLY LOOK INTO YOUR PATHETIC EYES IN PERSON.
THE EYES OF A FAILURE.
LET GO OF MY DAD!
NOW!
TSSSHHH!

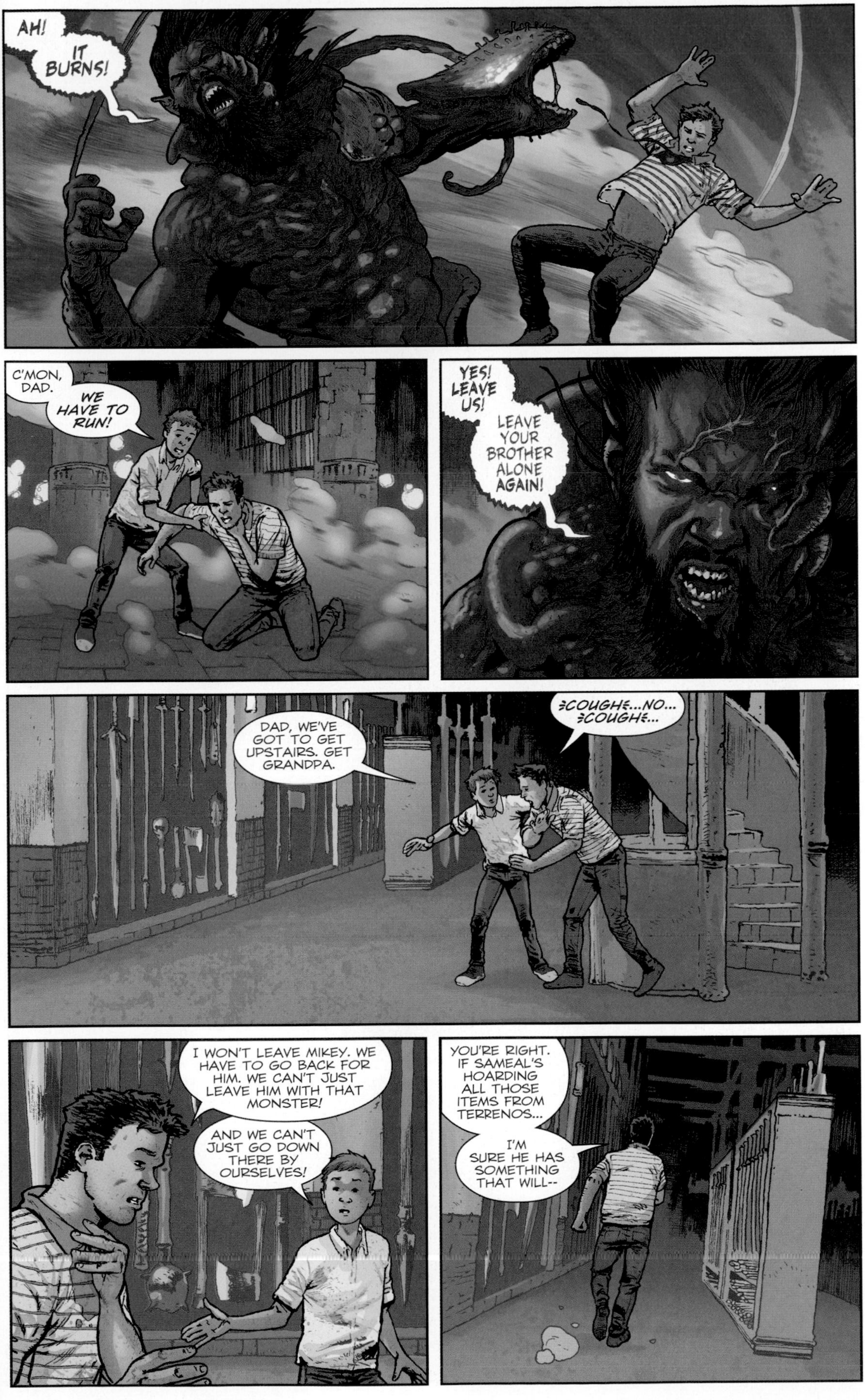
AH!
IT BURNS!
C'MON, DAD.
WE HAVE TO RUN!
YES! LEAVE US!
LEAVE YOUR BROTHER ALONE AGAIN!
DAD, WE'VE GOT TO GET UPSTAIRS. GET GRANDPA.
COUGH...NO... *COUGH*...
I WON'T LEAVE MIKEY. WE HAVE TO GO BACK FOR HIM. WE CAN'T JUST LEAVE HIM WITH THAT MONSTER!
AND WE CAN'T JUST GO DOWN THERE BY OURSELVES!
YOU'RE RIGHT. IF SAMEAL'S HOARDING ALL THOSE ITEMS FROM TERRENOS...
I'M SURE HE HAS SOMETHING THAT WILL--

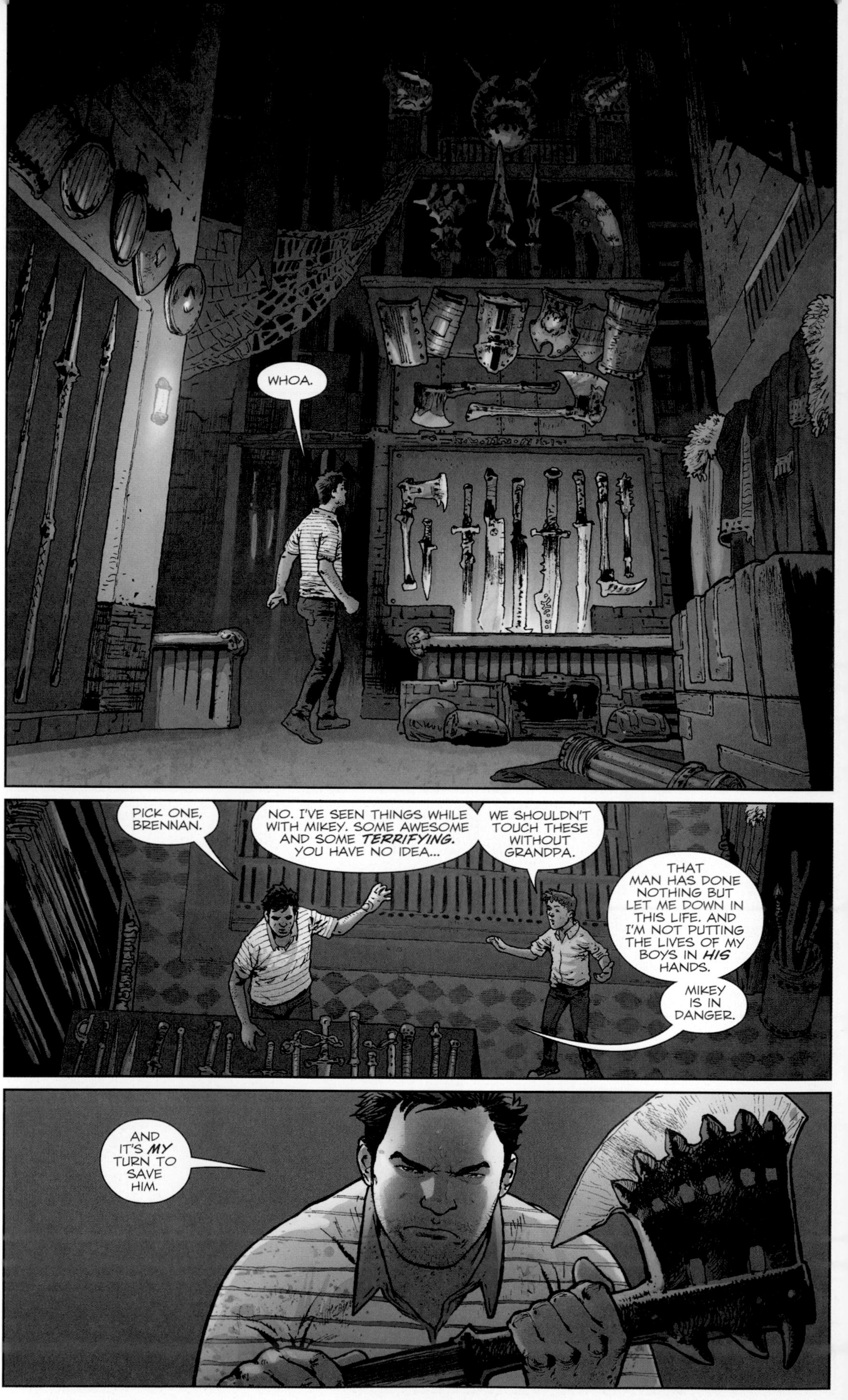
WHOA.
PICK ONE, BRENNAN.
NO. I'VE SEEN THINGS WHILE WITH MIKEY. SOME AWESOME AND SOME *TERRIFYING.* YOU HAVE NO IDEA...
WE SHOULDN'T TOUCH THESE WITHOUT GRANDPA.
THAT MAN HAS DONE NOTHING BUT LET ME DOWN IN THIS LIFE. AND I'M NOT PUTTING THE LIVES OF MY BOYS IN *HIS* HANDS.
MIKEY IS IN DANGER.
AND IT'S *MY* TURN TO SAVE HIM.

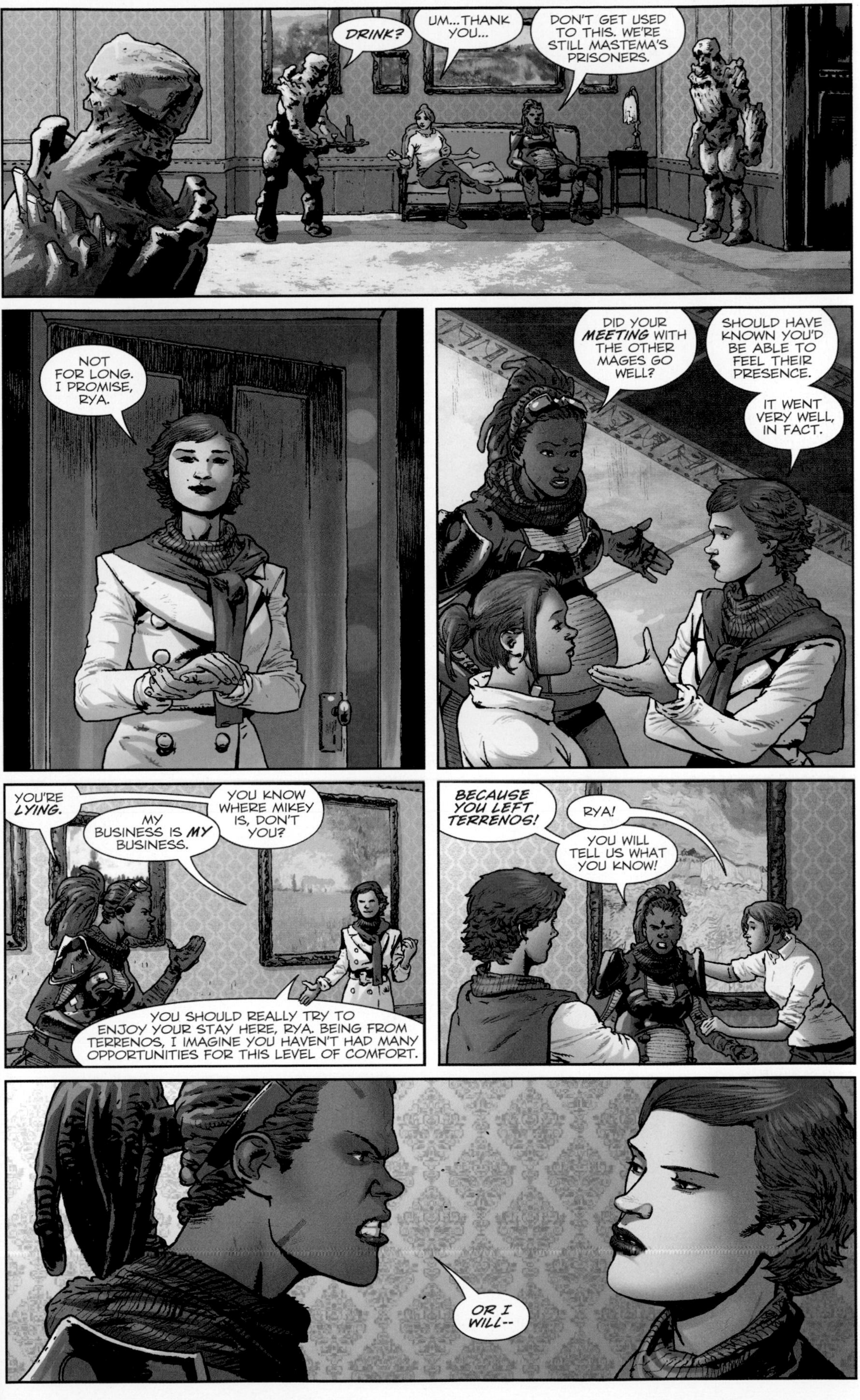
DRINK?
UM...THANK YOU...
DON'T GET USED TO THIS. WE'RE STILL MASTEMA'S PRISONERS.
NOT FOR LONG. I PROMISE, RYA.
DID YOUR MEETING WITH THE OTHER MAGES GO WELL?
SHOULD HAVE KNOWN YOU'D BE ABLE TO FEEL THEIR PRESENCE.
IT WENT VERY WELL, IN FACT.
YOU'RE LYING.
YOU KNOW WHERE MIKEY IS, DON'T YOU?
MY BUSINESS IS MY BUSINESS.
YOU SHOULD REALLY TRY TO ENJOY YOUR STAY HERE, RYA. BEING FROM TERRENOS, I IMAGINE YOU HAVEN'T HAD MANY OPPORTUNITIES FOR THIS LEVEL OF COMFORT.
BECAUSE YOU LEFT TERRENOS!
RYA!
YOU WILL TELL US WHAT YOU KNOW!
OR I WILL--

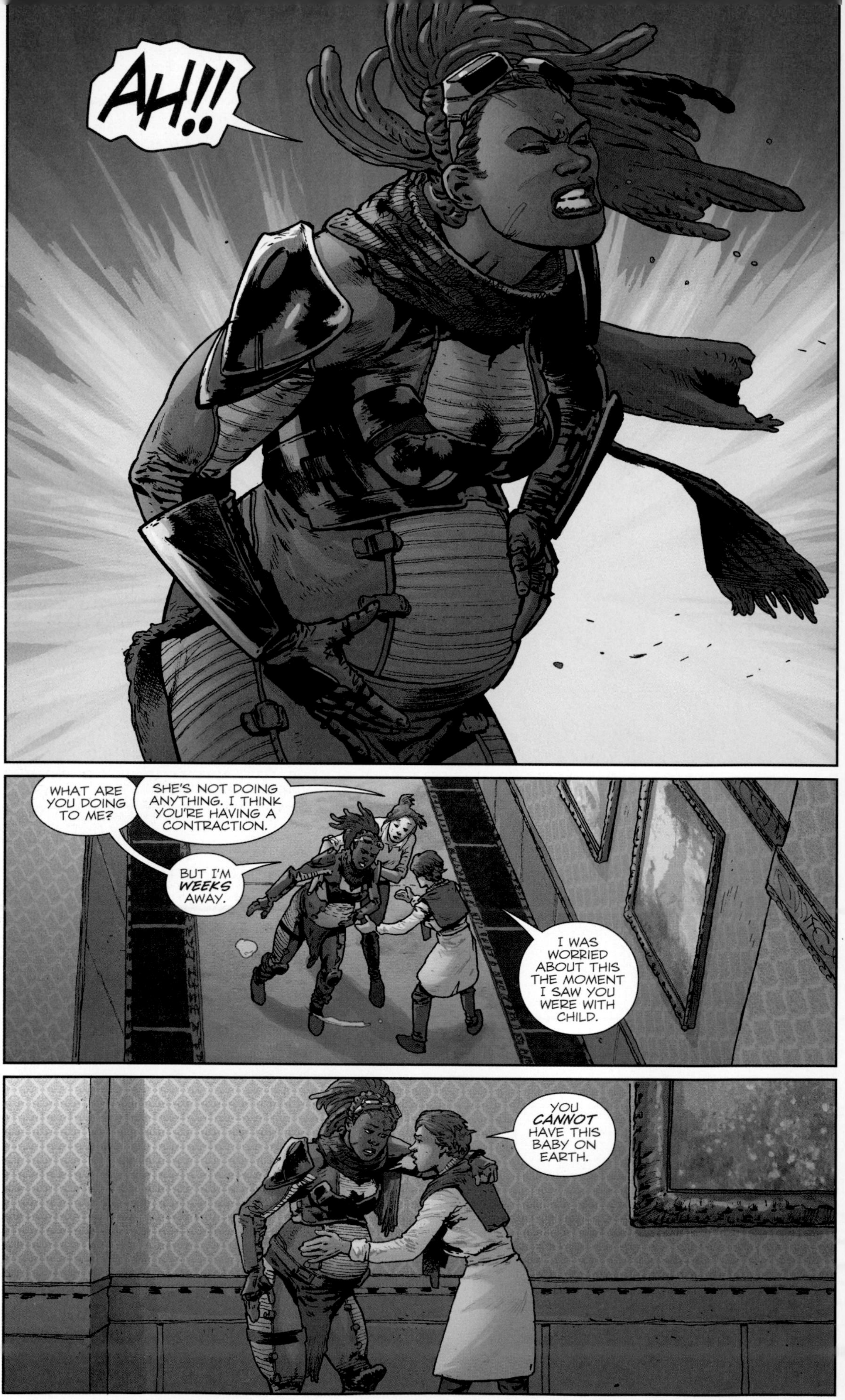
AH!!
WHAT ARE YOU DOING TO ME?
SHE'S NOT DOING ANYTHING. I THINK YOU'RE HAVING A CONTRACTION.
BUT I'M *WEEKS* AWAY.
I WAS WORRIED ABOUT THIS THE MOMENT I SAW YOU WERE WITH CHILD.
YOU *CANNOT* HAVE THIS BABY ON EARTH.

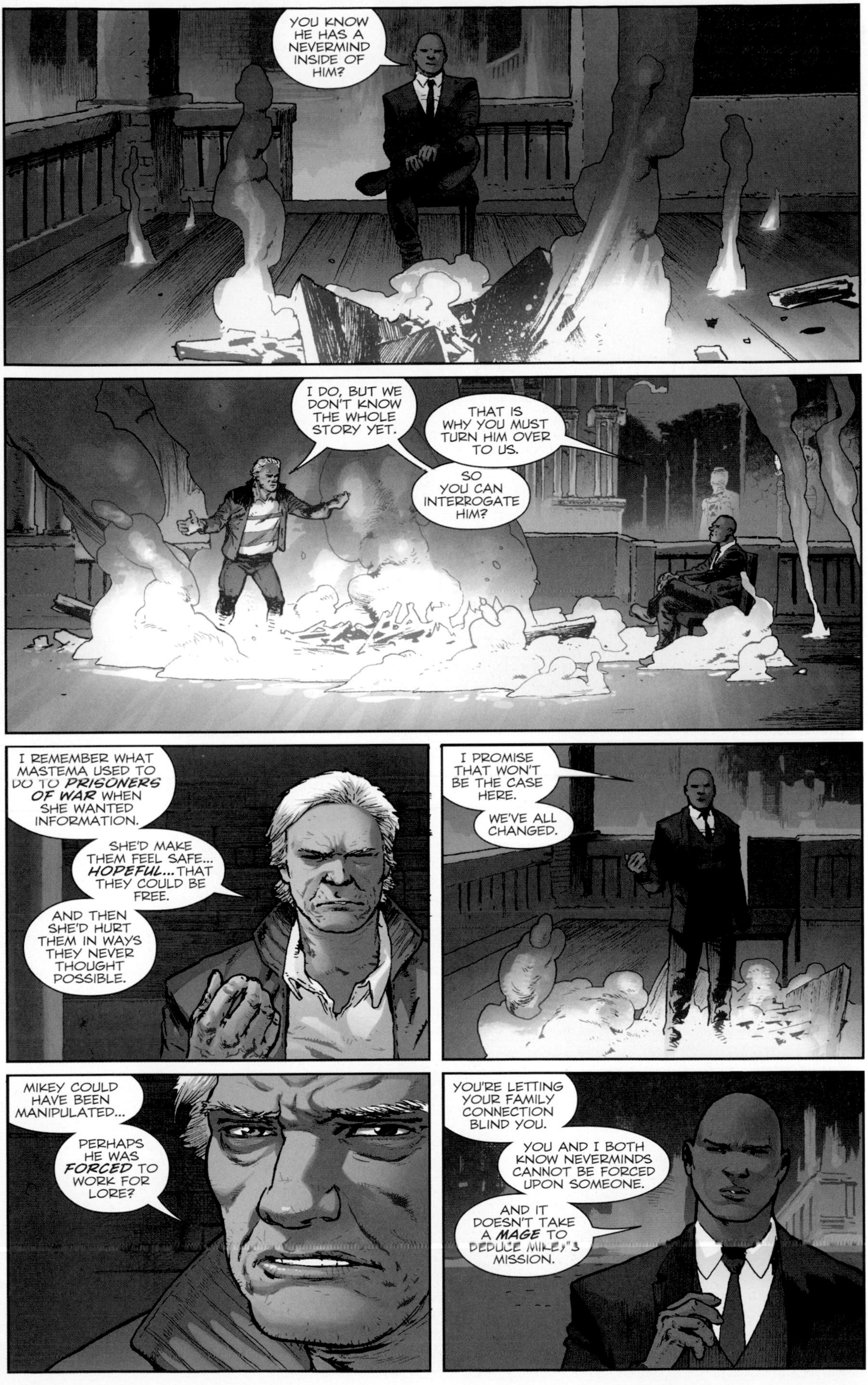
YOU KNOW HE HAS A NEVERMIND INSIDE OF HIM?
I DO, BUT WE DON'T KNOW THE WHOLE STORY YET.
THAT IS WHY YOU MUST TURN HIM OVER TO US.
SO YOU CAN INTERROGATE HIM?
I REMEMBER WHAT MASTEMA USED TO DO TO *PRISONERS OF WAR* WHEN SHE WANTED INFORMATION.
SHE'D MAKE THEM FEEL SAFE... *HOPEFUL*... THAT THEY COULD BE FREE.
AND THEN SHE'D HURT THEM IN WAYS THEY NEVER THOUGHT POSSIBLE.
I PROMISE THAT WON'T BE THE CASE HERE.
WE'VE ALL CHANGED.
MIKEY COULD HAVE BEEN MANIPULATED...
PERHAPS HE WAS *FORCED* TO WORK FOR LORE?
YOU'RE LETTING YOUR FAMILY CONNECTION BLIND YOU.
YOU AND I BOTH KNOW NEVERMINDS CANNOT BE FORCED UPON SOMEONE.
AND IT DOESN'T TAKE A *MAGE* TO DEDUCE MIKEY'S MISSION.

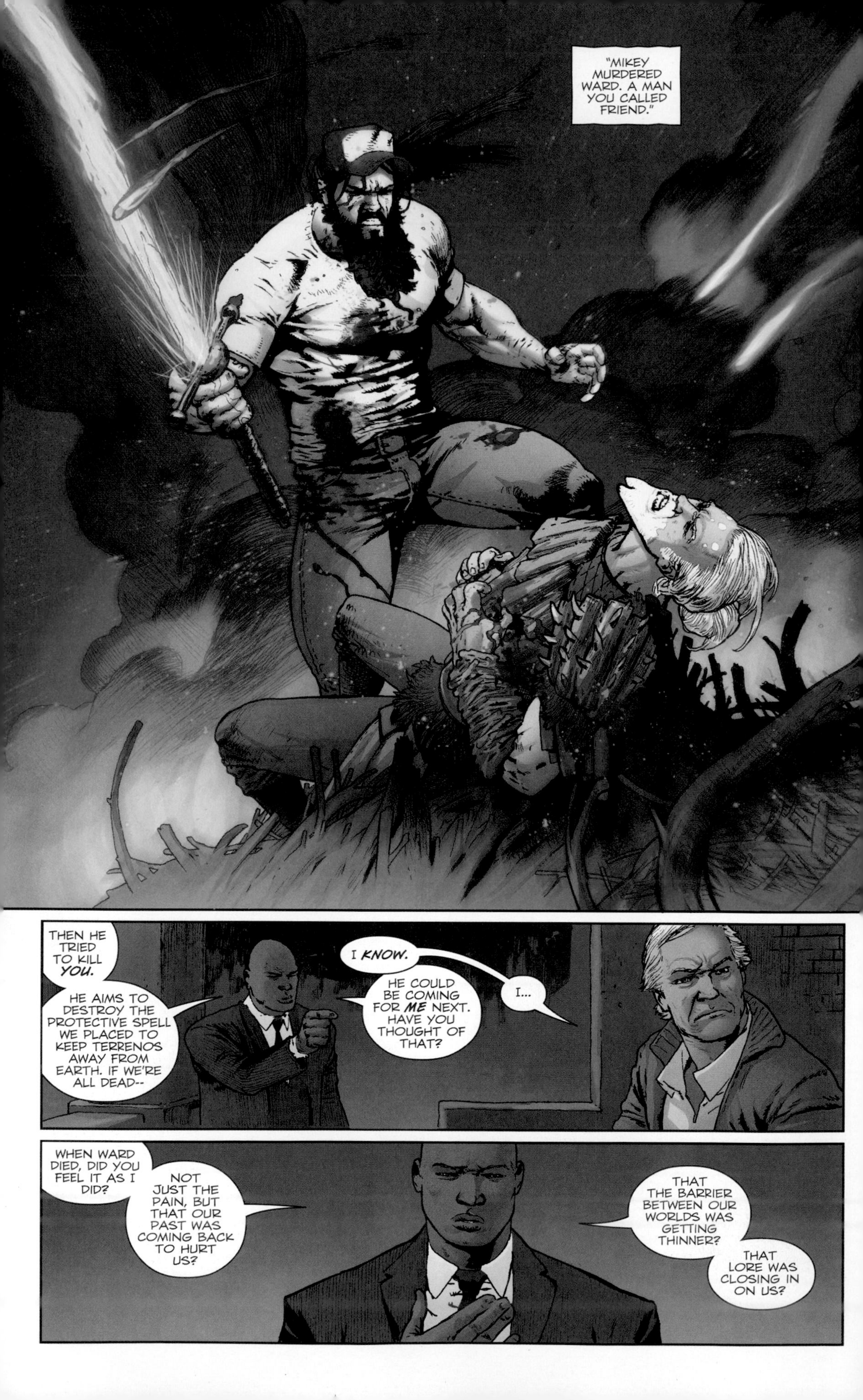
"MIKEY MURDERED WARD. A MAN YOU CALLED FRIEND."
THEN HE TRIED TO KILL *YOU.*
HE AIMS TO DESTROY THE PROTECTIVE SPELL WE PLACED TO KEEP TERRENOS AWAY FROM EARTH. IF WE'RE ALL DEAD--
I *KNOW.*
HE COULD BE COMING FOR *ME* NEXT. HAVE YOU THOUGHT OF THAT?
I...
WHEN WARD DIED, DID YOU FEEL IT AS I DID?
NOT JUST THE PAIN, BUT THAT OUR PAST WAS COMING BACK TO HURT US?
THAT THE BARRIER BETWEEN OUR WORLDS WAS GETTING THINNER?
THAT LORE WAS CLOSING IN ON US?

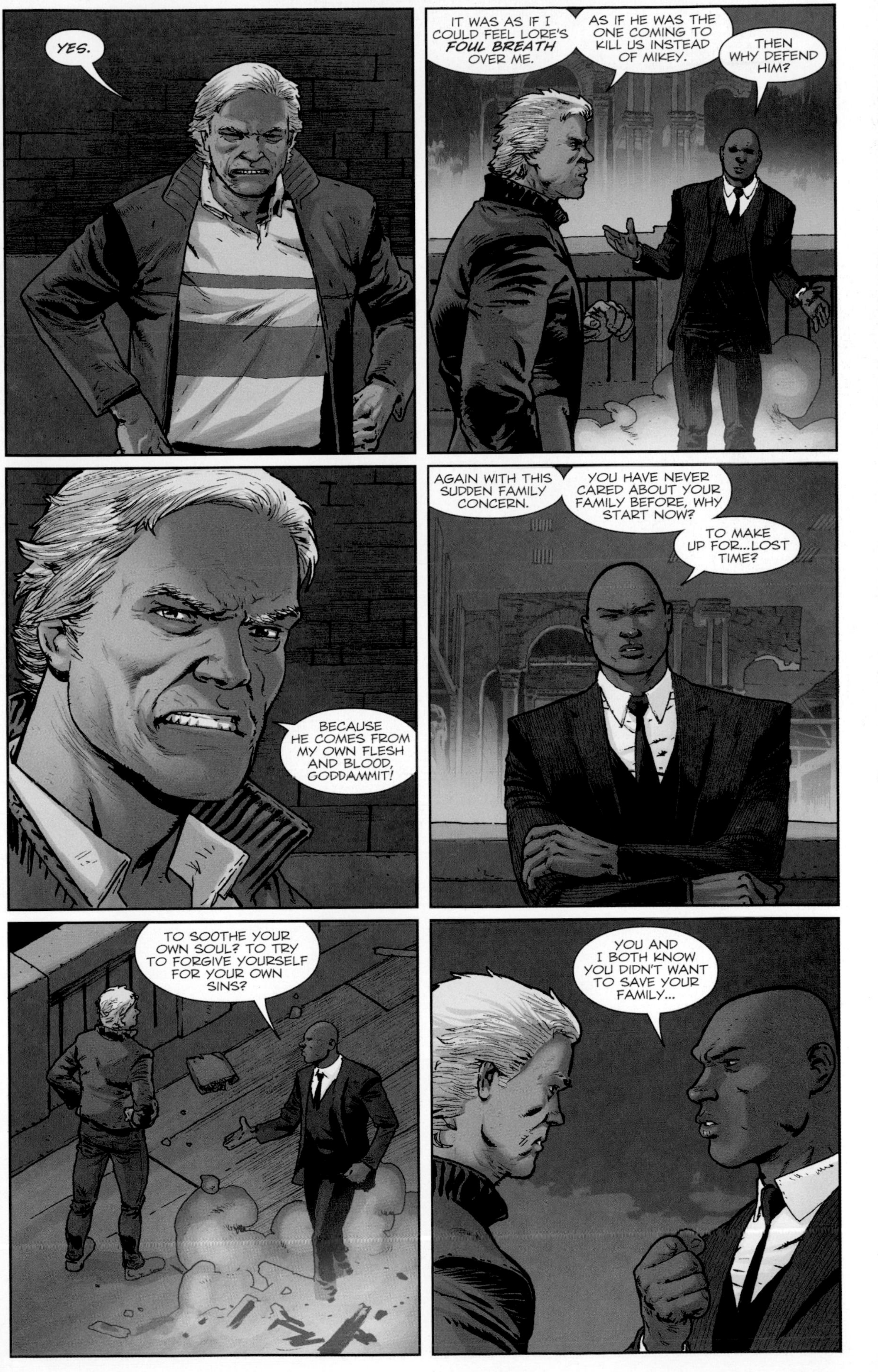
YES.
IT WAS AS IF I COULD FEEL LORE'S *FOUL BREATH* OVER ME.
AS IF HE WAS THE ONE COMING TO KILL US INSTEAD OF MIKEY.
THEN WHY DEFEND HIM?
BECAUSE HE COMES FROM MY OWN FLESH AND BLOOD, GODDAMMIT!
AGAIN WITH THIS SUDDEN FAMILY CONCERN.
YOU HAVE NEVER CARED ABOUT YOUR FAMILY BEFORE, WHY START NOW?
TO MAKE UP FOR...LOST TIME?
TO SOOTHE YOUR OWN SOUL? TO TRY TO FORGIVE YOURSELF FOR YOUR OWN SINS?
YOU AND I BOTH KNOW YOU DIDN'T WANT TO SAVE YOUR FAMILY...

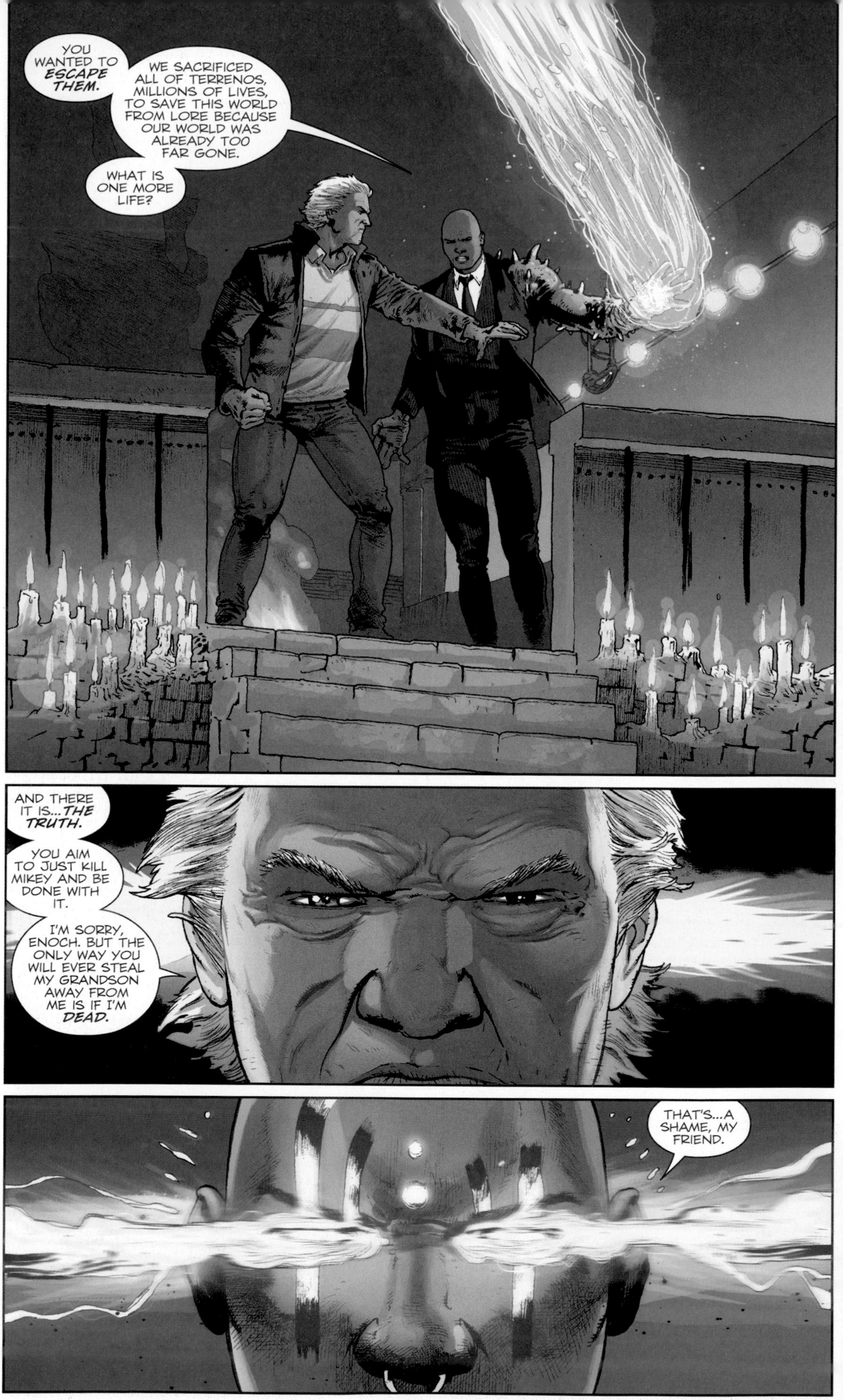
YOU WANTED TO *ESCAPE THEM.*
WE SACRIFICED ALL OF TERRENOS, MILLIONS OF LIVES, TO SAVE THIS WORLD FROM LORE BECAUSE OUR WORLD WAS ALREADY TOO FAR GONE.
WHAT IS ONE MORE LIFE?
AND THERE IT IS...*THE TRUTH.*
YOU AIM TO JUST KILL MIKEY AND BE DONE WITH IT.
I'M SORRY, ENOCH. BUT THE ONLY WAY YOU WILL EVER STEAL MY GRANDSON AWAY FROM ME IS IF I'M *DEAD.*
THAT'S...A SHAME, MY FRIEND.

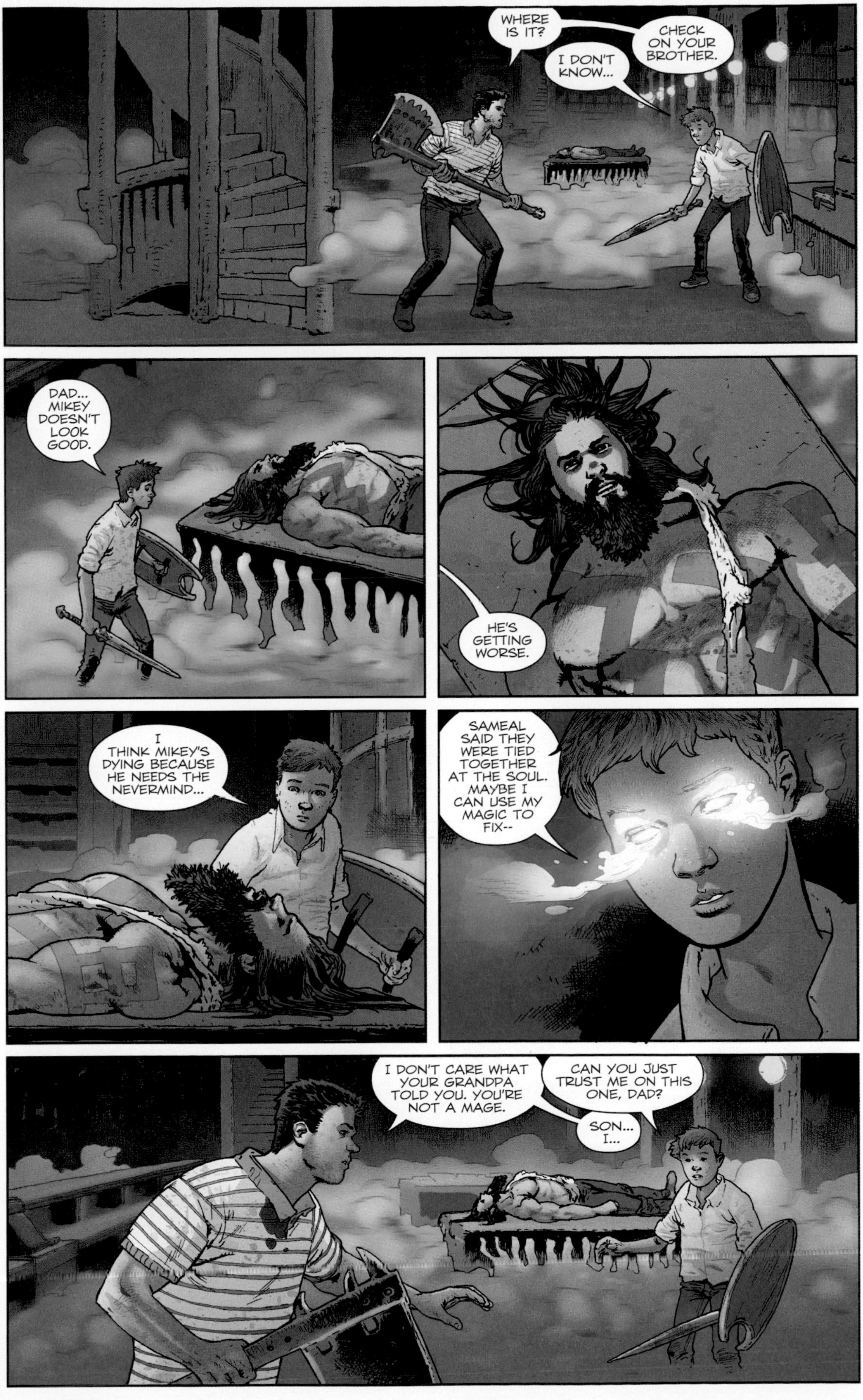
WHERE IS IT?
I DON'T KNOW...
CHECK ON YOUR BROTHER.
DAD... MIKEY DOESN'T LOOK GOOD.
HE'S GETTING WORSE.
I THINK MIKEY'S DYING BECAUSE HE NEEDS THE NEVERMIND...
SAMEAL SAID THEY WERE TIED TOGETHER AT THE SOUL. MAYBE I CAN USE MY MAGIC TO FIX--
I DON'T CARE WHAT YOUR GRANDPA TOLD YOU. YOU'RE NOT A MAGE.
CAN YOU JUST TRUST ME ON THIS ONE, DAD?
SON... I...

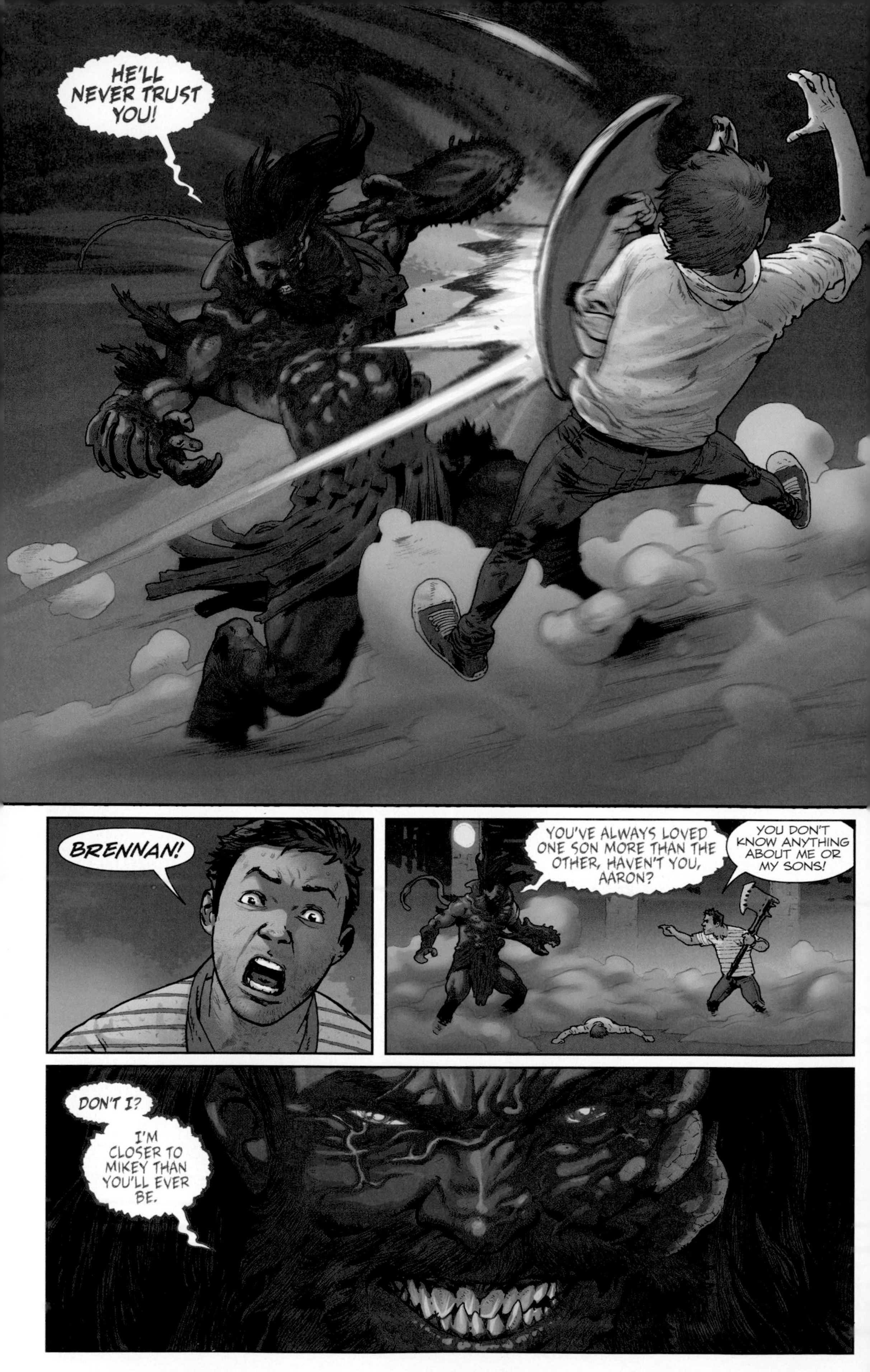
HE'LL NEVER TRUST YOU!
BRENNAN!
YOU'VE ALWAYS LOVED ONE SON MORE THAN THE OTHER, HAVEN'T YOU, AARON?
YOU DON'T KNOW ANYTHING ABOUT ME OR MY SONS!
DON'T I?
I'M CLOSER TO MIKEY THAN YOU'LL EVER BE.

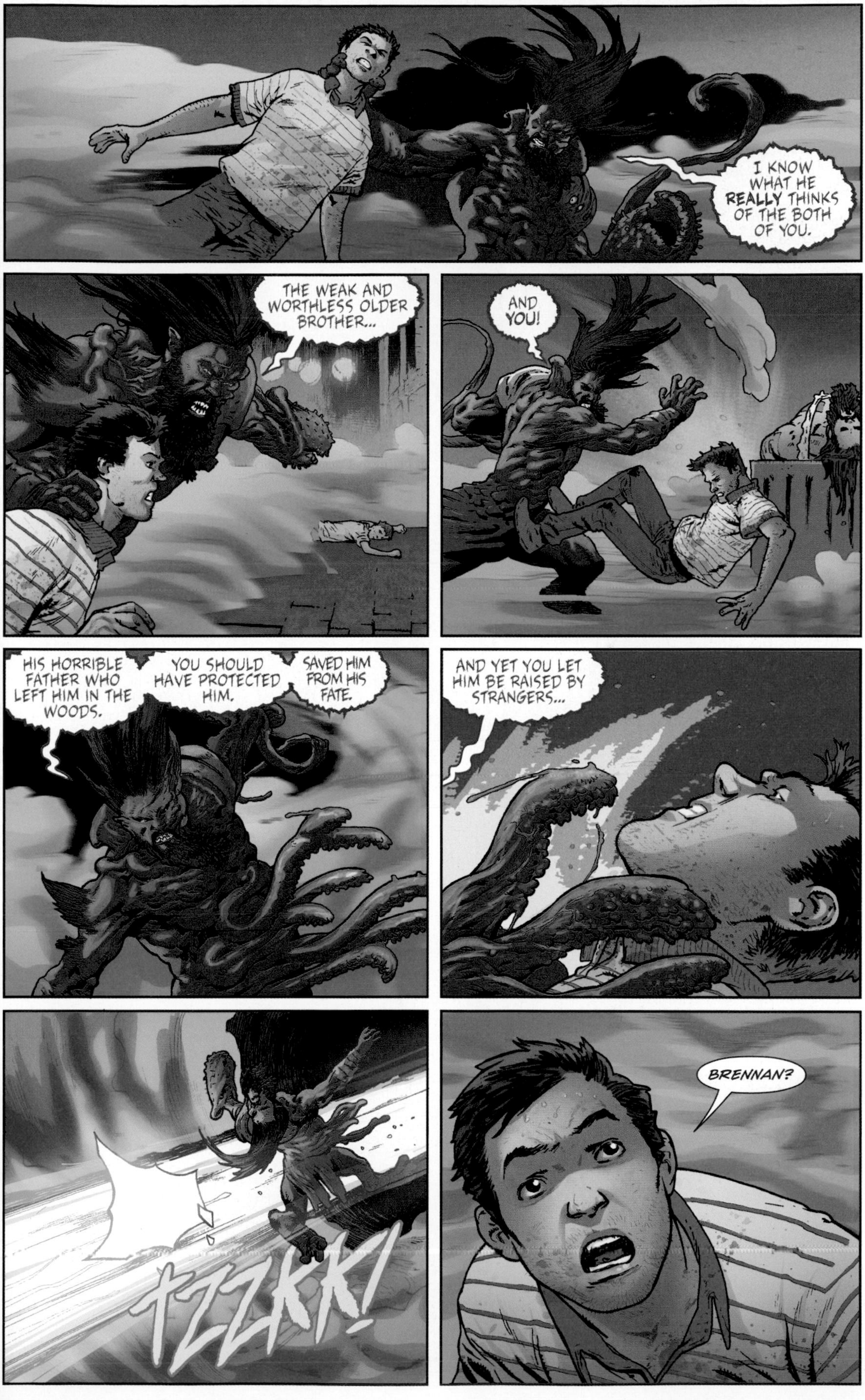
I KNOW WHAT HE REALLY THINKS OF THE BOTH OF YOU.
THE WEAK AND WORTHLESS OLDER BROTHER...
AND YOU!
HIS HORRIBLE FATHER WHO LEFT HIM IN THE WOODS.
YOU SHOULD HAVE PROTECTED HIM.
SAVED HIM FROM HIS FATE.
AND YET YOU LET HIM BE RAISED BY STRANGERS...
TZZKK!
BRENNAN?

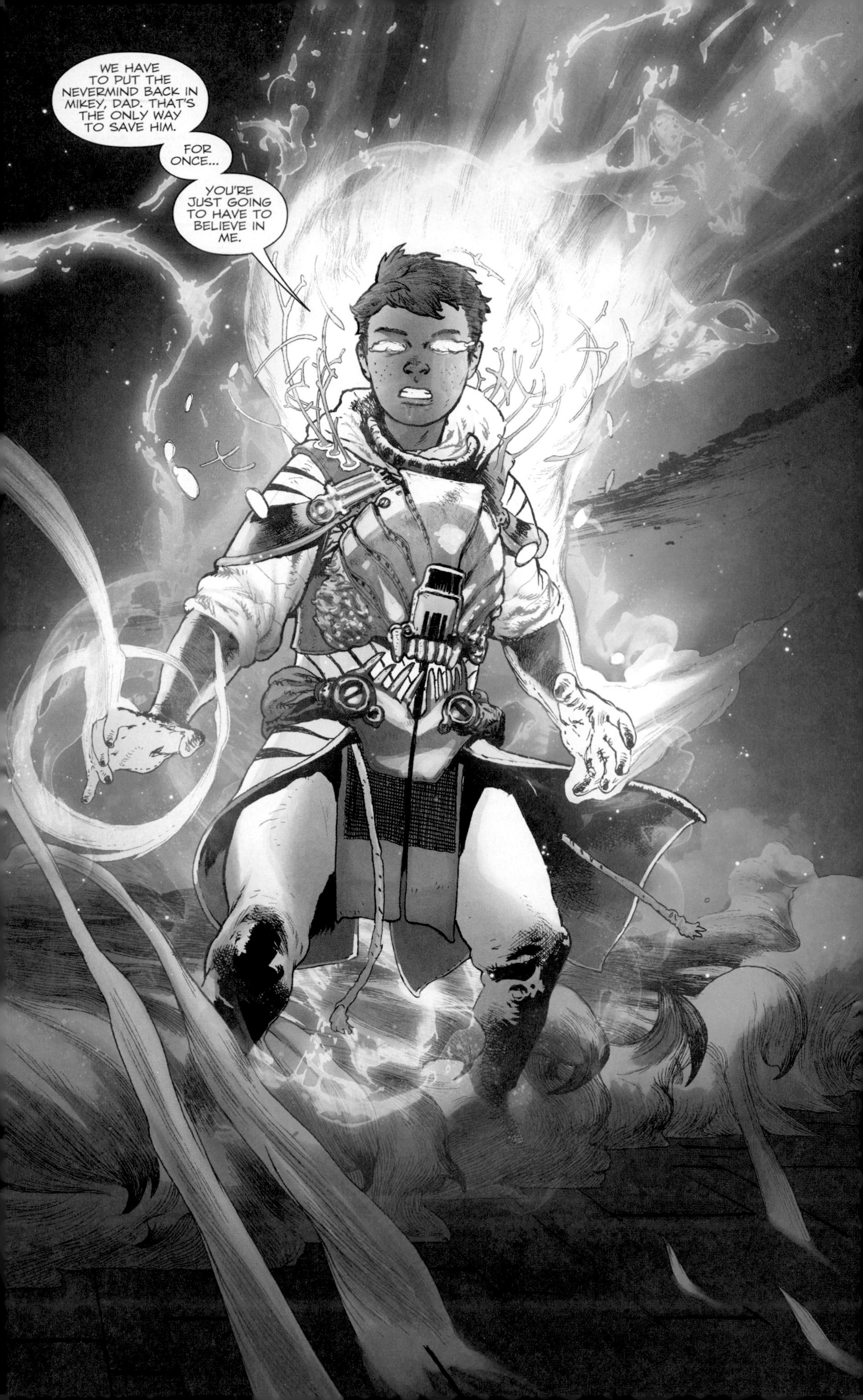
WE HAVE TO PUT THE NEVERMIND BACK IN MIKEY, DAD. THAT'S THE ONLY WAY TO SAVE HIM.
FOR ONCE...
YOU'RE JUST GOING TO HAVE TO BELIEVE IN ME.

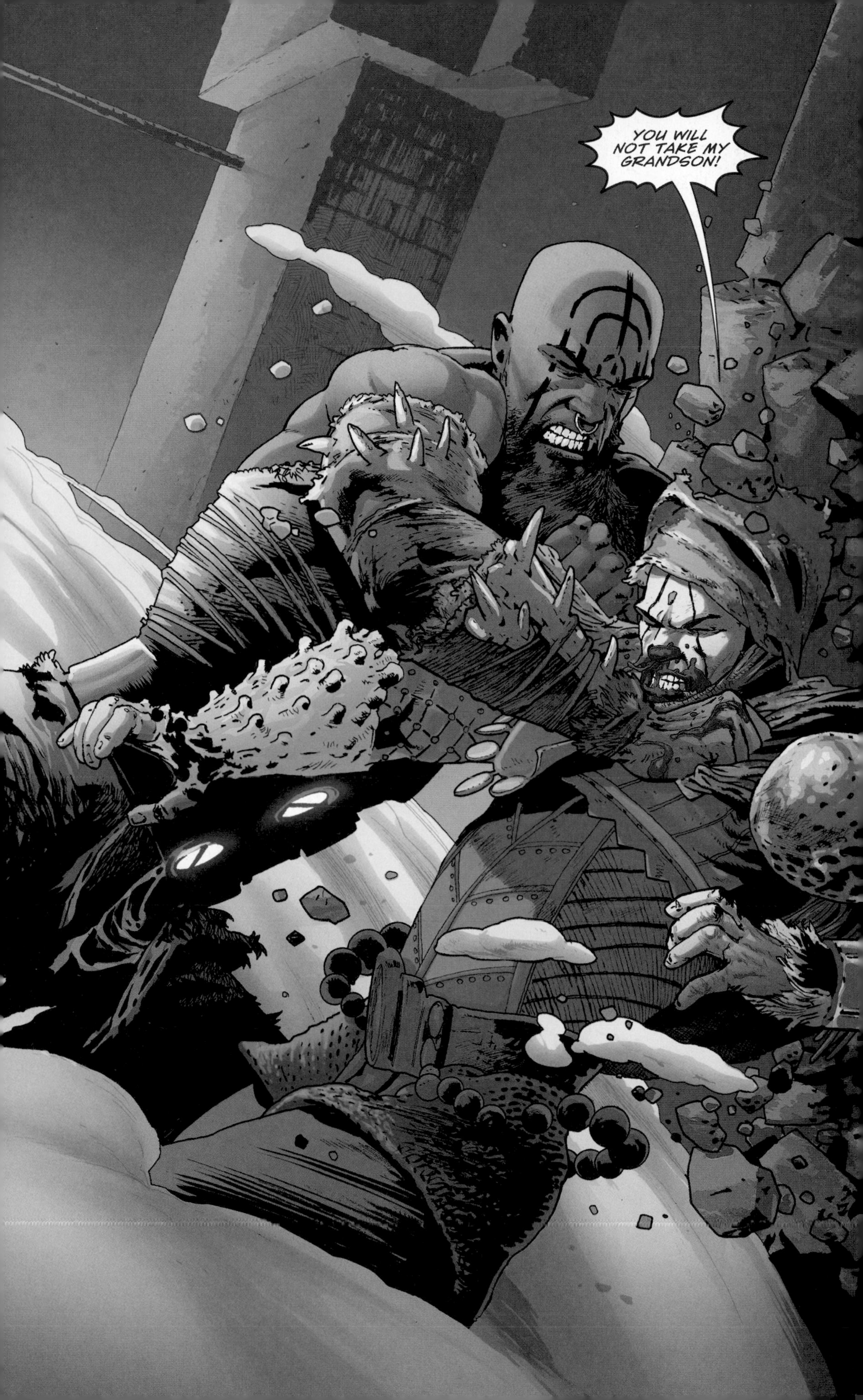
YOU WILL NOT TAKE MY GRANDSON!

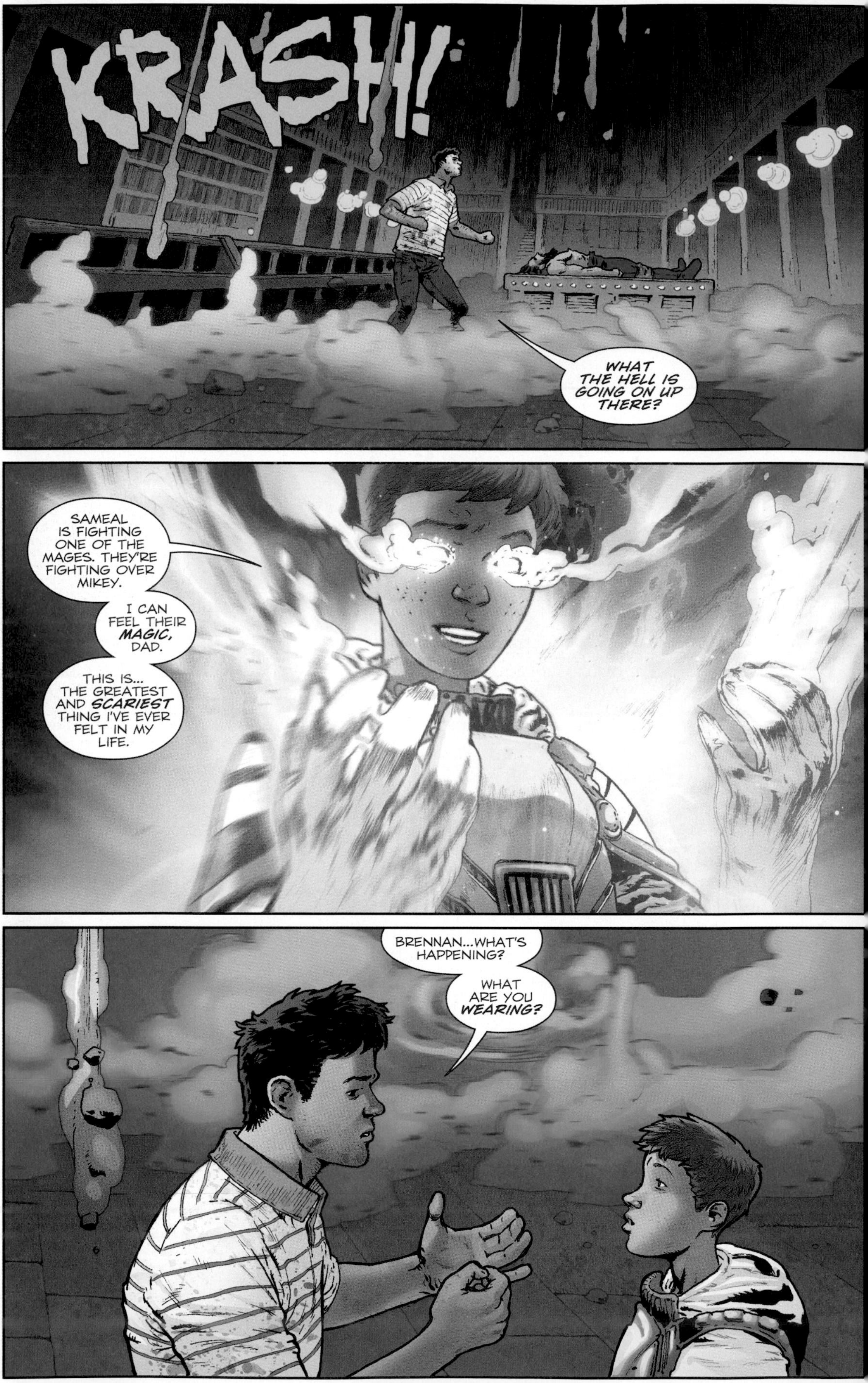
KRASH!
WHAT THE HELL IS GOING ON UP THERE?
SAMEAL IS FIGHTING ONE OF THE MAGES. THEY'RE FIGHTING OVER MIKEY.
I CAN FEEL THEIR *MAGIC,* DAD.
THIS IS... THE GREATEST AND *SCARIEST* THING I'VE EVER FELT IN MY LIFE.
BRENNAN...WHAT'S HAPPENING?
WHAT ARE YOU *WEARING?*

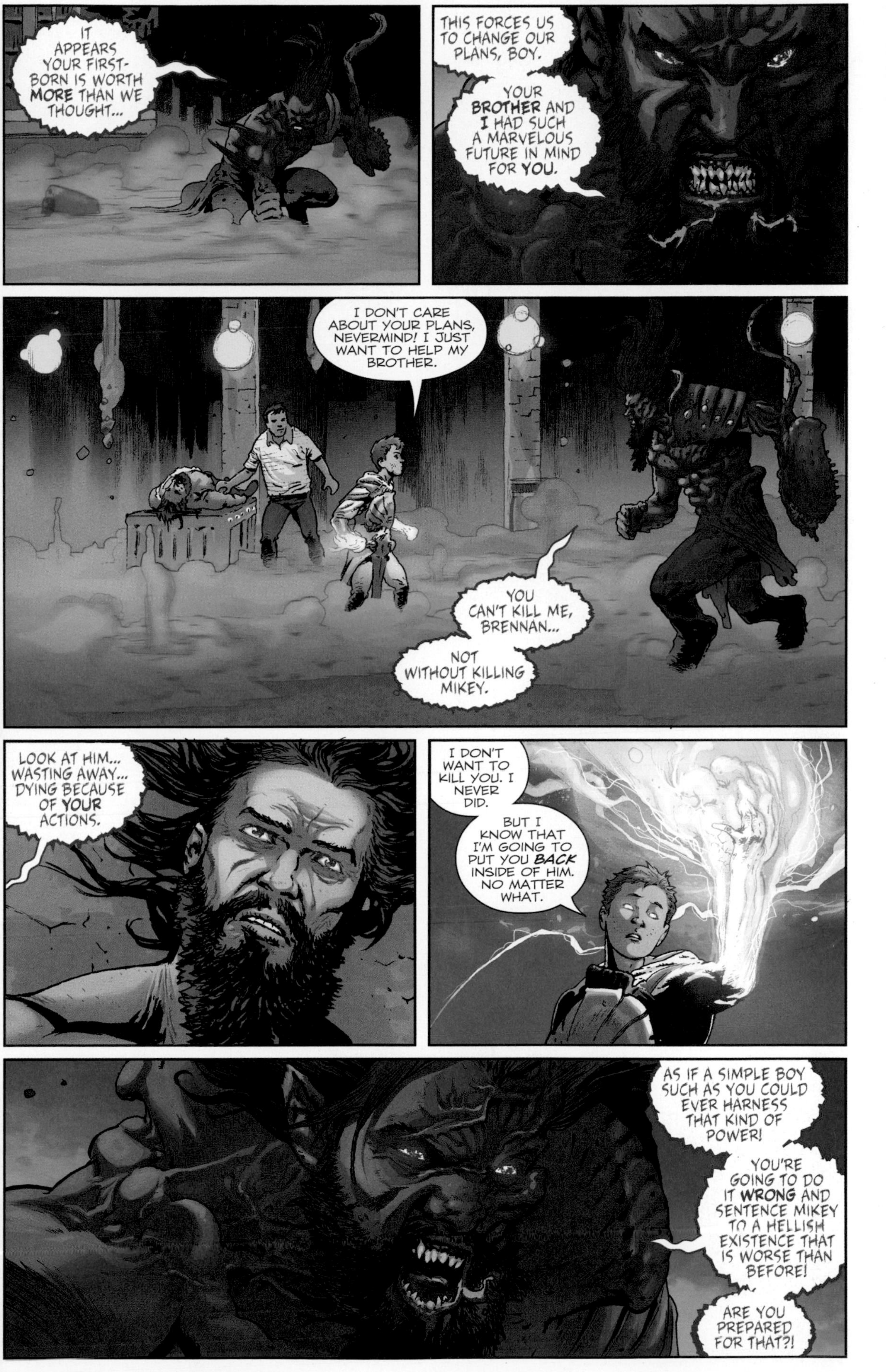
IT APPEARS YOUR FIRST-BORN IS WORTH **MORE** THAN WE THOUGHT...
THIS FORCES US TO CHANGE OUR PLANS, BOY.
YOUR **BROTHER** AND **I** HAD SUCH A MARVELOUS FUTURE IN MIND FOR **YOU.**
I DON'T CARE ABOUT YOUR PLANS, NEVERMIND! I JUST WANT TO HELP MY BROTHER.
YOU CAN'T KILL ME, BRENNAN...
NOT WITHOUT KILLING MIKEY.
LOOK AT HIM... WASTING AWAY... DYING BECAUSE OF **YOUR** ACTIONS.
I DON'T WANT TO KILL YOU. I NEVER DID.
BUT I KNOW THAT I'M GOING TO PUT YOU ***BACK*** INSIDE OF HIM. NO MATTER WHAT.
AS IF A SIMPLE BOY SUCH AS YOU COULD EVER HARNESS THAT KIND OF POWER!
YOU'RE GOING TO DO IT **WRONG** AND SENTENCE MIKEY TO A HELLISH EXISTENCE THAT IS WORSE THAN BEFORE!
ARE YOU PREPARED FOR THAT?!

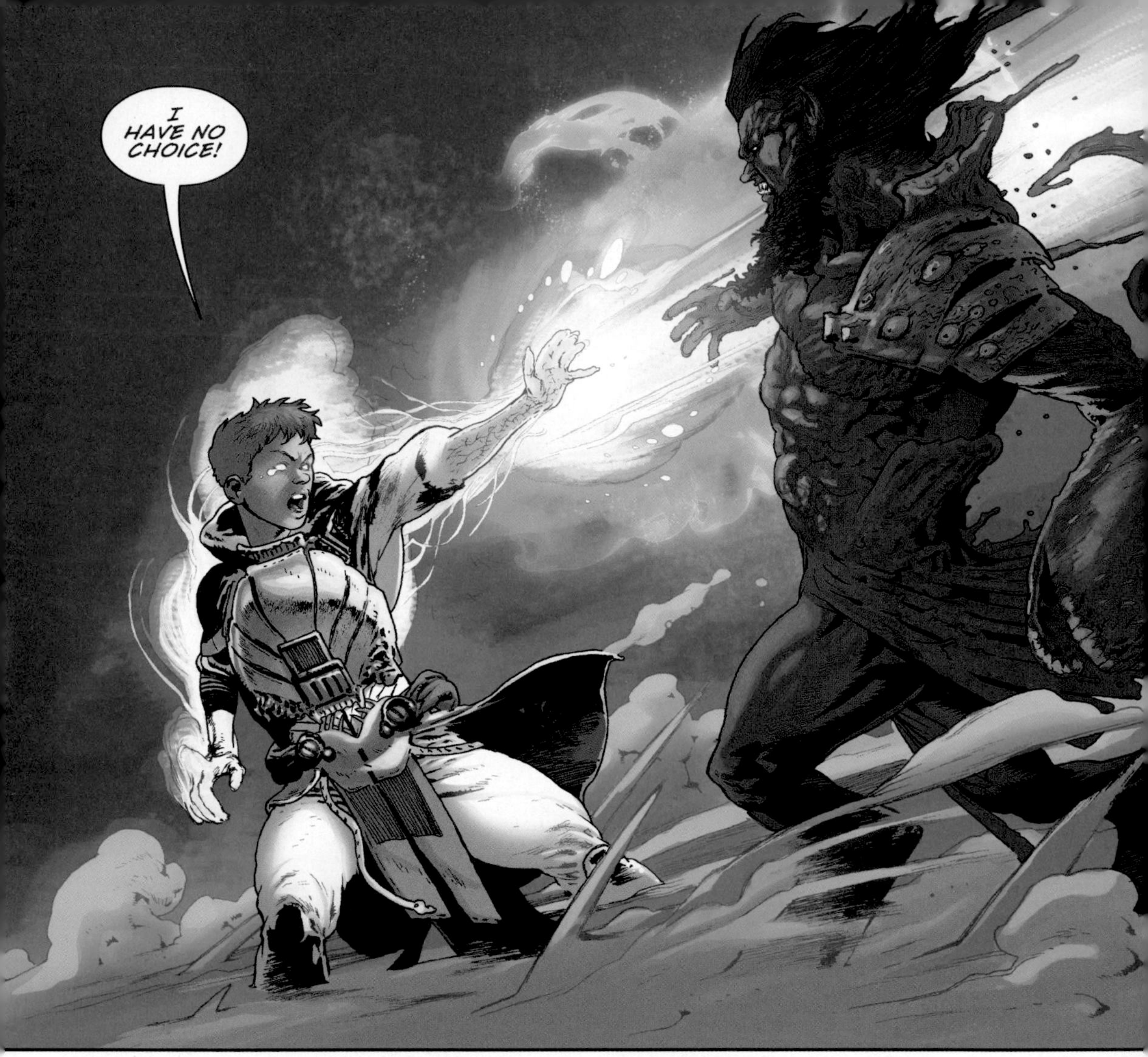
I HAVE NO CHOICE!

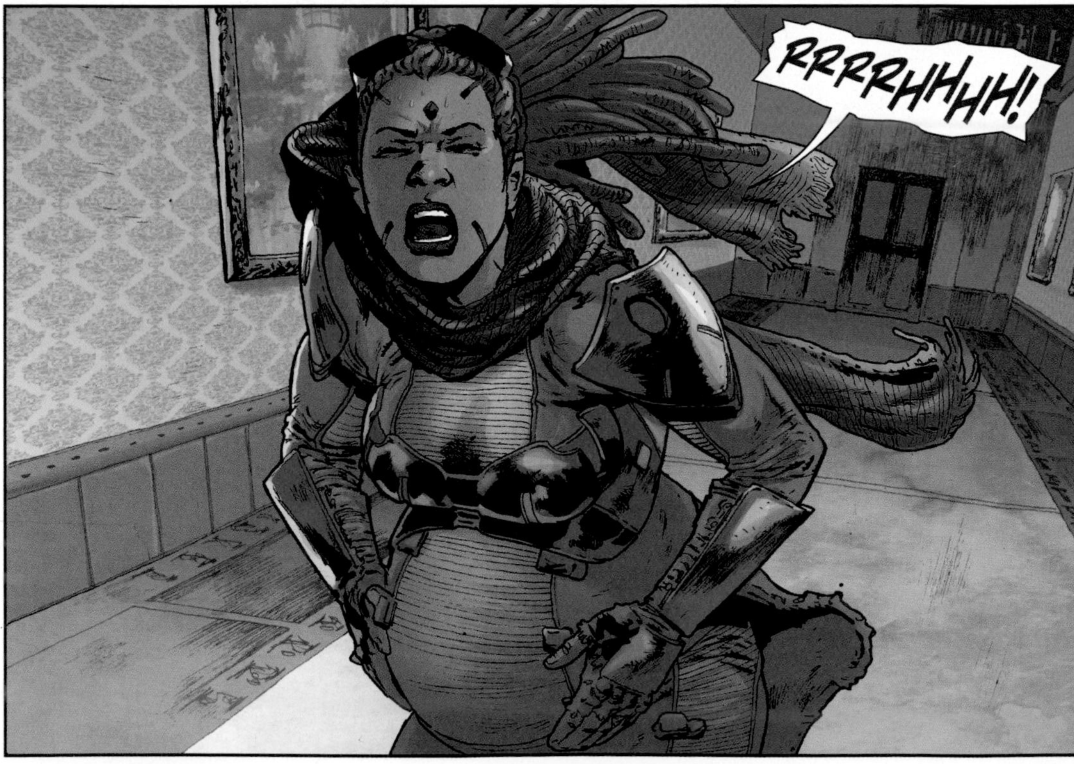
RRRRHHHHH!

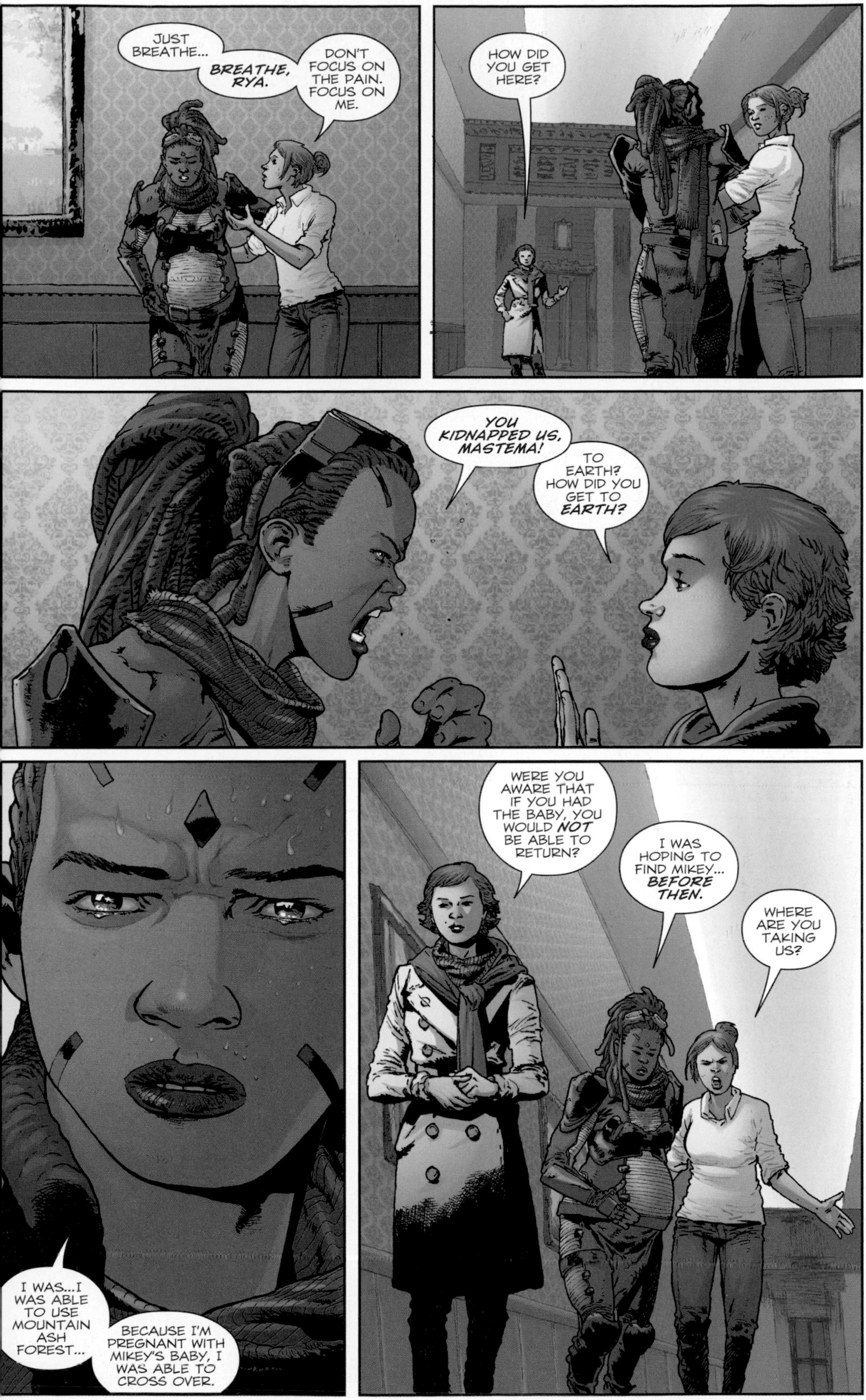
JUST BREATHE... BREATHE, RYA.
DON'T FOCUS ON THE PAIN. FOCUS ON ME.
HOW DID YOU GET HERE?
YOU KIDNAPPED US, MASTEMA!
TO EARTH? HOW DID YOU GET TO EARTH?
I WAS...I WAS ABLE TO USE MOUNTAIN ASH FOREST...
BECAUSE I'M PREGNANT WITH MIKEY'S BABY, I WAS ABLE TO CROSS OVER.
WERE YOU AWARE THAT IF YOU HAD THE BABY, YOU WOULD NOT BE ABLE TO RETURN?
I WAS HOPING TO FIND MIKEY... BEFORE THEN.
WHERE ARE YOU TAKING US?

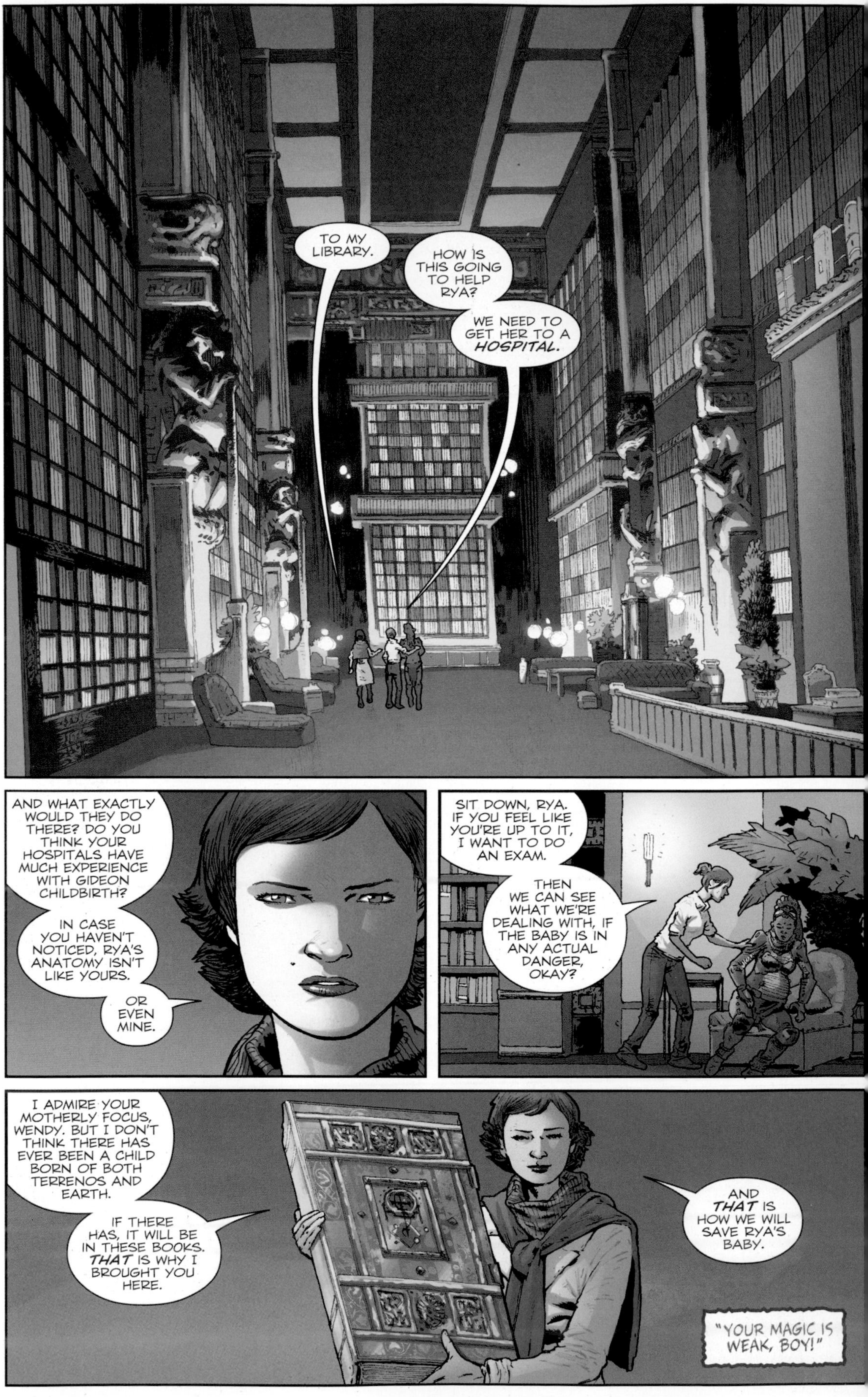
TO MY LIBRARY.
HOW IS THIS GOING TO HELP RYA?
WE NEED TO GET HER TO A *HOSPITAL*.
AND WHAT EXACTLY WOULD THEY DO THERE? DO YOU THINK YOUR HOSPITALS HAVE MUCH EXPERIENCE WITH GIDEON CHILDBIRTH?
IN CASE YOU HAVEN'T NOTICED, RYA'S ANATOMY ISN'T LIKE YOURS.
OR EVEN MINE.
SIT DOWN, RYA. IF YOU FEEL LIKE YOU'RE UP TO IT, I WANT TO DO AN EXAM.
THEN WE CAN SEE WHAT WE'RE DEALING WITH, IF THE BABY IS IN ANY ACTUAL DANGER, OKAY?
I ADMIRE YOUR MOTHERLY FOCUS, WENDY. BUT I DON'T THINK THERE HAS EVER BEEN A CHILD BORN OF BOTH TERRENOS AND EARTH.
IF THERE HAS, IT WILL BE IN THESE BOOKS. *THAT* IS WHY I BROUGHT YOU HERE.
AND *THAT* IS HOW WE WILL SAVE RYA'S BABY.
"YOUR MAGIC IS WEAK, BOY!"

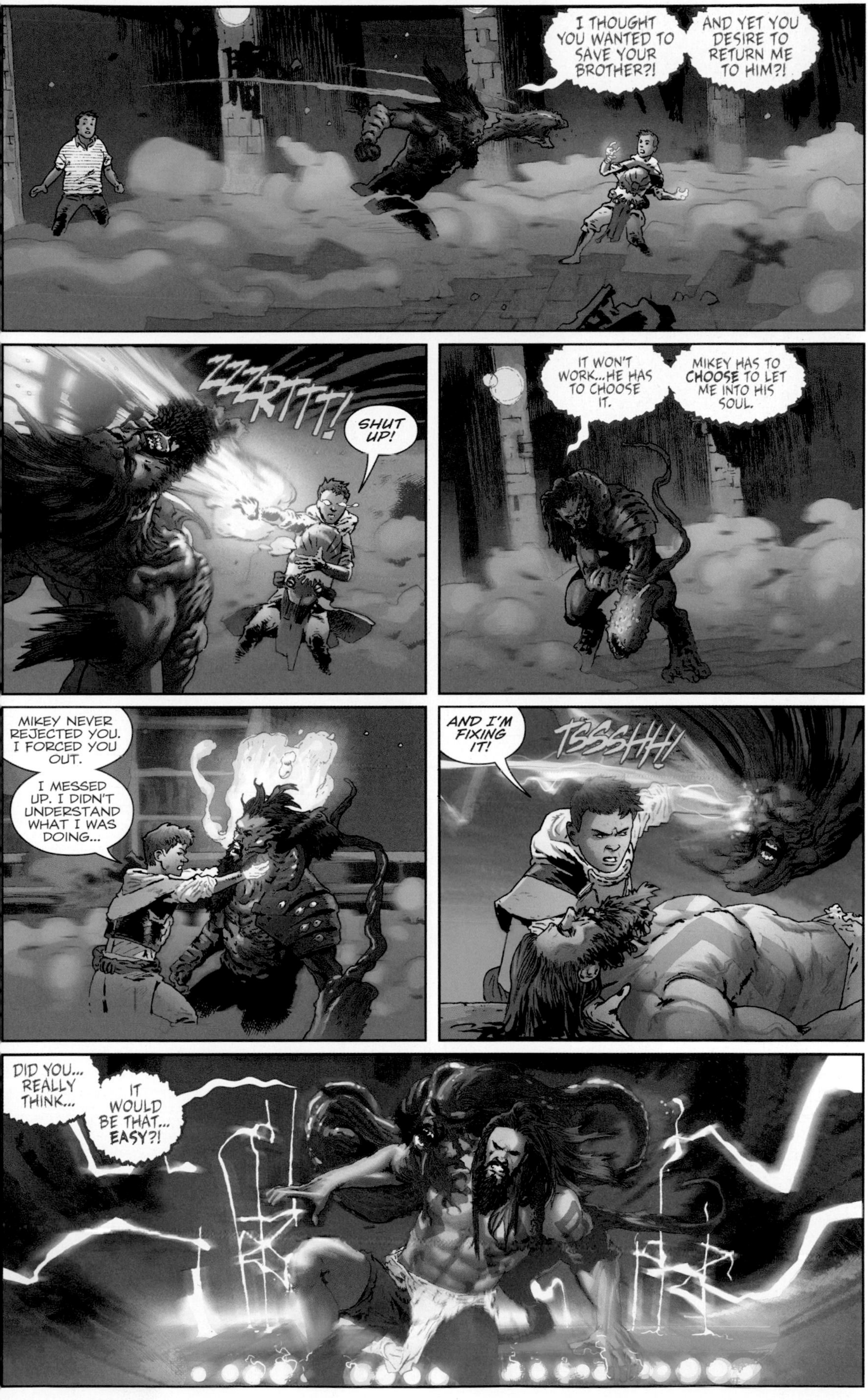

I THOUGHT YOU WANTED TO SAVE YOUR BROTHER?!
AND YET YOU DESIRE TO RETURN ME TO HIM?!
ZZZRTTTT!
SHUT UP!
IT WON'T WORK...HE HAS TO CHOOSE IT.
MIKEY HAS TO **CHOOSE** TO LET ME INTO HIS SOUL.
MIKEY NEVER REJECTED YOU. I FORCED YOU OUT.
I MESSED UP. I DIDN'T UNDERSTAND WHAT I WAS DOING...
AND I'M FIXING IT!
TSSSHH!
DID YOU... REALLY THINK...
IT WOULD BE THAT... **EASY**?!

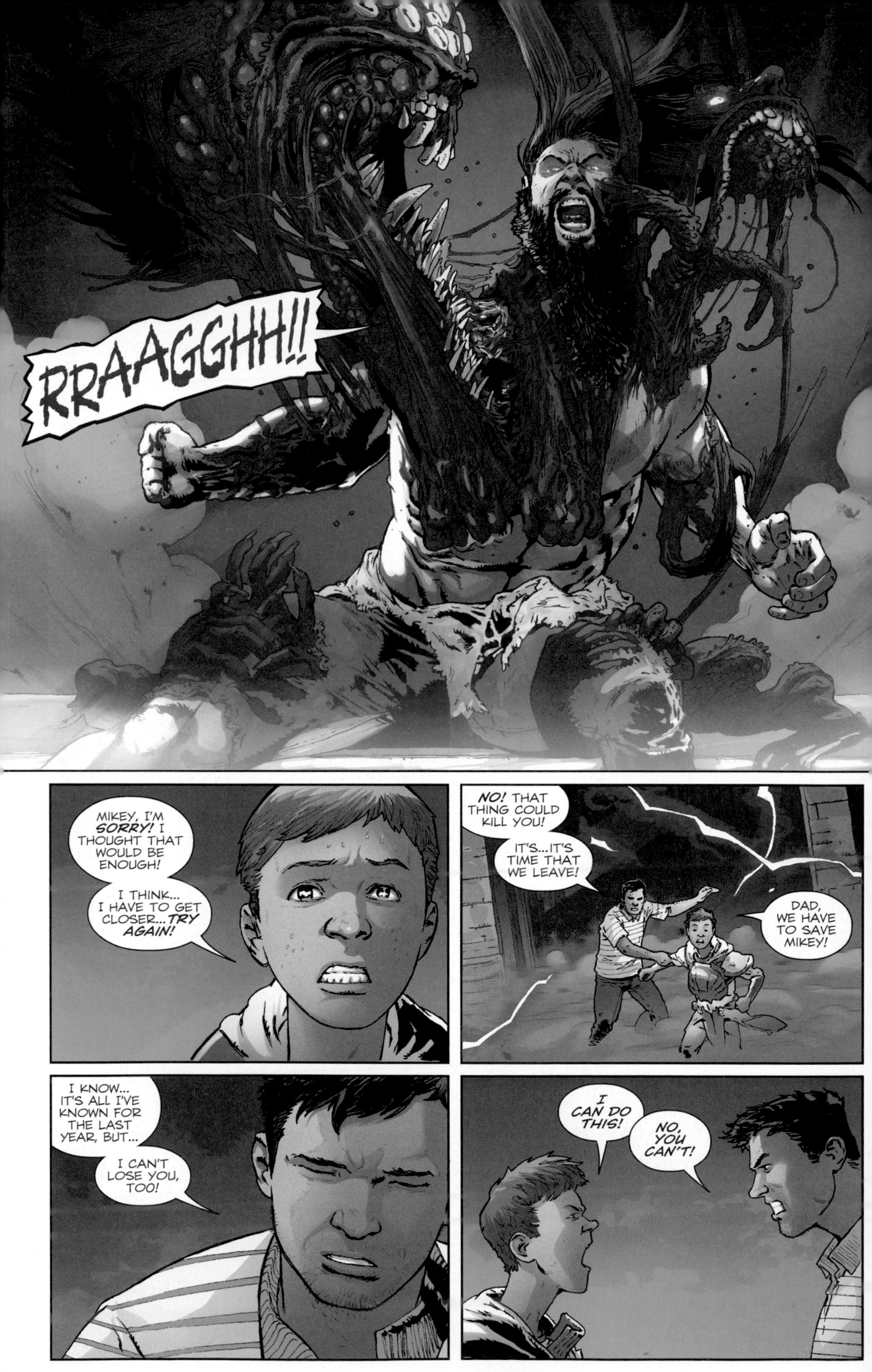
RRAAGGHH!!
MIKEY, I'M SORRY! I THOUGHT THAT WOULD BE ENOUGH!
I THINK... I HAVE TO GET CLOSER...TRY AGAIN!
NO! THAT THING COULD KILL YOU!
IT'S...IT'S TIME THAT WE LEAVE!
DAD, WE HAVE TO SAVE MIKEY!
I KNOW... IT'S ALL I'VE KNOWN FOR THE LAST YEAR, BUT...
I CAN'T LOSE YOU, TOO!
I CAN DO THIS!
NO, YOU CAN'T!

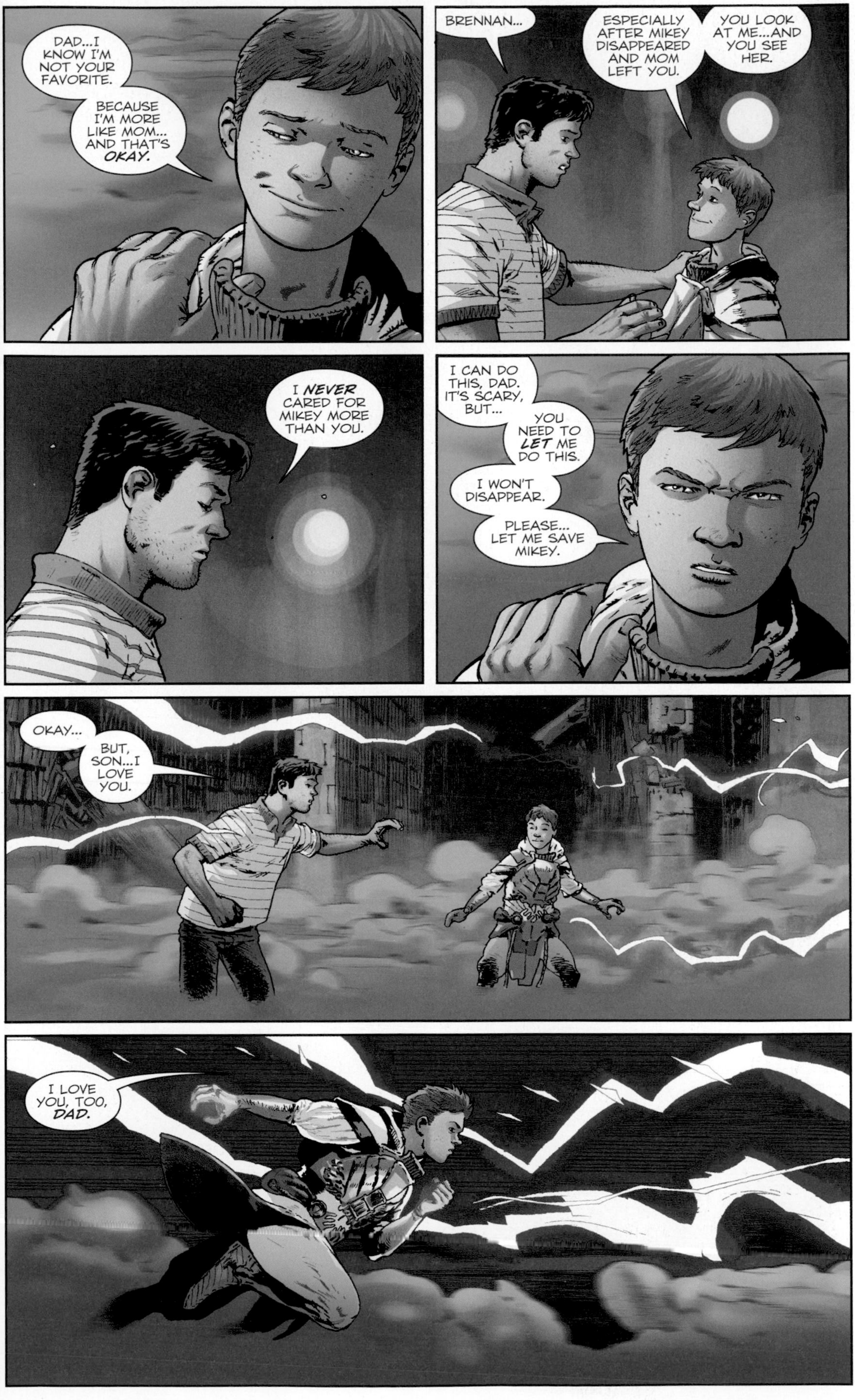
DAD...I KNOW I'M NOT YOUR FAVORITE.
BECAUSE I'M MORE LIKE MOM... AND THAT'S OKAY.
BRENNAN...
ESPECIALLY AFTER MIKEY DISAPPEARED AND MOM LEFT YOU.
YOU LOOK AT ME...AND YOU SEE HER.
I NEVER CARED FOR MIKEY MORE THAN YOU.
I CAN DO THIS, DAD. IT'S SCARY, BUT...
YOU NEED TO LET ME DO THIS.
I WON'T DISAPPEAR.
PLEASE... LET ME SAVE MIKEY.
OKAY...
BUT, SON...I LOVE YOU.
I LOVE YOU, TOO, DAD.

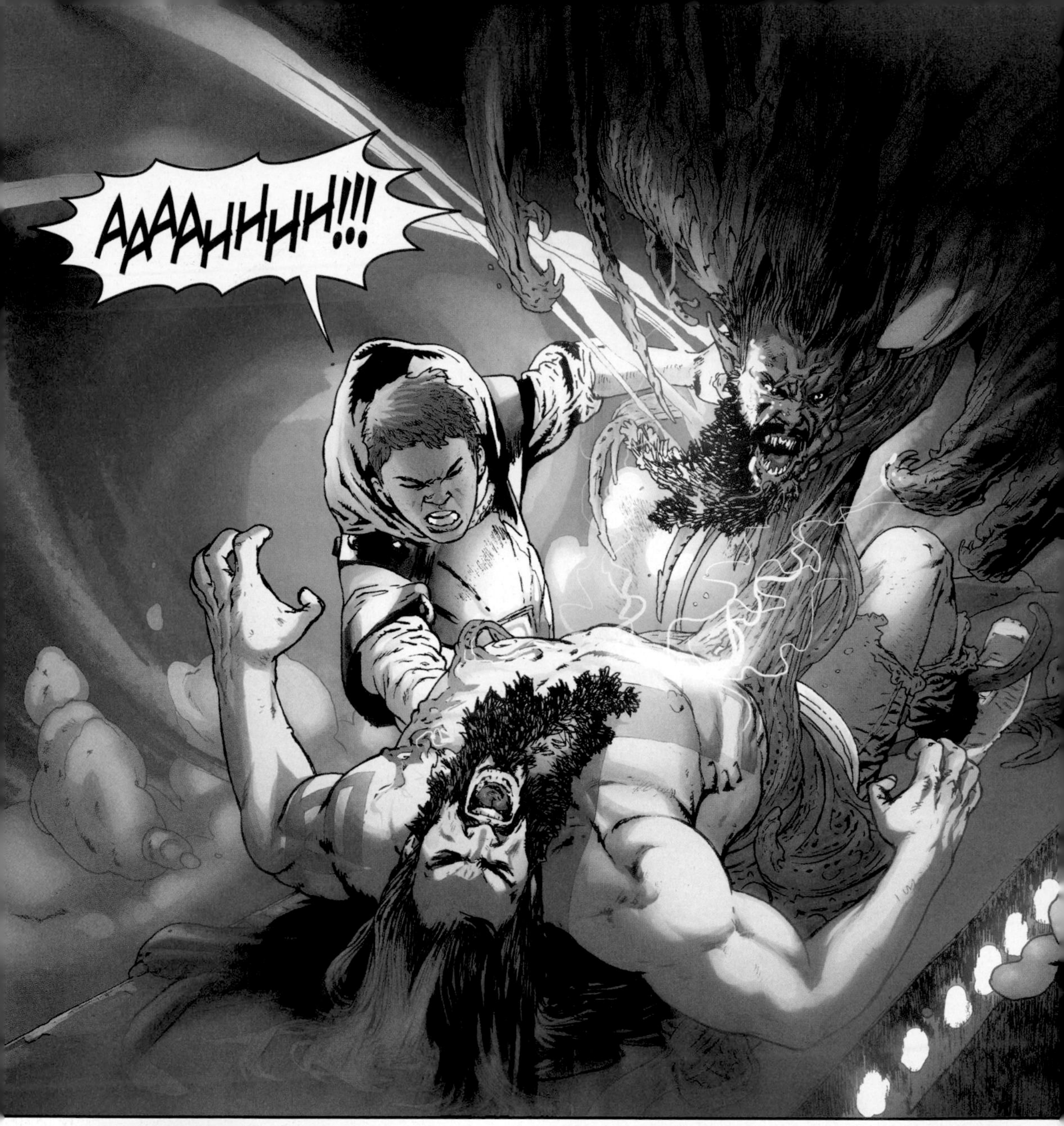
AAAAHHHH!!!

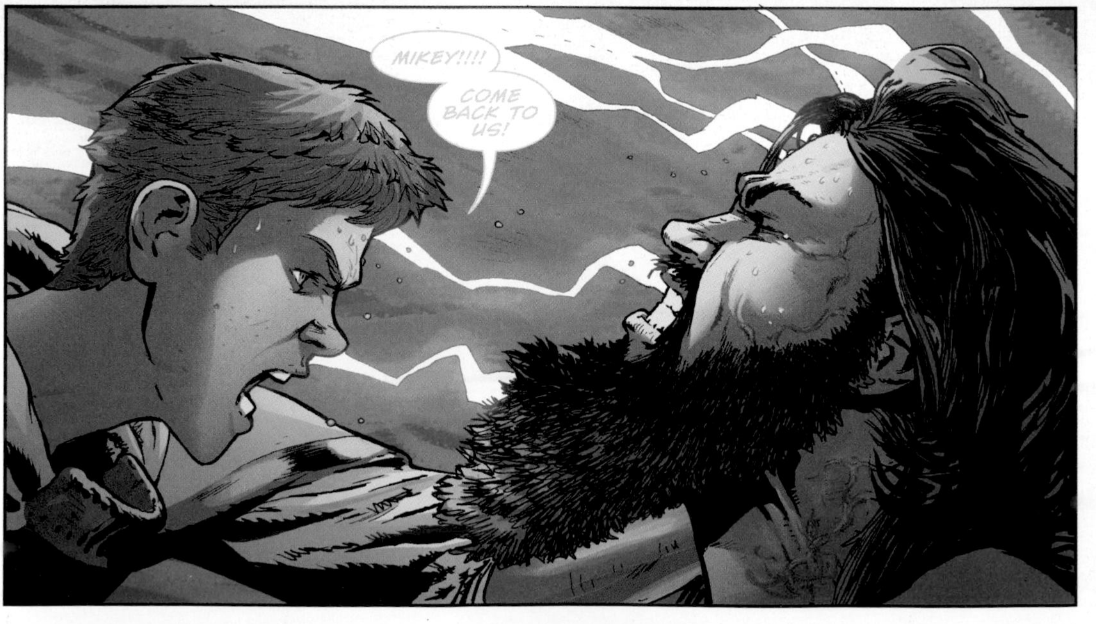
MIKEY!!!!
COME BACK TO US!

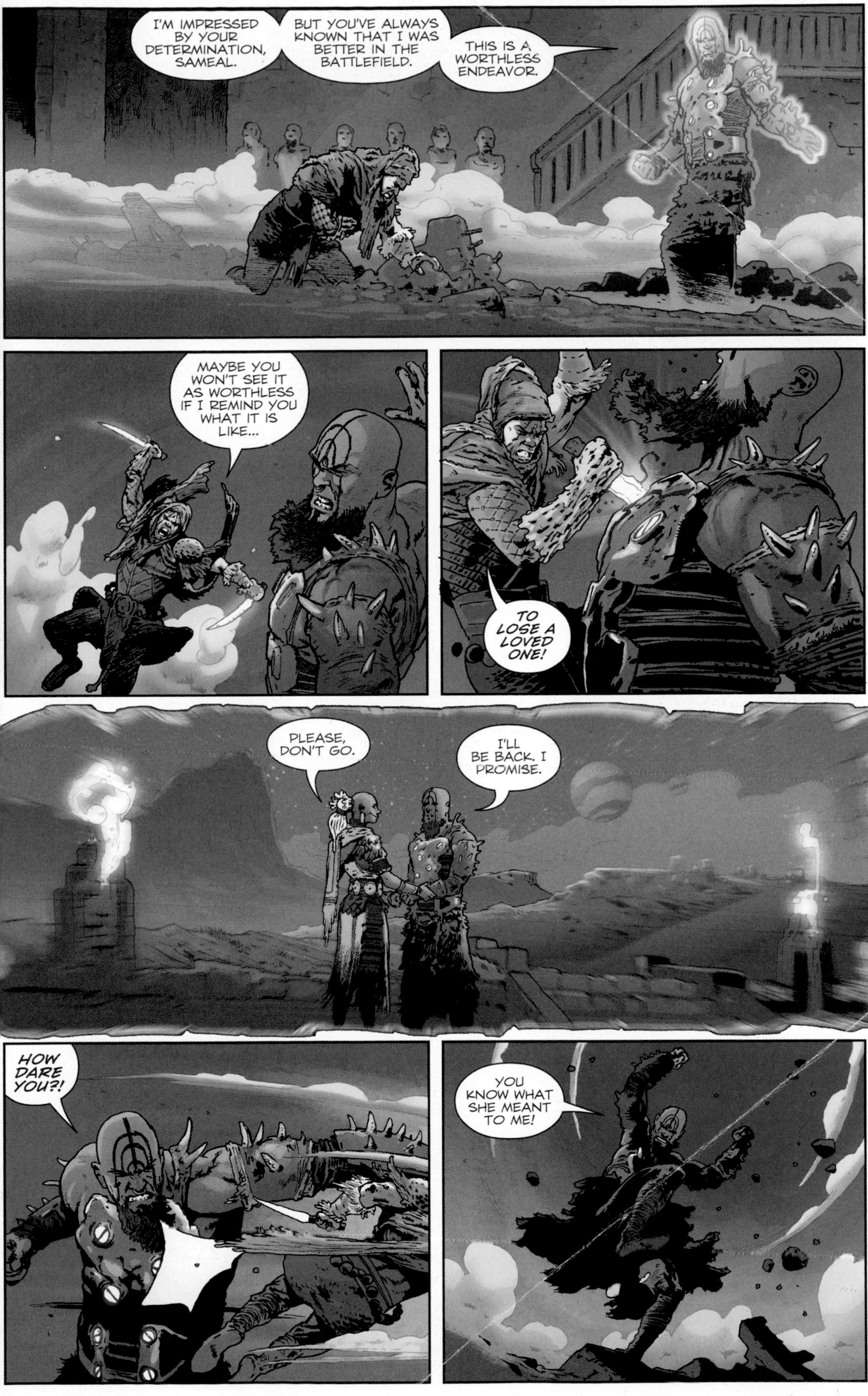
I'M IMPRESSED BY YOUR DETERMINATION, SAMEAL.
BUT YOU'VE ALWAYS KNOWN THAT I WAS BETTER IN THE BATTLEFIELD.
THIS IS A WORTHLESS ENDEAVOR.
MAYBE YOU WON'T SEE IT AS WORTHLESS IF I REMIND YOU WHAT IT IS LIKE...
TO LOSE A LOVED ONE!
PLEASE, DON'T GO.
I'LL BE BACK. I PROMISE.
HOW DARE YOU?!
YOU KNOW WHAT SHE MEANT TO ME!

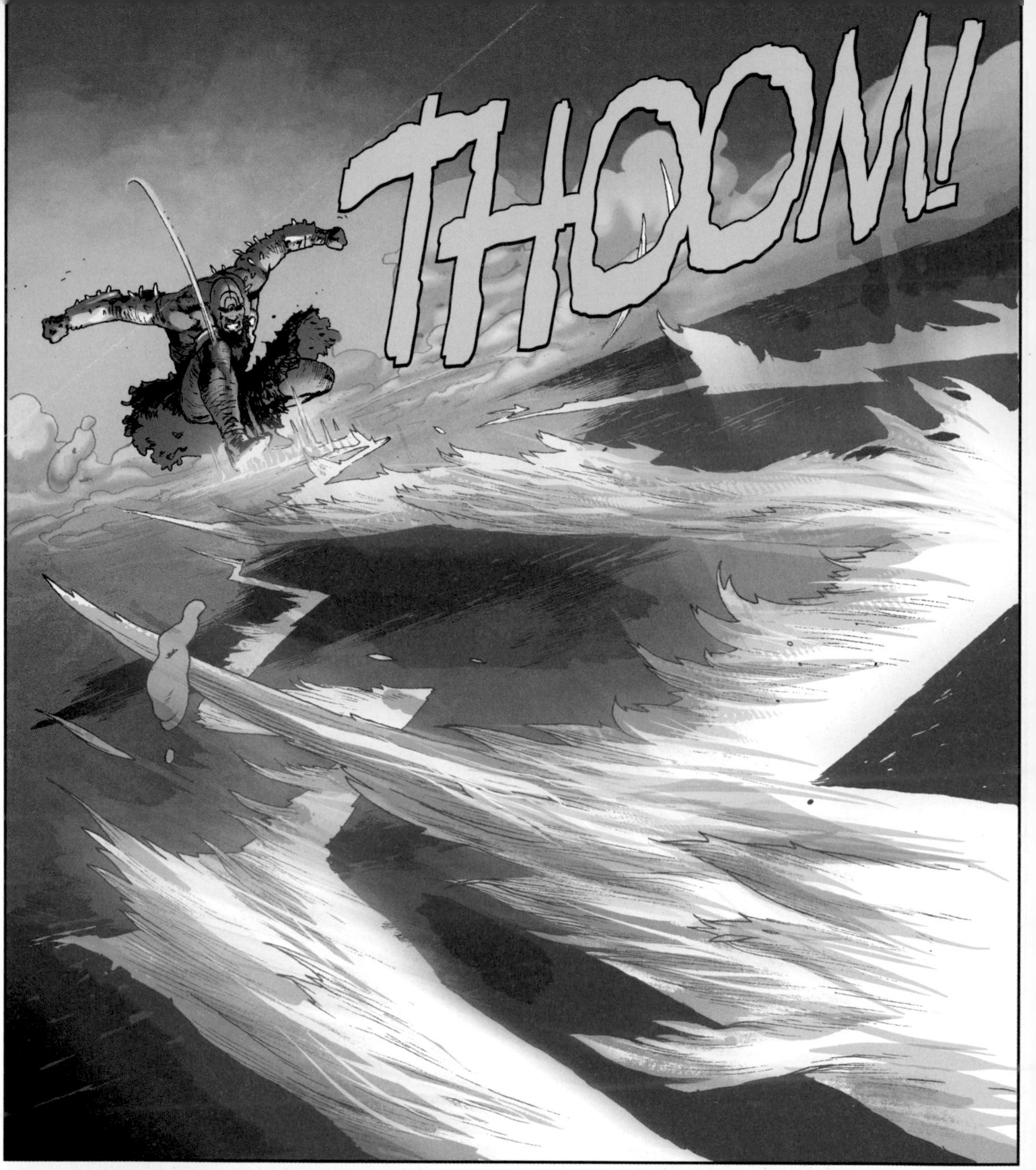
THOOM!

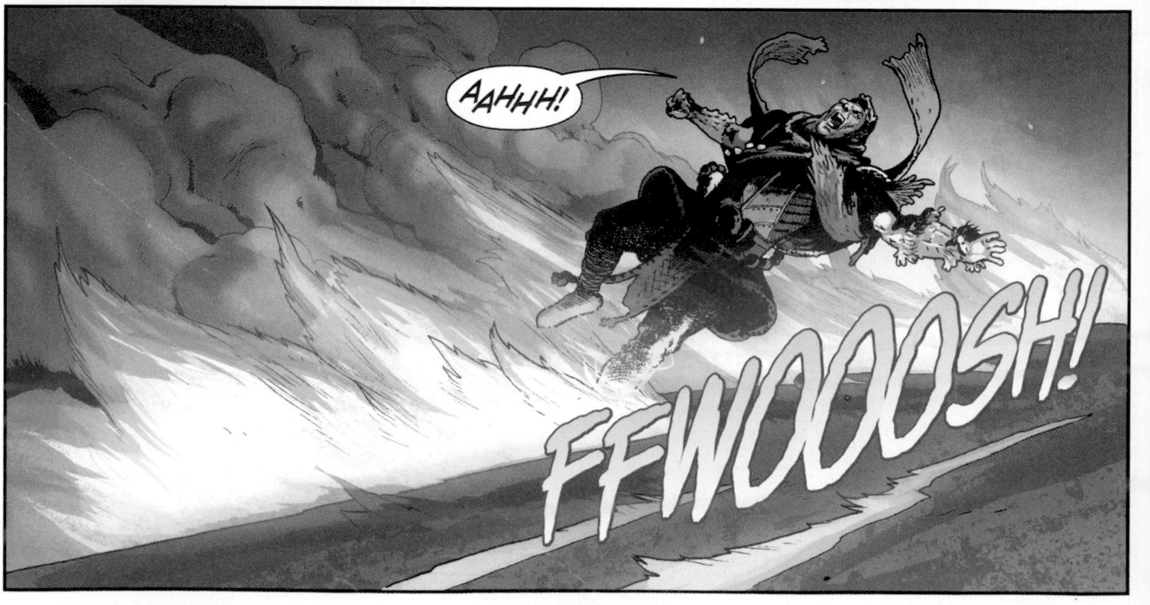
AAHHH!
FFWOOOSH!

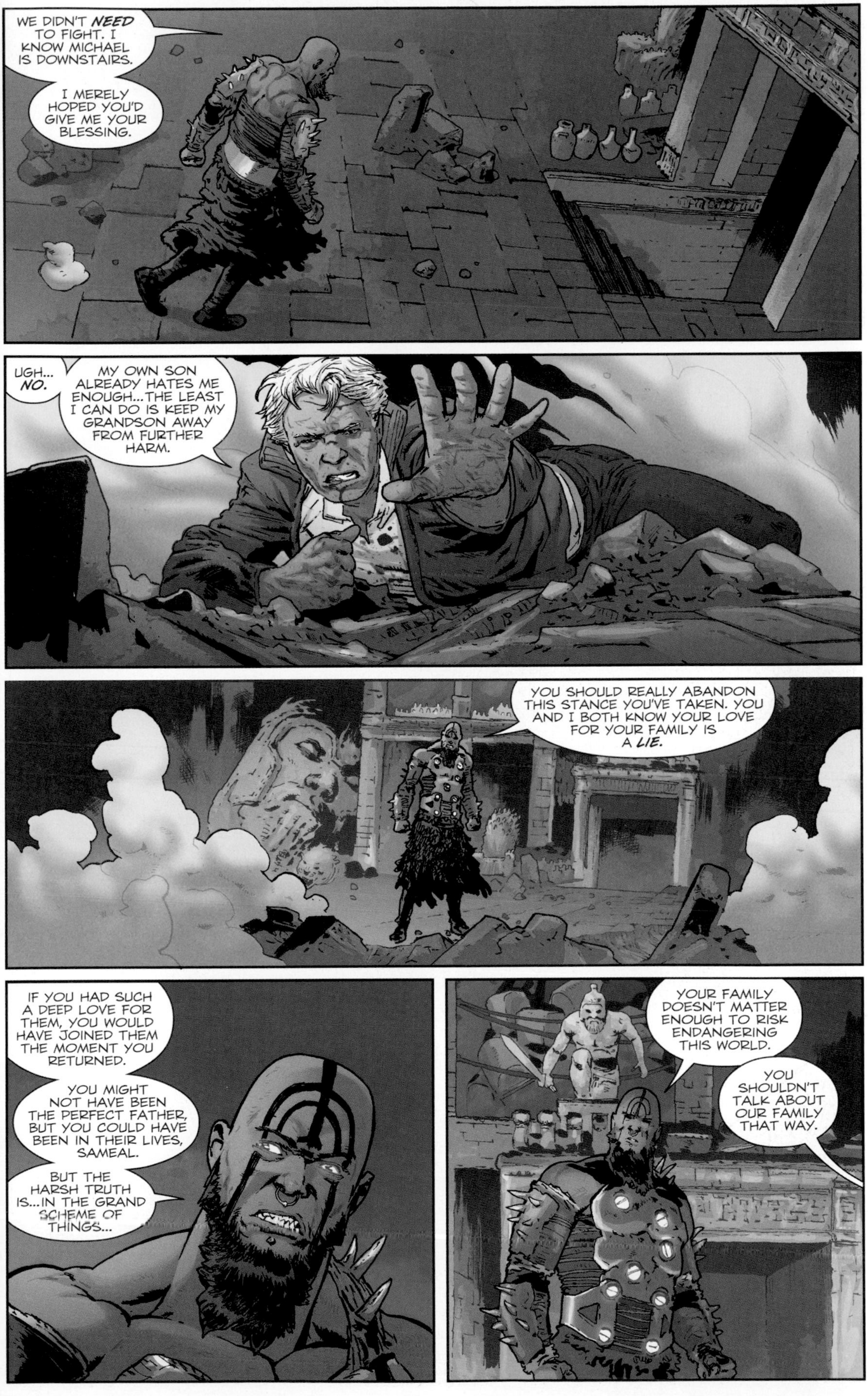
WE DIDN'T NEED TO FIGHT. I KNOW MICHAEL IS DOWNSTAIRS.
I MERELY HOPED YOU'D GIVE ME YOUR BLESSING.
UGH... NO.
MY OWN SON ALREADY HATES ME ENOUGH...THE LEAST I CAN DO IS KEEP MY GRANDSON AWAY FROM FURTHER HARM.
YOU SHOULD REALLY ABANDON THIS STANCE YOU'VE TAKEN. YOU AND I BOTH KNOW YOUR LOVE FOR YOUR FAMILY IS A LIE.
IF YOU HAD SUCH A DEEP LOVE FOR THEM, YOU WOULD HAVE JOINED THEM THE MOMENT YOU RETURNED.
YOU MIGHT NOT HAVE BEEN THE PERFECT FATHER, BUT YOU COULD HAVE BEEN IN THEIR LIVES, SAMEAL.
BUT THE HARSH TRUTH IS...IN THE GRAND SCHEME OF THINGS...
YOUR FAMILY DOESN'T MATTER ENOUGH TO RISK ENDANGERING THIS WORLD.
YOU SHOULDN'T TALK ABOUT OUR FAMILY THAT WAY.

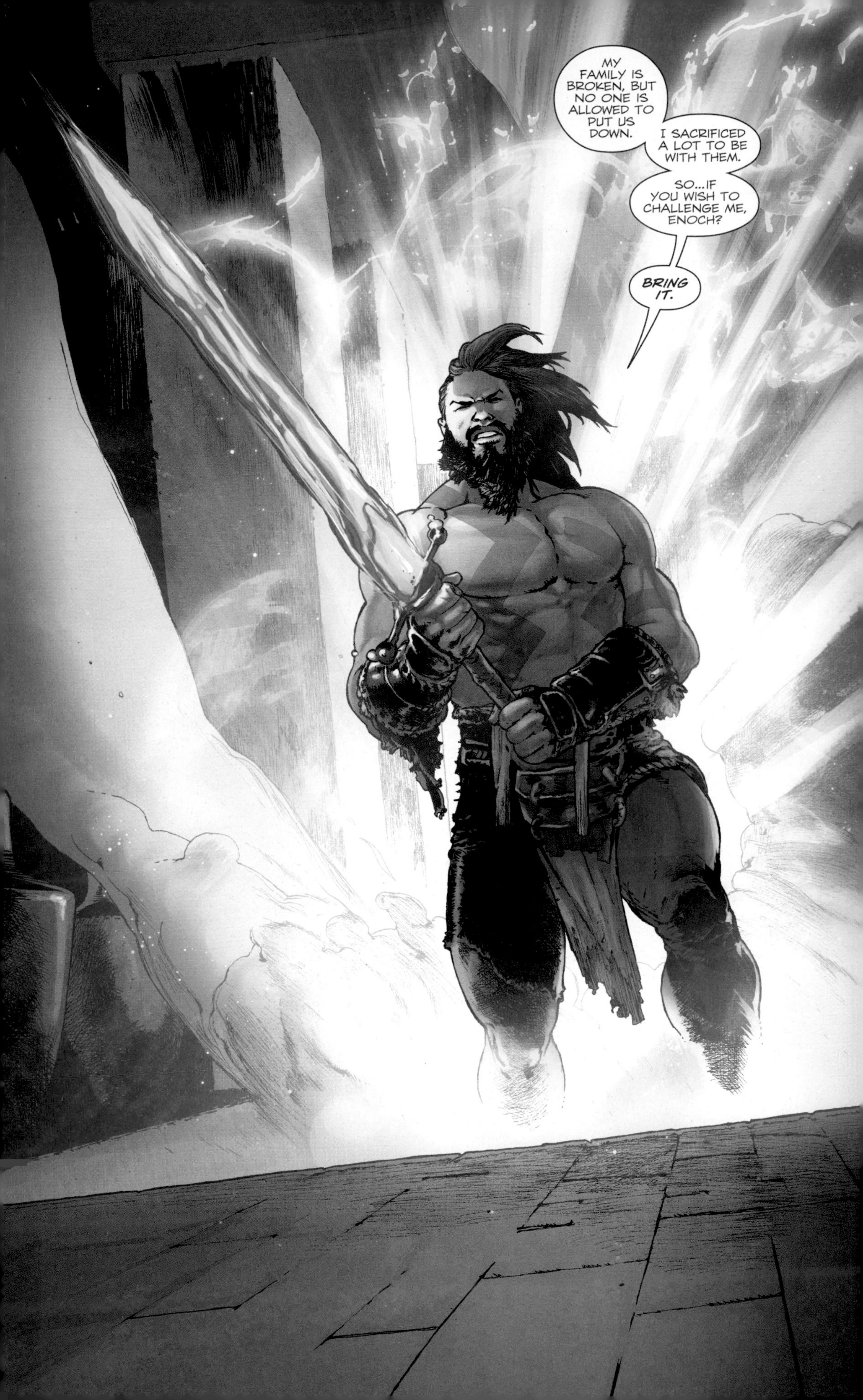
MY FAMILY IS BROKEN, BUT NO ONE IS ALLOWED TO PUT US DOWN.
I SACRIFICED A LOT TO BE WITH THEM.
SO...IF YOU WISH TO CHALLENGE ME, ENOCH?
BRING IT.

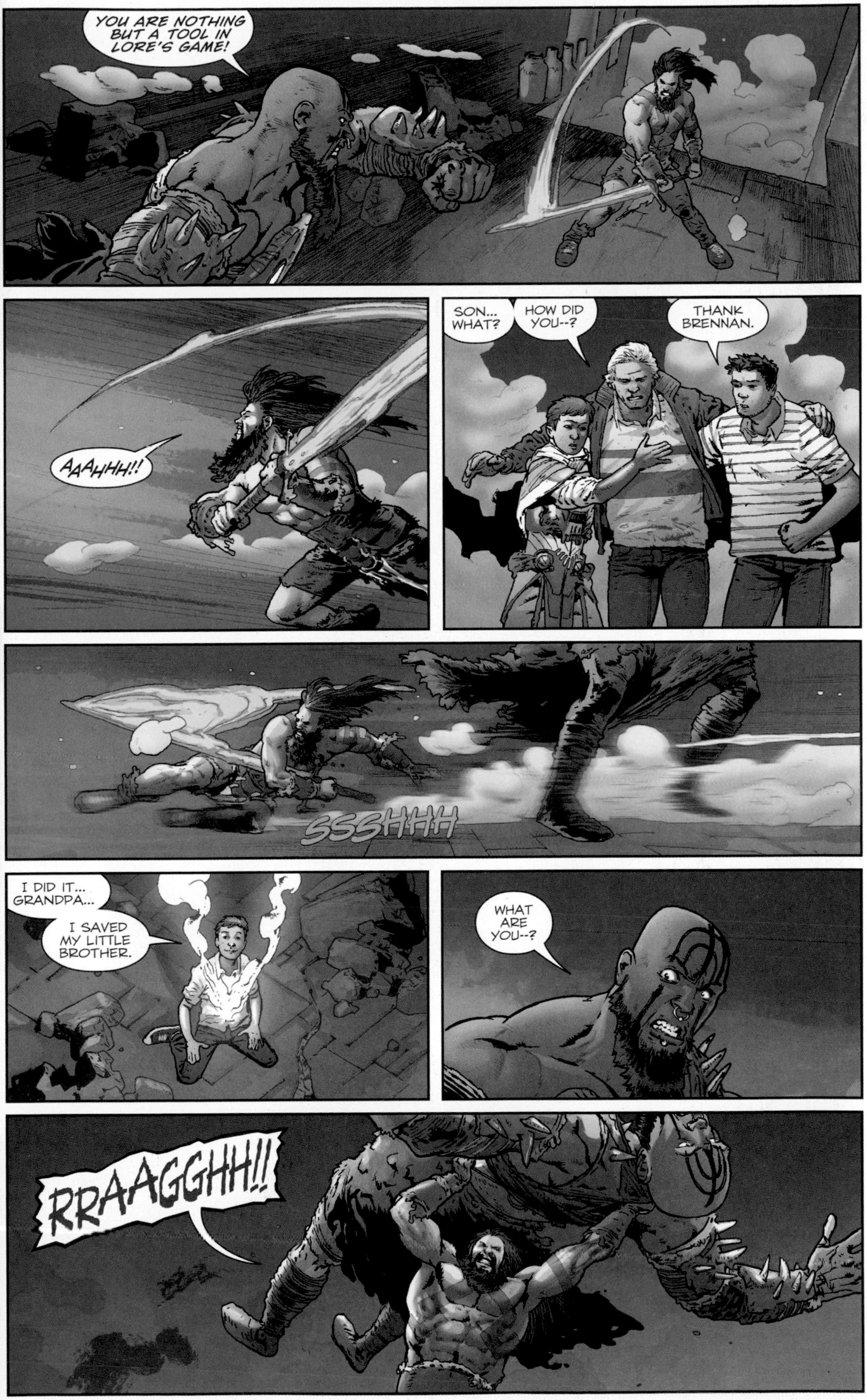
YOU ARE NOTHING BUT A TOOL IN LORE'S GAME!
AAAHHH!!
SON... WHAT?
HOW DID YOU--?
THANK BRENNAN.
SSSHHH
I DID IT... GRANDPA...
I SAVED MY LITTLE BROTHER.
WHAT ARE YOU--?
RRAAGGHH!!

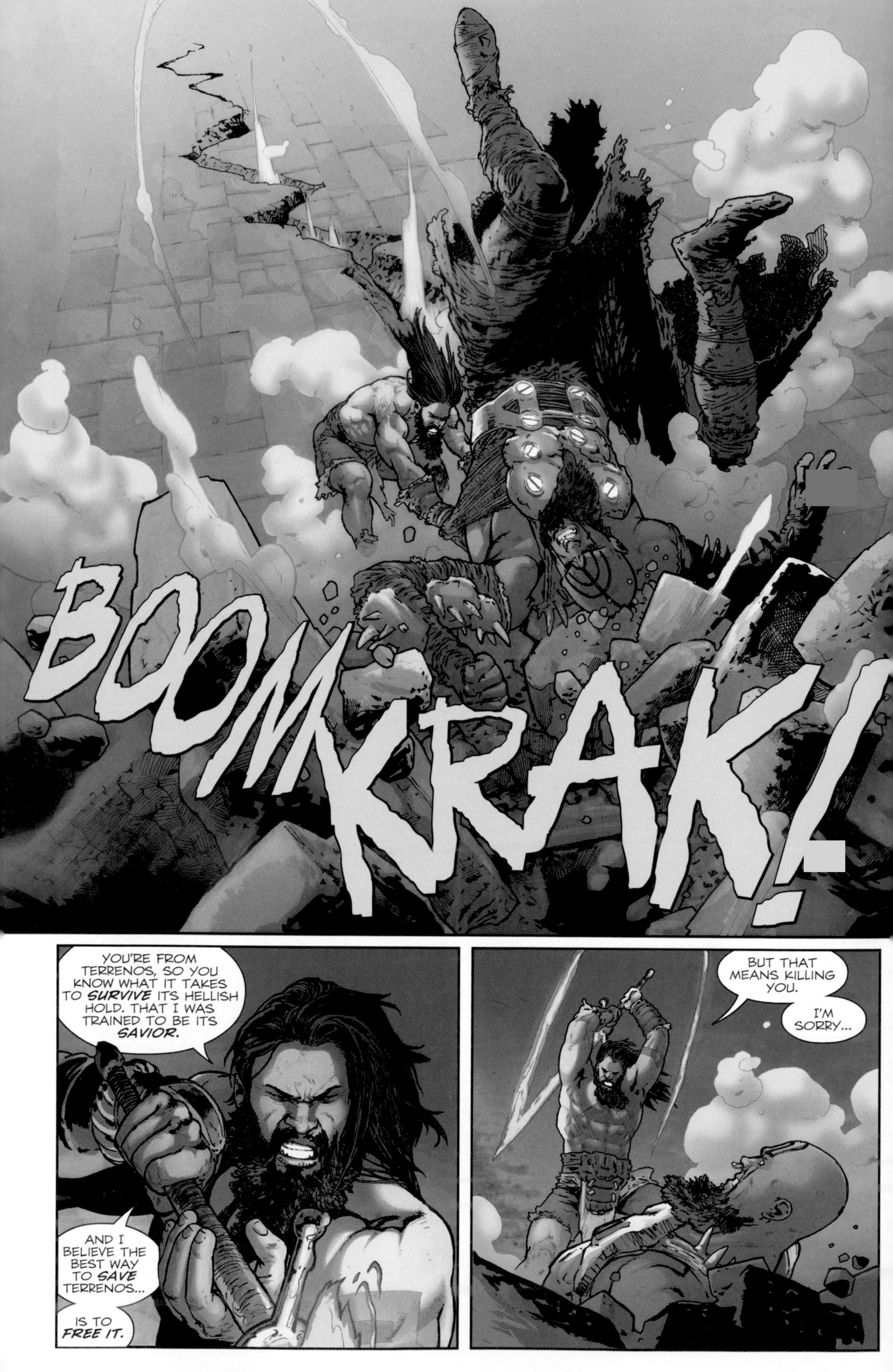
BOOM KRAK!
YOU'RE FROM TERRENOS, SO YOU KNOW WHAT IT TAKES TO SURVIVE ITS HELLISH HOLD. THAT I WAS TRAINED TO BE ITS SAVIOR.
AND I BELIEVE THE BEST WAY TO SAVE TERRENOS...
IS TO FREE IT.
BUT THAT MEANS KILLING YOU.
I'M SORRY...

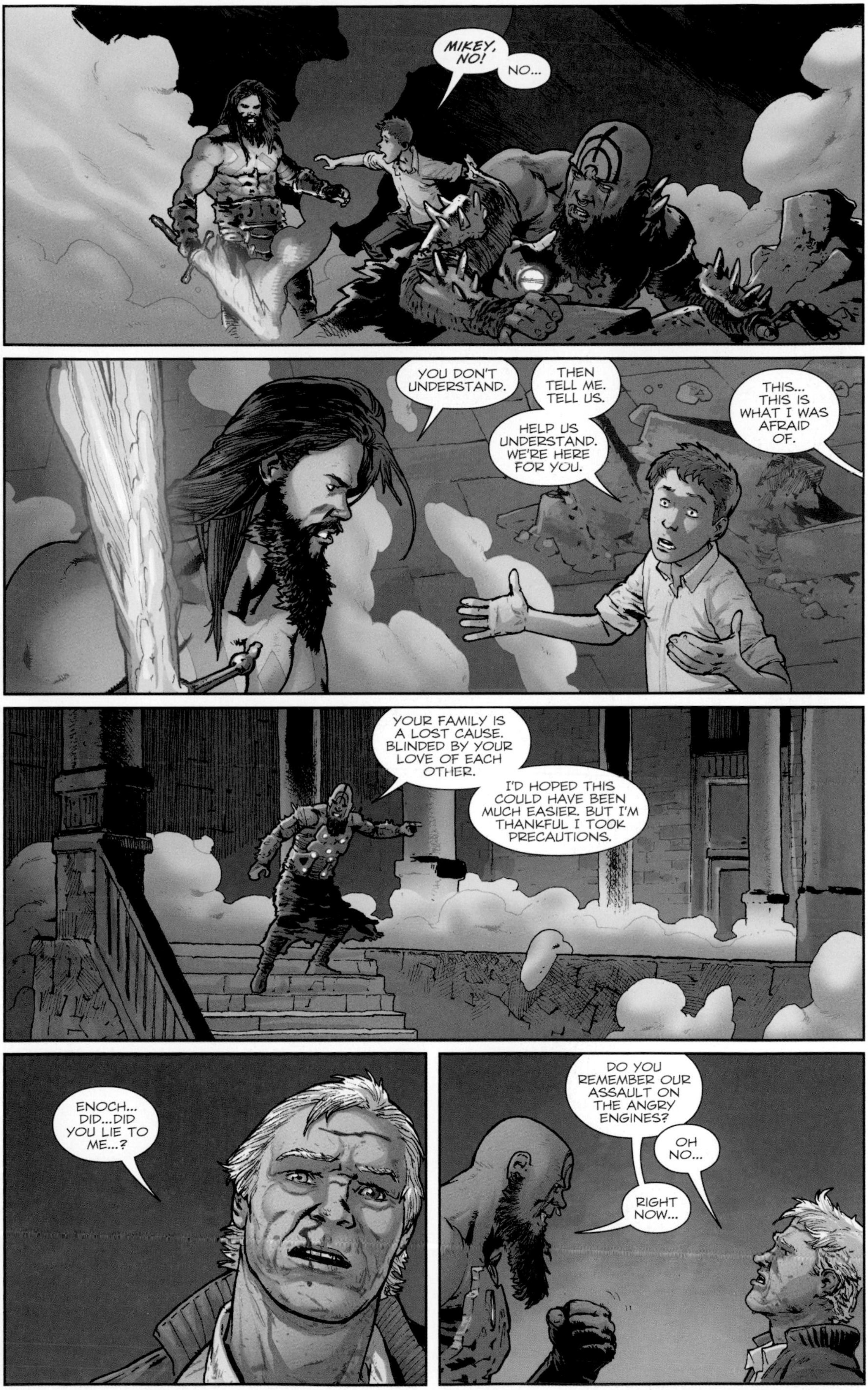

MIKEY, NO!
NO...
YOU DON'T UNDERSTAND.
THEN TELL ME. TELL US.
HELP US UNDERSTAND. WE'RE HERE FOR YOU.
THIS... THIS IS WHAT I WAS AFRAID OF.
YOUR FAMILY IS A LOST CAUSE. BLINDED BY YOUR LOVE OF EACH OTHER.
I'D HOPED THIS COULD HAVE BEEN MUCH EASIER. BUT I'M THANKFUL I TOOK PRECAUTIONS.
ENOCH... DID...DID YOU LIE TO ME...?
DO YOU REMEMBER OUR ASSAULT ON THE ANGRY ENGINES?
OH NO...
RIGHT NOW...

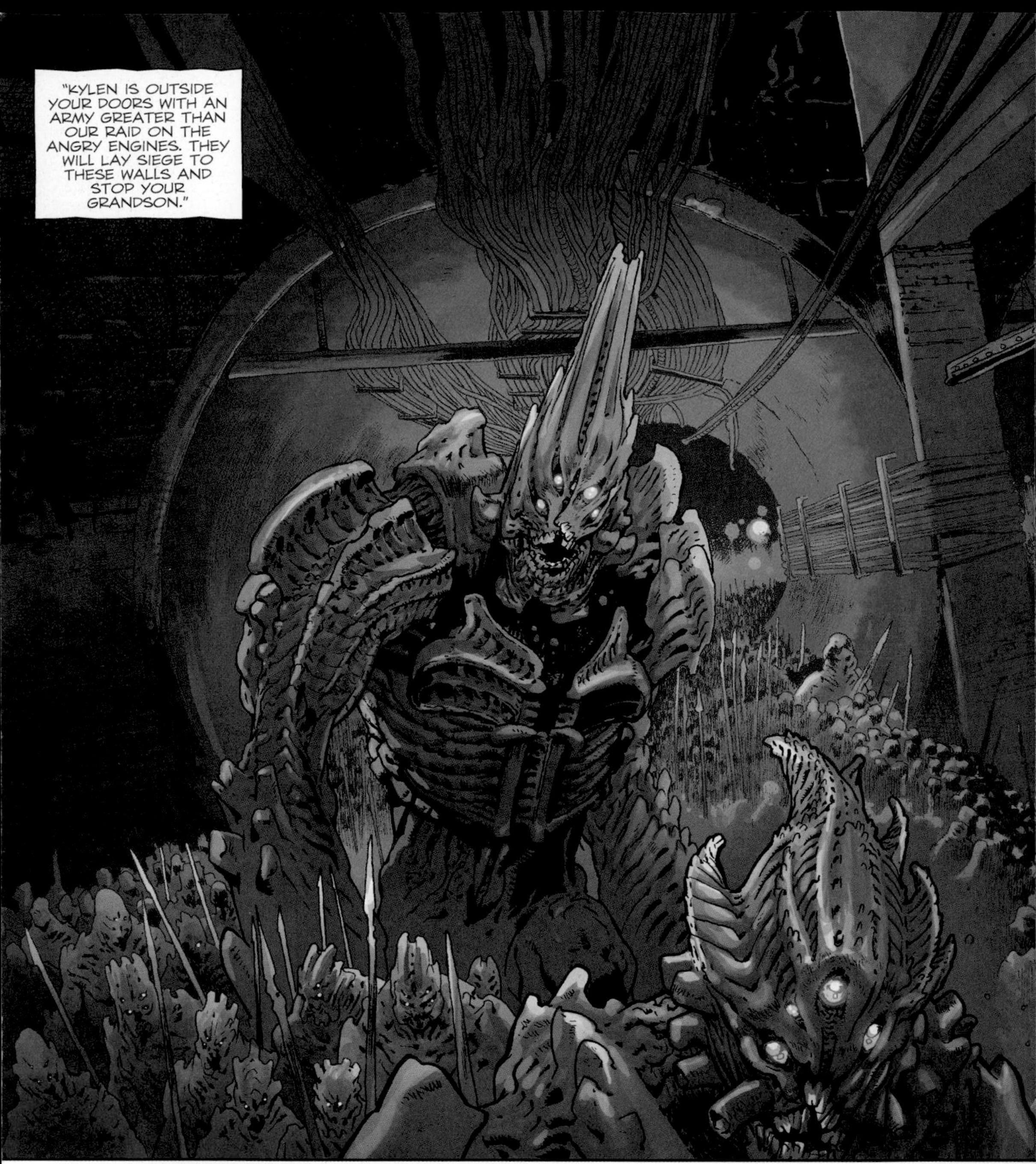
"KYLEN IS OUTSIDE YOUR DOORS WITH AN ARMY GREATER THAN OUR RAID ON THE ANGRY ENGINES. THEY WILL LAY SIEGE TO THESE WALLS AND STOP YOUR GRANDSON."

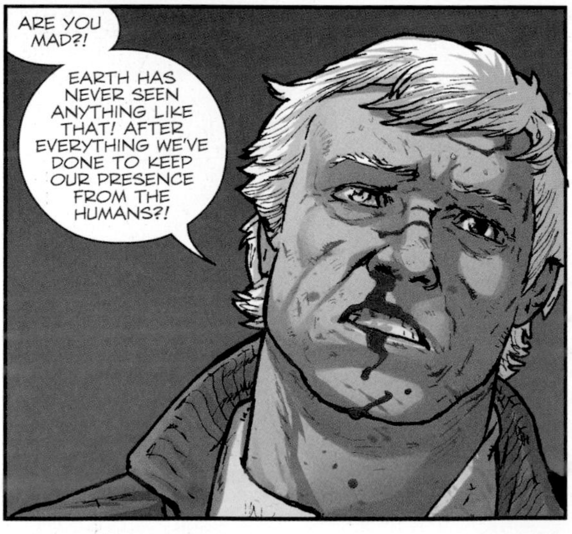
ARE YOU MAD?!
EARTH HAS NEVER SEEN ANYTHING LIKE THAT! AFTER EVERYTHING WE'VE DONE TO KEEP OUR PRESENCE FROM THE HUMANS?!

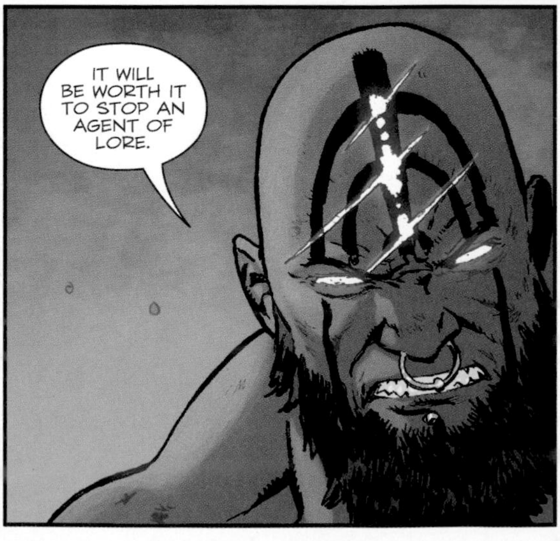
IT WILL BE WORTH IT TO STOP AN AGENT OF LORE.

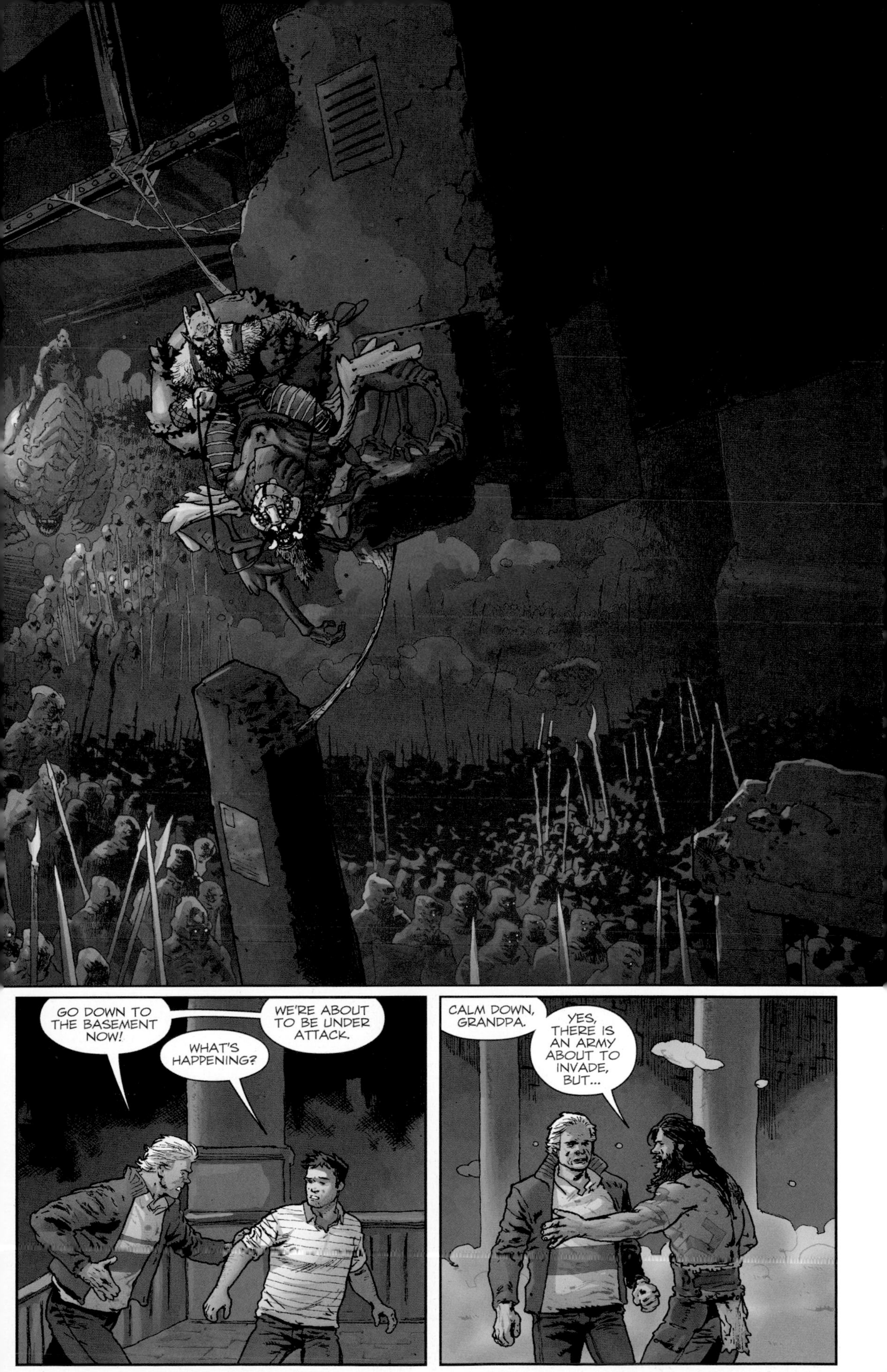
GO DOWN TO THE BASEMENT NOW!
WHAT'S HAPPENING?
WE'RE ABOUT TO BE UNDER ATTACK.
CALM DOWN, GRANDPA.
YES, THERE IS AN ARMY ABOUT TO INVADE, BUT...

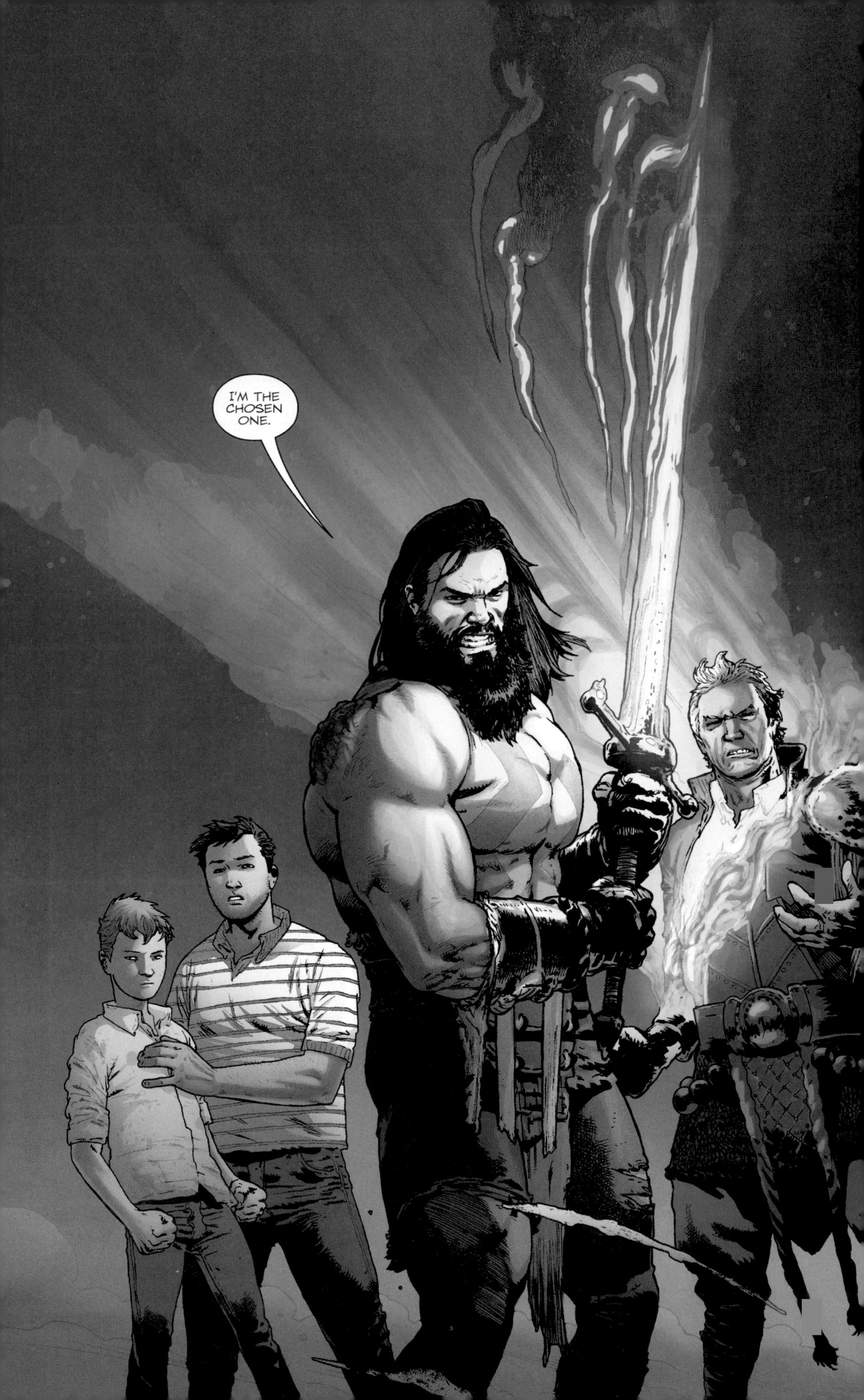
I'M THE CHOSEN ONE.

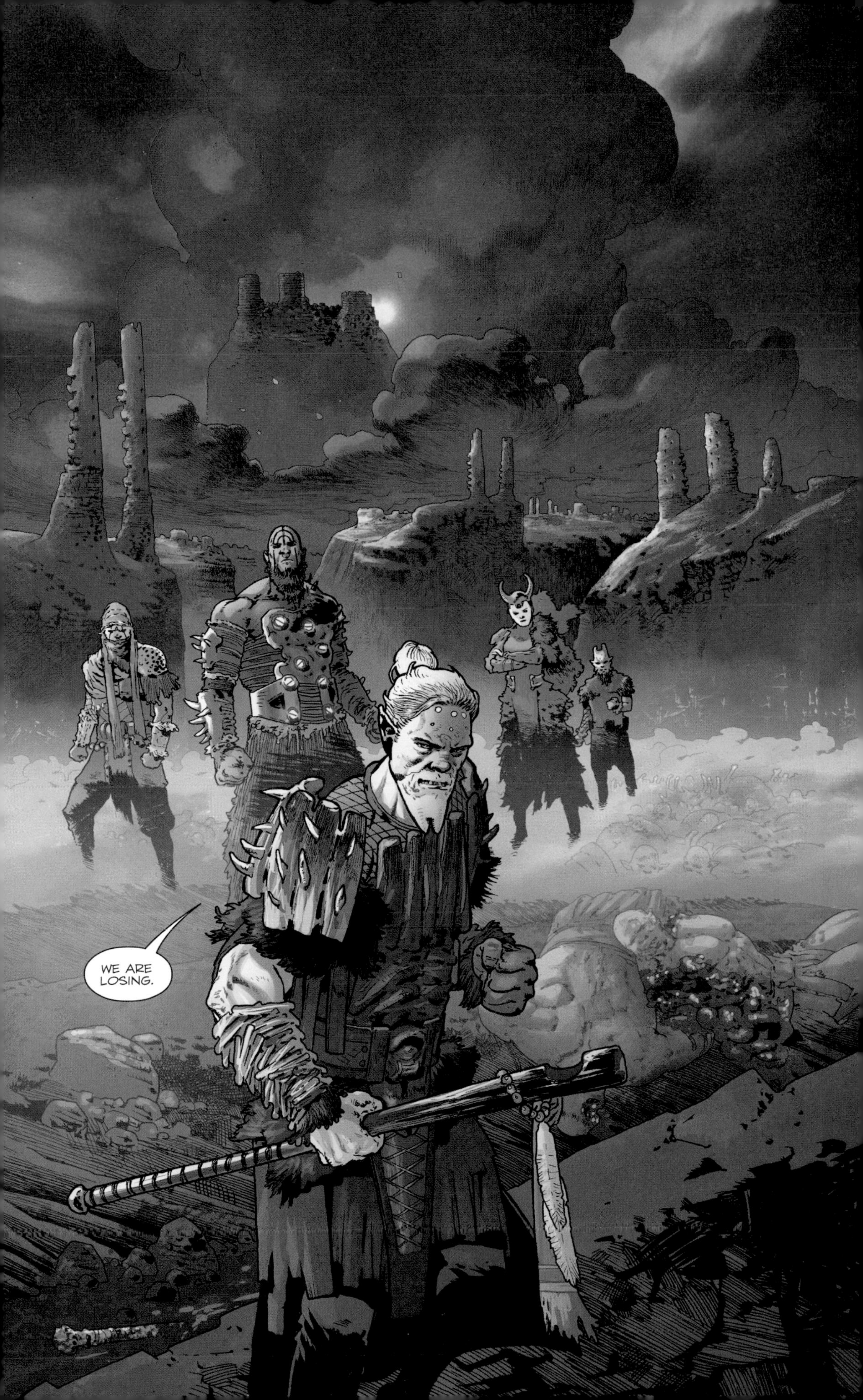
WE ARE LOSING.

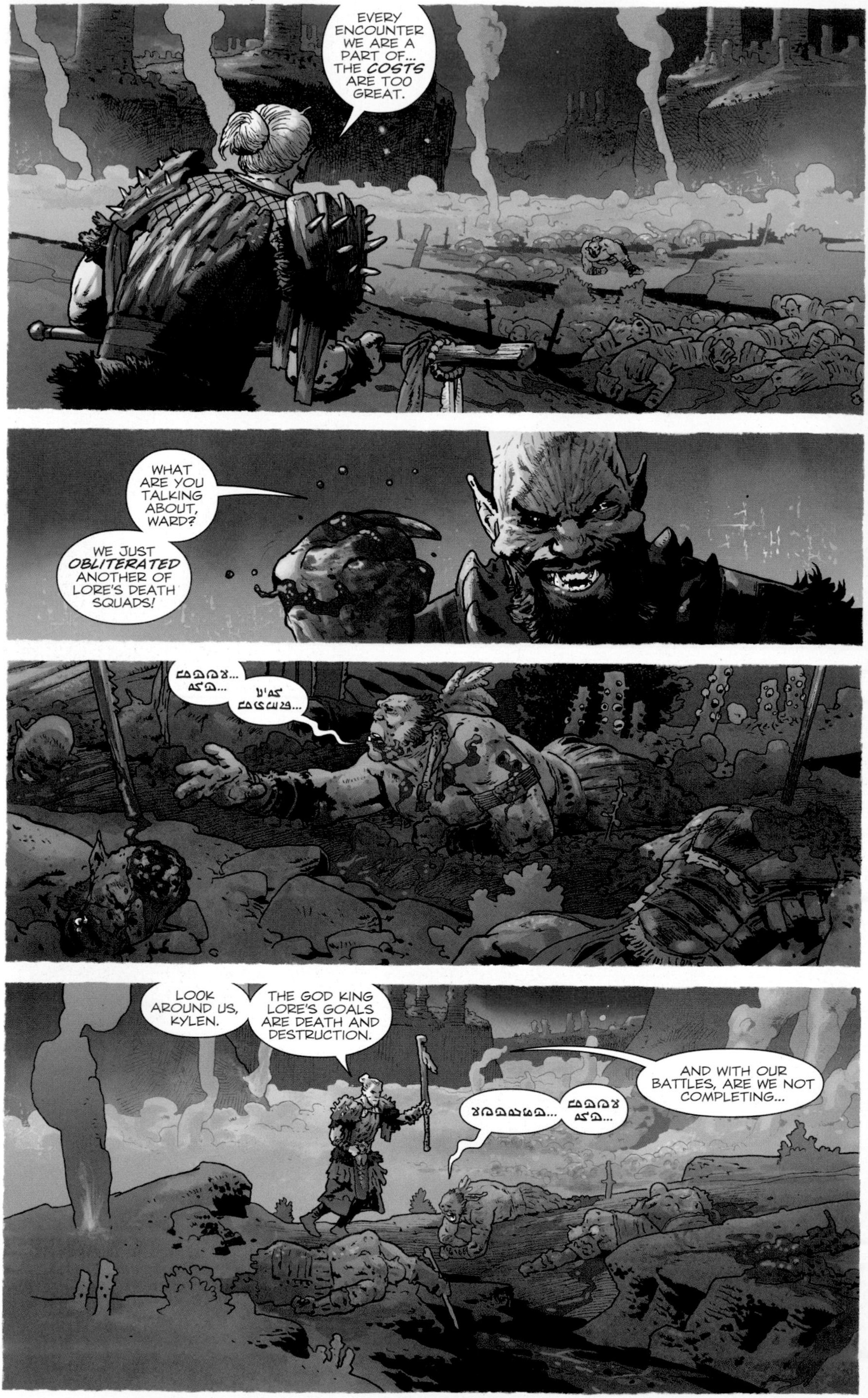
EVERY ENCOUNTER WE ARE A PART OF... THE COSTS ARE TOO GREAT.
WHAT ARE YOU TALKING ABOUT, WARD?
WE JUST OBLITERATED ANOTHER OF LORE'S DEATH SQUADS!
LOOK AROUND US, KYLEN.
THE GOD KING LORE'S GOALS ARE DEATH AND DESTRUCTION.
AND WITH OUR BATTLES, ARE WE NOT COMPLETING...

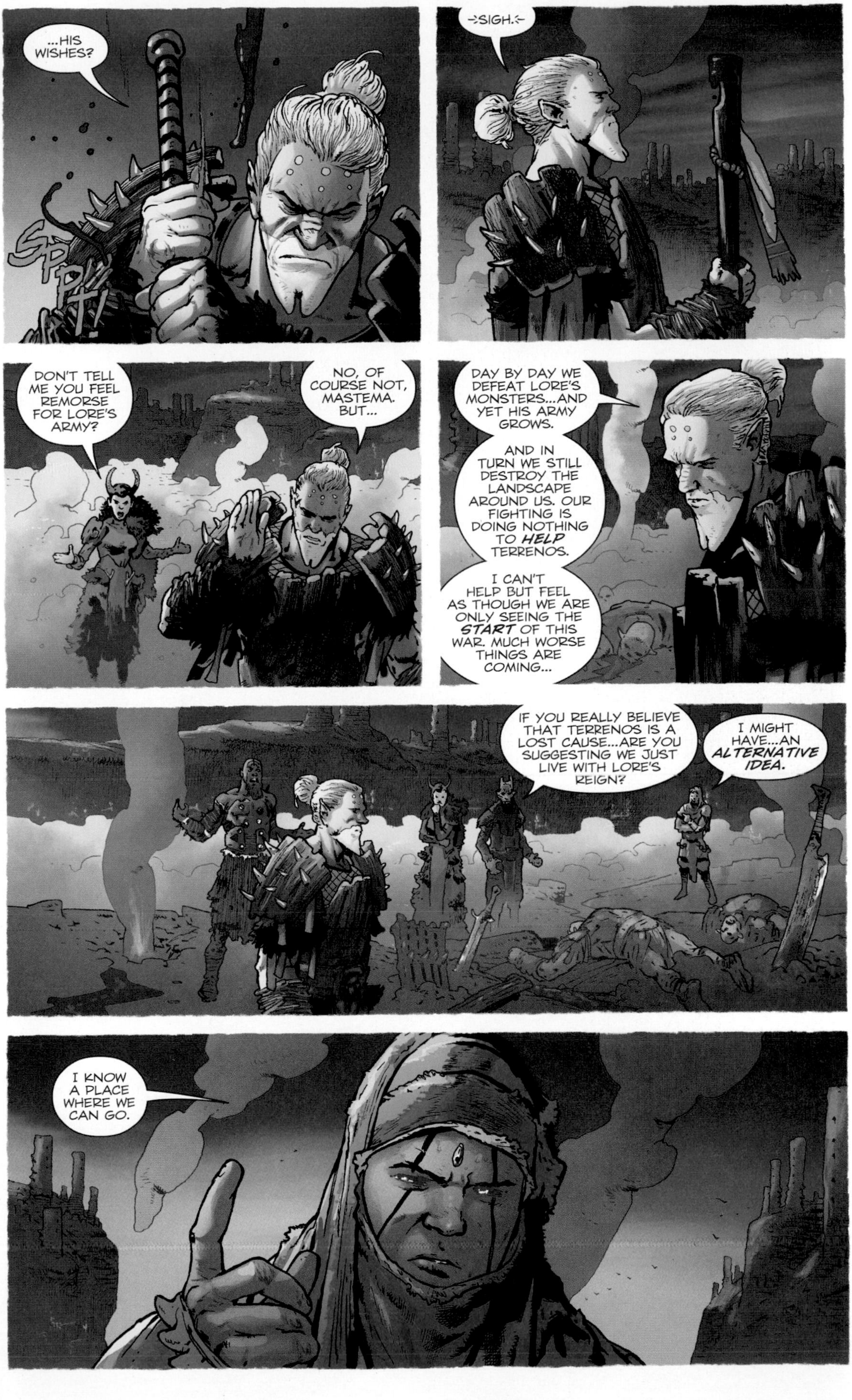
...HIS WISHES?
SPPT!
-SIGH.-
DON'T TELL ME YOU FEEL REMORSE FOR LORE'S ARMY?
NO, OF COURSE NOT, MASTEMA. BUT...
DAY BY DAY WE DEFEAT LORE'S MONSTERS...AND YET HIS ARMY GROWS.
AND IN TURN WE STILL DESTROY THE LANDSCAPE AROUND US. OUR FIGHTING IS DOING NOTHING TO HELP TERRENOS.
I CAN'T HELP BUT FEEL AS THOUGH WE ARE ONLY SEEING THE START OF THIS WAR. MUCH WORSE THINGS ARE COMING...
IF YOU REALLY BELIEVE THAT TERRENOS IS A LOST CAUSE...ARE YOU SUGGESTING WE JUST LIVE WITH LORE'S REIGN?
I MIGHT HAVE...AN ALTERNATIVE IDEA.
I KNOW A PLACE WHERE WE CAN GO.

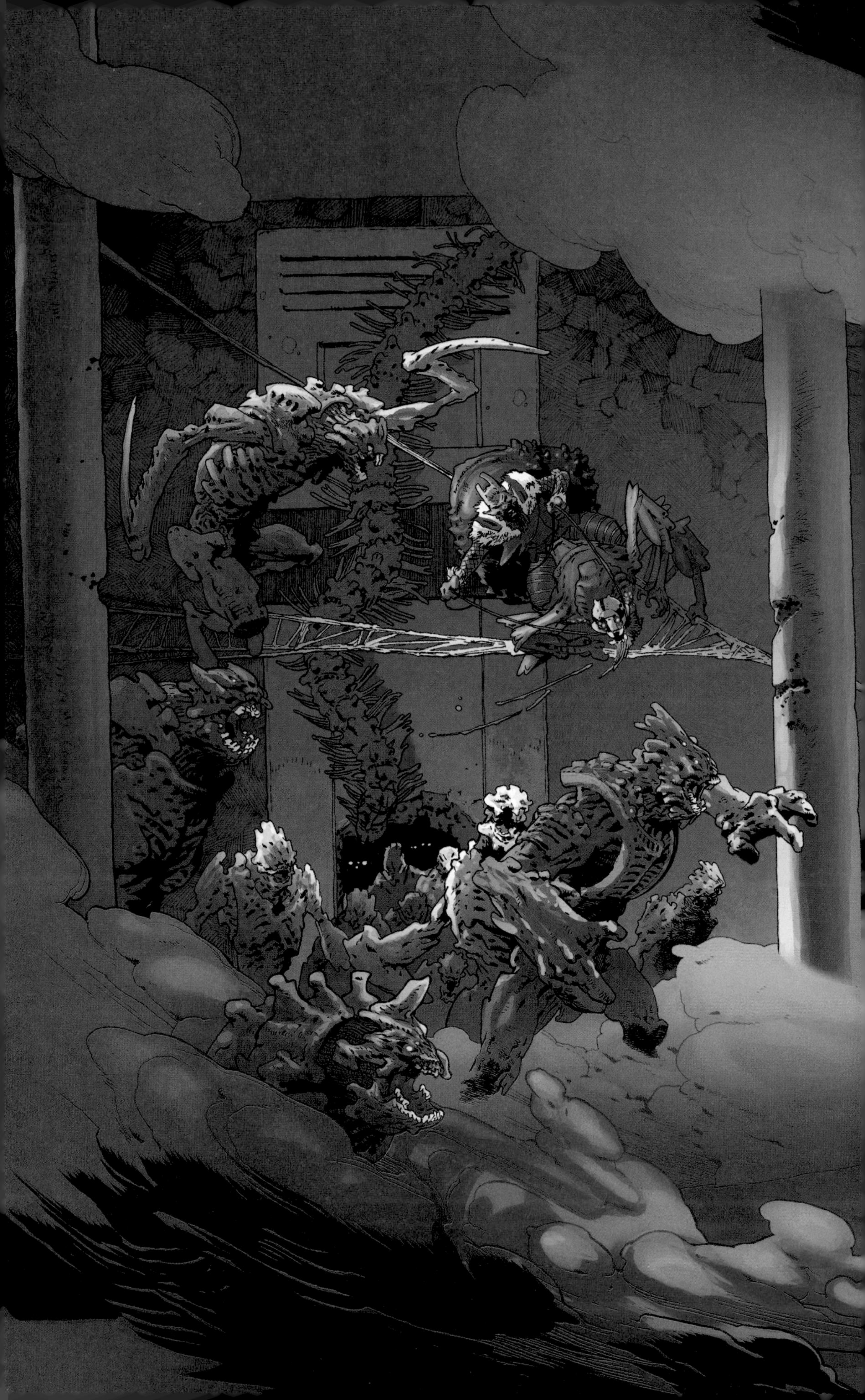

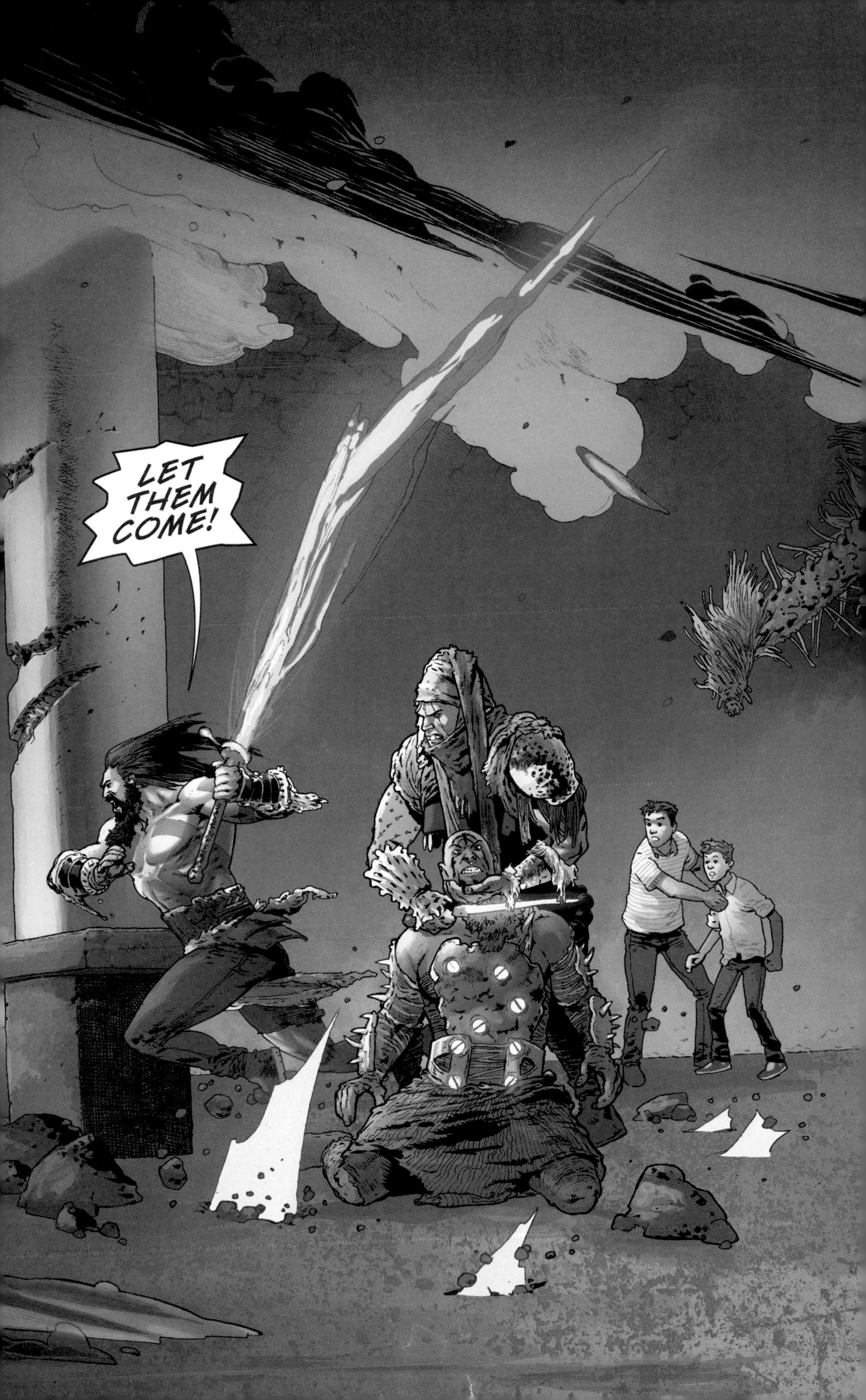
LET THEM COME!

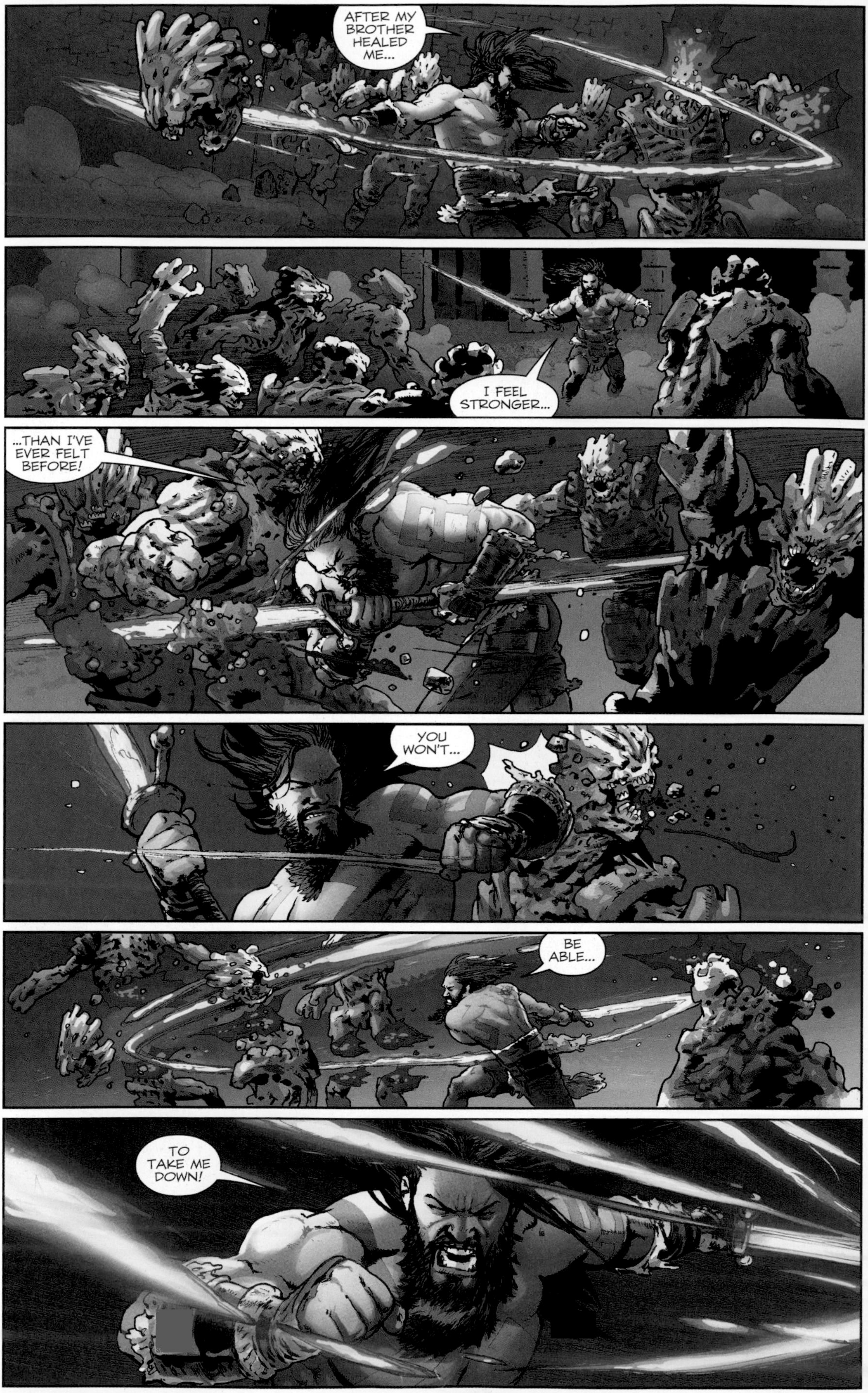
AFTER MY BROTHER HEALED ME...
I FEEL STRONGER...
...THAN I'VE EVER FELT BEFORE!
YOU WON'T...
BE ABLE...
TO TAKE ME DOWN!

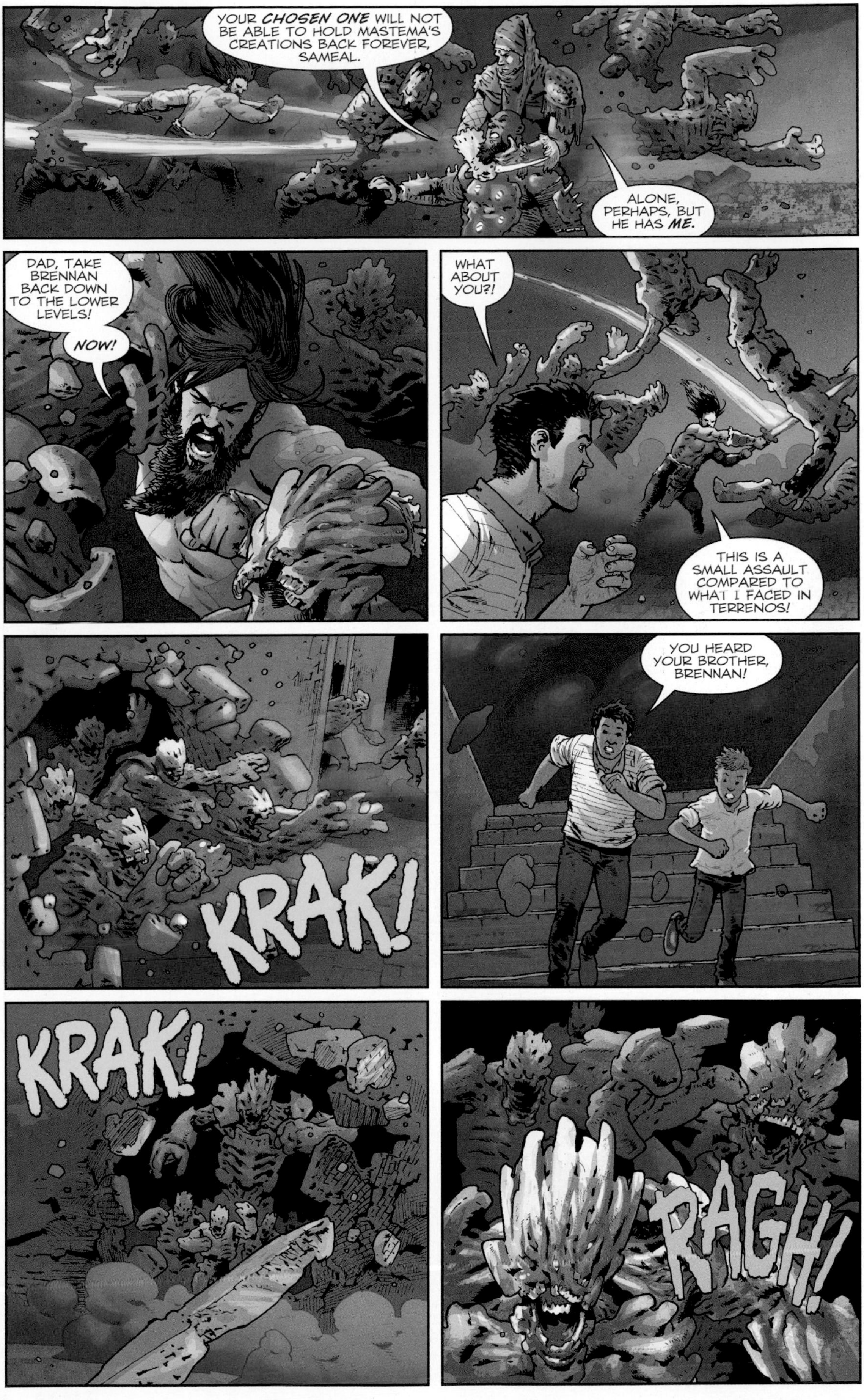

YOUR CHOSEN ONE WILL NOT BE ABLE TO HOLD MASTEMA'S CREATIONS BACK FOREVER, SAMEAL.
ALONE, PERHAPS, BUT HE HAS ME.
DAD, TAKE BRENNAN BACK DOWN TO THE LOWER LEVELS!
NOW!
WHAT ABOUT YOU?!
THIS IS A SMALL ASSAULT COMPARED TO WHAT I FACED IN TERRENOS!
KRAK!
YOU HEARD YOUR BROTHER, BRENNAN!
KRAK!
RAGH!

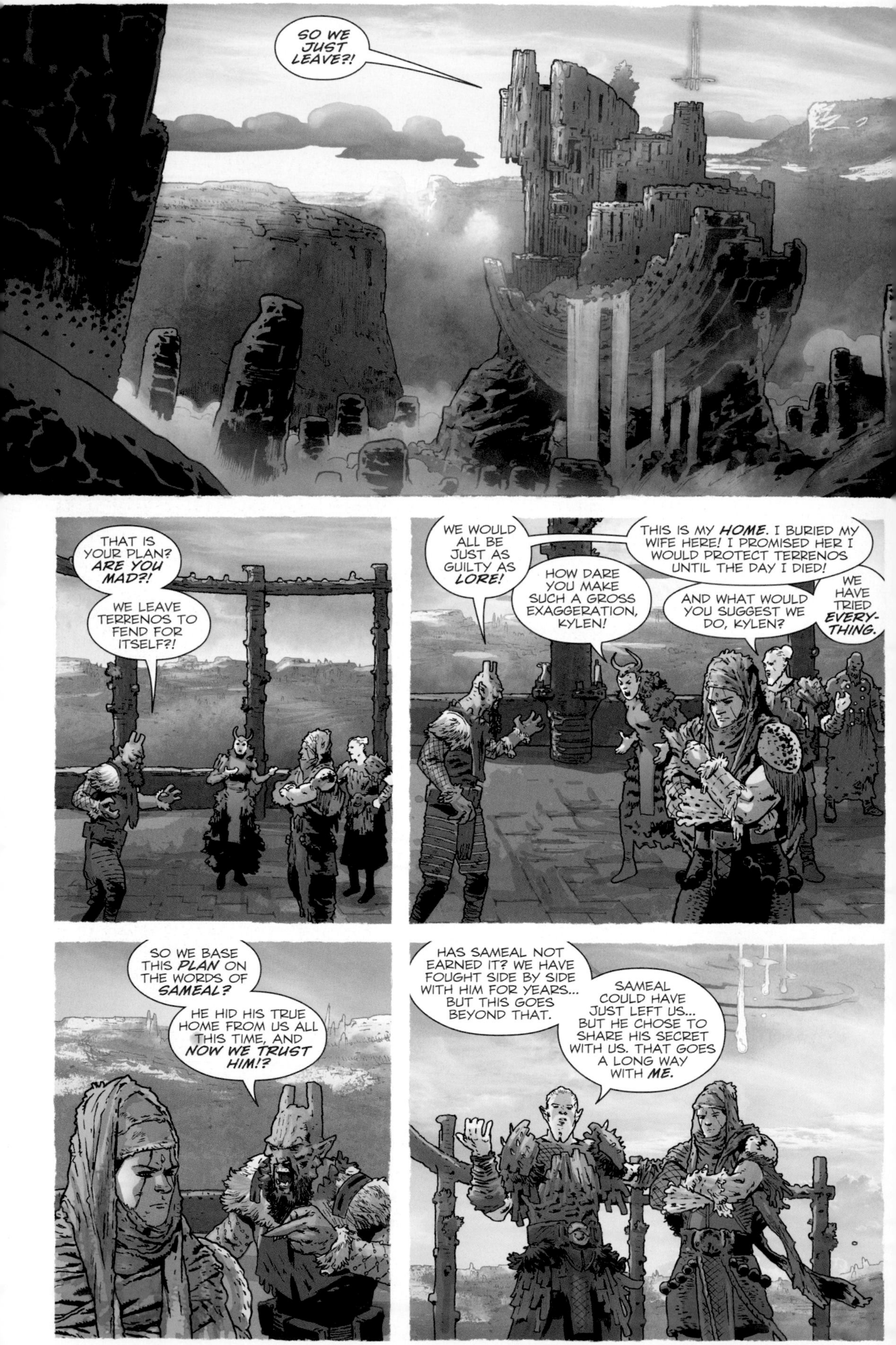
SO WE JUST LEAVE?!
THAT IS YOUR PLAN? ARE YOU MAD?!
WE LEAVE TERRENOS TO FEND FOR ITSELF?!
WE WOULD ALL BE JUST AS GUILTY AS LORE!
THIS IS MY HOME. I BURIED MY WIFE HERE! I PROMISED HER I WOULD PROTECT TERRENOS UNTIL THE DAY I DIED!
HOW DARE YOU MAKE SUCH A GROSS EXAGGERATION, KYLEN!
AND WHAT WOULD YOU SUGGEST WE DO, KYLEN?
WE HAVE TRIED EVERY-THING.
SO WE BASE THIS PLAN ON THE WORDS OF SAMEAL?
HE HID HIS TRUE HOME FROM US ALL THIS TIME, AND NOW WE TRUST HIM!?
HAS SAMEAL NOT EARNED IT? WE HAVE FOUGHT SIDE BY SIDE WITH HIM FOR YEARS... BUT THIS GOES BEYOND THAT.
SAMEAL COULD HAVE JUST LEFT US... BUT HE CHOSE TO SHARE HIS SECRET WITH US. THAT GOES A LONG WAY WITH ME.

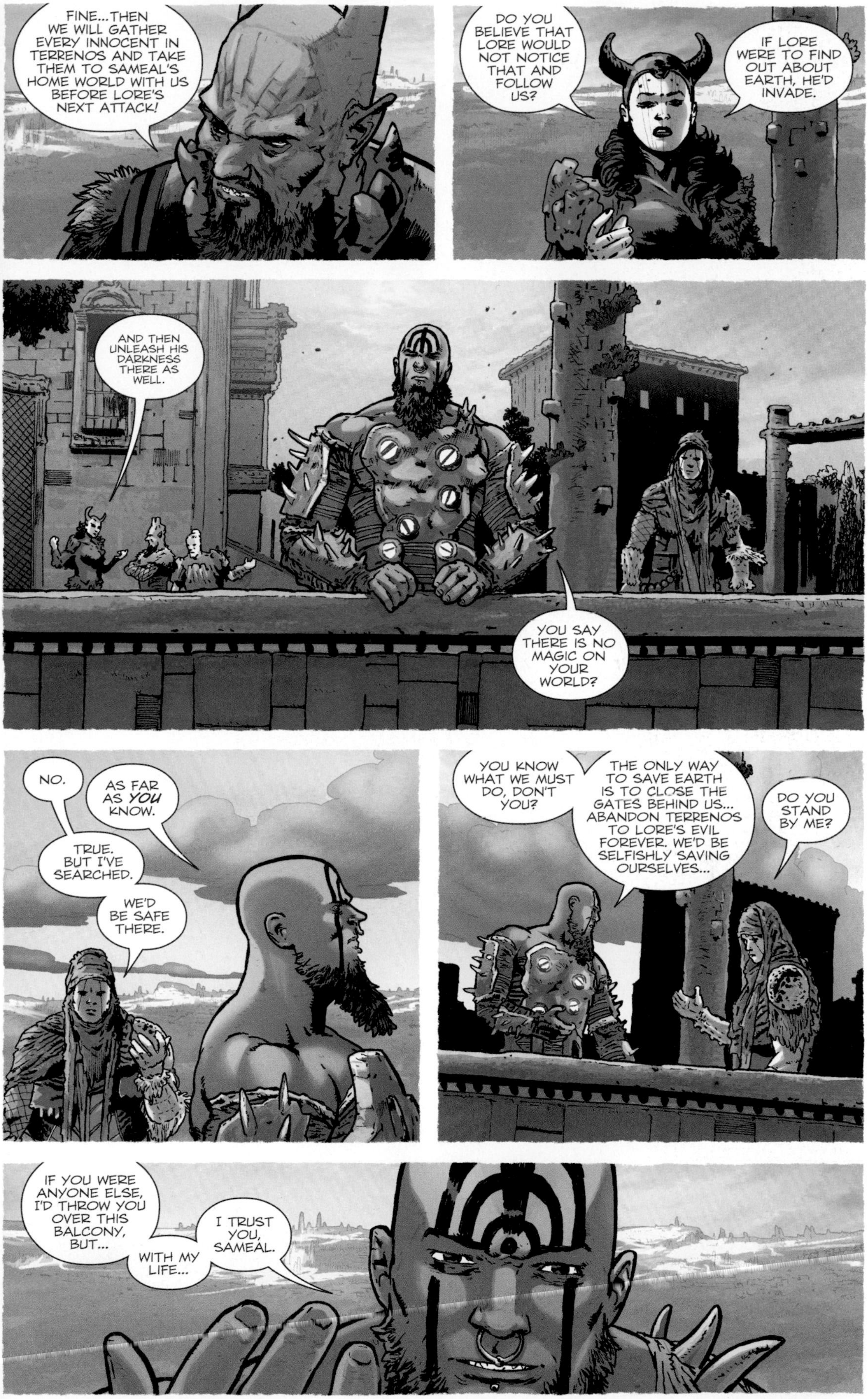
FINE...THEN WE WILL GATHER EVERY INNOCENT IN TERRENOS AND TAKE THEM TO SAMEAL'S HOME WORLD WITH US BEFORE LORE'S NEXT ATTACK!
DO YOU BELIEVE THAT LORE WOULD NOT NOTICE THAT AND FOLLOW US?
IF LORE WERE TO FIND OUT ABOUT EARTH, HE'D INVADE.
AND THEN UNLEASH HIS DARKNESS THERE AS WELL.
YOU SAY THERE IS NO MAGIC ON YOUR WORLD?
NO.
AS FAR AS YOU KNOW.
TRUE. BUT I'VE SEARCHED.
WE'D BE SAFE THERE.
YOU KNOW WHAT WE MUST DO, DON'T YOU?
THE ONLY WAY TO SAVE EARTH IS TO CLOSE THE GATES BEHIND US... ABANDON TERRENOS TO LORE'S EVIL FOREVER. WE'D BE SELFISHLY SAVING OURSELVES...
DO YOU STAND BY ME?
IF YOU WERE ANYONE ELSE, I'D THROW YOU OVER THIS BALCONY, BUT...
WITH MY LIFE...
I TRUST YOU, SAMEAL.

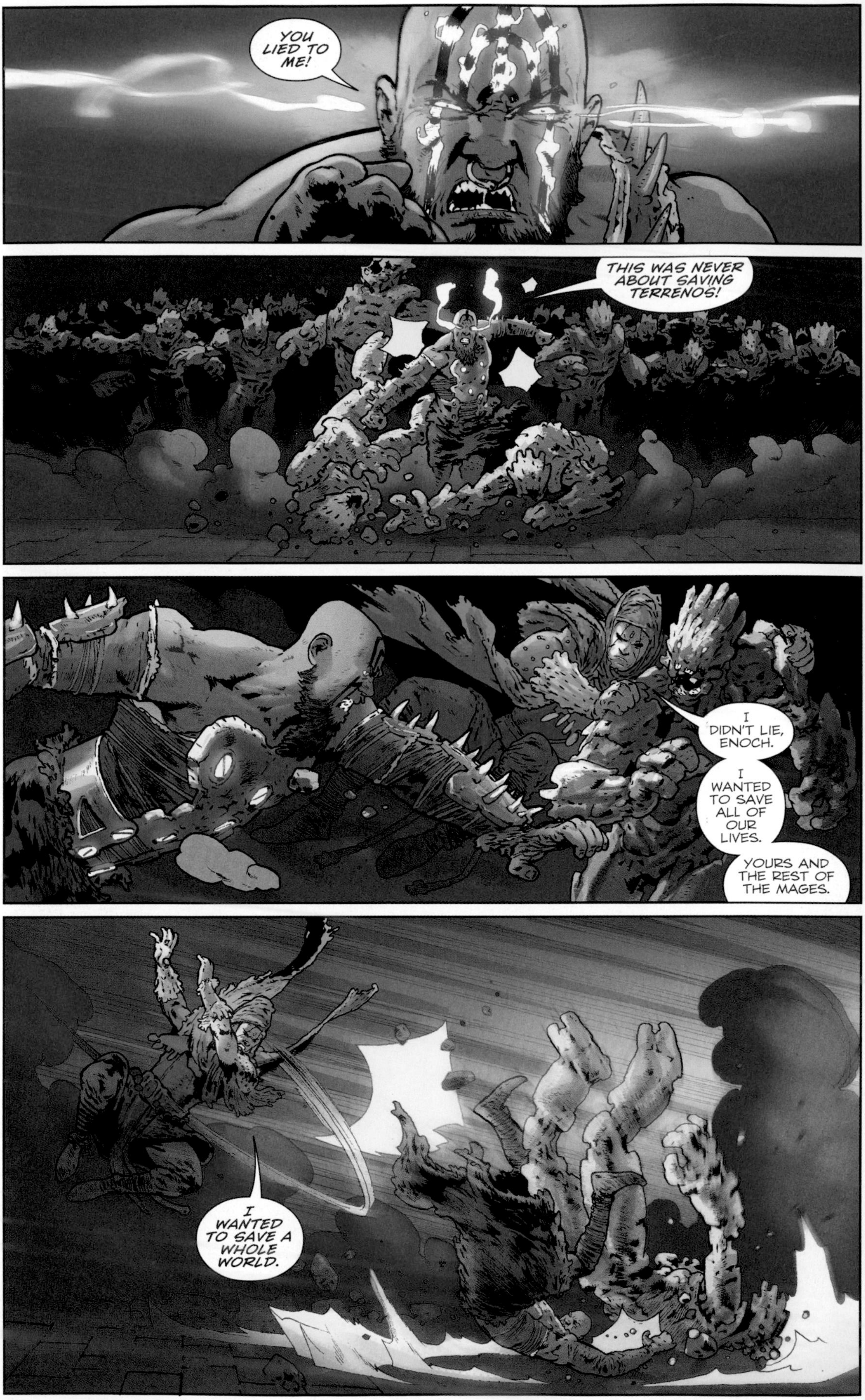
YOU LIED TO ME!
THIS WAS NEVER ABOUT SAVING TERRENOS!
I DIDN'T LIE, ENOCH.
I WANTED TO SAVE ALL OF OUR LIVES.
YOURS AND THE REST OF THE MAGES.
I WANTED TO SAVE A WHOLE WORLD.

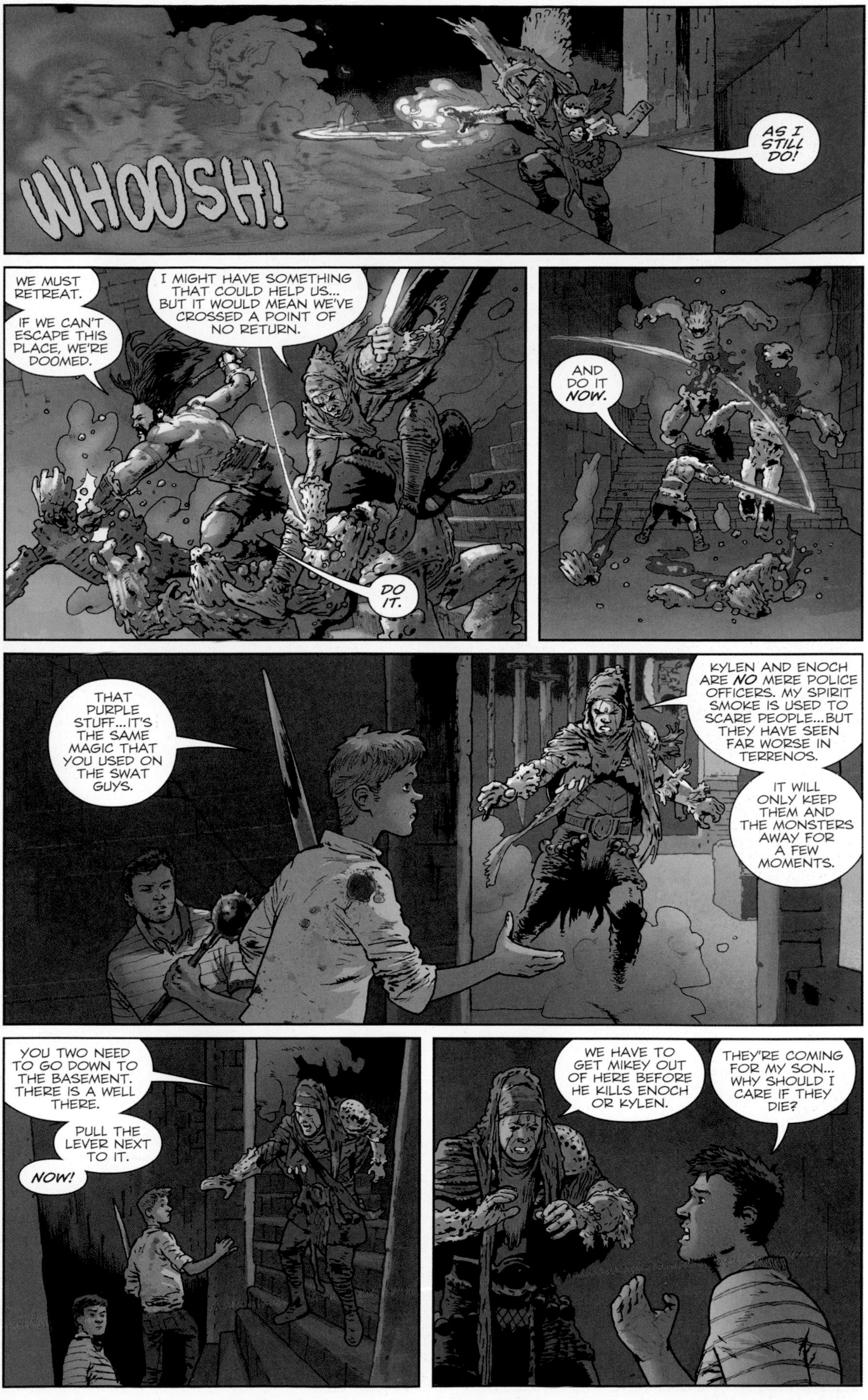
WHOOSH!
AS I STILL DO!
WE MUST RETREAT.
IF WE CAN'T ESCAPE THIS PLACE, WE'RE DOOMED.
I MIGHT HAVE SOMETHING THAT COULD HELP US... BUT IT WOULD MEAN WE'VE CROSSED A POINT OF NO RETURN.
DO IT.
AND DO IT NOW.
THAT PURPLE STUFF...IT'S THE SAME MAGIC THAT YOU USED ON THE SWAT GUYS.
KYLEN AND ENOCH ARE NO MERE POLICE OFFICERS. MY SPIRIT SMOKE IS USED TO SCARE PEOPLE...BUT THEY HAVE SEEN FAR WORSE IN TERRENOS.
IT WILL ONLY KEEP THEM AND THE MONSTERS AWAY FOR A FEW MOMENTS.
YOU TWO NEED TO GO DOWN TO THE BASEMENT. THERE IS A WELL THERE.
PULL THE LEVER NEXT TO IT.
NOW!
WE HAVE TO GET MIKEY OUT OF HERE BEFORE HE KILLS ENOCH OR KYLEN.
THEY'RE COMING FOR MY SON... WHY SHOULD I CARE IF THEY DIE?

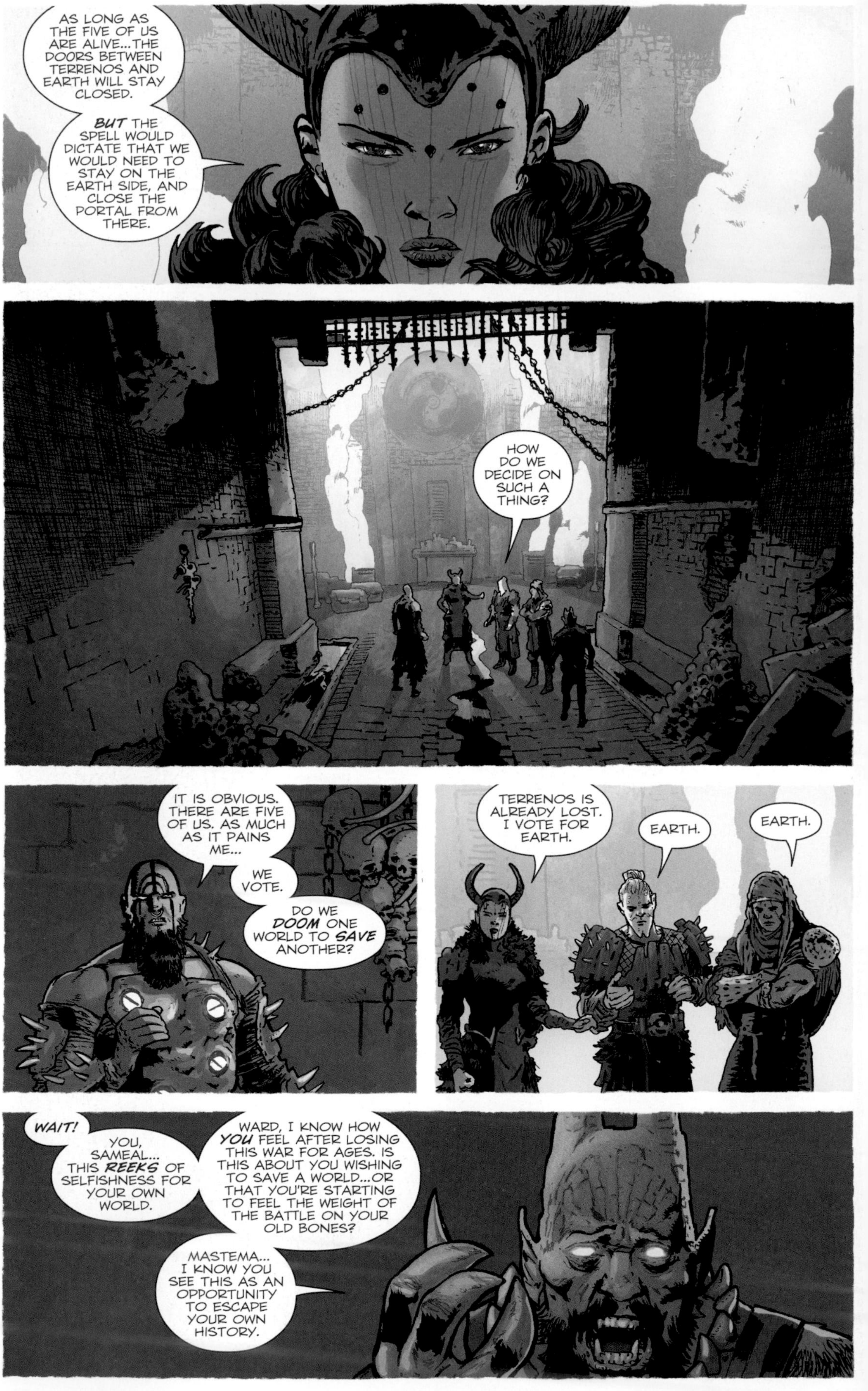
AS LONG AS THE FIVE OF US ARE ALIVE...THE DOORS BETWEEN TERRENOS AND EARTH WILL STAY CLOSED.
BUT THE SPELL WOULD DICTATE THAT WE WOULD NEED TO STAY ON THE EARTH SIDE, AND CLOSE THE PORTAL FROM THERE.
HOW DO WE DECIDE ON SUCH A THING?
IT IS OBVIOUS. THERE ARE FIVE OF US. AS MUCH AS IT PAINS ME...
WE VOTE.
DO WE DOOM ONE WORLD TO SAVE ANOTHER?
TERRENOS IS ALREADY LOST. I VOTE FOR EARTH.
EARTH.
EARTH.
WAIT!
YOU, SAMEAL... THIS REEKS OF SELFISHNESS FOR YOUR OWN WORLD.
WARD, I KNOW HOW YOU FEEL AFTER LOSING THIS WAR FOR AGES. IS THIS ABOUT YOU WISHING TO SAVE A WORLD...OR THAT YOU'RE STARTING TO FEEL THE WEIGHT OF THE BATTLE ON YOUR OLD BONES?
MASTEMA... I KNOW YOU SEE THIS AS AN OPPORTUNITY TO ESCAPE YOUR OWN HISTORY.

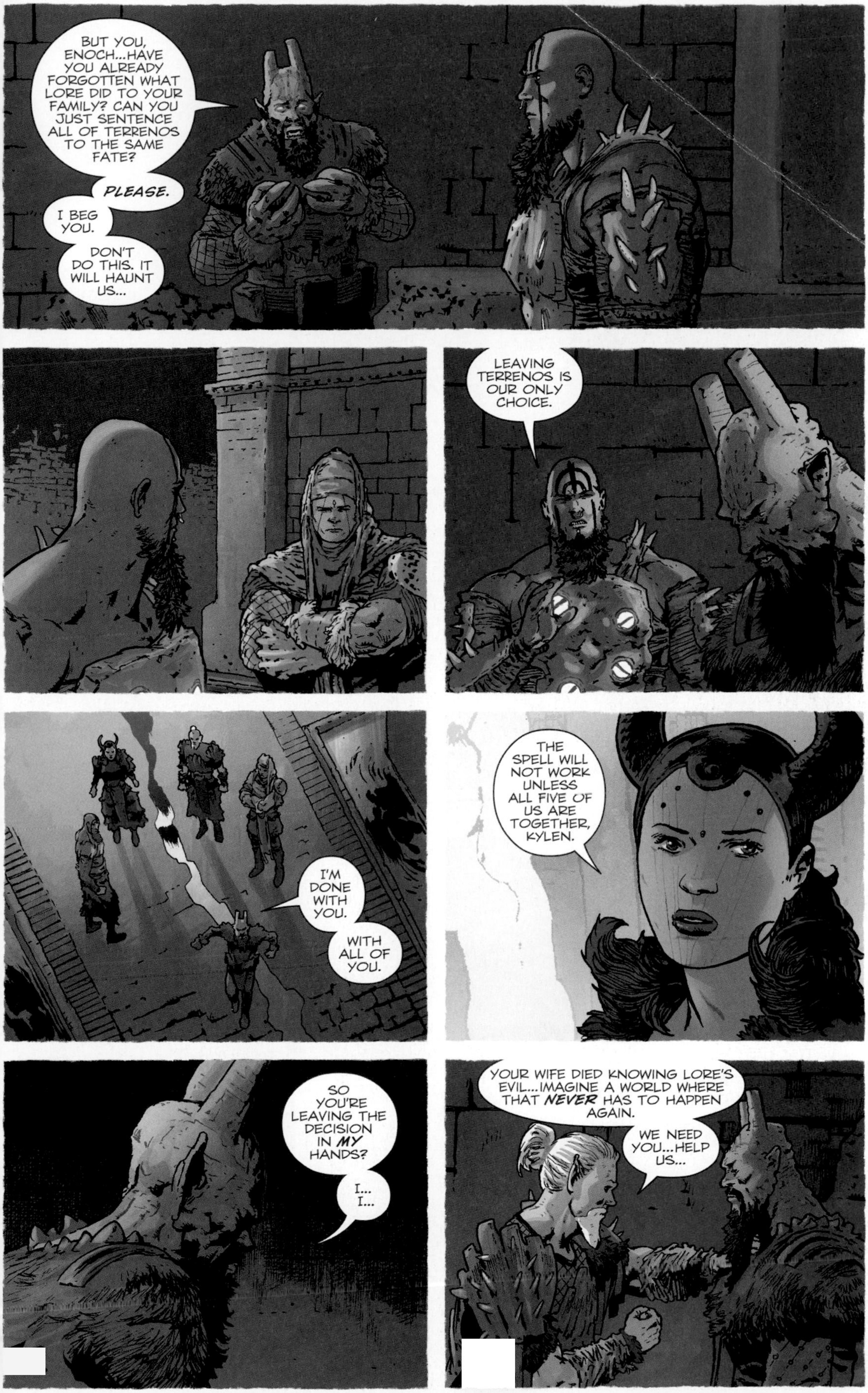
BUT YOU, ENOCH...HAVE YOU ALREADY FORGOTTEN WHAT LORE DID TO YOUR FAMILY? CAN YOU JUST SENTENCE ALL OF TERRENOS TO THE SAME FATE?
PLEASE.
I BEG YOU.
DON'T DO THIS. IT WILL HAUNT US...
LEAVING TERRENOS IS OUR ONLY CHOICE.
I'M DONE WITH YOU.
WITH ALL OF YOU.
THE SPELL WILL NOT WORK UNLESS ALL FIVE OF US ARE TOGETHER, KYLEN.
SO YOU'RE LEAVING THE DECISION IN MY HANDS?
I... I...
YOUR WIFE DIED KNOWING LORE'S EVIL...IMAGINE A WORLD WHERE THAT NEVER HAS TO HAPPEN AGAIN.
WE NEED YOU...HELP US...

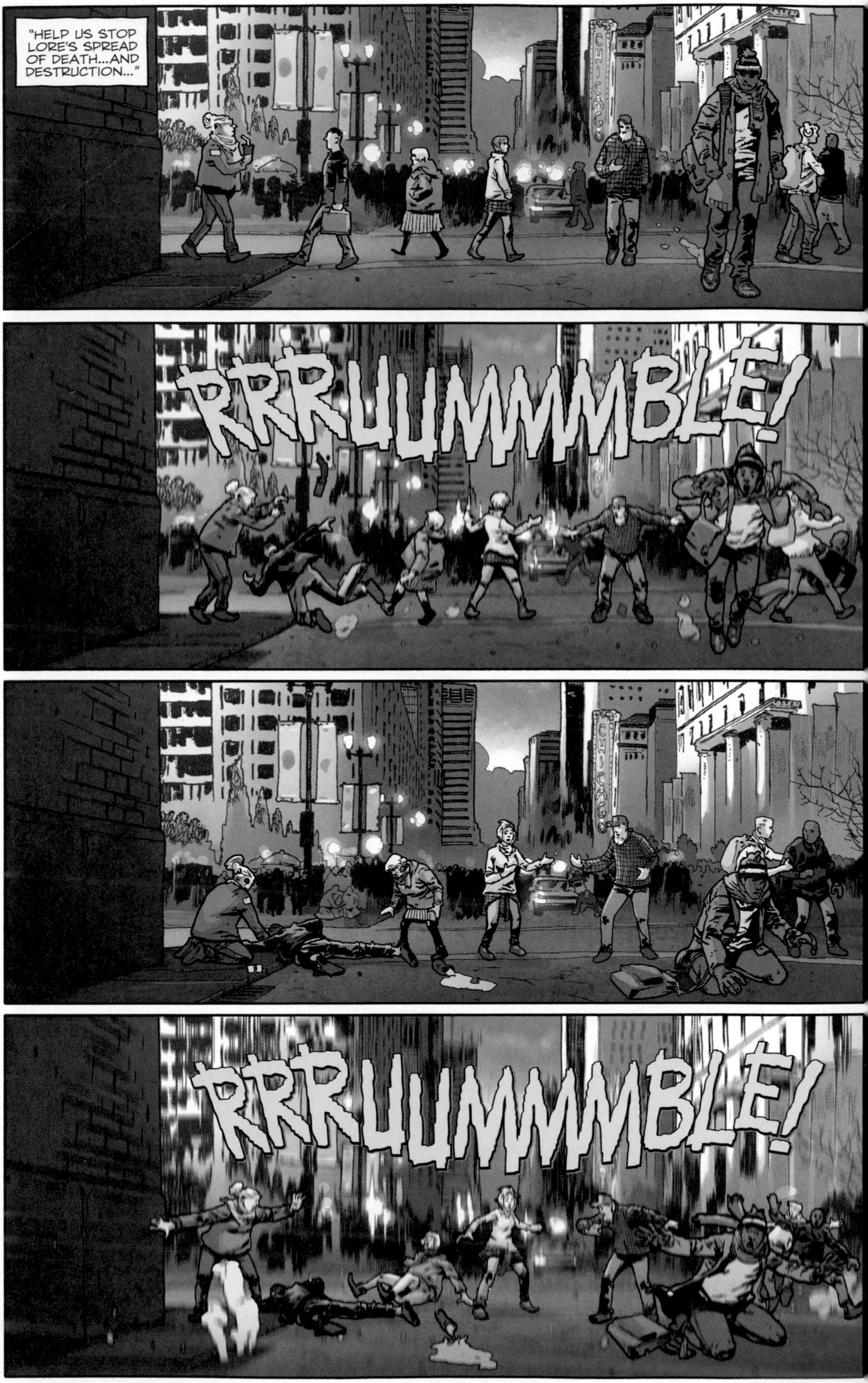
"HELP US STOP LORE'S SPREAD OF DEATH...AND DESTRUCTION..."
RRRUUMMMBLE!
RRRUUMMMBLE!

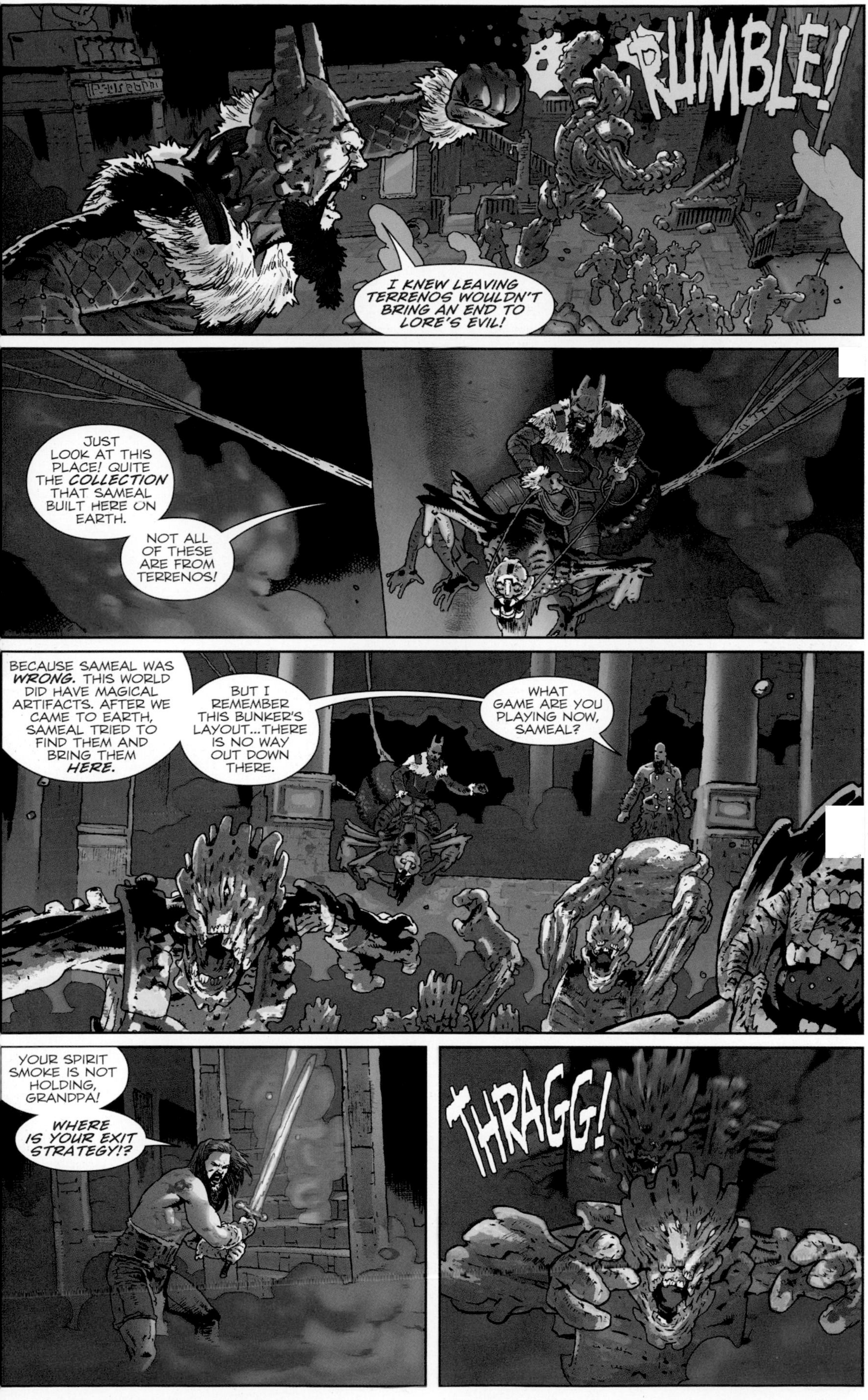
RUMBLE!
I KNEW LEAVING TERRENOS WOULDN'T BRING AN END TO LORE'S EVIL!
JUST LOOK AT THIS PLACE! QUITE THE COLLECTION THAT SAMEAL BUILT HERE ON EARTH.
NOT ALL OF THESE ARE FROM TERRENOS!
BECAUSE SAMEAL WAS WRONG. THIS WORLD DID HAVE MAGICAL ARTIFACTS. AFTER WE CAME TO EARTH, SAMEAL TRIED TO FIND THEM AND BRING THEM HERE.
BUT I REMEMBER THIS BUNKER'S LAYOUT...THERE IS NO WAY OUT DOWN THERE.
WHAT GAME ARE YOU PLAYING NOW, SAMEAL?
YOUR SPIRIT SMOKE IS NOT HOLDING, GRANDPA!
WHERE IS YOUR EXIT STRATEGY!?
THRAGG!

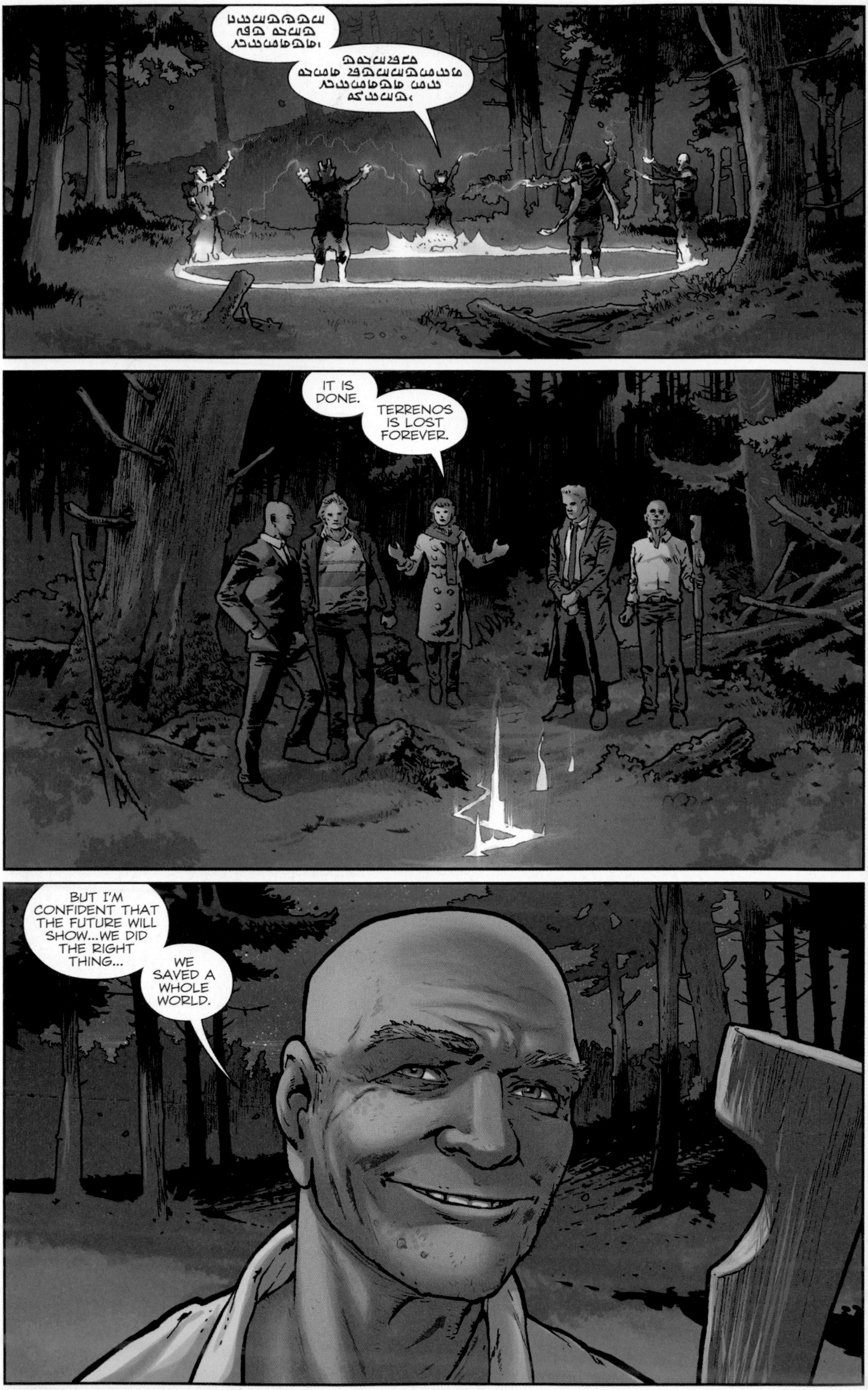
IT IS DONE.
TERRENOS IS LOST FOREVER.
BUT I'M CONFIDENT THAT THE FUTURE WILL SHOW...WE DID THE RIGHT THING...
WE SAVED A WHOLE WORLD.

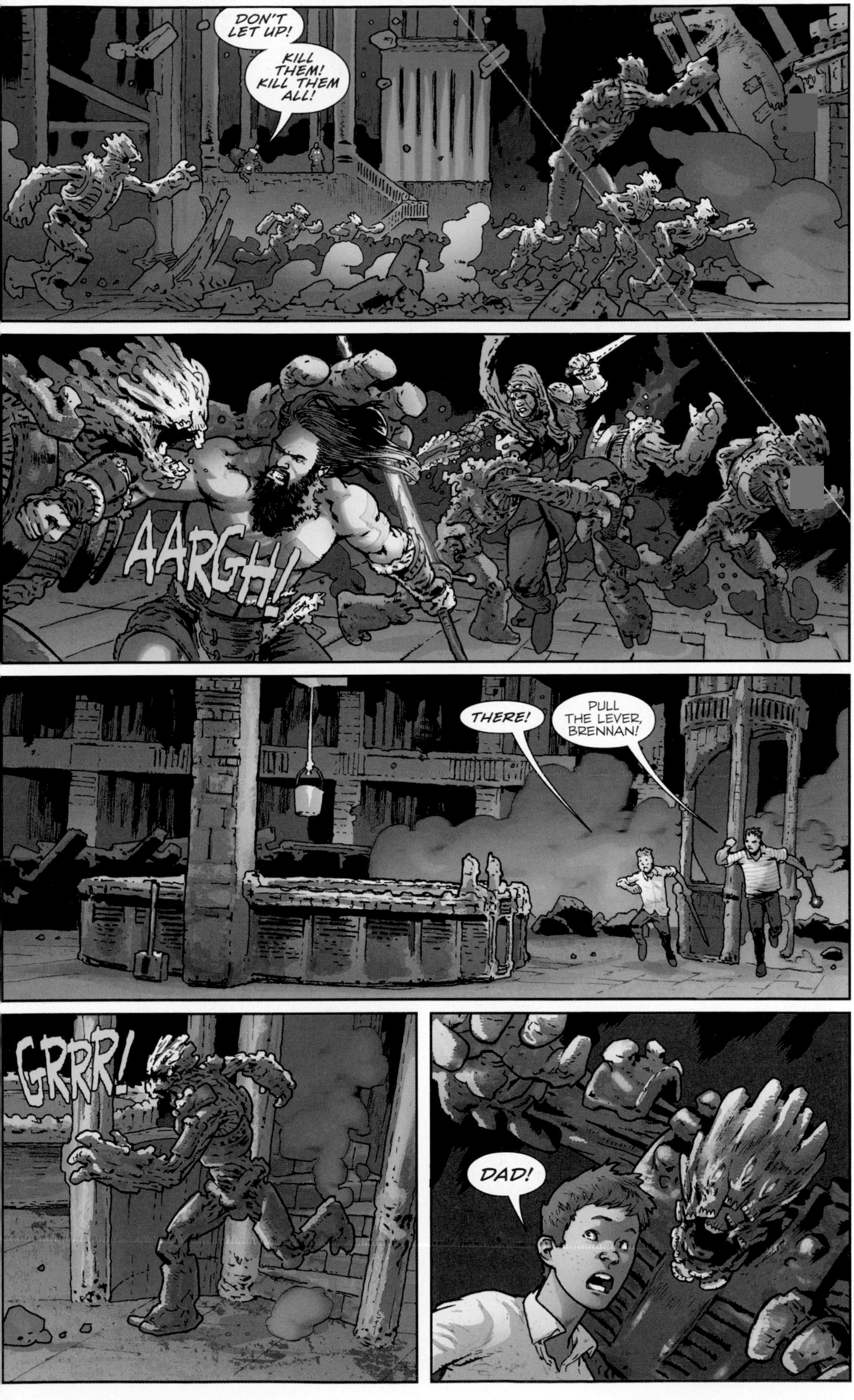
DON'T LET UP!
KILL THEM! KILL THEM ALL!
AARGH!
THERE!
PULL THE LEVER, BRENNAN!
GRRR!
DAD!

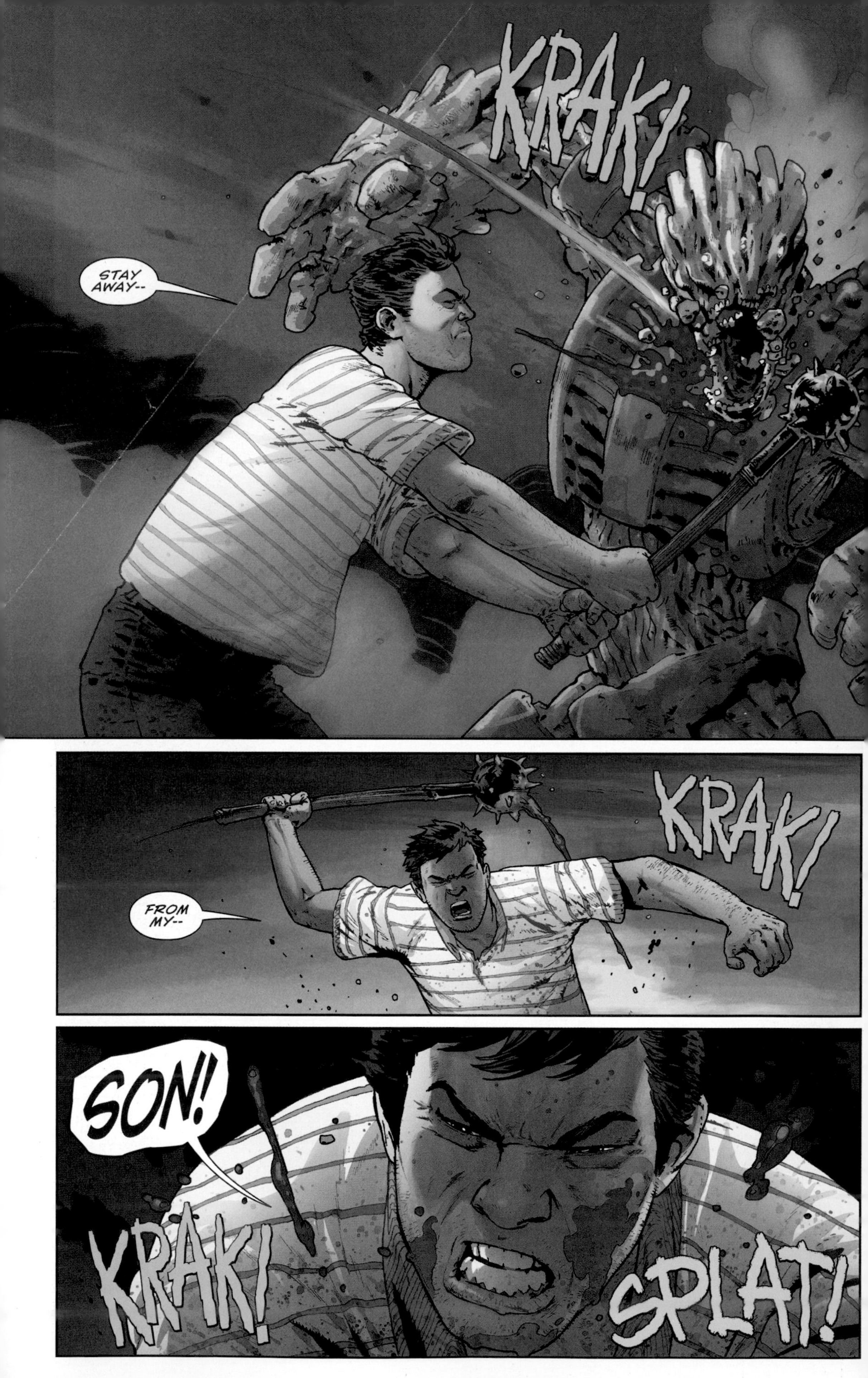
KRAK!
STAY AWAY--
FROM MY--
KRAK!
SON!
KRAK!
SPLAT!

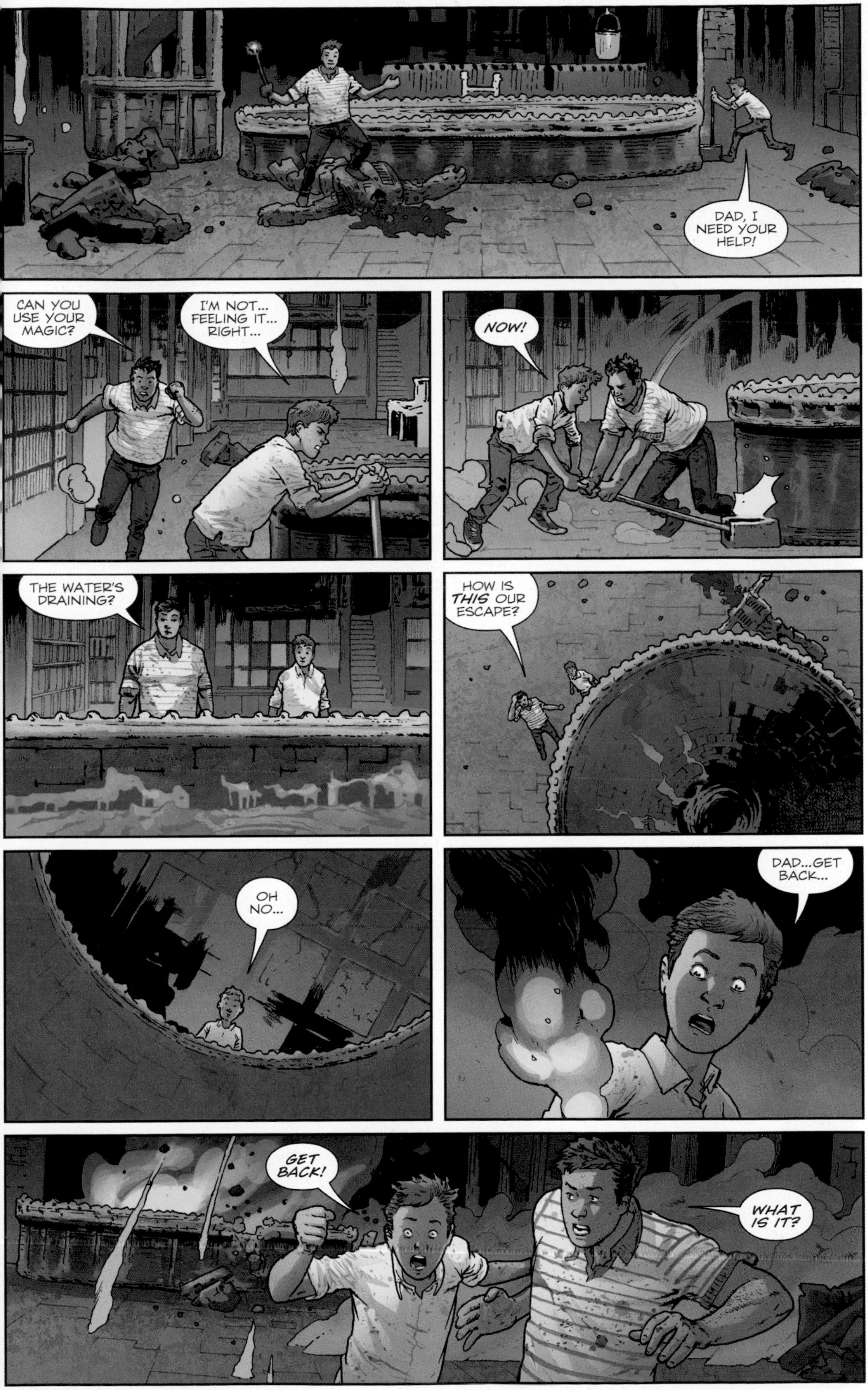
DAD, I NEED YOUR HELP!
CAN YOU USE YOUR MAGIC?
I'M NOT... FEELING IT... RIGHT...
NOW!
THE WATER'S DRAINING?
HOW IS THIS OUR ESCAPE?
OH NO...
DAD...GET BACK...
GET BACK!
WHAT IS IT?

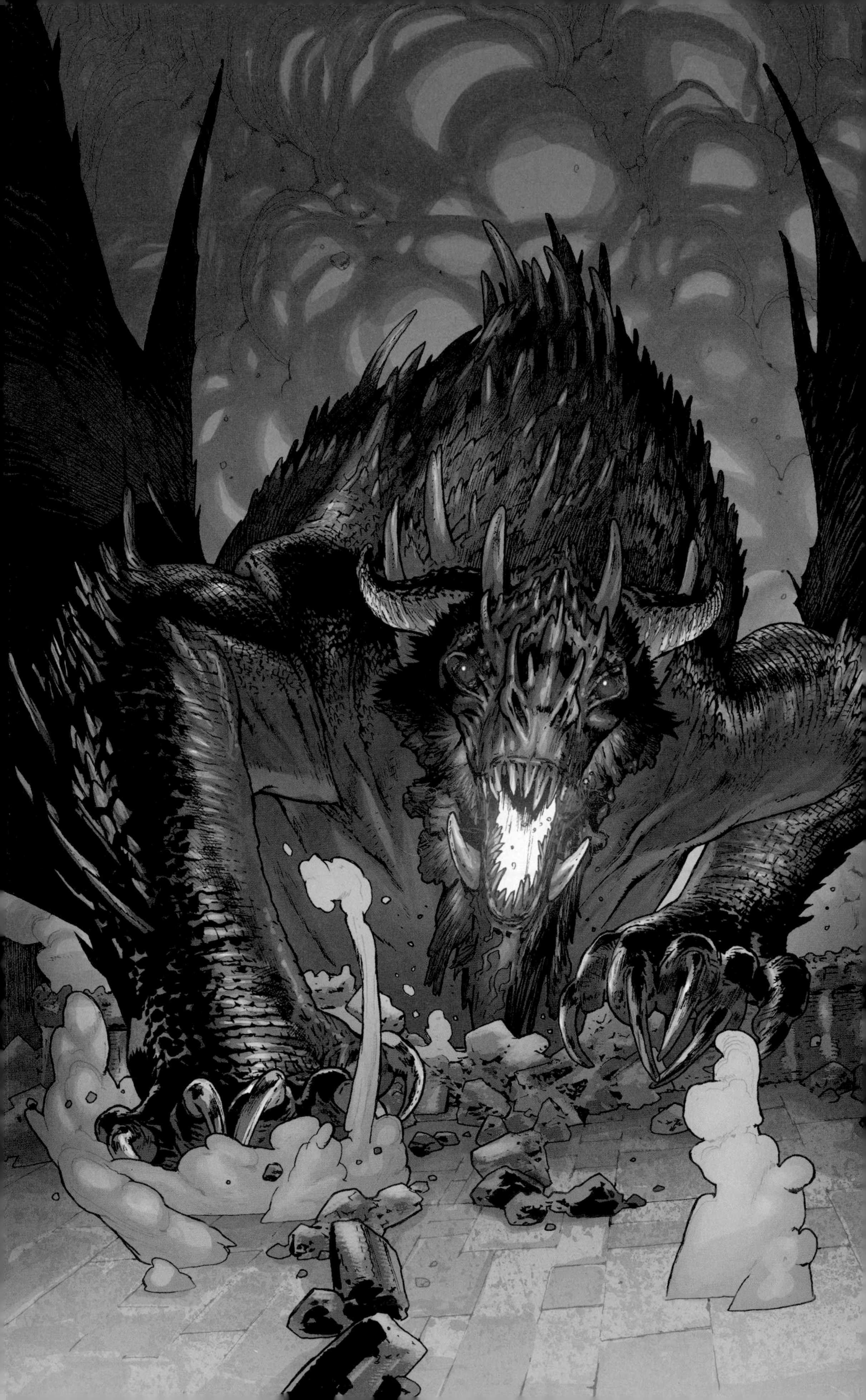

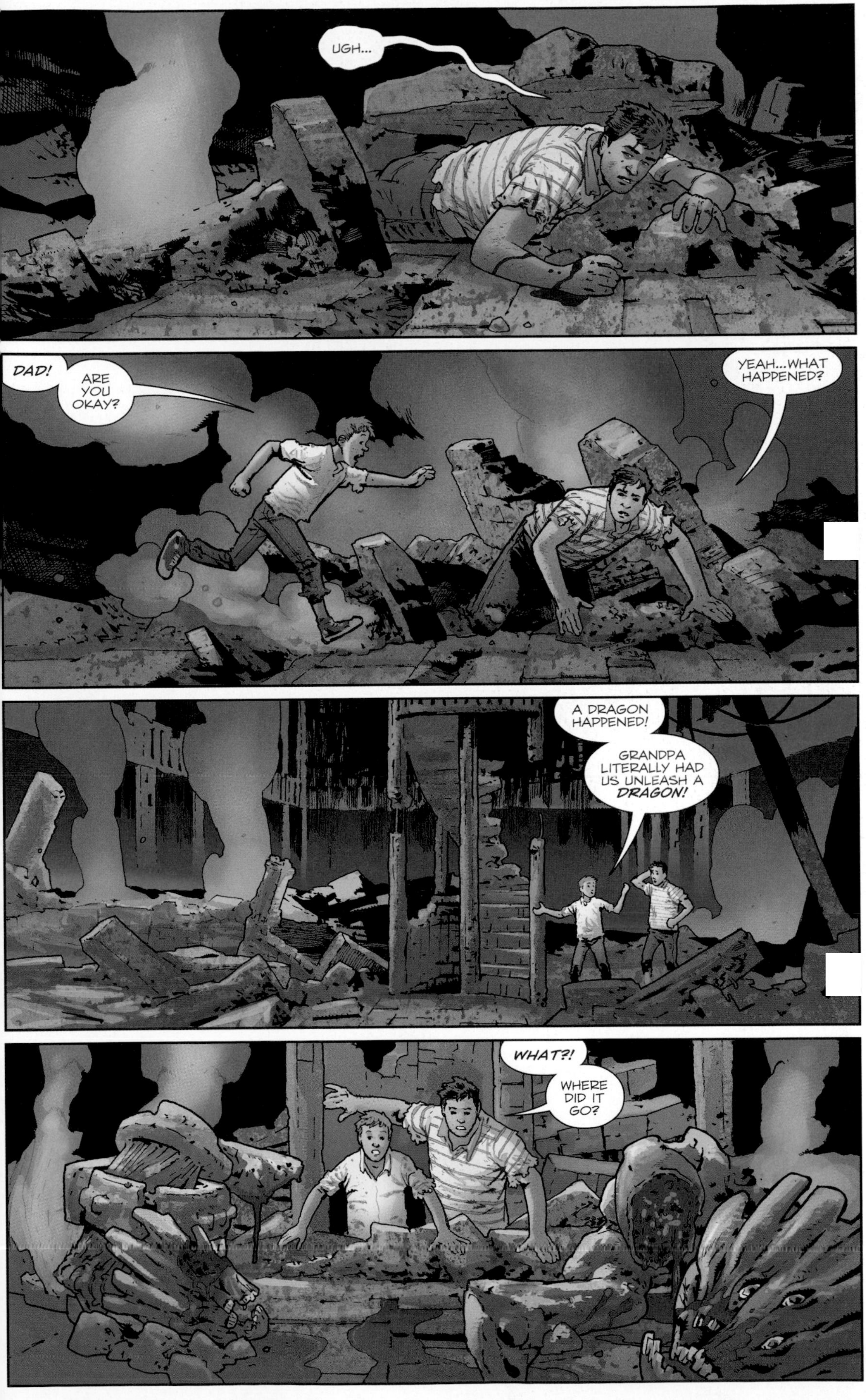
UGH...
DAD!
ARE YOU OKAY?
YEAH...WHAT HAPPENED?
A DRAGON HAPPENED!
GRANDPA LITERALLY HAD US UNLEASH A *DRAGON!*
WHAT?!
WHERE DID IT GO?

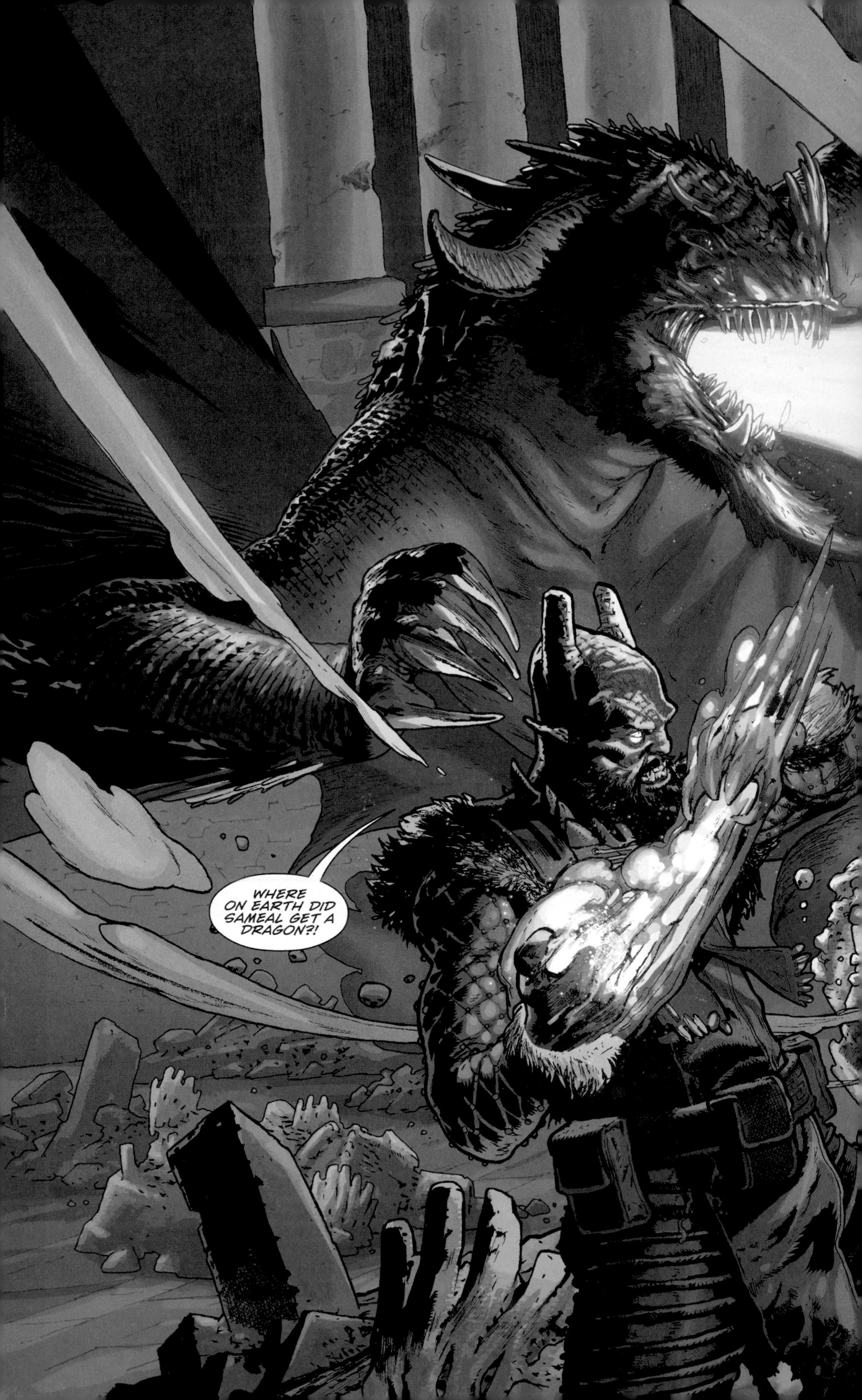
WHERE ON EARTH DID SAMEAL GET A DRAGON?!

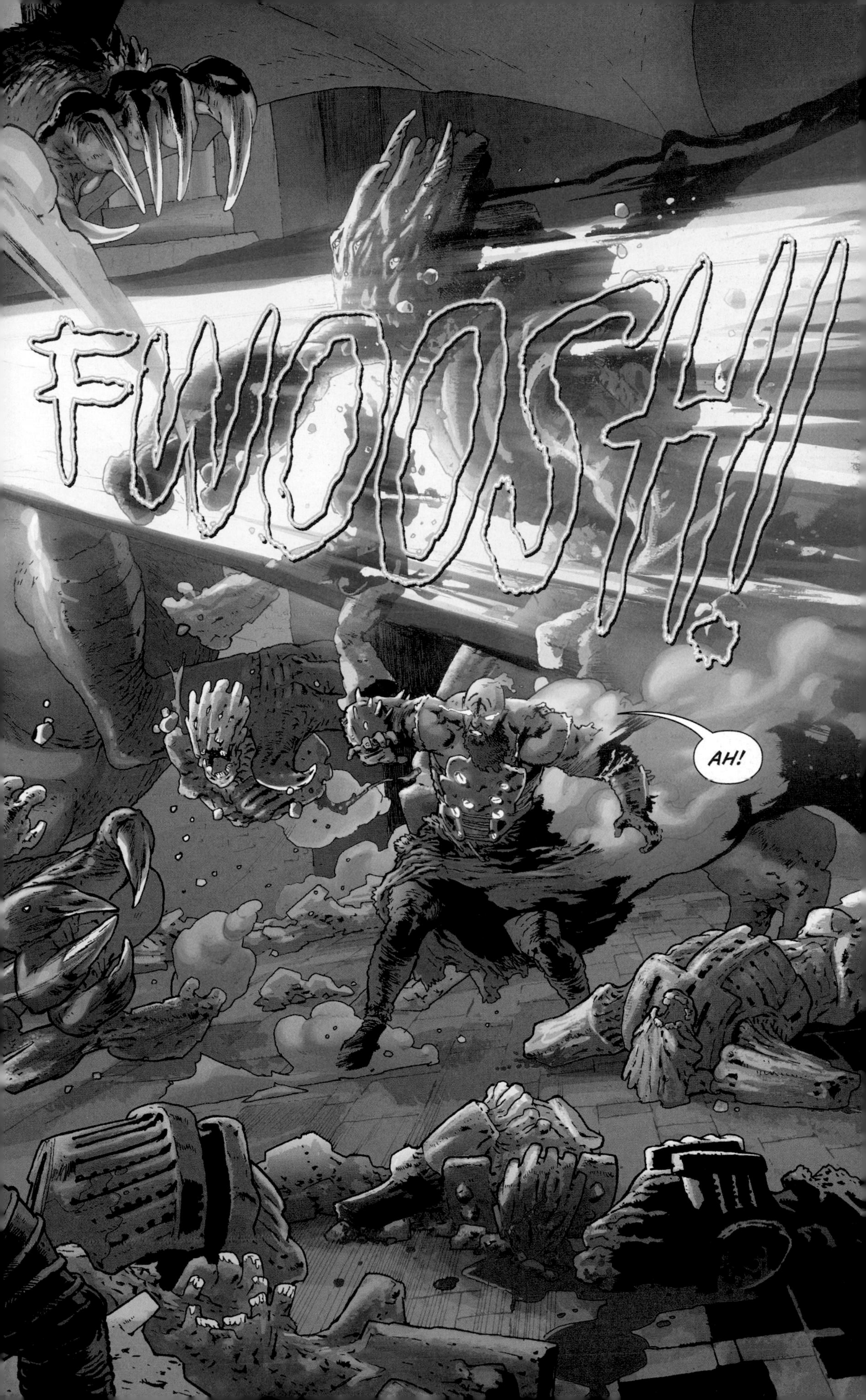
FWOOSH!!
AH!

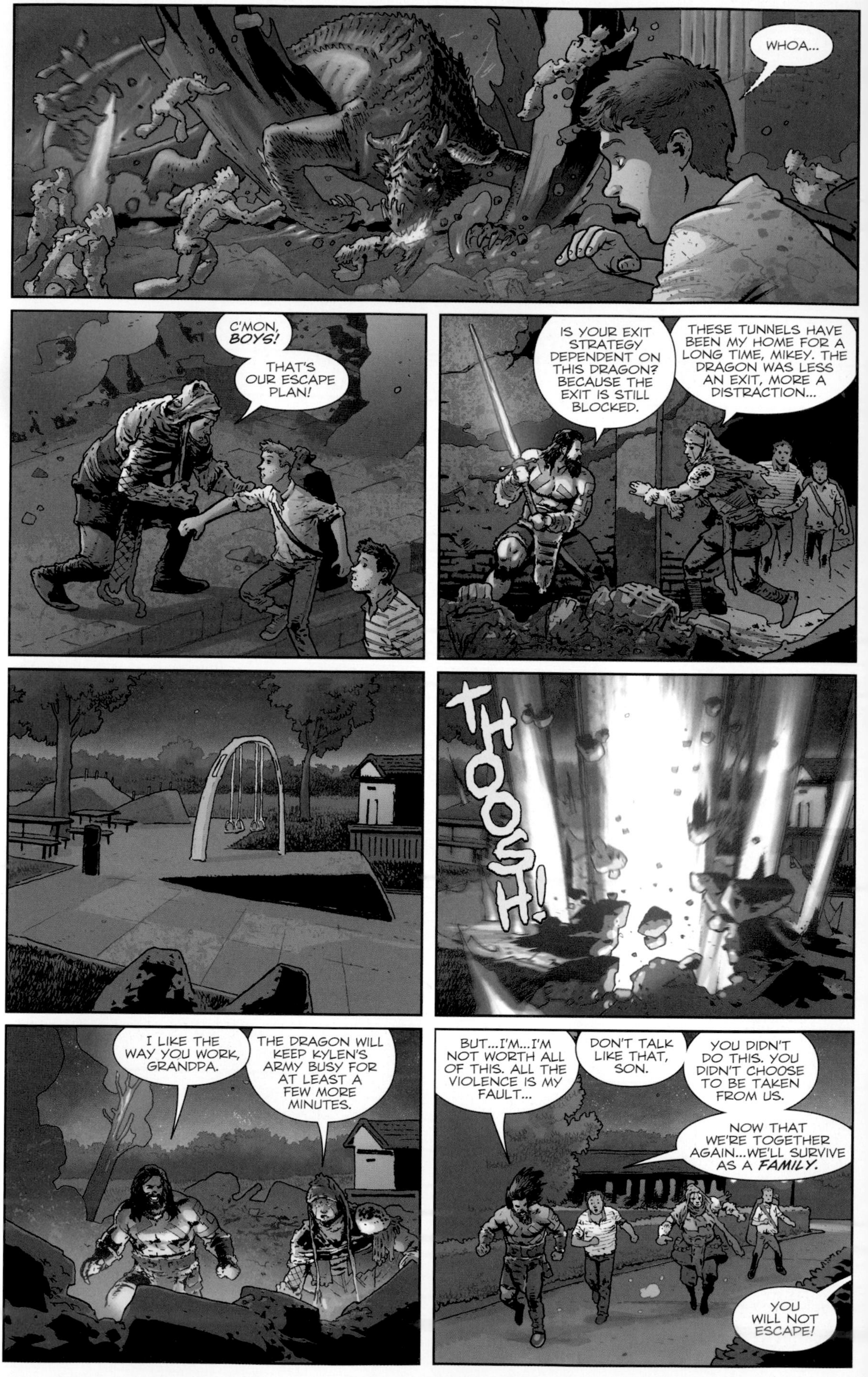
WHOA...
C'MON, *BOYS!*
THAT'S OUR ESCAPE PLAN!
IS YOUR EXIT STRATEGY DEPENDENT ON THIS DRAGON? BECAUSE THE EXIT IS STILL BLOCKED.
THESE TUNNELS HAVE BEEN MY HOME FOR A LONG TIME, MIKEY. THE DRAGON WAS LESS AN EXIT, MORE A DISTRACTION...
THOOSH!
I LIKE THE WAY YOU WORK, GRANDPA.
THE DRAGON WILL KEEP KYLEN'S ARMY BUSY FOR AT LEAST A FEW MORE MINUTES.
BUT...I'M...I'M NOT WORTH ALL OF THIS. ALL THE VIOLENCE IS MY FAULT...
DON'T TALK LIKE THAT, SON.
YOU DIDN'T DO THIS. YOU DIDN'T CHOOSE TO BE TAKEN FROM US.
NOW THAT WE'RE TOGETHER AGAIN...WE'LL SURVIVE AS A *FAMILY.*
YOU WILL NOT ESCAPE!

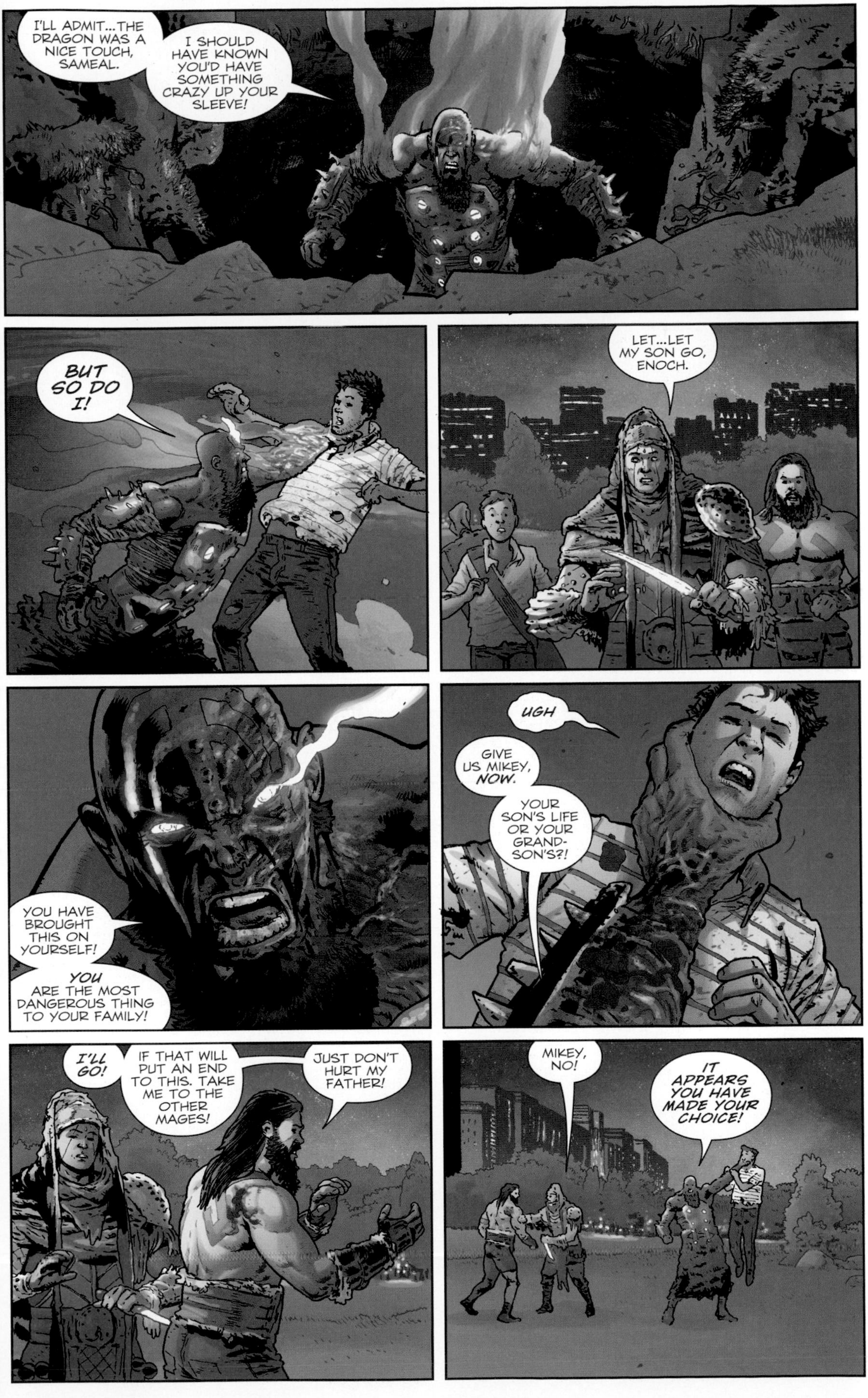
I'LL ADMIT...THE DRAGON WAS A NICE TOUCH, SAMEAL.
I SHOULD HAVE KNOWN YOU'D HAVE SOMETHING CRAZY UP YOUR SLEEVE!
BUT SO DO I!
LET...LET MY SON GO, ENOCH.
YOU HAVE BROUGHT THIS ON YOURSELF!
YOU ARE THE MOST DANGEROUS THING TO YOUR FAMILY!
UGH
GIVE US MIKEY, NOW.
YOUR SON'S LIFE OR YOUR GRAND-SON'S?!
I'LL GO!
IF THAT WILL PUT AN END TO THIS. TAKE ME TO THE OTHER MAGES!
JUST DON'T HURT MY FATHER!
MIKEY, NO!
IT APPEARS YOU HAVE MADE YOUR CHOICE!

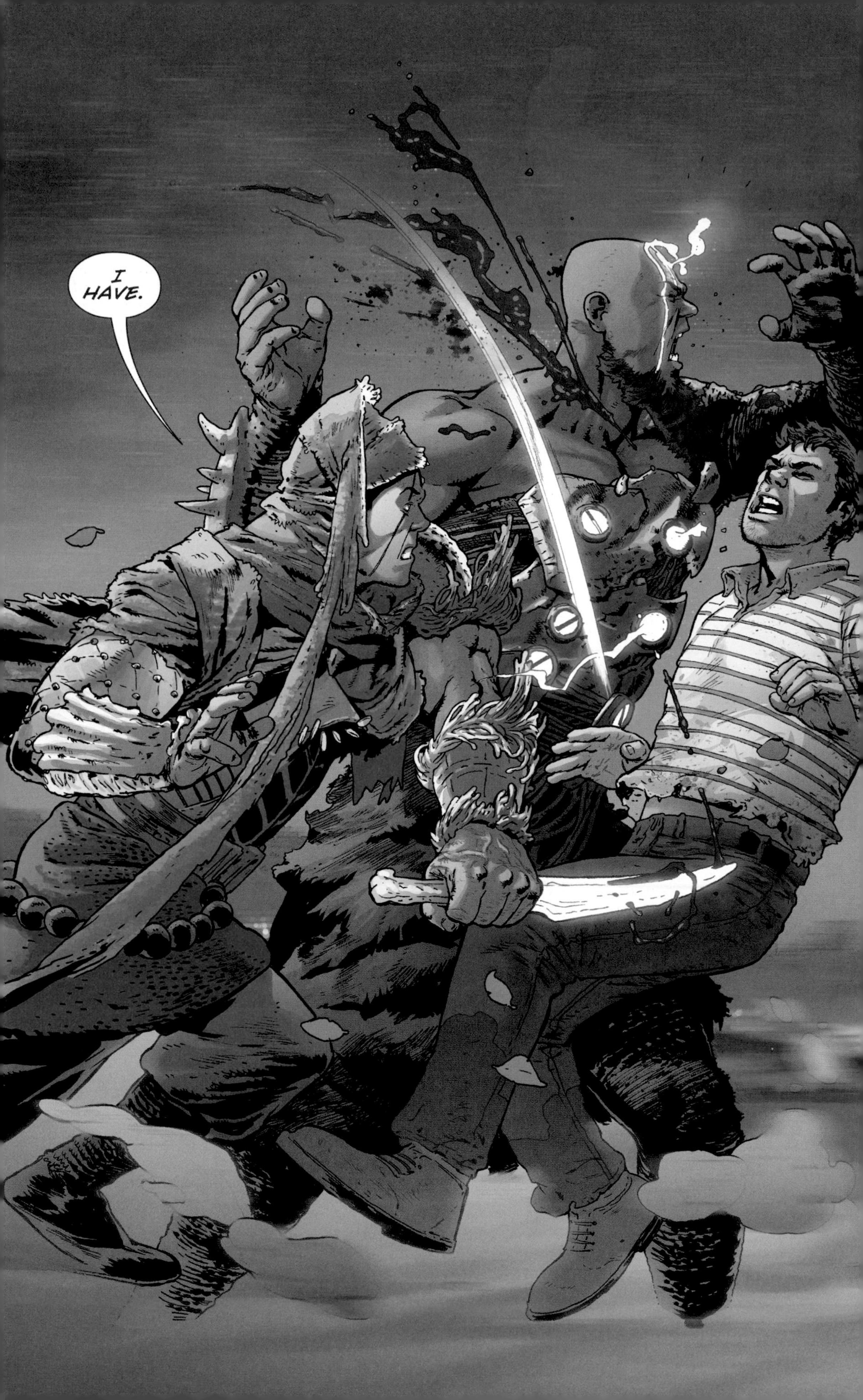
I HAVE.

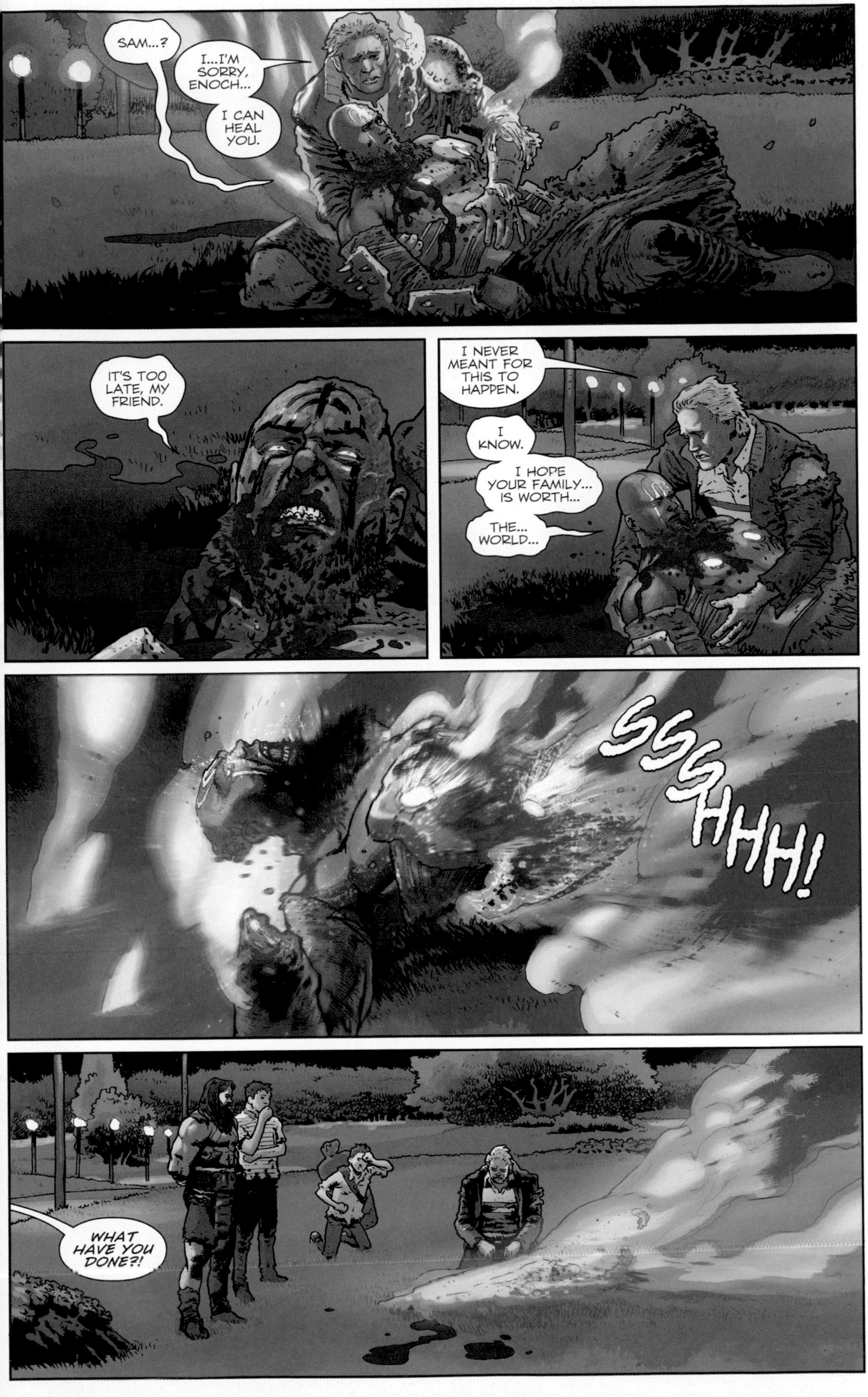
SAM...?
I...I'M SORRY, ENOCH...
I CAN HEAL YOU.
IT'S TOO LATE, MY FRIEND.
I NEVER MEANT FOR THIS TO HAPPEN.
I KNOW.
I HOPE YOUR FAMILY... IS WORTH...
THE... WORLD...
SSSHHHH!
WHAT HAVE YOU DONE?!

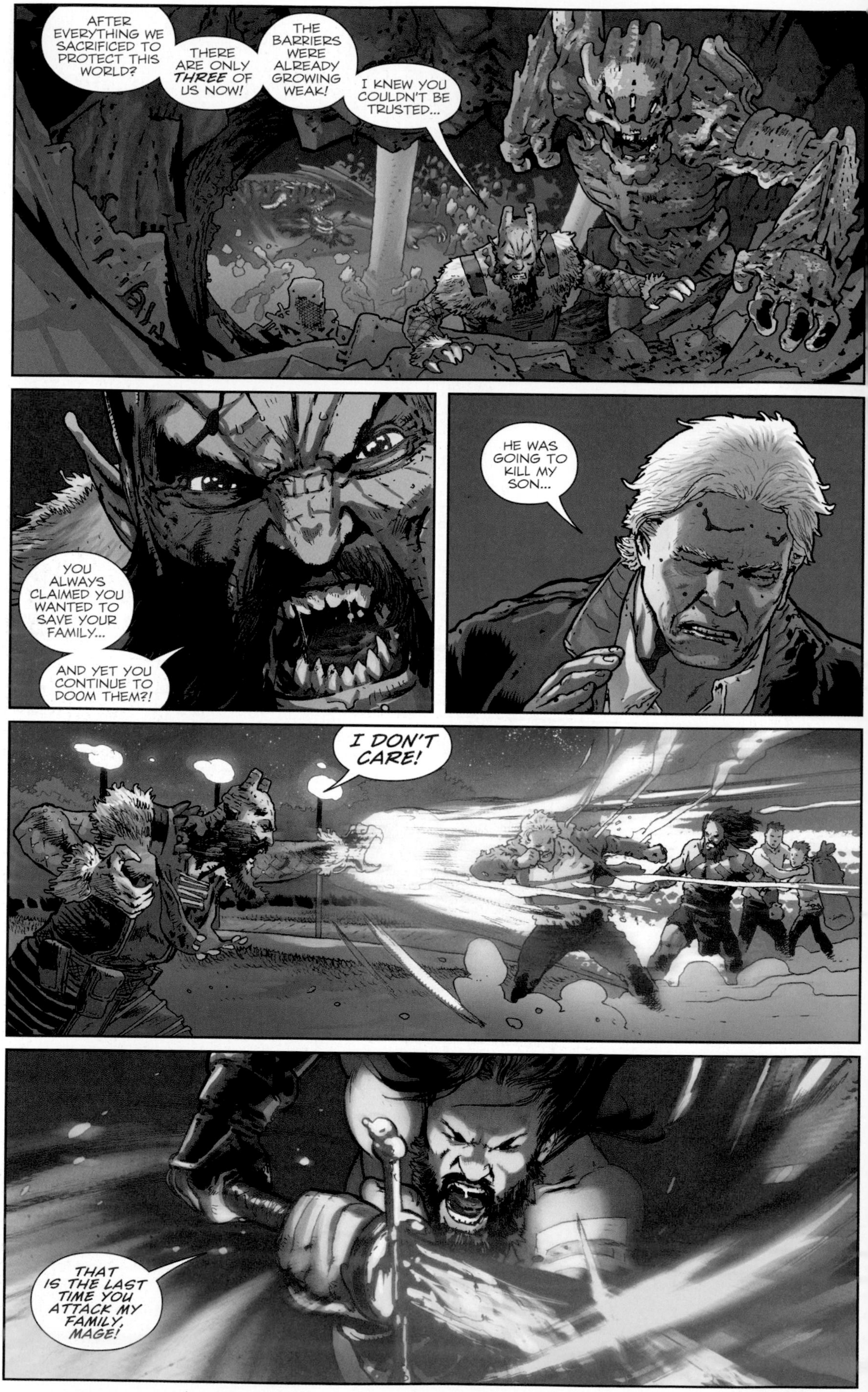
AFTER EVERYTHING WE SACRIFICED TO PROTECT THIS WORLD?
THERE ARE ONLY THREE OF US NOW!
THE BARRIERS WERE ALREADY GROWING WEAK!
I KNEW YOU COULDN'T BE TRUSTED...
YOU ALWAYS CLAIMED YOU WANTED TO SAVE YOUR FAMILY...
AND YET YOU CONTINUE TO DOOM THEM?!
HE WAS GOING TO KILL MY SON...
I DON'T CARE!
THAT IS THE LAST TIME YOU ATTACK MY FAMILY, MAGE!

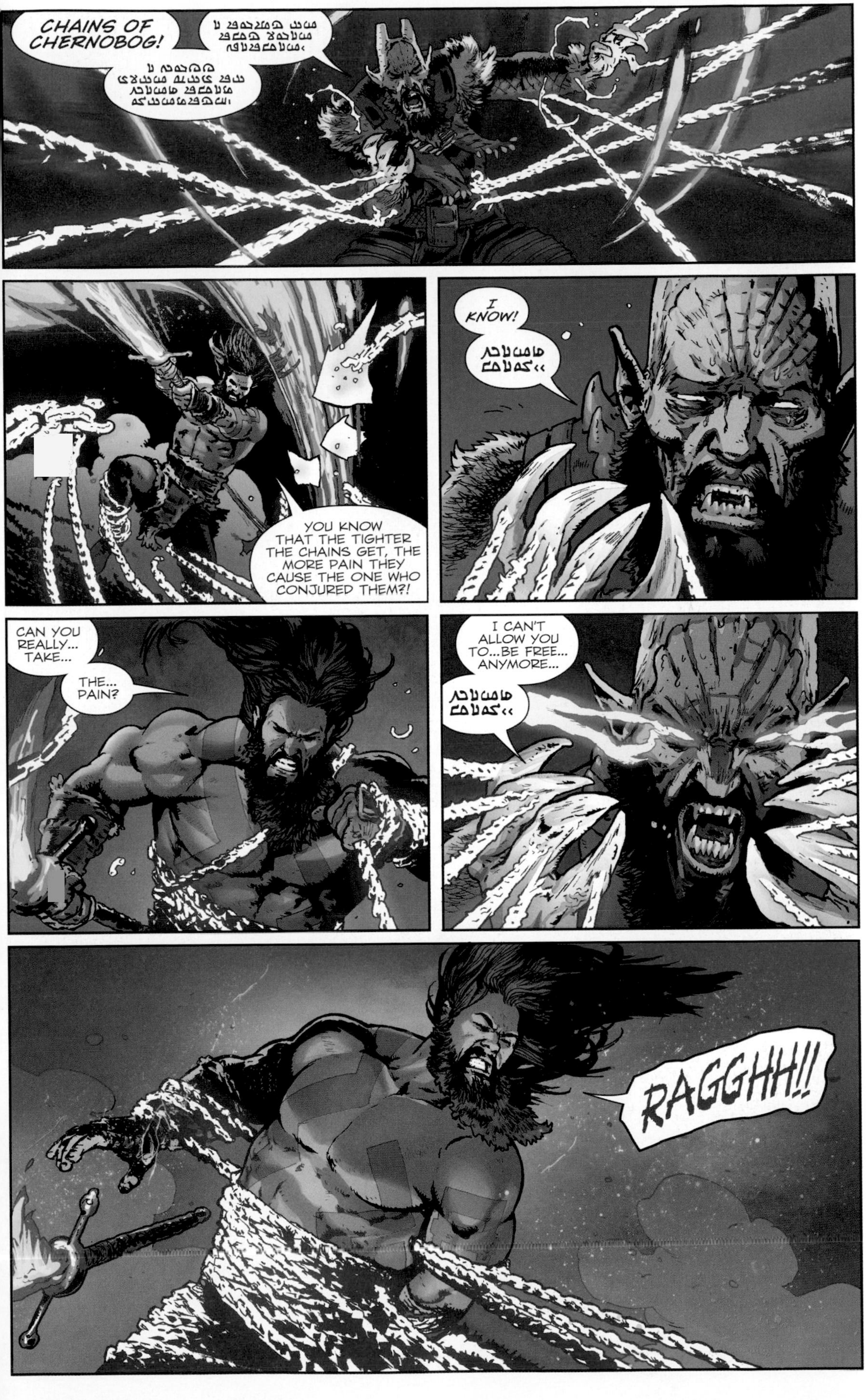
CHAINS OF CHERNOBOG!
YOU KNOW THAT THE TIGHTER THE CHAINS GET, THE MORE PAIN THEY CAUSE THE ONE WHO CONJURED THEM?!
I KNOW!
CAN YOU REALLY... TAKE...
THE... PAIN?
I CAN'T ALLOW YOU TO...BE FREE... ANYMORE...
RAGGHH!!

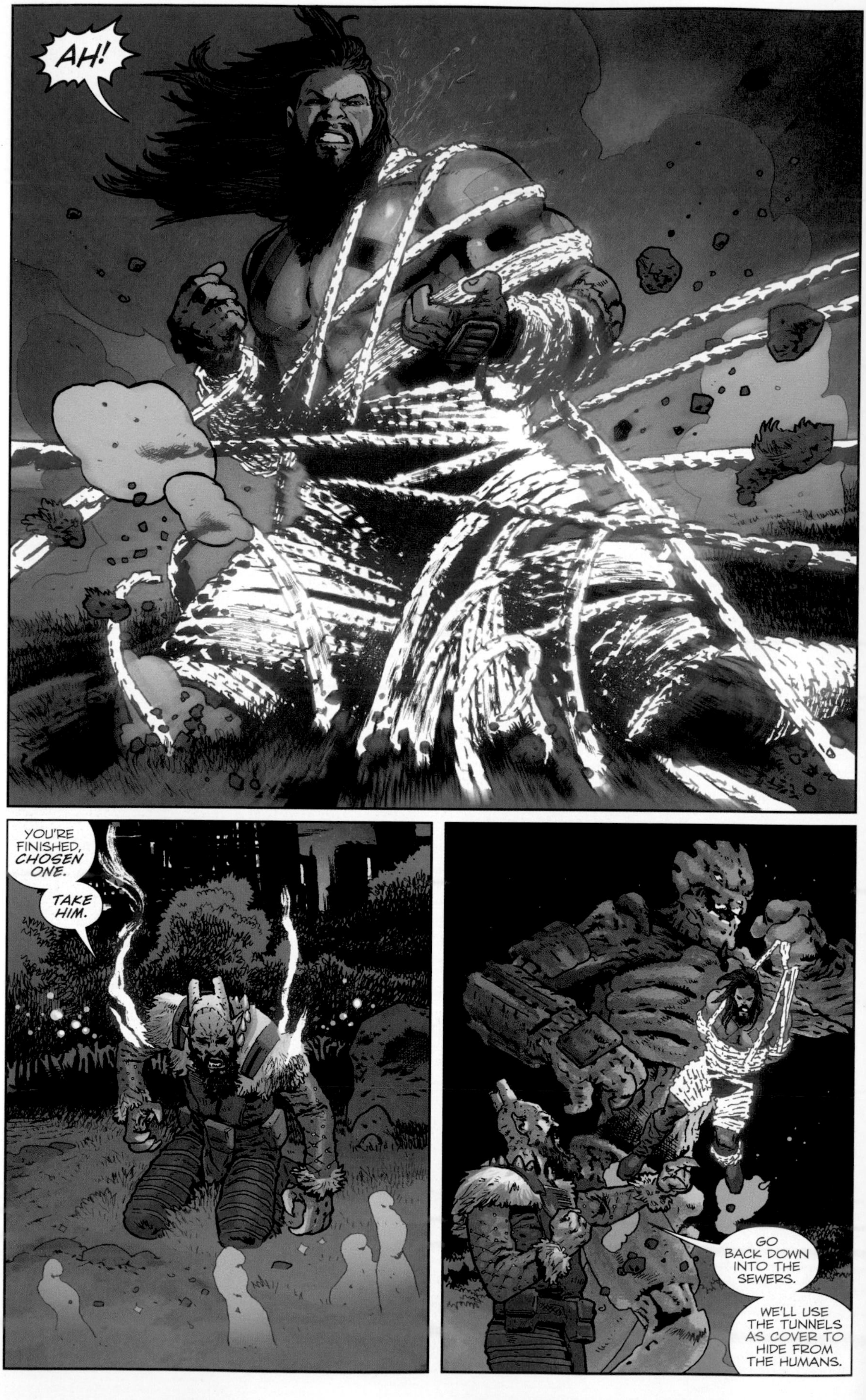
AH!
YOU'RE FINISHED, CHOSEN ONE.
TAKE HIM.
GO BACK DOWN INTO THE SEWERS.
WE'LL USE THE TUNNELS AS COVER TO HIDE FROM THE HUMANS.

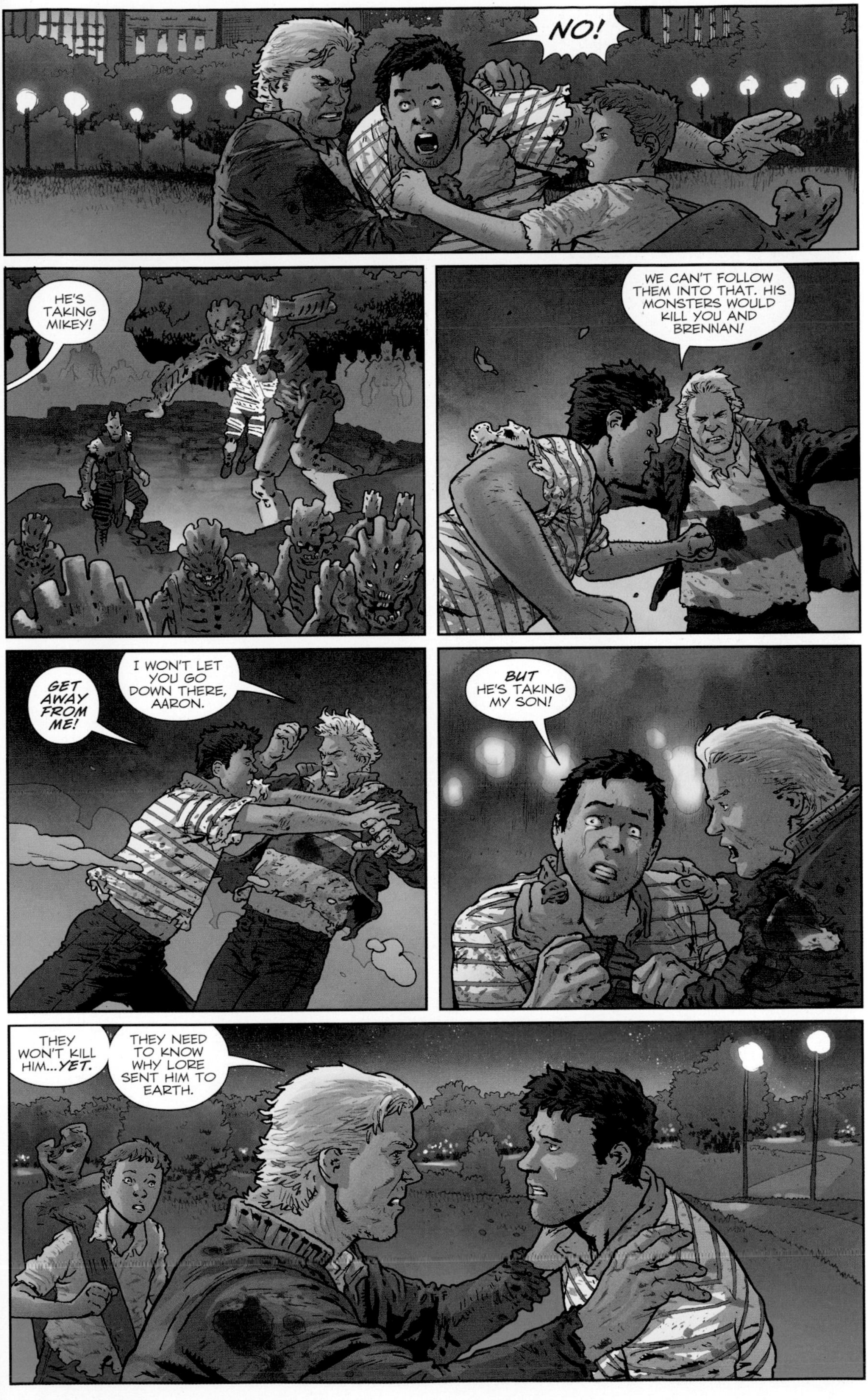
NO!
HE'S TAKING MIKEY!
WE CAN'T FOLLOW THEM INTO THAT. HIS MONSTERS WOULD KILL YOU AND BRENNAN!
GET AWAY FROM ME!
I WON'T LET YOU GO DOWN THERE, AARON.
BUT HE'S TAKING MY SON!
THEY WON'T KILL HIM...YET.
THEY NEED TO KNOW WHY LORE SENT HIM TO EARTH.

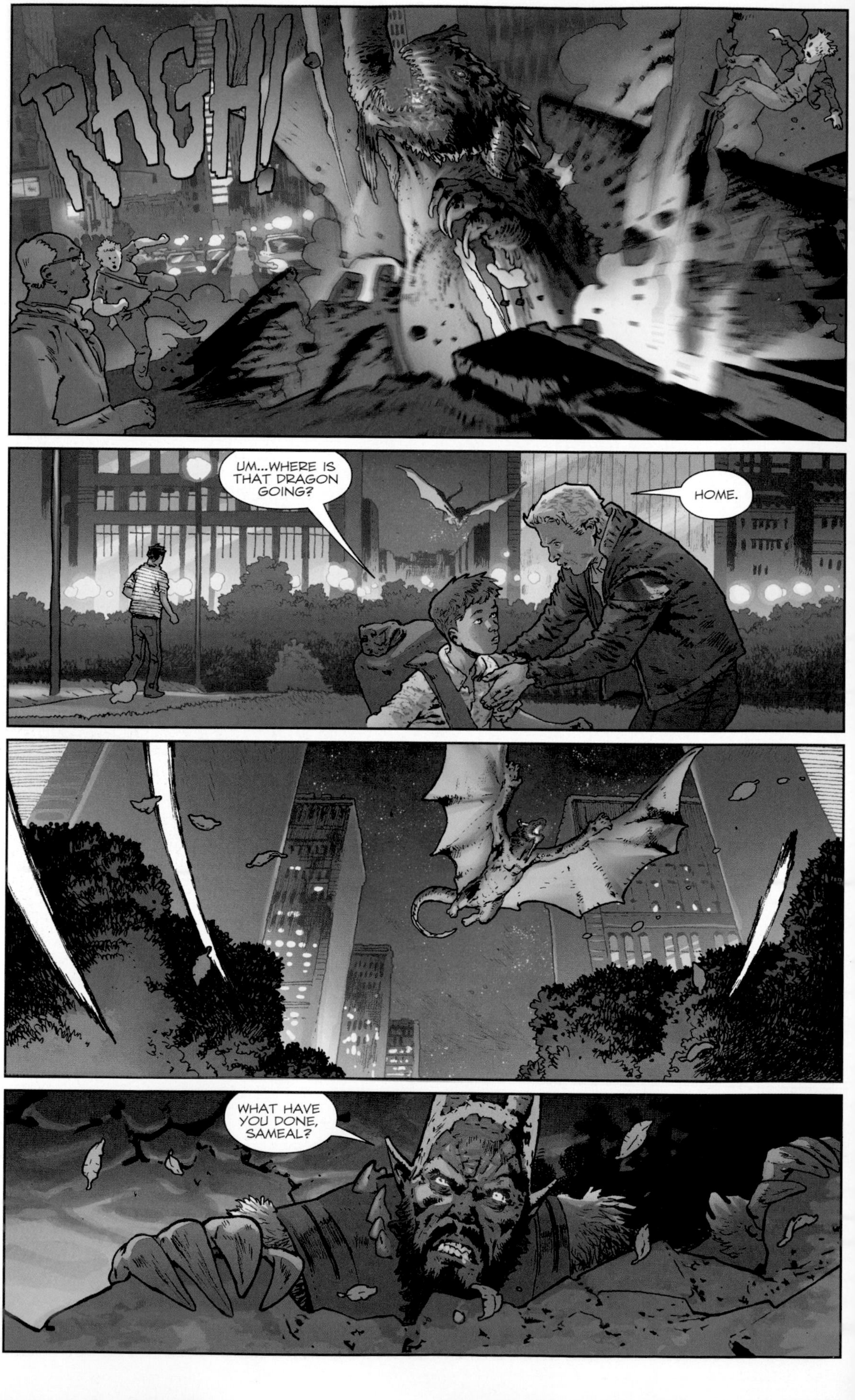
RAGH!
UM...WHERE IS THAT DRAGON GOING?
HOME.
WHAT HAVE YOU DONE, SAMEAL?

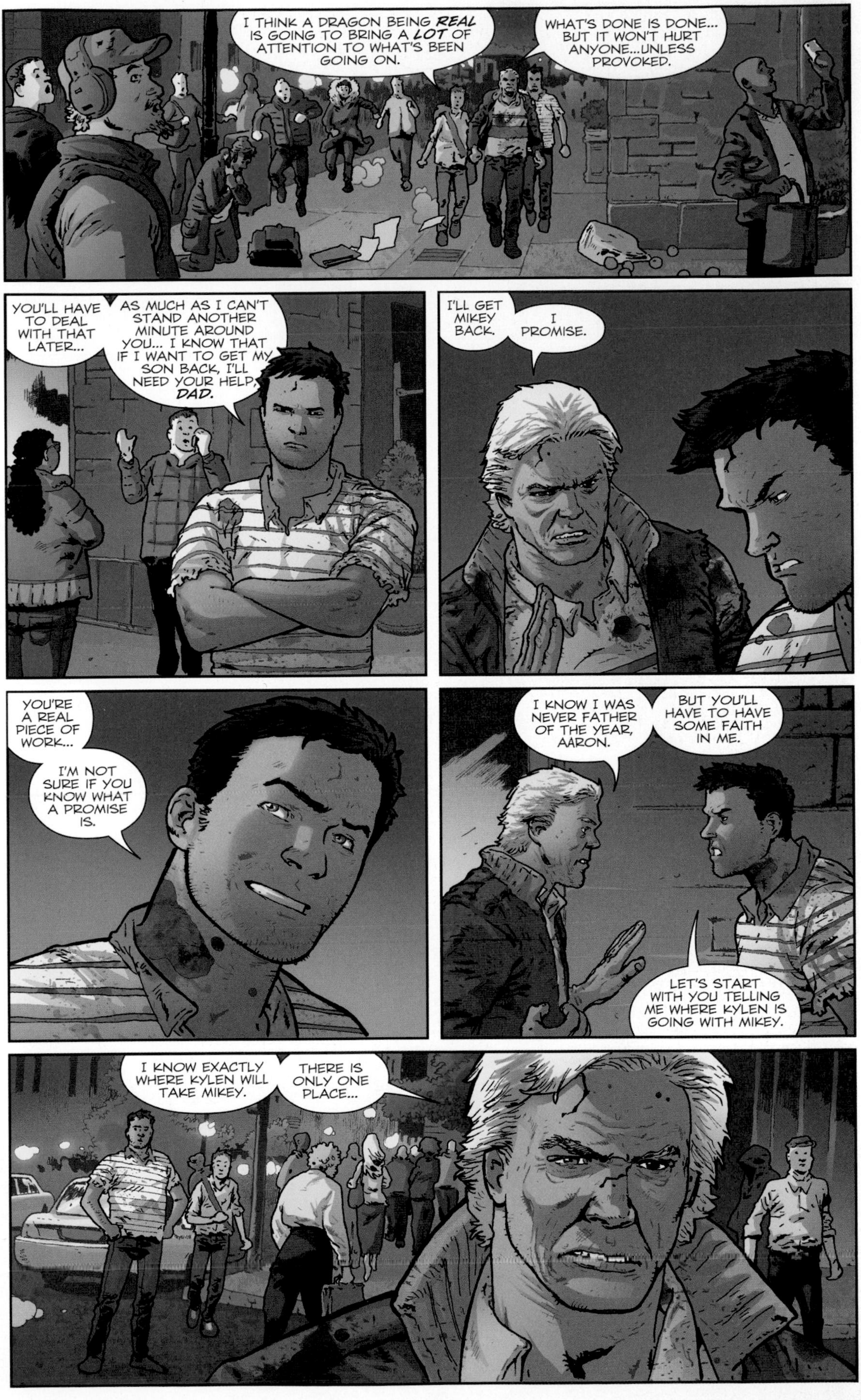
I THINK A DRAGON BEING *REAL* IS GOING TO BRING A *LOT* OF ATTENTION TO WHAT'S BEEN GOING ON.
WHAT'S DONE IS DONE... BUT IT WON'T HURT ANYONE...UNLESS PROVOKED.
YOU'LL HAVE TO DEAL WITH THAT LATER...
AS MUCH AS I CAN'T STAND ANOTHER MINUTE AROUND YOU... I KNOW THAT IF I WANT TO GET MY SON BACK, I'LL NEED YOUR HELP, *DAD.*
I'LL GET MIKEY BACK.
I PROMISE.
YOU'RE A REAL PIECE OF WORK...
I'M NOT SURE IF YOU KNOW WHAT A PROMISE IS.
I KNOW I WAS NEVER FATHER OF THE YEAR, AARON.
BUT YOU'LL HAVE TO HAVE SOME FAITH IN ME.
LET'S START WITH YOU TELLING ME WHERE KYLEN IS GOING WITH MIKEY.
I KNOW EXACTLY WHERE KYLEN WILL TAKE MIKEY.
THERE IS ONLY ONE PLACE...

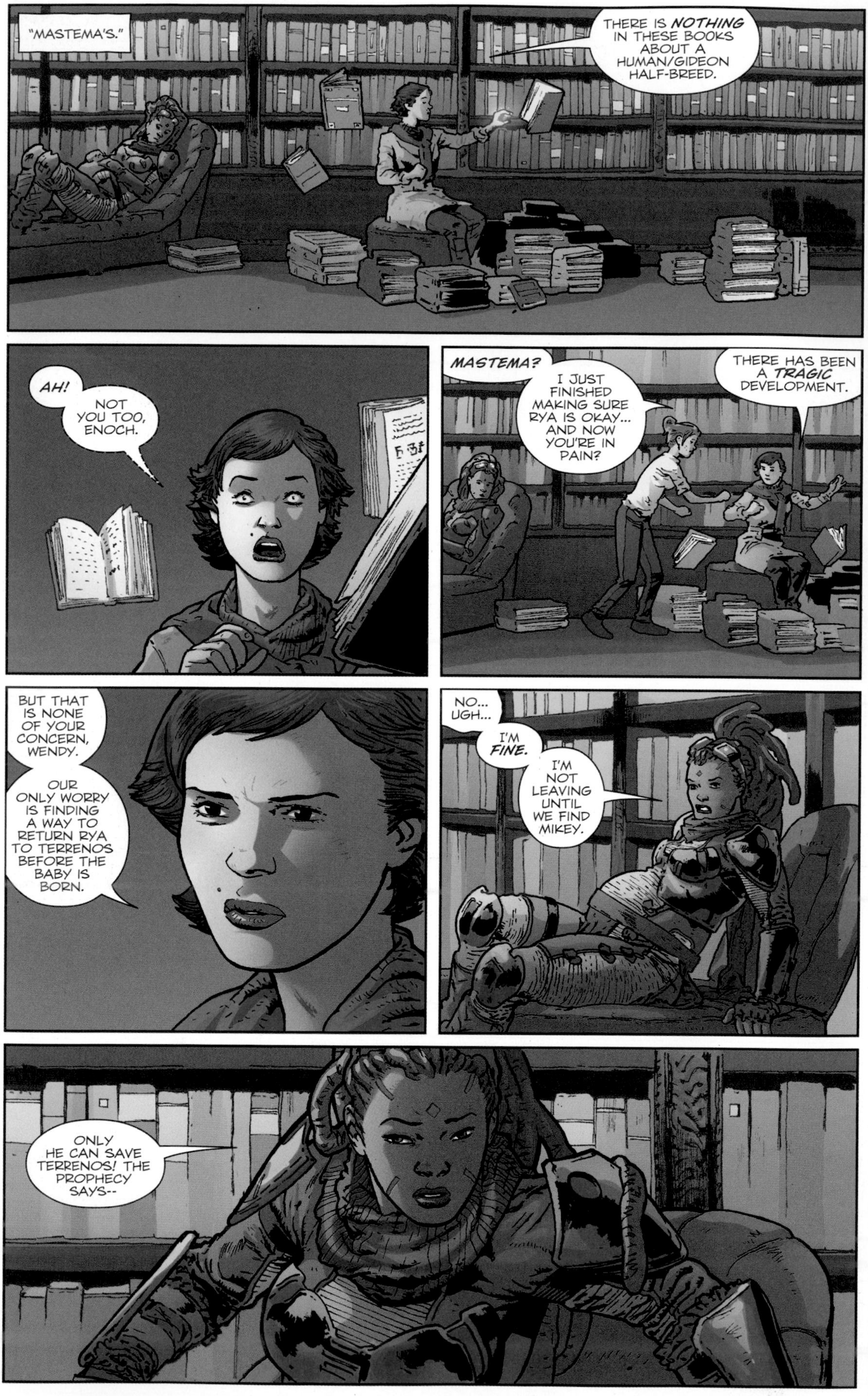
"MASTEMA'S."
THERE IS NOTHING IN THESE BOOKS ABOUT A HUMAN/GIDEON HALF-BREED.
AH!
NOT YOU TOO, ENOCH.
MASTEMA?
I JUST FINISHED MAKING SURE RYA IS OKAY... AND NOW YOU'RE IN PAIN?
THERE HAS BEEN A TRAGIC DEVELOPMENT.
BUT THAT IS NONE OF YOUR CONCERN, WENDY.
OUR ONLY WORRY IS FINDING A WAY TO RETURN RYA TO TERRENOS BEFORE THE BABY IS BORN.
NO... UGH...
I'M FINE.
I'M NOT LEAVING UNTIL WE FIND MIKEY.
ONLY HE CAN SAVE TERRENOS! THE PROPHECY SAYS--

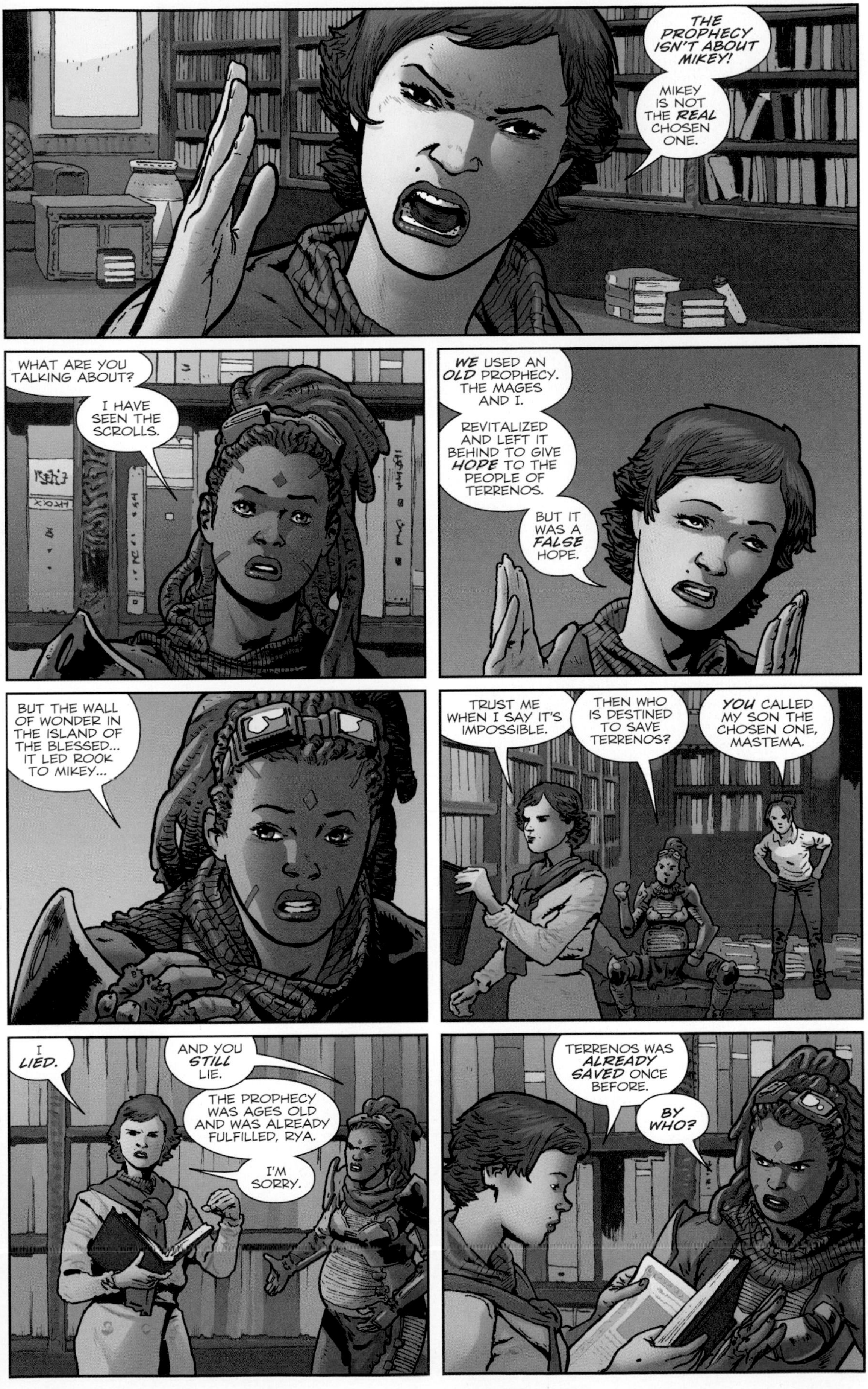
THE PROPHECY ISN'T ABOUT MIKEY!
MIKEY IS NOT THE REAL CHOSEN ONE.
WHAT ARE YOU TALKING ABOUT?
I HAVE SEEN THE SCROLLS.
WE USED AN OLD PROPHECY. THE MAGES AND I.
REVITALIZED AND LEFT IT BEHIND TO GIVE HOPE TO THE PEOPLE OF TERRENOS.
BUT IT WAS A FALSE HOPE.
BUT THE WALL OF WONDER IN THE ISLAND OF THE BLESSED... IT LED ROOK TO MIKEY...
TRUST ME WHEN I SAY IT'S IMPOSSIBLE.
THEN WHO IS DESTINED TO SAVE TERRENOS?
YOU CALLED MY SON THE CHOSEN ONE, MASTEMA.
I LIED.
AND YOU STILL LIE.
THE PROPHECY WAS AGES OLD AND WAS ALREADY FULFILLED, RYA.
I'M SORRY.
TERRENOS WAS ALREADY SAVED ONCE BEFORE.
BY WHO?

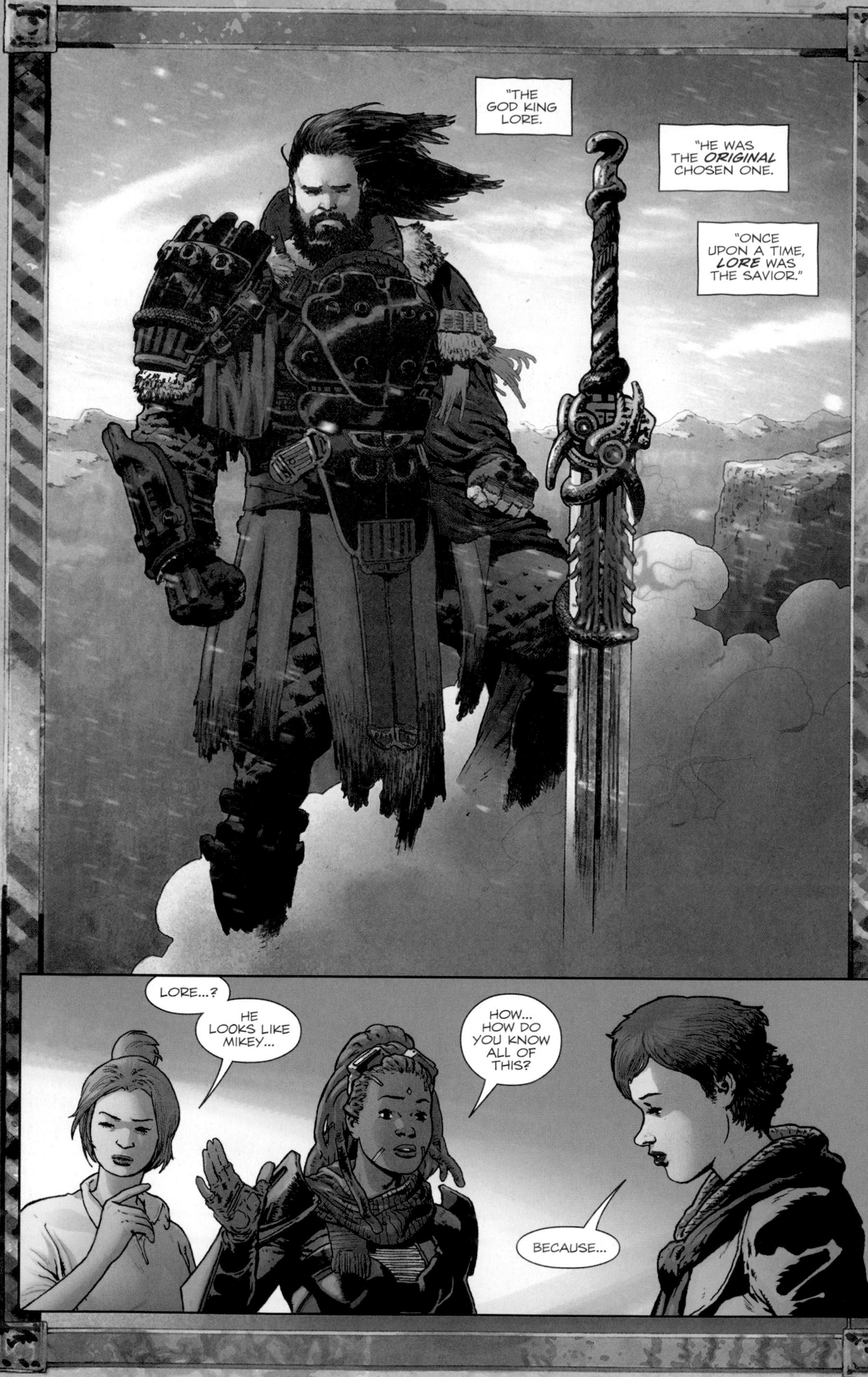
"THE GOD KING LORE.
"HE WAS THE ORIGINAL CHOSEN ONE.
"ONCE UPON A TIME, LORE WAS THE SAVIOR."
LORE...?
HE LOOKS LIKE MIKEY...
HOW... HOW DO YOU KNOW ALL OF THIS?
BECAUSE...

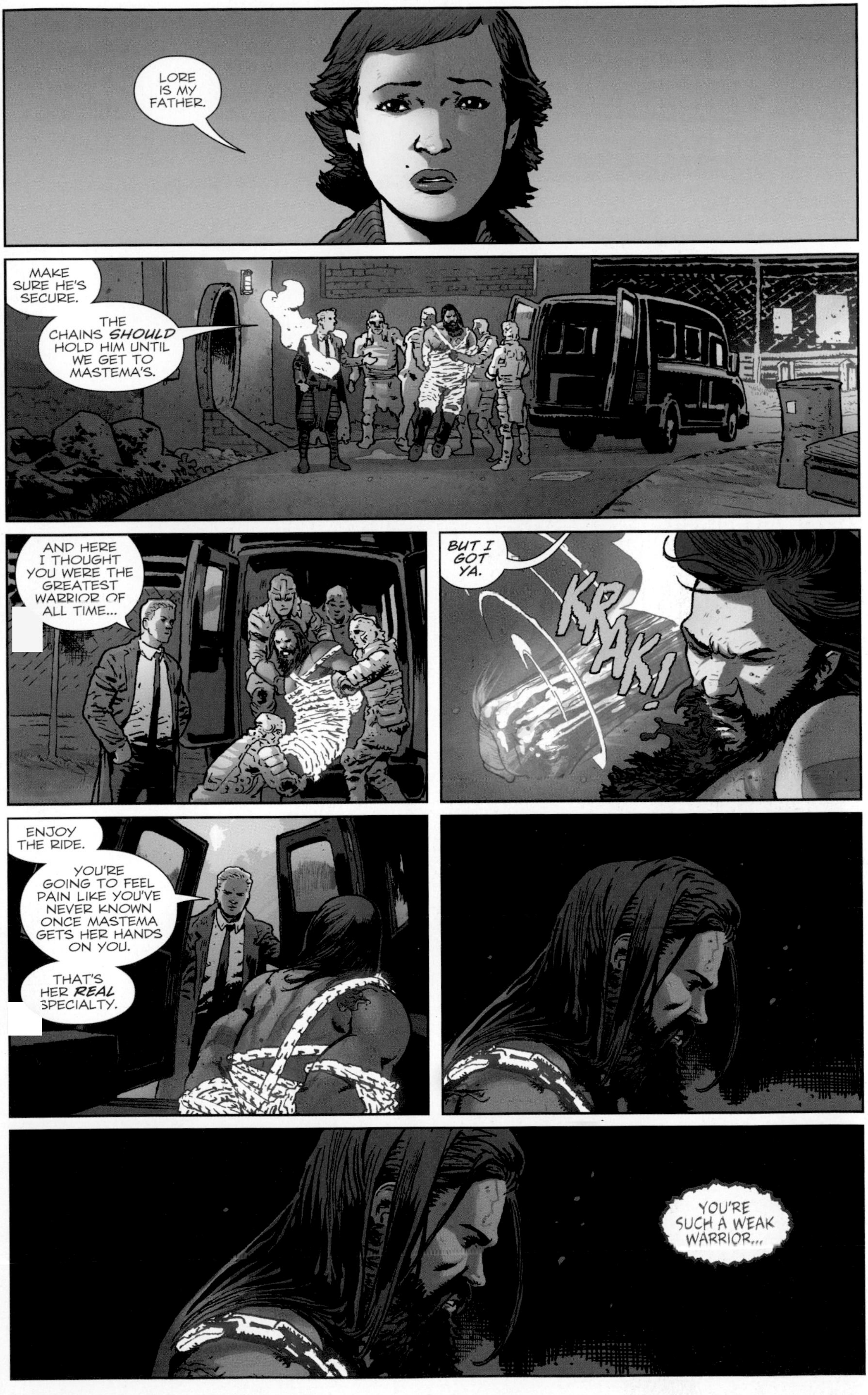
LORE IS MY FATHER.
MAKE SURE HE'S SECURE.
THE CHAINS SHOULD HOLD HIM UNTIL WE GET TO MASTEMA'S.
AND HERE I THOUGHT YOU WERE THE GREATEST WARRIOR OF ALL TIME...
BUT I GOT YA.
KRAK!
ENJOY THE RIDE.
YOU'RE GOING TO FEEL PAIN LIKE YOU'VE NEVER KNOWN ONCE MASTEMA GETS HER HANDS ON YOU.
THAT'S HER REAL SPECIALTY.
YOU'RE SUCH A WEAK WARRIOR...

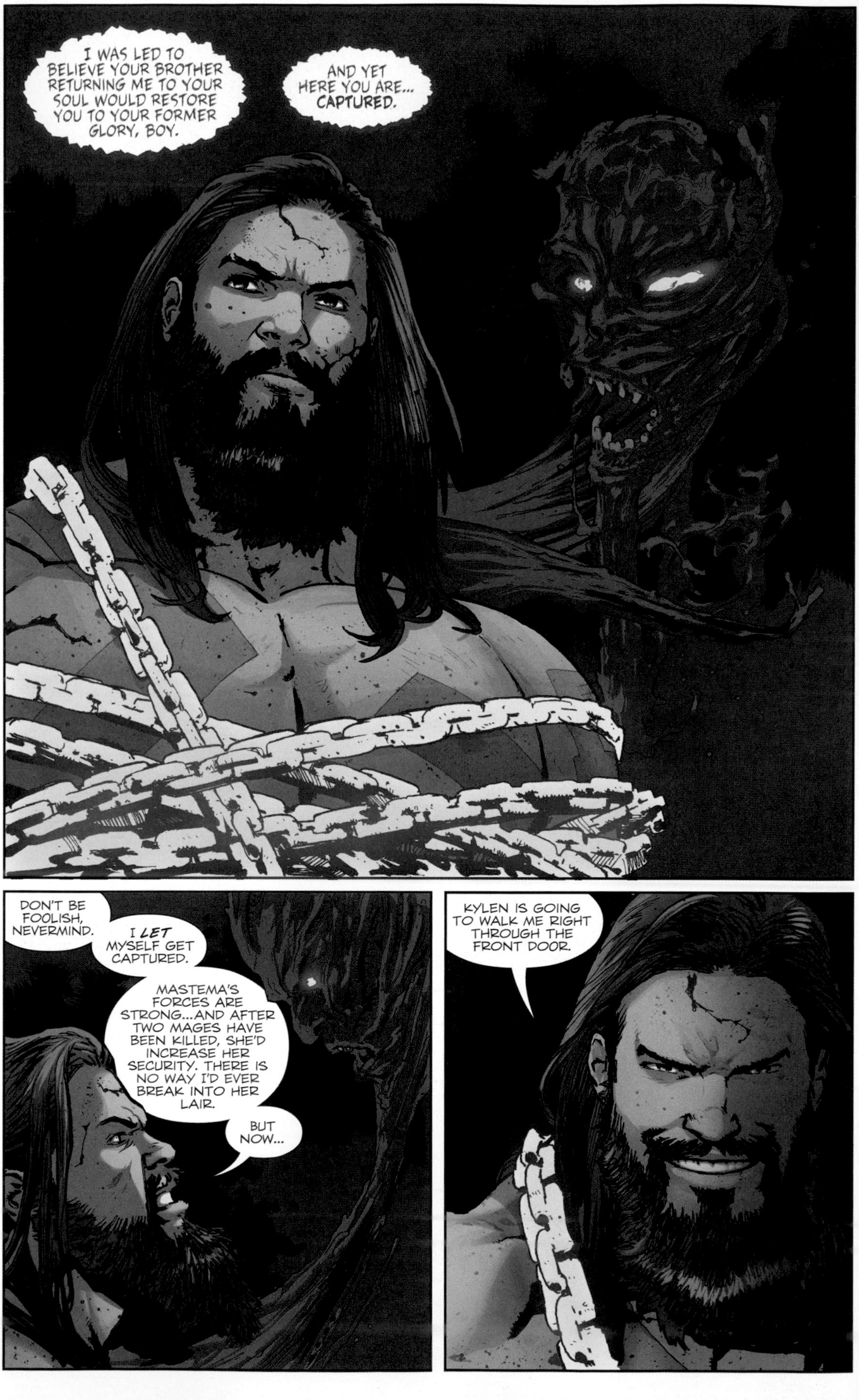

I WAS LED TO BELIEVE YOUR BROTHER RETURNING ME TO YOUR SOUL WOULD RESTORE YOU TO YOUR FORMER GLORY, BOY.
AND YET HERE YOU ARE... CAPTURED.
DON'T BE FOOLISH, NEVERMIND.
I LET MYSELF GET CAPTURED.
MASTEMA'S FORCES ARE STRONG...AND AFTER TWO MAGES HAVE BEEN KILLED, SHE'D INCREASE HER SECURITY. THERE IS NO WAY I'D EVER BREAK INTO HER LAIR.
BUT NOW...
KYLEN IS GOING TO WALK ME RIGHT THROUGH THE FRONT DOOR.

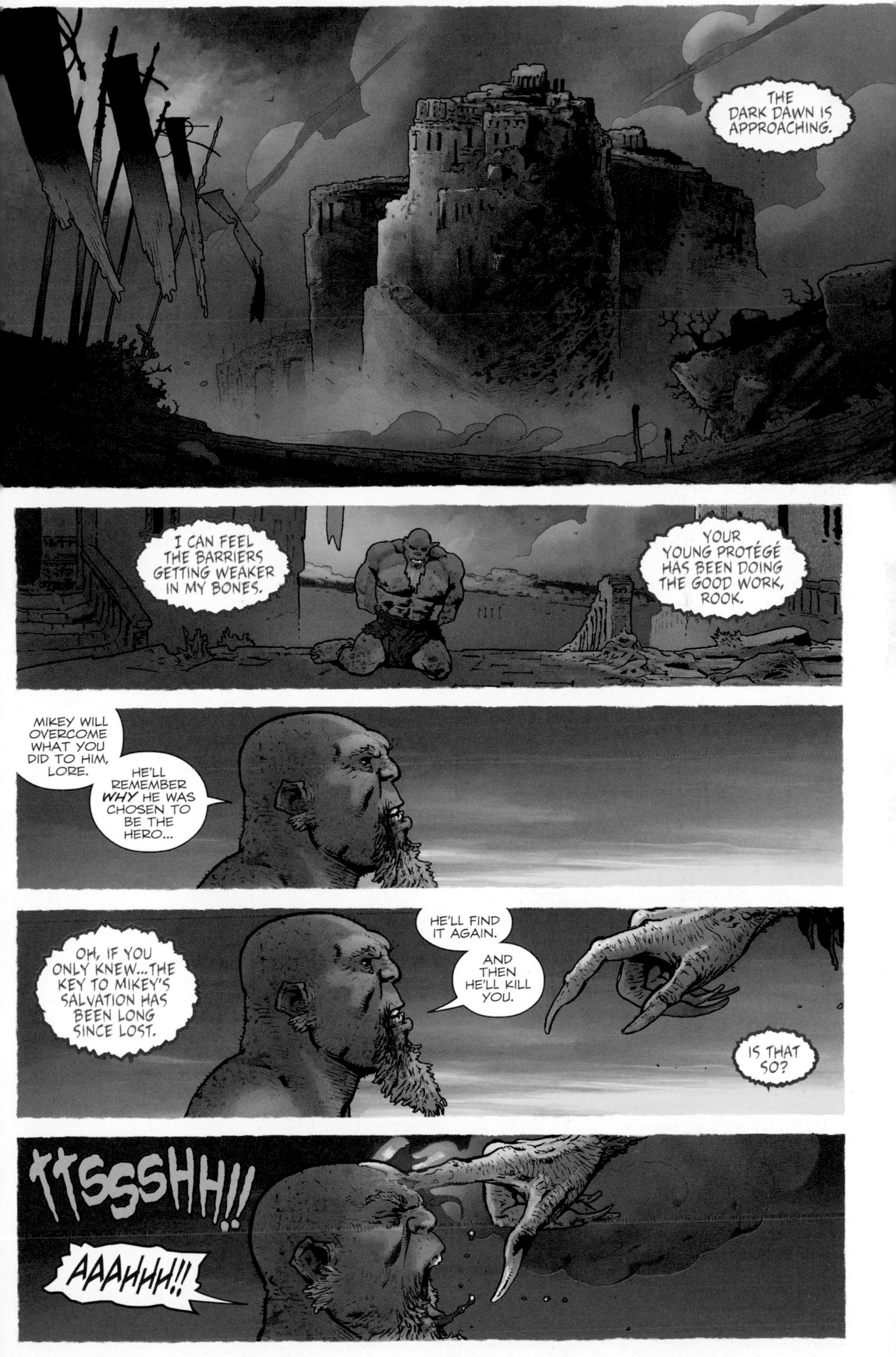
THE DARK DAWN IS APPROACHING.
I CAN FEEL THE BARRIERS GETTING WEAKER IN MY BONES.
YOUR YOUNG PROTÉGÉ HAS BEEN DOING THE GOOD WORK, ROOK.
MIKEY WILL OVERCOME WHAT YOU DID TO HIM, LORE.
HE'LL REMEMBER *WHY* HE WAS CHOSEN TO BE THE HERO...
OH, IF YOU ONLY KNEW...THE KEY TO MIKEY'S SALVATION HAS BEEN LONG SINCE LOST.
HE'LL FIND IT AGAIN.
AND THEN HE'LL KILL YOU.
IS THAT SO?
TTSSSHH!!
AAAHHH!!

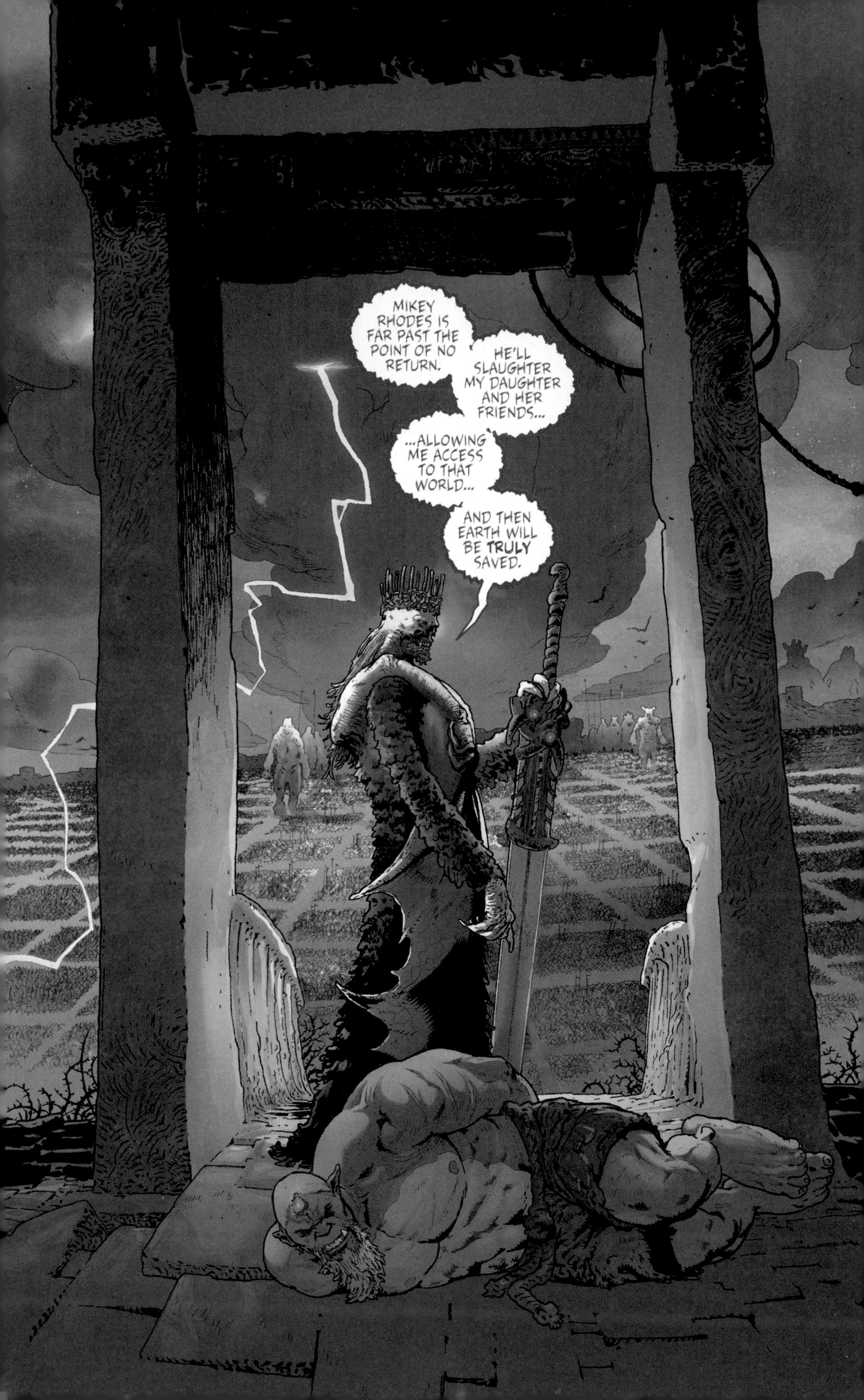
MIKEY RHODES IS FAR PAST THE POINT OF NO RETURN.
HE'LL SLAUGHTER MY DAUGHTER AND HER FRIENDS...
...ALLOWING ME ACCESS TO THAT WORLD...
AND THEN EARTH WILL BE **TRULY** SAVED.

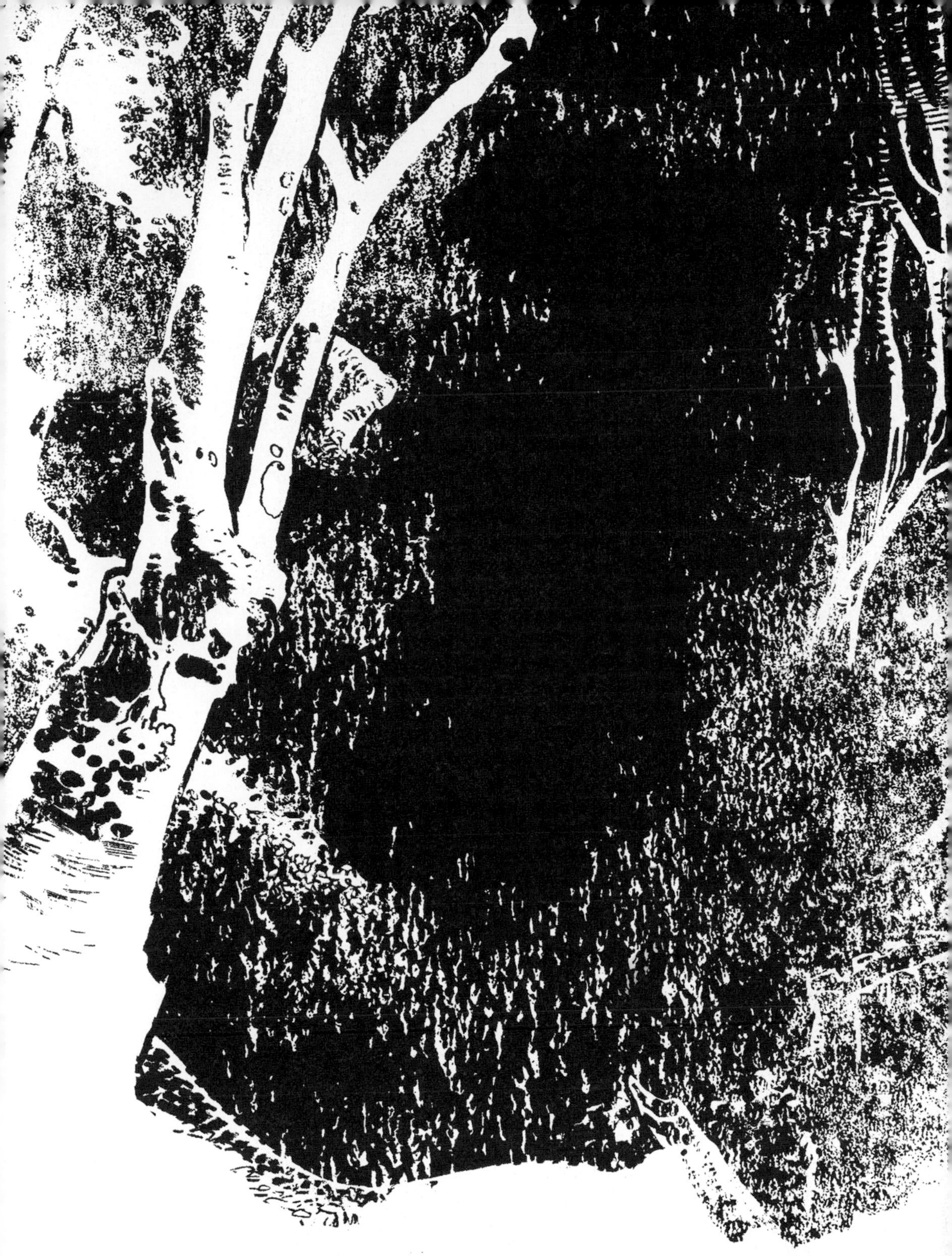

To be continued...

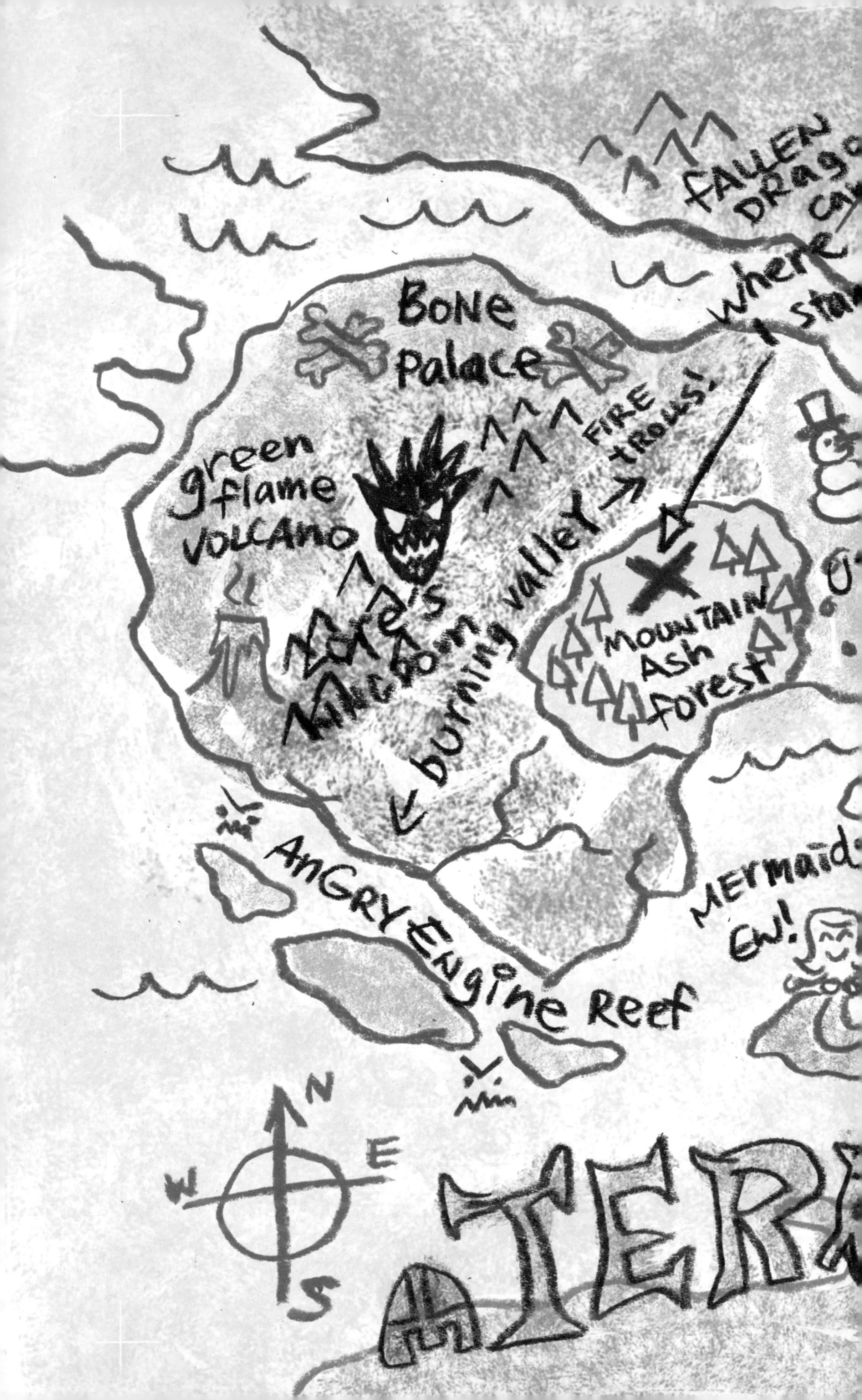
FALLEN
Bone Palace
FIRE TROLLS!
green flame VOLCANO
burning valley
MOUNTAIN Ash forest
ANGRY Engine Reef
Ew!
N
E
W
S

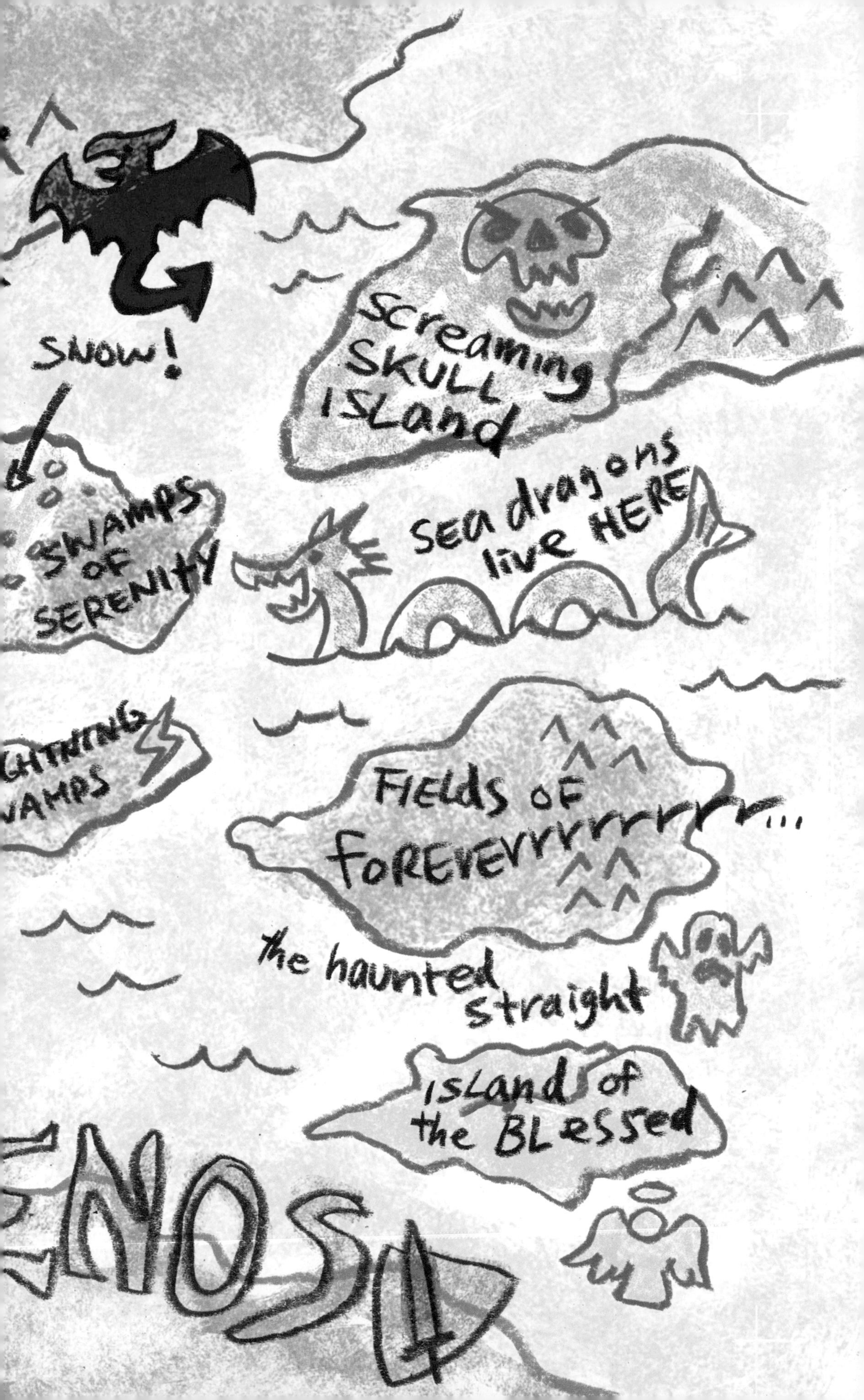

SNOW!
Screaming SKULL ISLand
SWAMPS OF SERENITY
Sea dragons live HERE
GHTNING WAMPS
FIELDS OF FOREVERRRRRRRRR...
the haunted straight
ISLand of the BLessed
NOS

"You brought this nightmare into our world."

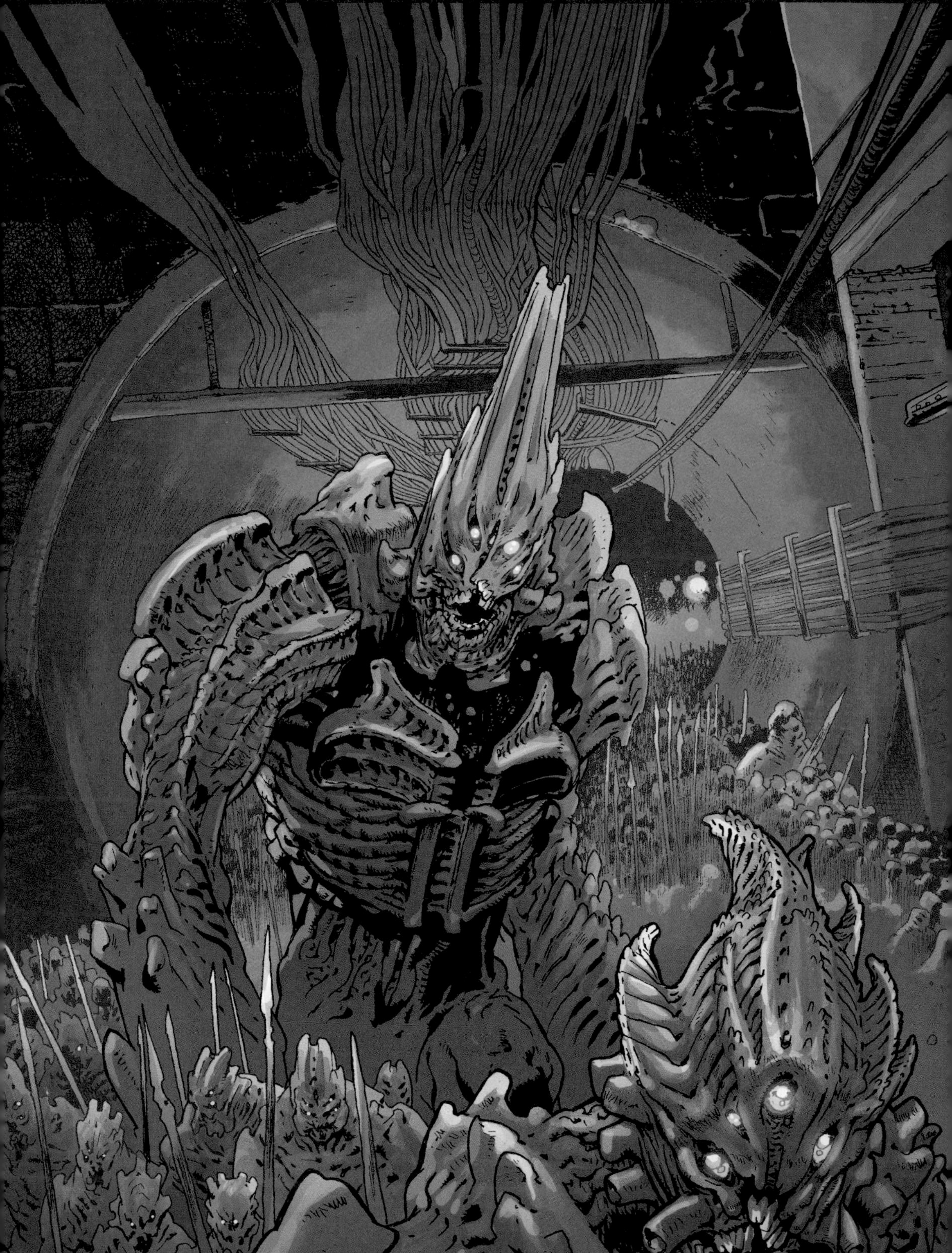

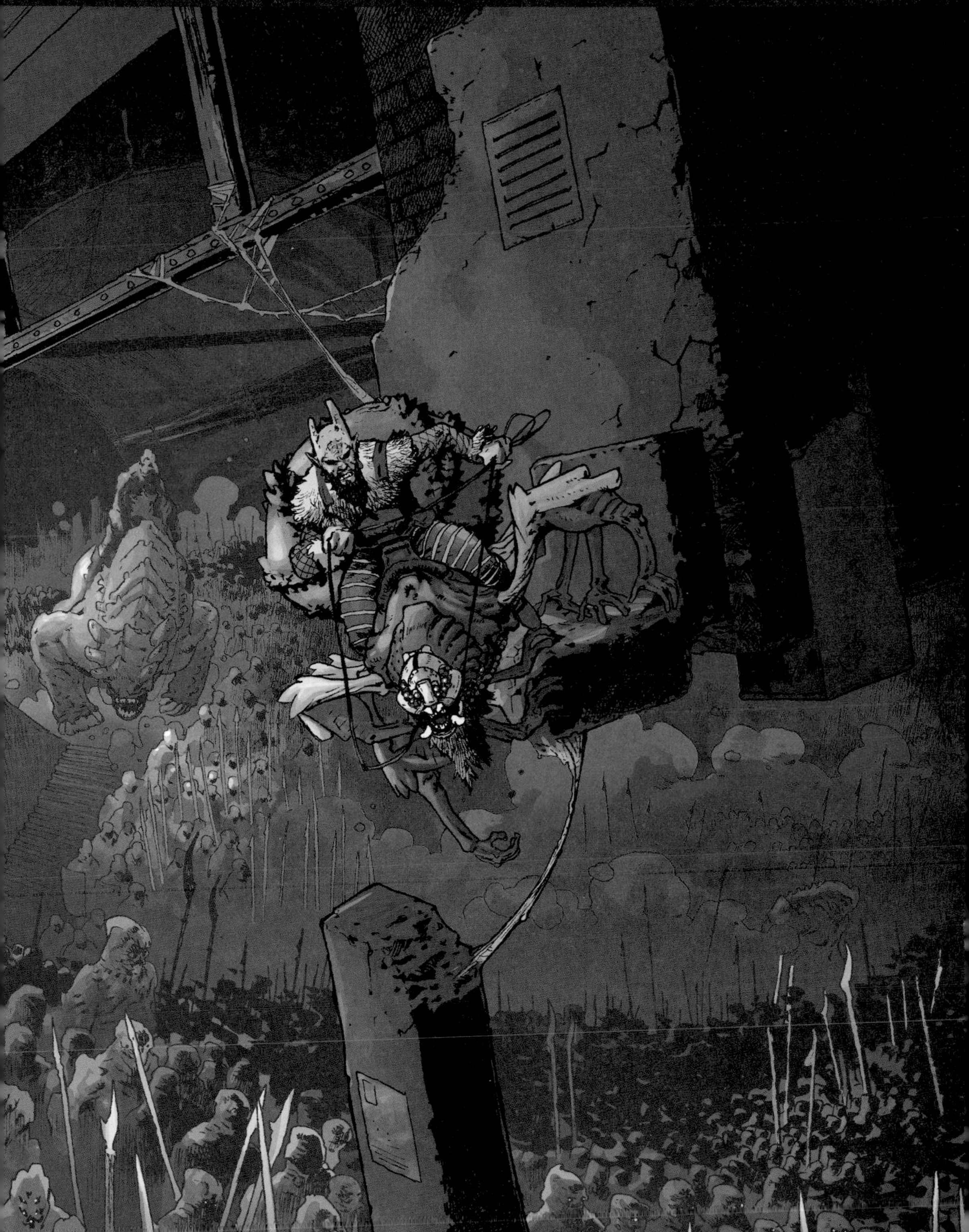

WE'RE ONLINE.

NEWS.

MERCH.

EXCLUSIVES.

GIVEAWAYS.

SALES.

LET'S BE FRIENDS.

 @SKYBOUNDENTERTAINMENT
@THEOFFICIALWALKINGDEAD

 @SKYBOUND
@THEWALKINGDEAD

FOR MORE OF THE WALKING DEAD

TRADEPAPERBACKS

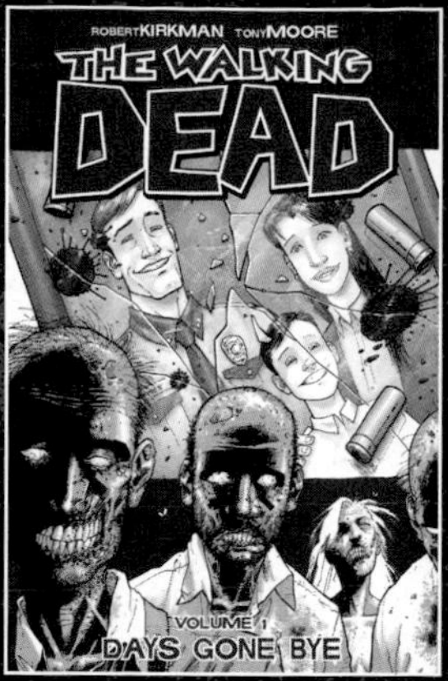

ROBERT KIRKMAN TONY MOORE
THE WALKING DEAD
VOLUME 1
DAYS GONE BYE

VOL. 1: DAYS GONE BYE TP
ISBN: 978-1-58240-672-5
$14.99

VOL. 2: MILES BEHIND US TP
ISBN: 978-1-58240-775-3
$14.99

VOL. 3: SAFETY BEHIND BARS TP
ISBN: 978-1-58240-805-7
$14.99

VOL. 4: THE HEART'S DESIRE TP
ISBN: 978-1-58240-530-8
$14.99

VOL. 5: THE BEST DEFENSE TP
ISBN: 978-1-58240-612-1
$14.99

VOL. 6: THIS SORROWFUL LIFE TP
ISBN: 978-1-58240-684-8
$14.99

VOL. 7: THE CALM BEFORE TP
ISBN: 978-1-58240-828-6
$14.99

VOL. 8: MADE TO SUFFER TP
ISBN: 978-1-58240-883-5
$14.99

VOL. 9: HERE WE REMAIN TP
ISBN: 978-1-60706-022-2
$14.99

VOL. 10: WHAT WE BECOME TP
ISBN: 978-1-60706-075-8
$14.99

VOL. 11: FEAR THE HUNTERS TP
ISBN: 978-1-60706-181-6
$14.99

VOL. 12: LIFE AMONG THEM TP
ISBN: 978-1-60706-254-7
$14.99

VOL. 13: TOO FAR GONE TP
ISBN: 978-1-60706-329-2
$14.99

VOL. 14: NO WAY OUT TP
ISBN: 978-1-60706-392-6
$14.99

VOL. 15: WE FIND OURSELVES TP
ISBN: 978-1-60706-440-4
$14.99

VOL. 16: A LARGER WORLD TP
ISBN: 978-1-60706-559-3
$14.99

VOL. 17: SOMETHING TO FEAR TP
ISBN: 978-1-60706-615-6
$14.99

VOL. 18: WHAT COMES AFTER TP
ISBN: 978-1-60706-687-3
$14.99

VOL. 19: MARCH TO WAR TP
ISBN: 978-1-60706-818-1
$14.99

VOL. 20: ALL OUT WAR PART ONE TP
ISBN: 978-1-60706-882-2
$14.99

VOL. 21: ALL OUT WAR PART TWO TP
ISBN: 978-1-63215-030-1
$14.99

VOL. 22: A NEW BEGINNING TP
ISBN: 978-1-63215-041-7
$14.99

VOL. 23: WHISPERS INTO SCREAMS TP
ISBN: 978-1-63215-258-9
$14.99

VOL. 24: LIFE AND DEATH TP
ISBN: 978-1-63215-402-6
$14.99

VOL. 25: NO TURNING BACK TP
ISBN: 978-1-63215-612-9
$14.99

VOL. 26: CALL TO ARMS TP
ISBN: 978-1-63215-917-5
$14.99

VOL. 1: SPANISH EDITION TP
ISBN: 978-1-60706-797-9
$14.99

VOL. 2: SPANISH EDITION TP
ISBN: 978-1-60706-845-7
$14.99

VOL. 3: SPANISH EDITION TP
ISBN: 978-1-60706-883-9
$14.99

VOL. 4: SPANISH EDITION TP
ISBN: 978-1-63215-035-6
$14.99

HARDCOVERS

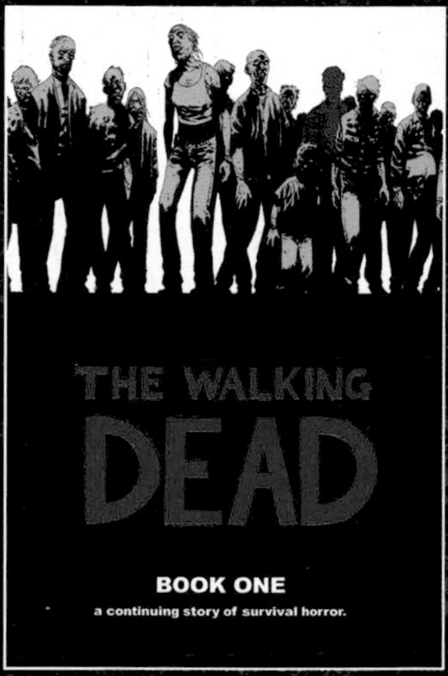

THE WALKING DEAD
BOOK ONE
a continuing story of survival horror.

BOOK ONE HC
ISBN: 978-1-58240-619-0
$34.99

BOOK TWO HC
ISBN: 978-1-58240-698-5
$34.99

BOOK THREE HC
ISBN: 978-1-58240-825-5
$34.99

BOOK FOUR HC
ISBN: 978-1-60706-000-0
$34.99

BOOK FIVE HC
ISBN: 978-1-60706-171-7
$34.99

BOOK SIX HC
ISBN: 978-1-60706-327-8
$34.99

BOOK SEVEN HC
ISBN: 978-1-60706-439-8
$34.99

BOOK EIGHT HC
ISBN: 978-1-60706-593-7
$34.99

BOOK NINE HC
ISBN: 978-1-60706-798-6
$34.99

BOOK TEN HC
ISBN: 978-1-63215-034-9
$34.99

BOOK ELEVEN HC
ISBN: 978-1-63215-271-8
$34.99

BOOK TWELVE HC
ISBN: 978-1-63215-451-4
$34.99

BOOK THIRTEEN HC
ISBN: 978-1-63215-916-8
$34.99

COMPENDIUMS

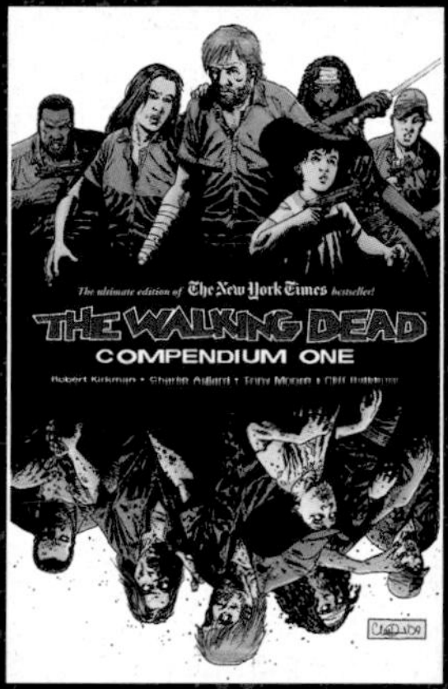

The ultimate edition of The New York Times bestseller!
THE WALKING DEAD
COMPENDIUM ONE

COMPENDIUM TP, VOL. 1
ISBN: 978-1-60706-076-5
$59.99

COMPENDIUM TP, VOL. 2
ISBN: 978-1-60706-596-8
$59.99

COMPENDIUM TP, VOL. 3
ISBN: 978-1-63215-456-9
$59.99

SPECIALTY BOOKS

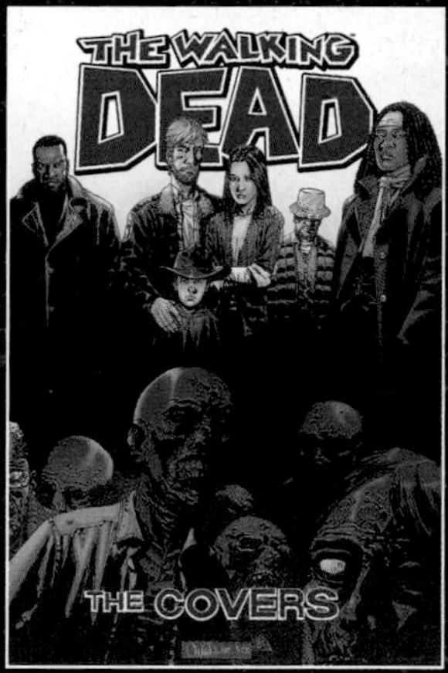

THE WALKING DEAD
THE COVERS

THE WALKING DEAD: THE COVERS, VOL. 1 HC
ISBN: 978-1-60706-002-4
$24.99

THE WALKING DEAD: ALL OUT WAR HC
ISBN: 978-1-63215-038-7
$34.99

THE WALKING DEAD COLORING BOOK
ISBN: 978-1-63215-774-4
$14.99

THE WALKING DEAD RICK GRIMES COLORING BOOK
ISBN: 978-1-5343-0003-3
$14.99

OMNIBUS

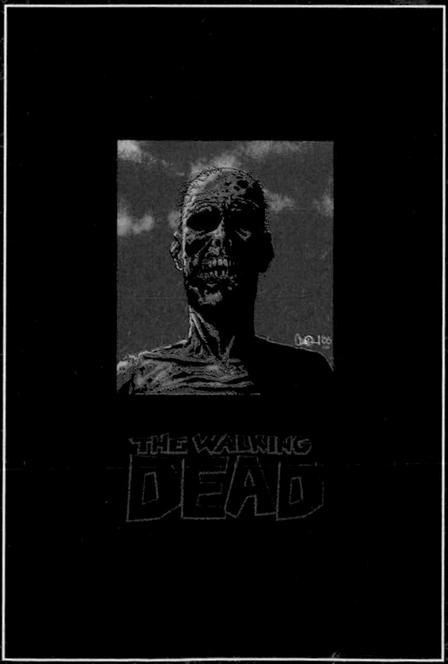

THE WALKING DEAD

OMNIBUS, VOL. 1
ISBN: 978-1-60706-503-6
$100.00

OMNIBUS, VOL. 2
ISBN: 978-1-60706-515-9
$100.00

OMNIBUS, VOL. 3
ISBN: 978-1-60706-330-8
$100.00

OMNIBUS, VOL. 4
ISBN: 978-1-60706-616-3
$100.00

OMNIBUS, VOL. 5
ISBN: 978-1-63215-042-4
$100.00

OMNIBUS, VOL. 6
ISBN: 978-1-63215-521-4
$100.00

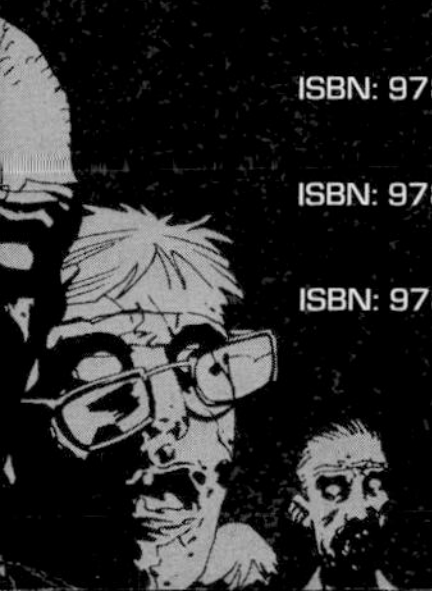

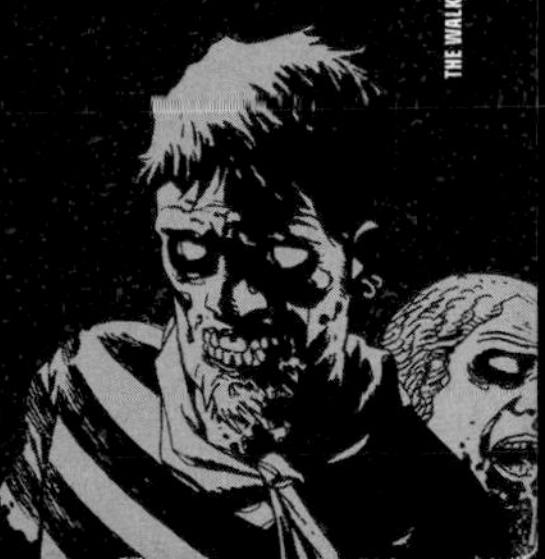

For more tales from ROBERT KIRKMAN and SKYBOUND

VOLUME 3: THIS LITTLE LIGHT
BY KIRKMAN & AZACETA
OUTCAST

CHRIS DINGESS · MATTHEW ROBERTS · OWEN GIENI
MANIFEST DESTINY
VOLUME 4 · SASQUATCH

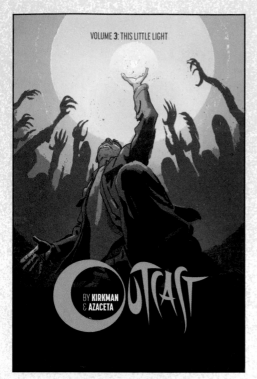

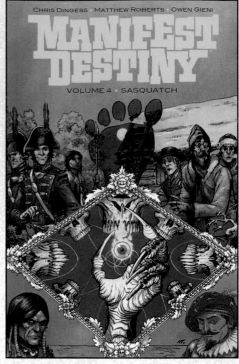

VOL. 1: A DARKNESS SURROUNDS HIM TP
ISBN: 978-1-63215-053-0
$9.99

VOL. 2: A VAST AND UNENDING RUIN TP
ISBN: 978-1-63215-448-4
$14.99

VOL. 3: THIS LITTLE LIGHT TP
ISBN: 978-1-63215-693-8
$14.99

VOL. 1: FLORA & FAUNA TP
ISBN: 978-1-60706-982-9
$9.99

VOL. 2: AMPHIBIA & INSECTA TP
ISBN: 978-1-63215-052-3
$14.99

VOL. 3: CHIROPTERA & CARNIFORMAVES TP
ISBN: 978-1-63215-397-5
$14.99

VOL. 4: SASQUATCH TP
ISBN: 978-1-63215-890-1
$14.99

CLONE
VOLUME 1
FIRST GENERATION

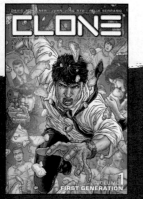

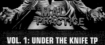

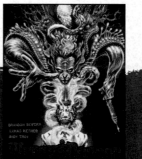

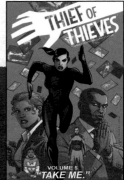

VOL. 1: FIRST GENERATION TP
ISBN: 978-1-60706-683-5
$12.99

VOL. 2: SECOND GENERATION TP
ISBN: 978-1-60706-830-3
$12.99

VOL. 3: THIRD GENERATION TP
ISBN: 978-1-60706-939-3
$12.99

VOL. 4: FOURTH GENERATION TP
ISBN: 978-1-63215-036-3
$12.99

GHOSTED
VOLUME ONE · HAUNTED HEIST

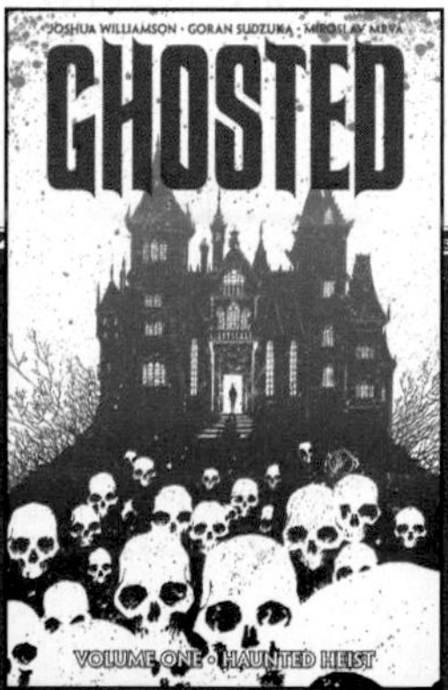

VOL. 1: HAUNTED HEIST TP
ISBN: 978-1-60706-836-5
$9.99

VOL. 2: BOOKS OF THE DEAD TP
ISBN: 978-1-63215-046-2
$12.99

VOL. 3: DEATH WISH TP
ISBN: 978-1-63215-051-6
$12.99

VOL. 4: GHOST TOWN TP
ISBN: 978-1-63215-317-3
$12.99

MAL PRACTICE

VOL. 1: UNDER THE KNIFE TP
ISBN: 978-1-60706-441-1
$12.99

VOL. 2: MAL PRACTICE TP
ISBN: 978-1-60706-693-4
$14.99

THIEF OF THIEVES
VOLUME 5
"TAKE ME."

VOL. 1: "I QUIT."
ISBN: 978-1-60706-592-0
$14.99

VOL. 2: "HELP ME."
ISBN: 978-1-60706-676-7
$14.99

VOL. 3: "VENICE."
ISBN: 978-1-60706-844-0
$14.99

VOL. 4: "THE HIT LIST."
ISBN: 978-1-63215-037-0
$14.99

VOL. 5: "TAKE ME."
ISBN: 978-1-63215-401-9
$14.99